CASTING OFF

Elizabeth Jane Howard was the author of fifteen highly acclaimed novels. The Cazalet Chronicles – *The Light Years*, *Marking Time*, *Confusion*, *Casting Off* and *All Change* – have become established as modern classics and have been adapted for a major BBC television series and most recently for BBC Radio 4. In 2002 Macmillan published Elizabeth Jane Howard's autobiography, *Slipstream*. In that same year she was awarded a CBE in the Queen's Birthday Honours list. She died in January 2014, following the publication of *All Change*.

ALSO BY ELIZABETH JANE HOWARD

The Amazing Adventures of Freddie Whitemouse
Love All
Falling
Getting It Right
Odd Girl Out
Mr Wrong
Something in Disguise
After Julius
The Sea Change
The Long View
The Beautiful Visit

The Cazalet Chronicles
The Light Years
Marking Time
Confusion
All Change

Non-Fiction
Slipstream
Green Shades
The Lover's Companion

CASTING OFF

Volume Four of The Cazalet Chronicles

ELIZABETH
JANE HOWARD

PAN BOOKS

First published 1995 by Macmillan

This edition published 2021 by Pan Books
an imprint of Pan Macmillan
The Smithson, 6 Briset Street, London EC1M 5NR
EU representative: Macmillan Publishers Ireland Ltd,
Mallard Lodge, Lansdowne Village, Dublin 4
Associated companies throughout the world
www.panmacmillan.com

ISBN 978-1-5290-4942-8

1 3 5 7 9 8 6 4 2

A CIP catalogue record for this book is available from the British Library.

Printed and bound by CPI Group (UK) Ltd, Croydon, CR0 4YY

Visit **www.panmacmillan.com** to read more about all our books
and to buy them. You will also find features, author interviews and
news of any author events, and you can sign up for e-newsletters
so that you're always first to hear about our new releases.

To Sybille Bedford
with love and homage

CONTENTS

PART FOUR

ACKNOWLEDGEMENT

I want to thank Jane Wood, who has been my patient, kind, vigilant and most encouraging editor through-out three of these four volumes . . . Without her, I don't think I would have managed to get this far.

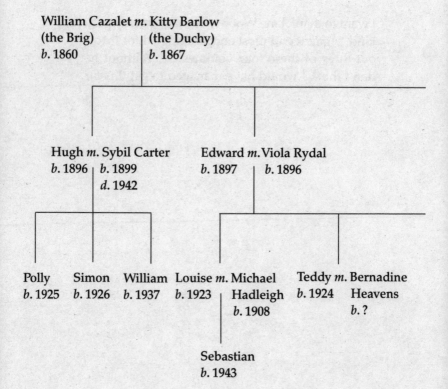

William Cazalet *m*. Kitty Barlow
(the Brig)   (the Duchy)
b. 1860   *b*. 1867

Hugh *m*. Sybil Carter   Edward *m*. Viola Rydal
b. 1896 *b*. 1899   *b*. 1897   *b*. 1896
         d. 1942

Polly   Simon   William   Louise *m*. Michael   Teddy *m*. Bernadine
b. 1925   *b*. 1926 *b*. 1937 *b*. 1923   Hadleigh   *b*. 1924 Heavens
                                             b. 1908   *b*. ?

Sebastian
b. 1943

THE CAZALET FAMILY TREE

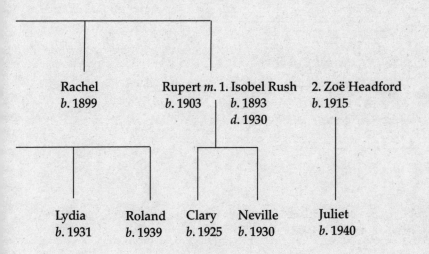

Rachel
b. 1899

Rupert *m.* 1. Isobel Rush
b. 1903   *b.* 1893
  d. 1930

2. Zoë Headford
b. 1915

Lydia
b. 1931

Roland
b. 1939

Clary
b. 1925

Neville
b. 1930

Juliet
b. 1940

THE CAZALET FAMILIES
AND THEIR SERVANTS

WILLIAM CAZALET, known as the Brig
  Kitty Barlow, known as the Duchy (his wife)
    Rachel, their unmarried daughter

HUGH CAZALET, eldest son
  Sybil Carter (his late wife)
    Polly
    Simon
    William, known as Wills

EDWARD CAZALET, second son
  Viola, known as Villy (his wife)
    Louise
    Teddy
    Lydia
    Roland, known as Roly

RUPERT CAZALET, third son
  Zoë (second wife)
  Isobel (first wife; died having Neville)
    Clarissa, known as Clary
    Neville
    Juliet

JESSICA CASTLE (Villy's sister)
  Raymond (her husband)
    Angela
    Christopher
    Nora
    Judy

Mrs Cripps (cook)
Ellen (nurse)
Eileen (maid)
Tonbridge (chauffeur)
McAlpine (gardener)

FOREWORD

The following background is intended for those readers who are unfamiliar with The Cazalet Chronicles, a series of novels whose first three volumes are *The Light Years*, *Marking Time* and *Confusion*.

In the summer of 1945 William and Kitty Cazalet, known to their family as the Brig and the Duchy, are living quietly in the family house, Home Place, in Sussex. The Brig is now blind. They have an unmarried daughter, Rachel, and three sons, who all work in the family timber firm. Hugh is a widower, Edward is married but entangled in a serious affair, and Rupert has just returned to England and his wife Zoë, having been missing in France since Dunkirk.

Edward's daughter Louise is struggling with her marriage to the portrait painter Michael Hadleigh. They have one son, Sebastian. Louise's brother Teddy, training in the RAF in Arizona, has not yet returned with his American bride.

Polly and Clary, Hugh's and Rupert's daughters, are sharing a flat in London. Polly works for an interior decorator and Clary for a literary agent. Polly's brother Simon is at Oxford, and Clary's brother Neville is still at Stowe.

While Rupert was away, Zoë gave birth to their daughter, Juliet.

FOREWORD

Rachel lives for others, which her great friend, Margot Sidney (Sid), who is a violin teacher in London, often finds hard.

Edward's wife, Villy, has a sister, Jessica Castle, married to Raymond. They have four children: Angela, who has become engaged to an American, Christopher, who lives in a caravan with his dog and works for a farmer, Nora, who married a paraplegic and has taken over the Castle house in Surrey as a nursing home for seriously wounded men, and Judy, who is still at boarding school.

Miss Milliment is the very old family governess, and is to live with Villy and Edward when they move back to London.

Diana Mackintosh, Edward's lady, has had a child by him.

Archie Lestrange, Rupert's oldest friend, is still working at the Admiralty, and is the recipient of most of the family's confidences.

Casting Off begins in July 1945, soon after Rupert's return to England.

PART ONE

THE BROTHERS

July 1945

'So I thought if I stayed until the autumn, it would give you plenty of time to find someone suitable. Naturally I wouldn't want to put you out.' In the silence that followed, she sought and discovered a small white lace handkerchief in the sleeve of her cardigan and unobtrusively, ineffectively, blew her nose. Her hay fever was always troublesome at this time of year.

Hugh gazed at her in dismay. 'I shall never find anyone remotely as suitable as you.' The compliment struck her as a small stone, and she flinched: one of the things she had been dreading about this conversation was his being nice to her.

'They say nobody is indispensable, don't they?' she returned, although when it came to the point, like now, she did not feel this to be true at all.

'You've been with me so long I shall be lost without you.' When she had first come, all the girls had had shingled hair; hers was now grey. 'It must be over twenty years. Goodness, how time flies.'

'That's what they say.' This, she thought, was not true either. But in all of the twenty-three years she would never have dreamed of arguing with him. She could see now that he was upset: a small pulse at the side of his forehead became noticeable, and any moment now he would run his hand fretfully on to it and up into his hair.

'And I suppose,' he said, when he had finished rubbing his head, 'that there is no way that I could get you to change your mind?'

She shook her head. 'It's Mother, you see. As I said earlier, she can't manage on her own all day any more.'

There was a short silence as he recognised that they were back at the beginning of the conversation. She moved his laurel-wood cigarette box towards him – she had filled it that morning as usual; it was so much easier for him with one hand than struggling to open packets – and waited while he took one and lit it with the silver lighter that Mrs Hugh had given him the year of the Coronation. That had been the year that the firm had supplied the elm for all of the stools for the Abbey; she had seen the one that Mr Edward had bought afterwards – lovely it had looked with its blue velvet and gold braid. She'd felt proud that it was *their* wood that had been chosen for a piece of history. Her retirement would be full of memories.

'I was wondering,' she said, 'whether you would care for me to assist you in finding a new person?'

'Do you know somebody who might do?'

'Oh, no! I just thought that perhaps I could have helped to sort out the people who applied for an interview.'

'I'm sure you'd do that far better than I should.' His head was beginning to throb.

'Would you like me to open the window?'

'Do. No good being hermetically sealed on a day like this.'

As soon as she had undone the window bolt and heaved up the heavy sash a few inches the warm breeze carried in with it the staccato, raucous cries of the old news-vendor from the street corner below. 'Election special! Two Cabinet ministers out! Big swing to Labour! Read all about it!'

'Send Tommy out for a paper, would you, Miss Pearson? It sounds like bad news, but we'd better know the worst.'

She went herself, as Tommy, the office boy, combined being chronically elusive with a capacity for slow motion that would, as Mr Rupert had once remarked in her hearing, do credit to a two-toed sloth. She would miss them *all*, she told herself, trying to spread the awful sense of impending loss. And this was just the beginning of it. There would be a farewell party in the office, everybody wishing her luck and drinking her health, and they might – probably *would* – have a whip-round for a leaving present. Then she would wait for the bus that took her to the station for the last time, walk the twenty minutes from New Cross to Laburnum Grove until she reached number eighty-four, insert the key in the door – then shut herself in and that would be that. Mother had always resented her because she had been born out of wedlock – was no better than she should be, as Mother would say whenever she got really fed up. She *would* get out, of course, to go to the shops and to change their library books and perhaps, occasionally, she might slip out to the cinema, although she was going to have to be very careful with money. By retiring so much earlier than she had meant to she would be forfeiting quite a proportion of her pension that the firm arranged for all its employees. Holidays, in any case, would be out of the question unless Mother's incontinence cleared up – which she supposed it might do if she was at home all day to prevent it.

It had crossed her mind these last weeks that Mother

was doing it on purpose, but it wasn't very kind to think like that.

When she got back to Mr Hugh with the paper it was clear that he'd got one of his heads. He'd pulled down the top blind on the window so that the sun no longer fell across the desk, winking on the large silver inkstand that he never used. She laid the paper on the desk.

'Good Lord!' he said. 'Macmillan and Bracken out. Landslide predicted. Poor old Churchill!'

'It does seem a shame, doesn't it? After all he's done for us.' She left him then, but before settling in the little back room where she typed and kept her files, she did feel it right to say that of course she would stay – until September anyway, and longer if he had difficulty in finding the right substitute.

'That's really very good of you, Miss Pearson. I don't have to say how sorry I am that you're going at all.'

Although he smiled at her, she could tell he was in pain.

In the ladies' lavatory, where she went for a short, noiseless weep, the thought flashed through her mind of how different everything would be if she was having to leave her job in order to look after someone like Mr Hugh instead of Mother. It was a ridiculous notion; she couldn't imagine how it had come up.

When she had closed the door behind her in the way that she always did when he had one of his heads (she had a dozen ways of showing that she knew about them that used to irritate him beyond measure, until years of familiarity had bred indifference), Hugh pushed away the paper, leaned back in his chair, shut his eyes and waited for the dope to work. A Labour government – it really looked as though that was the way things would go – was

8

a disturbing prospect. It showed that, when it came to the crunch, ideas *were* more important than people, which, while it might be morally superior, was vulgarly surprising. Churchill was, rightly, a national figure: everybody knew about him – his emotional flamboyance, his oratory, his bronchitis, his cigars – whereas very little, and for most people nothing at all, was known about Attlee. The Service vote, he decided, must be proving the decisive factor. These ruminations were interrupted by the appearance of Cartwright with his report on the condition of the firm's lorries, which had been causing concern. Most of them had reached a state where they were becoming uneconomic to maintain, but it would be some time before there was any appreciable number of new lorries available. 'You'll just have to do the best you can, Cartwright.' And Cartwright, whose smile was skeletal – exposing a fearsome quantity of yellowing teeth with the minimum of mirth – finished with his usual complaint about the repainting of the vehicles. Cazalet lorries were blue with gold lettering. They were unique in this respect, since the blue faded so quickly that they needed constant attention. Cartwright resented using his budget on this, particularly with the present antique fleet, but the Brig had decreed years ago that the lorries should be blue and thereby distinguishable from any other lorry on the road. Neither Hugh nor Edward felt that this was a tradition that could be broken, more since their father was no longer able to see that they had done so. 'Don't start that one, Cartwright, but lay off repainting until I've been on to Rootes to see if they can produce anything for us.'

'Seddons would be better than the Commers, sir, if we have any choice, the price of petrol being what it is.'

'Yes – right. Good point.'

Cartwright said well, he'd be off then, but showed no signs of doing so. It turned out that he had a nephew due to be demobbed in the near future – his wife's brother's son, he explained. The family lived in Gosport and he wondered whether there might be a job going at the new wharf in Southampton. Hugh said that he would ask his brother and Cartwright said thank you very much, sir, he'd be obliged. Then he did go.

The twinge of irritation and anxiety that Hugh always felt whenever Southampton was mentioned occurred, setting off at the same time a larger and more immediate twinge of the same about Miss Pearson leaving. He did not feel at all like breaking in a new secretary after all these years. 'You don't like changing *anything*, my darling,' Sybil had said, when he had exclaimed at her altering the parting of her hair. My God, he wouldn't mind *what* she did with her hair, if only she was still alive! It was three years now – three years and four months – since she had died and it seemed to him that all that had happened in that time was that he had got horribly *used* to missing her. This was described by other people as getting over it.

At this point he resorted as usual to telling himself that at least she was out of pain – he could never have wanted, could not have *borne* any more of that for her. It was better that she should die and leave him than continue to be so racked.

He finished reading and signing the letters that Miss Pearson had brought in when she gave her notice. She would collect and pack them into their envelopes while he was at lunch. He buzzed her to call a taxi for him and to say that he might be late returning.

He was lunching with Rachel – at least it was not

10

going to be one of those alcoholic business lunches that he always found particularly trying after his headaches. He found that he was constantly reassuring himself with small mercies of this kind.

He was meeting her at a small Italian restaurant in Greek Street – chosen because it was quiet and likely to proffer food that Rachel would accept. Like the Duchy, who absolutely never ate out of her own house, Rachel had a profound distrust for 'bought food' – it was either too rich, or too elaborate, or else menacing in some other way. But on this occasion it had been she who had suggested lunch – she was going to be in London for the night anyway as she was going to a concert with Sid. 'I simply must talk to you about Home Place and Chester Terrace and all that,' she had said. 'They each keep talking to me about it and saying what they want to do, but they don't want the same things. It's hopeless trying to talk at weekends – we're bound to be interrupted.'

But when he arrived at the restaurant he was greeted by Edda, the elderly proprietress, who said that the ladies were upstairs, and when he reached the table there was Rachel – with Sid.

'Darling, I do hope you don't mind. Sid and I had sort of arranged to spend the day and I'd forgotten about our lunch when I made the plan with her.'

'Of course not. Lovely to see you,' he said heartily. Privately, he thought Sid a bit odd: in her rather bulky tweed suit that she seemed to wear all the year round with a shirt and tie, her unfashionably short hair and her face with the complexion of a nut, she looked like a little old boy, but she was darling Rachel's best, if not her oldest and only friend and therefore merited his goodwill. 'I always think of you as practically one of the family,' he added, and was rewarded by the faint colour that came and went on his sister's anxious face. 'I told you,' she was saying to Sid. 'I had to persuade her to come,' she was now saying to him.

'I know you have family matters to discuss – didn't want to be in the way, you know. I promise I'll sit as quiet as a mouse. I won't say a word.'

This turned out to be quite untrue. They did not get down to things at first: food had to be chosen. Rachel, having perused the menu, eventually asked whether she could simply have a plain omelette – just a small one? This was after he and Sid had decided upon minestrone and braised liver and he and Sid were drinking Martinis that Rachel had refused.

They smoked while they were waiting for their food: he had bought a packet of Passing Clouds for Rachel, which he knew she liked best after her Egyptian ones that were hardly ever to be found.

'Oh, darling, thank you! But Sid has magicked my old brand from somewhere – I don't know how she does it.'

'There's just one place that sometimes has them,' Sid said offhandedly, as one for whom small triumphs made up for their lack of size by their frequency.

'Well, keep them anyway – as a reserve,' he said.

'I feel very much spoiled.' Rachel put them in her bag.

When the minestrone arrived, he suggested that she start on the parents' problems. The Brig wanted to move back to Chester Terrace so that he would be nearer the office, 'although the poor old boy can't do much when he gets there', but the Duchy, who had always hated the house, describing it as gaunt and dark and too large for

12

them anyway, wanted to stay in Home Place. 'She doesn't really like London at all, poor darling, she wants her rock garden and her roses. And she thinks it would be bad for the grandchildren if they didn't have the house for holidays. But *he* gets so restless there, now that he can't ride or shoot or do any more building . . . And they keep telling *me* what they want, but they don't talk to each other about it. So you *do* see . . .'

'Couldn't they just go back to what they did before the war? Keep both houses and then the Duchy could be in the country as much as she liked.'

'No, I don't think they could. Eileen really wouldn't be up to the stairs in London any more, and the Brig has promised the cottage over the garage to Mrs Cripps and Tonbridge when they're married – it seems unfair to move them. Chester Terrace would need at least three servants, and I'm told that it's almost impossible to get anyone reliable. The agencies say that girls simply aren't going into service any more.' She stopped and then said, 'Oh dear! I do hope I'm not spoiling your soup – it looks so delicious.'

'Like to try it?' Sid held out a spoonful.

'Oh, no, thank you, darling. If I have any soup, I wouldn't have room for anything else.'

'What would *you* like to do?'

'Good question,' Sid said at once.

Rachel looked nonplussed. 'I hadn't thought. Whatever would make them happiest, I suppose.'

'He wasn't asking you that. He was asking you what *you* would like.'

'Wouldn't you like to be in London?'

'Well, in some ways it would be rather nice.'

While the soup plates were being removed and the

main course brought and served Rachel explained that it would be easier for her to do a third day in the office if she was in London. She could not really keep up with the work in the two days she was now working. By the time she had listened to everybody's troubles . . . and she was off with the latest hard luck story: Wilson, whose wife had to go into hospital – no grandparents to look after the children, and they'd been bombed out, lived in two damp basement rooms, and his sister – who might have taken the children, was being divorced – her husband, shortly to come out of the Navy, wanted to marry a girl he'd met in Malta . . . anyway, she was so upset that she was in no state to look after anyone . . .

Her omelette was congealing on the plate.

'Oh dear,' she said, taking a tiny mouthful, 'I'm boring you both with my silly office troubles . . .'

But they *weren't* her troubles, he thought, they were other people's. He wondered, for a moment, what on earth the staff had done before she joined the firm. Officially, her job had been to deal with salaries, insurances and holiday dates for the staff, together with petty-cash accounts and office supplies. In fact, she had become the person to whom everyone went with their problems – either in the office or out – and she now knew far more about everyone who worked for the Cazalets than he or his brothers had ever done.

Sid said, 'But none of this has anything to do with what *you* would like to do.' There was an edge to her voice, Hugh thought; she sounded almost accusing.

'Well, of course it would be nice in other ways, but one can't make this sort of decision for purely selfish reasons.'

'Why not?' There was a short, charged silence and

14

then Sid repeated: 'Why on earth not? Why are everybody's feelings more important than yours?'

It was almost as though she was talking about *her*
feelings, he thought – he was beginning to feel out of his
depth somehow, and certainly rather uncomfortable. Poor
Rach! She simply wanted everything to be right for
everyone; it wasn't fair to bully her about it. She had gone
rather pale, he noticed, and had given up even a pretence
of eating her omelette.

'Well,' he said, 'it seems to me that Chester Terrace
should go. It's far too big, and it would be better to sell the
lease while there's a reasonable amount of it left, and then
they won't be liable for the repairs. So what about keeping
Home Place and getting a flat for you and the Brig when
he wants to be in London? Then the Duchy could stay in
the country. You'd only need one servant and a daily to
run a flat, wouldn't you?'

'A flat. I don't know whether either of them would
consider a *flat*. The Brig would think it was poky, and the
Duchy would think it was *fast*. She thinks flats are for
bachelors until they get married.'

'Nonsense,' Sid said. 'Hundreds of people will be
taking to flats in the same way that they will have to learn
to cook.'

'But not at the Duchy's age! You can't expect someone
of seventy-eight to start learning to cook!' There was an
uncomfortable silence, and then she said, 'No. If anyone
has to learn to cook, it should be me.'

Sid, looking contrite, put out her hand to touch
Rachel's arm. '*Touché*! But it's your life we're talking
about, isn't it?'

Hugh felt obscurely irritated at her trying to include
him. In spite of what she had said about not saying a

15

word, she was interfering in what he felt was none of her business. He signalled the waiter to get a menu, and said, to Rachel, 'Don't worry, darling. I'll have a word with the Brig about an alternative to Chester Terrace and you and I can hunt for a suitable place. If the worst comes to the worst, you could always move in with me as an interim. Now, who would like an ice or fruit salad or both?'

When Rachel, who immediately said that she couldn't possibly eat any more, had been persuaded to have some fruit salad and he and Sid had settled for a bit of both and he'd ordered coffee for everyone, he raised his glass and said, 'What shall we drink to? Peace?'

Rachel said, 'I think we should drink to poor Mr Churchill as we seem to be letting him down so badly. Doesn't it seem extraordinary that they should want to chuck him out the moment the war's over?'

'The war isn't completely over. There's another good two years' fighting in Japan, I should think. I suppose one has to say that at least the other lot are used to government – at Cabinet level anyway.'

Sid said, 'I'm rather in favour of the other lot. It's time we had a change.'

Hugh said: 'I think what most people want is to get back to normal as soon as possible.'

'I don't think we shall be going *back* to anything,' Rachel said. 'I think it's all going to be different.'

'You mean the Welfare State and a brave new world?'

He saw her face puckering in a little flurry of frowns and remembered suddenly how he and Edward had called her Monkey when they wanted to tease her.

'No, what I meant is that I think the war has changed people, they've got kinder to one another.' She turned to

16

Sid. '*You* think that, don't you? I mean, people have shared things more – particularly the awful ones, like being bombed and separated and all the rationing and men getting killed—'

'I think there isn't the same kind of arrogant indifference,' Sid said, 'but if we don't have a Labour government there jolly soon will be.'

'I'm absolutely no good at politics, as you well know, but surely both sides are saying the same things, aren't they? Better housing, longer education, equal pay for equal work . . .'

'They always say that sort of thing.'

'We're *not* saying the same thing. We aren't going to nationalise the railways and the coal mines, et cetera.' He glared at Sid. 'That's going to cause chaos. And, from our point of view, it means that we shall be faced with only one customer instead of a comforting number.'

The waiter brought their coffee – just as well, he thought: he really didn't want to have a political argument with Sid – he was afraid he might be rude to her and that would upset Rachel.

Now she was saying, 'What are you going to do? About your house, I mean. Are you going to stay in it? Edward and Villy are selling theirs and looking for somewhere smaller, which seems sensible.'

So that he can afford a second place to put that woman in, he thought. He said, 'I don't know. I'm fond of it. Sybil said she never wanted to leave it.'

There was a short silence. Then Sid said she would join them in a minute.

'Miss Pearson is leaving me,' he said, to deflect their thoughts.

'Oh dear. I was afraid she might. Her mother's

become such an invalid. She told me she got back last week and found the old lady on the floor. She'd fallen trying to get out of her chair, and she couldn't get up.'

'I shall miss her.'

'I'm sure you will. It's pretty awful for her because she won't get her full pension. I was going to talk to you about that. I'm afraid she's going to be rather hard up.'

'She must have saved a bit – she's been working for us for at least twenty years.'

'Twenty-three, actually. But her mother's only got a very small widow's pension that dies with her. Except for the house, Muriel won't get left anything, and I should think that by the time her mother dies she'll be too old to get another job. Don't you think, in the circumstances, that perhaps we ought to see that she gets her full pension?'

'The Old Man would say that it was setting a dangerous precedent. If *she* gets it, everyone else will think they're entitled to the same treatment.'

'That's absurd,' she said – quite sharply for her. '*He* needn't know, and nor need any of the staff.'

He looked at her; her expression was uncharacteristically ferocious – an expression so ill-suited to her that it made him want to laugh. 'You're absolutely right, of course. You've completely melted my stony Tory heart.'

She smiled then, wrinkling her nose in the way she always did when she wanted to add affection to a smile. 'Your heart isn't in the *least* stony, dear old boy.'

Then Sid returned; he called for the bill, and Rachel said that she would go and find the ladies'.

As soon as she was gone, Sid said, 'Thanks for the lunch, it was very good of you to have me.'

He looked up from writing the cheque; she was

fiddling with the coffee sugar and he could not help noticing her strong, elegant, but somehow mannish hands.

'The thing is,' she said, 'that I know I should have shut up about what are, from your point of view, purely family matters, but she *never* gives herself a chance! She's *always* worrying about other people – never gives herself a thought. And I supposed that now the war is over – here anyway – at last she might consider some life of her own.'

'Perhaps she doesn't want one.'

For some reason, although he couldn't for the life of him think why, this quite harmless remark seemed to go home. For a split second she looked positively stricken; then she said so quietly that he could barely hear her, 'I do hope you're not right.'

Rachel returned. They parted in the street outside, he to go back to the office, and they for a shopping spree in Oxford Street, at HMV for records, and Bumpus for books – 'It's so handy that they're practically next door to each other.' There was a faint, mutual atmosphere of apology.

Much later, in the early evening when he'd finished at the office, had caught a 27 bus back to Notting Hill Gate and walked down Lansdowne Road to Ladbroke Grove and let himself into his silent house, he remembered Rachel's remark about his heart not being stony. To him it seemed not so much a matter of the texture of his heart, more a question of whether it still existed at all. The effort of trying to turn grief into regret, to live entirely on past nourishment, even to keep the sharper parts of nostalgia credible (he found himself beginning to doubt and struggle with the intricacies of the smaller memories), and, most of all, the fearful absence of anything that could begin to take their place, had worn him down. Feeling had become an exercise that no longer enhanced the present; he slogged from one day to the next without expectation that one would be different from another. He was capable of irritation, of course, with small things like his car not starting, or Mrs Downs failing to collect his laundry, and anxiety – or was it simply anger? – at Edward's behaviour over Diana Mackintosh (he had refused point blank to meet her); since the time when he had failed to get Edward to see that he must give her up, Hugh had refused even to discuss the matter. This resulted in it being very difficult to discuss anything with Edward in the old, easy way that they had used to do, and left them in a state of mutual disagreement and irritation about things like the Southampton project, which he thought thoroughly ill-advised, a dotty way to use their capital and something which, if there had not been this other profound, private rift, he might have been able to reason Edward out of. At any rate, he missed their old intimacy and affection, compounded by the fact that in the old days it was exactly the kind of thing that he would have been able to resolve by talking it over with Sybil, whose attention and good sense he had come to value even more now that they were no longer available. He tried to have conversations with her about it, but it was no good – he missed her precisely because he could not become her in the duologue. He would have his say – and there would be silence while he battled with his failure to imagine how she would have responded. He had never had the same intimacy with Rupert – his being six years younger had been crucial. When he and Edward had gone to France in 1914, Rupert had been at school. When he and Edward had gone into the firm together,

Rupert had gone to the Slade and had been determined to be a painter and have nothing to do with the family business. When he *had* come in, it had been after a lot of dithering, and had been largely, Hugh now felt, because he wanted more money to please Zoë. Then, since his amazing reappearance – long after (although it was not voiced) everyone had given up hope of it – he had seemed, after the initial family celebration, to be curiously withdrawn. Hugh had had one good evening with him – had taken him out to dinner the evening after the Navy had relinquished him, and before it they had drunk a bottle of champagne together at home. Rupert had asked about Sybil and he had told him about those last days when he and Sybil had talked and talked and discovered that they had both known that she was going to die and had each tried to shield the other and the sweet relief when this was no longer something that either of them felt the need to do. He remembered how Rupert had stared at him without speaking, his eyes filled with tears, and how, for the first time since her death, he had felt comforted, felt some of the rigid, blocked grief begin to dissolve from this silent, complete sympathy. They had gone out together afterwards to dine, and he had felt almost light-hearted. But it had never been like that again; he sensed that there was some mystery about Rupert's long time away and his reticence about it, and after one tentative attempt, he did not pry. He imagined that if one had been so isolated for so long, a return to ordinary family life must be difficult and left it at that.

There were the children, but his affection for them was beginning to be tainted by anxiety and feelings of inadequacy about them. Without Sybil, he felt that he was losing his nerve. For instance, with Polly – he was fairly sure that she had fallen in love, some time about last Christmas was when he had noticed this, but she hadn't told him, had brushed off his (probably clumsy) attempts to give her openings for confidence. Nothing seemed to have come of it; for months she had been listless, polite, without her usual spirit. He worried about her, felt shut out, was afraid of boring her (this was the worst thing because if that was true, or became true, she would only spend time with him from pity). When he had discovered that Louise and Michael were giving up the house in St John's Wood, he had thrown out a very casual suggestion that she and Clary would always be welcome to take up their old rooms at the top of the house, but Poll had only said, 'That's jolly kind of you, Dad,' and changed the subject, so he was pretty sure that she wouldn't. And that made staying on in this house absurd. He only used his bedroom, the kitchen and the small back drawing room; everything else was shut up and probably getting filthy dirty, as Mrs Downs could not possibly clear the whole place in the two mornings a week that she came. The place needed some staff, a family – above all, a mistress . . . The thought of moving appalled him: it was something he had only ever done with Sybil. With her it had been an exciting adventure each time. They had begun married life in a flat in Clanricarde Gardens – all they could afford. It wasn't a nice place at all, being the ill-converted floor of a huge, tall stucco house whose owner needed the income. It had enormously high ceilings with paint-encrusted friezes, huge, draughty sash windows and a gas meter for the fires that swallowed shillings as voraciously as the wide cracks in the floorboards devoured Sybil's hairpins or the buttons off his clothes. Poll had been born there, but soon after they had moved to the house in Bedford Gardens. That had been a wonderful move. Their own little house with its tiny front and back gardens and a wisteria that reached the iron balcony outside their bedroom. He remembered their first night there, eating their first Bellamy pork pie and drinking the bottle of champagne that Edward brought when he came to fetch Poll to stay until they had got her room decorated. Hugh had taken a week of his holiday, and he and Sybil had painted the house together, had picnic meals and slept on a mattress in the sitting room while he laid the hardwood floor in their new bedroom. It had been one of the happiest weeks of his life. Simon had been born in that house, and they had only moved where he was now when Sybil became pregnant for the third time.

By now he had changed his shoes, washed, made himself a whisky and soda and settled down to listen to the six o'clock news. It was even more depressing than he had expected. Churchill, who had not been opposed by either Labour or Liberal candidates, had lost over a quarter of the poll to an independent – a man he had never heard of. He leaned over and switched off the wireless. Silence invaded the room. He sat for some minutes, trying to think of something that he could do, could have, to distract himself. He could go to his club where he would probably find someone to dine with and perhaps have a game of billiards, but everyone would be full of election talk, and collective depression was not an inviting prospect. He could ring up Poll – he *could*, but he knew that he wouldn't. He rationed himself to ringing her once a week, did not want her to feel that he was interfering with her life or being a burden. Simon was off somewhere with his friend Salter – a bicycling holiday in Cornwall. He realised now that Simon had worked so hard this last year at school in order to get into Oxford because that was where Salter was going. Well, why not? He knew that Sybil would have been keen on it, partly, of course, because it deferred his being called up, and now might even mean that when he was, he would not actually have to fight. And she would, anyway, have approved of Simon going to a university, attaching far more importance to education than the family did. The Brig thought it was a waste of time and Edward was pretty dismissive, but then he had hated his school life and had been delighted that their war had curtailed it. Whenever universities were mentioned, Edward would bring up the pre-war debate in the Oxford Union where there had been some ghastly pacifist vote, which had showed, Edward had repeatedly said, how degenerate the young had become, the implication being that places like Oxford simply filled the young with decadent ideas. Of course, the war, when it came, had utterly disproved this, but it had not really allayed the male Cazalet view that education should stop as soon as possible in order that real life could begin. That Simon was to read medicine had made the whole project more respectable: the Duchy, Villy and Rachel were deeply in favour; it was really only the Brig and Edward who passively disapproved, and that, he knew, was because they thought that all male Cazalets should go into the family firm. Anyway, Simon was not available for company. Tomorrow he would be going down to Sussex, and he'd think of things to do with Wills who, he felt, suffered from too much female company. Tonight he could not be bothered to go out. He made himself another drink and descended to the basement, where, after some searching, he found a tin of Spam, the rather stale remains of a loaf from which he had been making his morning toast all week, and a couple of tomatoes brought up from Home Place last weekend. He put these things on a tray with the tin opener and went back to the drawing room. A quiet evening at home, he told himself, would do no harm.

∞ ∞ ∞

They were running late, Edward reflected, although he ought to have known they would be. Whenever he went to Southampton unexpected problems came up, and today had been no exception. He'd gone down to interview a couple of blokes to be assistant wharf manager, and he'd taken Rupert with him because Rupert hadn't even seen the place and – as it was beginning to look as though he would be the only candidate for running it – it was high time that he was put in the picture. He'd meant just to interview the chaps and then they'd have a jolly good lunch and he would show Rupe round and generally enthuse him with the project. But it hadn't turned out like that. The first bloke had been hopeless – far too full of himself and of pointless breezy little anecdotes that were meant to show him in a good light but actually put them off him – and pretty cagey about his previous experience. The second man was late, on the old side and very nervous, clearing his throat every time before he spoke and sweating, but his track record was good: he'd run a softwoods sawmill throughout the war and was only leaving because the firm was taking somebody back out of the Army who had had the job before. Edward had the impression that he was older than he said he was, but he didn't push that one, and when the interview was over he asked Rupert what he thought.

'He seemed all right, but I wouldn't know whether he could do the job.'

'Well, it's all we've got to choose from.'

'Now it is. But any moment there'll be hundreds – or dozens, anyway – of men wanting a job.'

'But we need someone *now*. Unless you think you could do it as a stop-gap.'

'Good God! I couldn't begin to! I don't know the first thing about it.' He looked appalled. After a pause, he said, 'And it would mean living here, wouldn't it? Zoë has set her heart on London.'

This was not at all what he wanted to hear. He knew that Hugh would not consider running the place as he was dead against it – had been all along – and his own private life was far too complicated for him to conduct it so far from London. But there ought to be a Cazalet on the spot.

'Oh, well,' he said, 'let's sleep on it. I want to show you round, but let's get some lunch first.'

Lunch – at the Polygon Hotel – had taken ages. The place was unusually full, and the bar, where they had a drink while they waited for a table, was full of men poring over the election results in the early edition of the local evening paper. The banner headlines could be read across the room. LABOUR SWEEPING TO VICTORY! CONSERVATIVES ROUTED!

'There's not much to drink to,' he said, when their pink gins arrived, but Rupert said that he thought it was probably a good thing. They had a bit of an argument. Edward was shocked. 'Get rid of Churchill?' he said, more than once. 'It seems to me sheer bloody-minded madness. After all, he got us through the war.'

'But the war's over. Or over here, anyway.'

'The other lot are only bent on running down the Empire, ruining the economy with their blasted Welfare State. It's simply because people want something for nothing.'

'Well, they've put up with nothing for something for quite a while.'

'Really, old boy, you're turning into some sort of Red!'

'I'm not turning into anything. I've never been much of a Tory, but that doesn't make me a communist. I'd just like things to be a bit fairer.'

'What do you mean by "fairer"?'

There was a short silence; his brother seemed intent upon twisting a bit of the foiled paper from his packet of Senior Service.

'Bodies,' he said eventually. 'I don't mean dead ones. I noticed it when I was Number One on that destroyer. Men used to strip down, swabbing decks or in the engine room, or I just saw them when I was doing the rounds. I noticed that most of the Ordinary Seamen's bodies were a different *shape*: narrower shoulders, barrel-chested, bandy legs, scrawny-looking, terrible teeth – you'd be surprised how many of them had false ones. They just looked as though they'd never had a chance to grow to what they were originally meant to be. Of course, there were excep- tions – husky chaps who'd been stevedores or dockers or miners – but there were a hell of a lot who'd come from cities, from indoor jobs. I suppose it was mostly them I noticed. Anyway, compared to the officers they looked very different. It seemed to me then that except for our uniforms, we should have looked the same.' He looked up at his brother with a small smile – like a silent and mirthless apology. 'There were other things . . .'

Perhaps he's going to tell me about France, Edward thought. He's never talked about that – at all. 'Things?'

'Er – well, like if you haven't got much to lose, it's far worse when you lose it. One of our gunners lost his house in the bombing. If *we* lost a house, we've got another one, haven't we? Or we could get one. He lost his house and his furniture, everything in it.'

'That could happen to anyone – *has* happened—'

'No doubt – but it's what happens afterwards that's different.'

He *wasn't* going to talk about it – get whatever it was off his chest. Edward felt relieved when the waiter came to tell them that their table was ready.

But even when they got their table, the service was very slow and they didn't get back to the wharf until after three. He'd decided to do a quick tour with Rupert and then get away as he'd promised Diana he'd be at her place in time for dinner and spend Friday night with her before going on to Home Place. But when they got back the man who was overseeing the building and repairs to the sawmill said that the borough surveyor wanted to see him with a list of changes to be made for fire precautions. This meant going over the list on site, and one way and another it took nearly three hours. Rupert left him after a bit, and said he'd have a prowl round on his own.

A good many of the modifications should have been done during the rebuilding of the sawmill – it was going to be far more expensive to do them now. He told Turner, the man in charge, to send him a copy of the list and said he would tackle their own surveyor about why he hadn't called the borough surveyor earlier. Then he couldn't find Rupert, and after he sent someone to go and look for him, he rang Diana to tell her that he wouldn't be able to make it in time for dinner. 'I'm still in Southampton. Got to get Rupert back to London before I come down to you – sorry, sweetie, but it can't be helped.'

She was obviously very upset, and by the time he'd finished talking to her, and swivelled round in his chair to put out his cigarette, Rupert was standing in the open doorway to the office.

'Look here, I'd no idea I was putting you out. I can easily get back on a train.'

'It's all right, old boy.' He felt intensely irritated: Rupert must have heard every word he'd been saying – probably given the whole show away . . .

'I didn't realise that you were going on somewhere – much better if you put me on a train.'

If he drove straight from the station to Diana's he could get there in an hour and a half . . .

'Well, if it's all the same to you . . . Let's have a quick one first. There's quite a nice little pub up the road.'

While they were having the drink he told Rupert about Diana, about how long the affair had been going on, about how he really didn't feel 'that way' about Villy any more, about Diana's husband having died leaving her with practically not a bean and four children. 'It's a hell of a mess,' he said, 'I don't know what to do.' It was an enormous relief, he discovered, to have someone to talk to about it.

'Do you want to marry her?'

'Well, that's the problem, you see.' As he said this, he realised that he *did* want to very much indeed. 'You know, if you've had somebody's child—'

'You didn't say that—'

'Didn't I? As a matter of fact, she's almost certainly had two of mine. You can see how it is – it makes you feel responsible – difficult just to walk out – leave her and all that.'

Rupert was silent. Edward began to be afraid that he was going to start disapproving of him – like Hugh. He couldn't bear the idea of that: he desperately wanted someone on his side. 'I really do love her,' he said. 'It wouldn't have gone on so long if I didn't love her more than anyone I've ever met. And, anyway, how do you think she'd feel if I simply walked out on her?'

'I don't suppose Villy would feel too good if you left *her*. Does she know about it?'

'Good God, no! Not a thing.'

As Rupert remained silent, he said, 'What do you think I should do?'

'I suppose you feel that whichever you did would be wrong.'

'That's it! That's it exactly.'

'And I suppose that she – Diana – wants to marry you?'

'Well – we haven't actually talked about it, but I'm pretty sure that she does.' He gave a small, embarrassed laugh. 'She keeps saying she adores me – that kind of thing. Do you want another?' He'd noticed that Rupert had been staring into the bottom of his glass for some minutes now, but he shook his head.

'I suppose you'll just have to decide one way or the other.'

'It's a hell of a decision to make, though, isn't it?' It was all very well for Rupert to say that – he was not exactly known in the family as a decision-maker. 'I thought,' he said, 'that perhaps I ought to wait until Villy's found a house that she likes – get her installed in it, you know – before I – do anything. We ought to be off.

I'll just give her – Diana, I mean – a ring to tell her I will be back for dinner.'

On the way to the station he said, 'I would love you to meet her.'

'All right.'

'You will? Hugh has absolutely refused to.'

'Hugh knows about her, then?'

'He sort of knows, but he refuses to understand the situation, simply buries his head in the sand, whereas Diana and I have agreed it's much better to talk about things quite openly and frankly.'

'Except to Villy?'

'That's different, old boy, you must see that. I can't exactly *discuss* it with her until I've made up my mind to take the plunge.'

As he let Rupert out of the car he said, 'Nobody else knows about this, by the way.'

Rupert said all right.

'I'm really grateful to you letting me go off like this.'

'I'm not *letting*—'

'I mean, taking the train so that I don't have to let Diana down.'

'Oh, that! That's OK by me – I've got all the time in the world.'

It was a clear, sunny evening and Edward drove east with the sun behind him, on his way to have dinner and stay the night with his mistress. The prospect, which usually made him feel excited and carefree – as he always felt on the nights before his holiday – seemed now to have other dimensions: the watertight compartments in which he had kept his two lives throughout the war were no longer sound; guilt was leaking steadily from one to the other. He supposed that talking to Rupert had somehow

31

made everything seem more urgent. When he had said that Diana and he had not actually talked about marriage, he had rather simplified the point. Although she never said the word, she managed to bring all kinds of conversation to the outskirts of marriage. She couldn't go on in the cottage, for instance. Well, that was fair enough: it was cut off and a mean little place where she was hopelessly isolated. But what should she do? she had asked – more than once – her lovely eyes fixed on his face. She also asked many small, trapping questions about whether Villy was to continue in the country or go back to London. He hadn't told her about selling Lansdowne Road as he'd been afraid she would jump to conclusions. It was dreadfully hard on her, poor darling, having all this uncertainty. But, after all, he had it too. There was nothing he would like better than to have settled Villy comfortably, so that he needn't worry about her, and then be free to start a wonderful new life with Diana. Perhaps, he thought, reaching for his snuff box (marvellous stuff if you got sleepy driving), perhaps I should tell her this, and resolved that he would.

So, after dinner when they were drinking brandy, he did tell her, and she was overcome, said, 'Oh, darling, how wonderful!' and was awfully understanding about the terribly difficult problem of Villy. 'Of *course* I understand! Of course you must think of her first. We must *both* put her first, darling.'

∞ ∞ ∞

When he had bought his ticket and discovered that the next train to London would be in twenty minutes, he wandered up and down the platform, past the news-stall

32

– closed – to the station buffet. He went in: they might have some cigarettes and he was running out. They hadn't. The place was disconsolately dirty and smelt of beer and coal dust; the walls, once decorated in pale green high-gloss paint, were cracked and blistering, and the long counter had heavy glass domes that contained sandwiches writhing with antiquity. Just as he was wondering how on earth anybody could face them, a sailor came in and bought one with a bottle of Bass. Rupert left the buffet and walked to the very end of the platform. It was a beautiful evening full of tender yellow light and moth-coloured shadows; moth was a cop-out – they were all kinds of colours, really. He stopped looking: he was not a painter, he was a timber merchant. Like the rest of his life now, that seemed a completely unreal statement – he'd better think of something else. He thought about his brother, his older, once glamorous brother, whom he had felt was a kind of hero, or at least an heroic figure, although that, originating from when he was still a schoolboy during the First World War, had simply congealed into a habit. Poor old Edward! he now thought. He *has* got himself into a mess. Whatever he does now will make someone miserable . . . He suddenly found that he couldn't think about that, either. 'I suppose in the end she will get used to it,' came into his head – he might even have spoken it aloud; the cat's mother must be Villy. He knew, somehow, that Edward would do what he thought was the easier thing. He might well be wrong about what that might be, but when he did it that was what he would think. If whatever one did made one unhappy, might it not be best for Edward to do the harder thing? The harder thing was implicitly right, he knew, but that did not, he also knew, often provide much comfort. After all, Edward had been having it both ways for years; it was high time he had to face the music, make a decision one way or the other. His life must, for years, have been a tissue of lies, evasions, a withholding of essential truths.

He was no good at anger. Any resentment or disapproval he manufactured against Edward evaporated as fast as he put words to it; it wasn't just a question of deciding, it was living afterwards, according to the decision, dealing with the lifelong consequences . . .

His train had arrived; he did not know how long it had been there, and hurried to catch it. He found an empty compartment and settled himself in a corner of it to sleep. But the moment that he closed his eyes his head was full of familiar, silent images that seemed waiting to become animate in his dreams – to speak, to repeat themselves, to re-enact the key moments of the last three months: Michèle's head, sinking back upon her pillow after he had kissed her, then (he imagined) lying motionless as she listened to his departing footsteps – he had looked back once at the house to see if she had come to the window but she had not; the interim in the boat, which had seemed so painful and now seemed an almost blessed interlude when that image of her recurred and he could indulge in pure grief. He had wanted to stay one night in London on his own before embarking upon the last leg of his journey home, but he had no money except for the rail fares borrowed from the captain of the boat. He had not thought to ask for more – as it was, he walked from Waterloo Station to Charing Cross. The shabby, battered appearance of London appalled him. So he had bought his ticket and watched the familiar countryside and smoked his last cigarette from the packet they had given him on the boat and tried to imagine meeting Zoë.

He had not been able to imagine that. Nothing that came to his mind on the journey to Battle had any life, any credence at all. She might be disaffected, overjoyed, not even *there*: he knew nothing and, least of all, how he would feel at first sight. In fact, when he finally reached Home Place, in the middle of the afternoon, she was out. He walked through the old white gate that led to the front of the house, and there was his mother on her knees by her rock garden. Just as it occurred to him that his sudden appearance would be too much of a shock for her, she turned her head and saw him. He went quickly to her then, knelt down and put his arms round her; the expression on her face brought tears to his eyes. She clung to him, speechless, then put her hands on his shoulders to hold him away from her. 'Let me look at you,' she said, she was laughing – a little high-pitched gasping sound; tears were streaming down her face.

'Oh, my darling boy!'

'Now!' she said later. 'We must be sensible. Zoë's taken Juliet to Washington to the shop. You will want a little peace and quiet together.' She had taken the small white handkerchief from its place under her wristwatch to wipe her eyes, and he noticed with a pang of affection the strawberry mark on the back of that hand.

'Is she all right?'

She met his eye, and as he was rediscovering the familiar simple frankness of her gaze, it seemed to falter.

'Yes,' she said. 'It's been a very hard time for her. I have become very fond of her. Your daughter is a pearl. Why don't you walk to meet them?'

So he had done that – had walked back down the drive and up the steep road and at the top of the hill he met them by a gate into their fields. Juliet was sitting on the gate, and Zoë stood beside her and before he could hear what they were saying he recognised an argument.

'. . . *always* go back this way. Even *Ellen* knows it's my best way . . .'

He quickened his pace.

'I just don't feel like playing charabancs today.'

'You *never* feel like it!' She was wearing a scarlet beret but her head was turned away – he could not see her face.

'Well, I—' Zoë began, and then she saw him, stood motionless as he came up to her.

They stared at one another; she had gone white. When she spoke, she sounded frightened, husky and incredulous: 'Rupert! Rupert? *Rupert!*' The third time she put out a hand and touched his shoulder.

'Yes.' I should put my arms round her, he thought, but before he could do that, she had moved to Juliet.

'This is your father,' she said.

He turned to find her gazing at him.

'She has a picture of you in her nursery.'

He went to lift her off the gate, but as he drew near, she clutched it with both hands.

'Will you give me a kiss?'

She looked at him consideringly. 'If you had a beard I wouldn't. Because of birds. It's in a poem.' She was incredibly pretty – a miniature of Zoë with Cazalet eyes.

'As you can see, I haven't got a beard.'

She leaned towards him and gave him a smacking kiss. Her mouth was pale red and translucent, like the skin of a redcurrant. He kissed her back and she turned her head away and shut her eyes.

'Do you want to get down?'

She shook her head and renewed her grip on the top bar of the gate. He turned to Zoë: she was wearing an old

36

riding mac with a green foulard scarf round her neck. She was still very pale.

'I didn't mean to give you such a shock.'

'I know,' she said quickly. 'I know you didn't.'

'Are we going to play? I really want to play charabancs. I *really* want to.'

So they did what Juliet wanted and went to play on the fallen tree in the wood near the house. He thought afterwards that they had both been grateful for her presence: it postponed intimacy or, rather, excused the lack of it – he sensed that Zoë, too, felt awkward and intensely shy. The first time he touched her was when he helped her down from a branch of the tree after she had called a halt to the game. She blushed when he took her hand.

'I can hardly believe – it seems so extraordinary—' she began, in a low, hurried voice, but she was interrupted by Juliet who was standing precariously on the higher bit of the fallen tree, shouting, 'Someone catch me when I jump!'

He caught her and she wriggled from his arms to the ground and said, 'Now we'll all hold hands for going home.' So they walked back through the wood separated by their daughter who marched between them. It was during that walk that he learned that Sybil had died, that his father was blind, that Neville was at Stowe and that Clary was living in London and working for a literary agent and living in Louise's house – oh, yes, she had married Michael Hadleigh, the portrait painter . . . Telling and hearing the family news seemed to make things a little easier between them. Archie had been wonderful, she said – finding the right school for Neville after he had tried to run away, looking after Clary and Polly, coming down for weekends and cheering them all up. For a moment, he wondered whether she had fallen in love with Archie, then dismissed it as an ignoble thought; but when it returned later that same evening, he discovered that what frightened him about it was his lack of concern . . . It was true that when he walked into the house for the first time and was assailed by all the deeply familiar scents – of woodsmoke, damp mackintosh, the wallflowers that every year the Duchy put in a large bowl in the hall, the warm vanilla of a freshly baked cake on the large table now laid for tea – he felt a rush of simple, recognising pleasure, could for a moment feel himself home, and glad of it. He realised that he was ravenous, almost faint with hunger – he'd eaten nothing since the boat, which already seemed an immense, an almost unreal distance away – but he had only to say that he was looking forward to tea for a succession of dishes to be brought to him. Two boiled eggs, a Welsh rarebit, a chicken sandwich, two slices of cake. All this he ate, watched with joyful indulgence by the Duchy, Villy, Miss Milliment and Ellen, and with growing envy and insurrection by the children: Lydia, Wills – no longer a baby, a boy of *eight* – Roland and his own daughter. It was the children who underlined the length of his absence. 'We only get boiled eggs for tea on our birthdays,' one of them said. 'We don't get eggs. We get one miserable little egg. Once a year,' and so on.

It was the children who fired a series of direct questions at him. What was being a prisoner *like*? How had he escaped? Why hadn't he escaped sooner when the war stopped? Lydia wanted to know, but Villy told her that her uncle was tired and didn't want to be cross-examined the moment he got home. Villy's hair had gone completely white, he noticed, but her strong eyebrows had remained dark.

To deflect curiosity about himself he had asked about Clary and Neville, but before any adult could answer him Lydia said: 'Neville's voice has changed, but I can't honestly say his character has improved at all. He's simply awful in slightly different ways. He gambles with money and he hardly ever plays any decent games with us. Clary's much nicer. You ought to ring her up, Uncle Rupert, she'll be so frightfully pleased. She always thought you'd come back – even when everybody else thought you were dead.'

'Lydia! Don't talk such nonsense!'

'I wasn't. I'm not.' She looked at her mother defiantly, but she didn't say any more.

He had glanced involuntarily at Zoë, seated beside him, but she was staring at her empty plate. It had been then that he had been assailed by senses of guilt and unreality – both so violent and so evenly balanced that he was paralysed. His decision to stay on in France all those months after he could legitimately have left, a decision that had seemed romantically moral at the time, now seemed mere self-indulgent folly, selfish in the extreme. And he was not even returning with a pure, undivided heart . . .

The train was slowing down for a station – Basingstoke. He hoped that nobody would get into this compartment; he spent much of his life hoping to be left alone these days, not because he enjoyed the solitude but simply because he found it less demanding. He felt tired all the time, kept thinking he wanted to sleep, but usually the attempt simply provided a replay of small, disparate, disturbing pieces of his life. The only person he felt

39

comfortable with was Archie, to whose flat he was now bound. He had rung Archie that first evening at Home Place, and somehow Archie's pleasure ('I say! What a thing!') had felt completely all right – he hadn't felt guilty or inadequate or dishonest at all. It was Archie who had said that he should not ring Clary, he should *see* her; he had also, after he'd heard about the fishing boat, asked immediately whether the Navy knew he was back, and when he'd said no, they didn't, had said, 'Well, you'd better come up at once and I'll fix an appointment for you at the Admiralty. I warn you, they won't be pleased.'

They hadn't been. He'd gone up the next morning, met Archie at the Whitehall entrance and been taken by him to see a Commander Brooke-Caldwell by name, who was distinctly hostile. He'd had to go over the whole thing. Why hadn't he got in touch with any of the British services still in France? Why had he waited so long? What the hell had he been up to and who did he think he was? Who had been concealing him all these years? Was she a member of the *Maquis*? Did MI6 know anything about her? Why hadn't she tried to move him on? She hadn't been a member of anything, he'd said. Well, that could be checked out – and would be. It was a good thing, he'd finished grimly, that Lieutenant Commander Lestrange was able to vouch for his identity. He'd read the relevant action report from Rupert's captain, so the first part of the story was accredited. But he still hadn't accounted for his delay in returning, had he? A stony glare from the overgrowth of black bushy eyebrows. Personal reasons, sir, he had eventually admitted. Commander Brooke-Caldwell had snorted.

'Personal reasons come second in this service, a fact which I am quite sure you are well aware of.'

Yes, he was.

'Report back here in two days. Ask my secretary on your way out what is a convenient time for me.'

He had left feeling distinctly small. It was Archie who had fixed him up with a temporary ration card, who'd got him some money, who'd arranged for Clary to come to his flat for their reunion. 'She often comes to supper with me, so she won't think it odd. I'll see that there's some food, or you can take her out, whichever you like.'

'What will you do?'

'Oh, I can easily make myself scarce. Much better for her to have you to herself. She bloody well deserves it.'

They had been eating a fairly horrible lunch in a café off Leicester Square. Archie had to go back to his desk but said he'd be through by five; Rupert had the afternoon to himself. He walked, aimlessly, for about two hours. The state of London appalled him. Sandbags, boarded-up windows, dirty buildings, blistering paint – there was a general feeling of dinginess and exhaustion. People in the streets looked grey and shabby, tired as they stood patiently at bus stops in straggling queues. The conductors were women, dressed in stiff dark blue serge trouser suits. The queues daunted him – he decided not to take a bus. Every now and then there was another of the posters he had seen at the railway station, 'Is Your Journey Really Necessary?', and another that said, 'Careless Talk Costs Lives', and a third one that simply said, 'Dig For Victory' – all a bit out of date now, he should have thought.

He walked – across Trafalgar Square and up Haymarket and then along Piccadilly. The church there had been bombed; loosestrife and ragwort grew out of its broken walls. He had some vague idea of buying a present for Clary, but he could not think of what to get. Five years

41

ago he would have been in no doubt, but now . . . the gap between fifteen and twenty was enormous; he had not the slightest notion of what she would like or want – should have asked Archie when they were having lunch. He tried to buy her a man's shirt in one of the shops in Jermyn Street, but when he had finally chosen one, in wide pink and white stripes, it turned out that he couldn't have it because he hadn't any clothes coupons. 'I've been away a long time,' he explained to the very old salesman, who looked at him over his gold-rimmed half-glasses and said, 'Ah, well, sir, that is the unfortunate situation, I'm afraid. Would you like me to keep the shirt for you until you acquire the requisite coupons?'

'Better not. I don't know whether I'm entitled to any.'

He wandered along the street until he came to a stationer's. He would buy her a fountain pen. She had always loved them. When he had chosen one, he thought he had better buy a bottle of ink to go with it. She had always liked brown ink: he remembered her saying, 'It makes my writing look nice and old and settled on the paper.' As he wondered whether she was still writing stories he began to feel vaguely frightened, afraid that he might, in some way, fail her. His record so far, from the reunion point of view, was hardly a blazing success. It had been a relief to have to come to London this morning after the enforced, nervous intimacy of the previous evening. He had been so terrified of not being able to perform with Zoë that he had dreaded touching her. With the old Zoë this would at once have led to passionate declarations, demands, small seductive dishevelments – he remembered how the wide white satin ribbons of her shoulder straps would slip off her shoulders, how the combs would slide from her hair . . . He had not dared to embark upon such a course.

After dinner, they had been left alone in the drawing room. He had been turning over music for the Duchy, who had played at his request. Now he stood, irresolute, by the piano looking across the room at her – his wife. She sat in the large armchair, whose linen cover had been elaborately patched and mended, sewing some frothy white muslin concoction that was to be a summer frock for Juliet. She wore a pale green shirt that made her eyes a darker green and a little turquoise heart slung on a silver chain round her neck. She must have felt his eyes on her, for she looked up as they both spoke at once. Both stopped in mid-sentence waiting for the other.

'I was only asking whether you wanted a whisky.'

'No thanks.' He'd had one before dinner with his father, and discovered that he'd lost the taste for it.

'What were you going to say?'

'Oh! *I* was wondering what you thought of Pipette.' That story had come up at dinner, but Zoë then, as during the whole evening, had hardly said anything.

'I never met him. I was visiting my mother when he came. On the Isle of Wight. She still lives with her friend Maud Witting.'

'How *is* your mother?'

'Quite well, really.'

There was a short silence. Then he said, 'Do the family always go to bed as early as this?'

'Not usually. I think they're trying to be tactful.'

Her timid smile made him recognise that she was used to deprivation, sadness, the absence of any lightness. He said involuntarily, 'It has been far harder for you.' He

43

pulled a stool nearer to sit before her. 'Even after you got the message. You must have thought that I had died. But you couldn't be sure. That must have been so – *difficult*. I'm so sorry.'

'It couldn't be helped. It wasn't your fault. Any of it.'

He saw that her hands, folding the white muslin, were trembling.

She said, 'Your family have been wonderful to me. Especially your mother. And I had Juliet.' She looked quickly at him and away. 'Seeing you walking towards me in the lane was such a shock. I can still hardly *believe* you. Believe you're back, I mean.'

'It seems extraordinary to me too.'

'It must.'

They had come to another full stop. Exhaustion hit him like a freak wave. 'Shall we turn in?'

'Perhaps we'd better.' She put her sewing on the table.

He held out his hand to pull her to her feet and saw a faint blush – she was paler than he remembered; her hand was very cold.

'Time,' he said. 'We both need some time to get used to one another again, don't you think?'

But in the bedroom – astonishingly unchanged, with its faded wallpaper of monstrous, mythical birds – there was the business of undressing in the uncompromising presence of the small double bed. Had she kept any of his pyjamas? Yes: most of them had been passed on to Neville, but she had kept one pair. The clothes he had been wearing, a pair of cotton trousers, a fisherman's sweater that had belonged to Miche's father, a threadbare shirt that she had washed and patched and ironed for his

44

journey back – had now been discarded. He undressed while Zoë went to the bathroom – gathered the shirt to his face to conjure the hot, peppery, baked smell that had permeated the large kitchen when Miche was ironing . . . He rubbed his eyes with the shirt and then put it on the chair that he had always used for his clothes.

When Zoë returned, she had undressed. She was wearing the very old peach-coloured kimono that the Brig had given her years ago, soon after they were married. She put her clothes almost furtively on the other chair and went to the dressing table to unpin her hair. Usually, he remembered, this had been the beginning of a long evening ritual, when she would clean her face with lotion, put some cream on it, brush her hair for three minutes, massage some special lotion she used to have made up at the chemist into her hands, take off her jewellery – it could all take what had seemed to him ages. He went to find the bathroom.

That, too, was just the same. The same dark green paint, the same bath with its claw feet and viridian stain from the leaking taps, the window-sill covered with toothpaste-encrusted mugs and contorted tubes of Phillips Dental Magnesia. There was a new clothes-horse covered with damp bath towels. From habit, he opened the window, now stripped of its blackout blind. The fresh, soft air revived him. Away from Zoë, even for a few minutes, he was able to consider *her*, and he recognised now that in her presence he was encapsulated by guilt, unable to perceive anything but his own responses. She felt shy with him, unsure of herself and uncertain of him. One would think, he thought wearily – *anyone* outside the situation would presume – that after this long, enforced absence their coming together again was the happy ending, containing nothing but delight and relief. He remembered the old chestnut that fellow officers had quoted on the destroyer about the rating who had written, 'I hope you are getting plenty of fresh air because once I get back you won't be seeing nothing but the bedroom ceiling.' Reunions were regarded as occasion for sexual abandon and unconfined joy. He shut the window. I was in love with her, he thought. She is beautiful – that hasn't changed; she is the mother of my daughter and she has spent five years waiting for me to come back. Somehow or other, I've got to make a go of it. But even as he reached his last resolution he remembered that it was not new: it had lain in him during most of the marriage, unvoiced for years before he had gone away.

When he got back to the bedroom, she was in bed, lying on her side and turned away from him; she seemed asleep and, grateful for this deception, he kissed her cold cheek and turned out the light . . .

∞ ∞ ∞

He was not used to walking – and particularly not on pavements. His feet hurt: he was not used to wearing English leather – he'd lived for so long in canvas shoes. He decided to go back along Jermyn Street, down St James's and into the park where he could find a bench to sit down.

Clary. When Archie had said, 'She bloody well deserves it,' he had suddenly remembered Clary face down on her bed sobbing her heart out because he was going to take Zoë on holiday to France. He had sat on the bed and tried to comfort her – it was only for two weeks. '*Two weeks*! It doesn't feel like that to me at all. You're just *saying* that to make it sound bearable.' He had turned her over so that she faced him. How often he remembered her face covered with freckles and tears and usually dirt because she was always rubbing the tears off. How often he remembered her eyes dark with defiance and grief. 'How do I *know* you'll ever come back?' she had cried on that occasion. When he did come back she was shy, sulky, unresponsive, until somehow he could break through and make her laugh. Then she would throw herself into his arms and say, 'Sorry I clang so much.' And a few days later she would accuse him: 'Dad! You should have told me not to say clang. You know perfectly well it's clung. Sometimes you can be very treacherous and unhelpful.' She had been jealous of Neville, jealous of Zoë. He wondered whether she was now jealous of Juliet. He had always felt protective towards her: of the three girls it was always she whose knees were permanently grazed, whose hair seemed never out of tangle, who invariably spilt things down a new dress or tore an old one, whose bitten nails were always fringed with black, who seemed always either to have comic gaps where milk teeth had fallen out, or heavy wire bars holding in the new ones. She had never had a vestige of Louise's dramatic glamour, or Polly's fastidious elegance. He had known also that Ellen, who had been such a tower of strength to him in every other way, had favoured Neville, had always found Clary difficult, and although she had faithfully performed the duties of nanny, had bestowed very little natural affection – Clary had been entirely dependent upon him. So, when he was lying in that ditch with his ankle hurting like hell and all hope of escape with Pipette gone, he had scribbled the note to Zoë and had written another little message for her as the only comfort he could give. But she had been still a child then: children got over things – she had, after all, never once mentioned her mother to him after Isobel had died. Perhaps he, too, would seem like a distant stranger . . . He felt daunted. When it came to getting over things – something he recognised one always hoped other people would do – he wondered how it applied to himself. How long would it take him to get over Miche? He had thought that making the decision to leave her would be the hardest part of it; he had expected, he now realised, to be rewarded for the decision by finding it less painful in practice than in anticipation. Even on the boat he had thought that. He had thought that, once home, he would find it possible to slot into his old life, upheld by the virtue of having made the right decision. But this was not so: not only did it seem to be difficult in ways he had not imagined – sharing a double bed with someone who seemed like an intimate stranger – but the hours without her had simply made his longing for Miche more agonising. Morality, too, had developed horns: he could neither act nor even feel towards one of them without damage of some kind to the other – at least that was how it was beginning to seem. And once out of the Navy, he would be expected to return to the family business, and absence from that had made it clear to him that he had no heart for it. But how could he expect Zoë to go back to complete penury if he reverted to teaching somewhere and trying to sell pictures? He supposed he would have to get over wanting to be a painter as well, but getting over things now seemed to be a shabby, inconclusive way of dealing with them.

In the bus going back to his flat with Archie, he managed to say that he was nervous about the meeting with Clary. 'Don't you think it might be better if we had the evening *à trois*? I mean, it sounds as though she knows you far better.'

'I think she should be allowed to choose about that.' Then, after a pause, Archie asked, 'What was it like going home?'

'Oh – you know – very *odd*. Not exactly how I expected.' After a pause, he added, 'Amazing to come back to a five-year-old ready-made daughter.'

'I bet.' There was another silence in which he noticed how Archie had carefully not mentioned Zoë.

'I didn't know what to get her. In the end I bought her a pen. Will that go down well, do you think?'

'Sure to. She loves anything like that.'

'Is she still writing?'

'She's a bit cagey about it – but probably. She wrote a journal for you during the war. For you to read when you came back. She always believed that you would, you know.'

As he was putting his key in the door of a large, rather gloomy-looking red-brick building, he said, 'Perhaps you'd better wait and let her tell you about the journal.' Archie's flat was small, but it had a balcony looking on to a square garden, now full of may and lilac and laburnum.

'What time is she coming?'

'Straight after work. Between half past six and seven. Like a whisky?'

'No, thanks.'

'Gin, then. I think I've got some of that left. Oh, no – it's vodka. Vodka has become rather a fashionable drink because of our Russian allies. You can have vodka and ice, vodka and tonic, or just vodka. I don't advise that – it has a sort of oily taste when remotely warm.'

'I think vodka and ice would be just the thing.' He didn't really, but he felt tired and a drink might pep him up.

Archie seemed to sense that he was nervous, because he began talking about the coming election, the end of the coalition and party politics back with a vengeance. 'They can hardly hear themselves speak in the House,' he said. 'I must say, I think it would have been better if they'd waited until we've finished off Japan.'

'Do you want to talk about France?' he asked a few minutes later, when it was clear he wasn't getting much response about politics.

'Not at the moment,' possibly not ever, he thought, and then wondered whether he would ever bring himself to say even that – even to Archie.

Archie said, 'When the bell rings I'm going down to fetch her. It's going to be a tremendous shock for her. I'd like to give her some sort of warning.'

'You make me sound like a catastrophe.'

'No, I don't. Shocks come in all shapes and sizes.'

When the bell rang – at last – they both jumped and Rupert realised that Archie was nervous as well. He put down his drink and limped quickly to the door, where he stopped.

'Er. One thing. She really *has* – minded about you. She – oh, well.' He shrugged and went. His uneven footsteps on the stairs faded; there was temporary silence. He got up and walked over to the balcony, which was further from the door. He heard voices, Archie's and hers, and then Archie saying, 'A bit of a surprise for you,' and hers, 'Oh, Archie! Another one? I'm not going to guess because last time you *got* me what I guessed it might be before – if you see what I . . .'

50

She was in the room, struck motionless at the sight of him, silent, and then, as though released by a spring, she shot into his arms.

'Only crying because I'm so pleased,' she said moments later. 'I always cry about things.'

'You always did.'

'Did I?' She stood in front of him – nearly as tall as he, stroking his shoulders with small uneven movements. Looking at her eyes was like looking at the sun. 'Wouldn't it be awful,' she said, and he saw her luxuriating in the fantasy, 'if you weren't actually real? If I'd just imagined you.'

'Awful. Darling Clary, I have missed you.'

'I know. I got your note that you thought of me every day. It made a great difference. Oh, Dad! Here you *are*! Could we sit down? I feel I'm going to *break*.'

Archie, who had put a drink for her on the table by the sofa, had disappeared.

'He's probably having a bath. He spends ages in them doing the crossword,' she said.

They sat on the sofa.

'Let me examine you,' he said. 'You've grown up so much.'

'Well, *up*,' she said. 'But not sort of – in other ways. Not like the others. Louise has become rather a beauty – it's generally acknowledged – and Poll is *so* pretty and elegant. They're both quite exotic, but I've just become a larger caterpillar – or a moth compared to butterflies.'

He looked at her. Her face was thinner, but still rounded, flushed now with excitement and streaked with tears, her eyelashes wet around eyes the frankness of whose love struck him then with an almost painful force.

'This is the most joyful day of my life,' she said.

'You have eyes just like your mother's.'

'You never told me that.' She began to smile, but her mouth trembled.

'And you've lost your freckles, I see.'

'Oh, Dad! You know I don't get them properly until the summer.'

He gave her hand a reassuring squeeze. 'I shall look forward to them immensely.'

During the rest of that first evening with her, which they persuaded Archie to share, he saw both how much she had grown up and also how intensely she had missed him: this last was revealed to him obliquely in various things that she asked or said. When Pipette had gone to Home Place and described the journey west, she'd realised that a lot of her imagining about him had been right. 'Not exactly the same adventures,' she said, 'but the same sort of ones.'

'And after D-day,' she had remarked later, 'I thought you might turn up at any minute. I suppose that was rather silly?' But she had immediately sensed that this was back to dangerous ground: earlier, she had asked him why he hadn't come earlier and what had been happening to him, and when he had said it was too long a story for now, she had at once desisted; the old or, rather, younger Clary would have continued with a relentless cross-examination, but that first evening she seemed to know that he did not want to talk about that . . .

Which, he reflected now as he sat in the train on his way to London and Archie's flat, had been quite unlike the behaviour both of the Admiralty and the rest of the family. The Admiralty, of course, had a right: he recognised – belatedly – that he had behaved very badly from their point of view, that the four years of isolation and intense intimacy had impaired his sense of reality, or values. Different things had imperceptibly come to seem important: saving his own skin had evolved to continual anxiety about Miche's – if she was discovered to be harbouring him she would be shot. They had made a number of hiding places and he had become as wary as an animal of any activity near the farm – could hear the sound of a motorbike or any other engine even before she did. For the Germans did turn up from time to time, at infrequent intervals, to extract food from them and other farms. They would take chickens, eggs, fruit, butter if it was to be had, and once, on an occasion that had after-wards caused Miche to sob with rage, one of her three pigs. Sometimes these things were punctiliously paid for, sometimes not. But apart from the major preoccupation of staying alive there had been two other elements to his life then – each unpromisingly begun from the lack of any alternative – that had gradually come to absorb him completely. The drawing had started because he had nothing better, or even else, to do. She had a pad of thin, lined paper on which she wrote the occasional family letter – to her sister in Rouen, to an aunt who was a nun in a convent near Bayeux. Even on the blank side the lines showed through, but he became used to this. He had started by drawing aspects of the kitchen, which was large and accommodated all indoor life except sleep. There, Michèle cooked and washed and ironed and mended, packed up eggs or chickens or rabbits – the last two live – for selling in the market where she went every other week. In season, she would put fruit she had picked into punnets, or preserved into jars, bundle herbs: any-thing she grew or raised to sell was got ready to carry on her bicycle with the small wooden cart behind it. Here he passed much of his time, idle, unless she found some task for him, but always he had to be poised for flight. The first drawings had been merely pleasant distraction, but quite soon he found himself becoming more serious, more critically responsible about them; he recognised that he was out of practice, and some time afterwards that it had been years since he had done any drawing without feeling faintly guilty and self-indulgent (Zoë had always resented him spending any of his spare time on what she called his Art). Now he had time to practise as much as he liked. And Michèle, once she realised that it was more to him than an idle ploy, went to great lengths to provide him with materials – chiefly paper, some pencils and once some charcoal. These she obtained occasionally on market days – there was not much there, she said, only things for the pupils of the local school, but once she came back with a small box of watercolours.

His second preoccupation had been, of course, Michèle. He had first gone to bed with her after about four months at the farm. It had been a matter of straight-forward lust and the comfort it provided. They had had a bad day – in the morning the goat was found mysteriously dead, a disaster since it had recently produced a kid who would now have to be fed by bottle on the precious cow's milk. She had been deeply upset because she could think of no reason for the goat's death. She brought the kid into the kitchen and tethered it in a corner, and while they were improvising a teat out of a piece of chamois leather, they heard a car door slam and men's voices. There was no time for him to get to the concealed cellar (which meant removing floorboards) or out to the loft in the barn. She had pointed to the stairs and he had gone up them just as there was a rapping on the door. He had not dared to mount the second stairway – a mere ladder – to the attics for fear of the noise it might make. Her bedroom door was open, but the large bedstead stood high from the floor with no bedclothes voluminous enough to conceal anyone lying under it. There was nothing to do but to stand behind the open door and hope to God that if they did search the house they would not look behind it. There was an element of murky farce about the whole thing, he felt, before he heard the sounds of their departure, but even then he waited, as Michèle had taught him to do, until she called him.

She was standing in the open doorway of the kitchen, watching the dust settle on the cart track that led to the road. She walked to the sink and spat out the clove of garlic she had been chewing. He knew now that she always put garlic in her mouth when the Germans came. 'They do not like,' she had said the first time they had come. There had been three of them, an officer, his driver and another one whom she thought was SS – the only one who spoke any French. They had asked a lot of questions of the usual kind: who else lived at the farm? How did she manage, then, on her own? What did the farm produce? and so on. It had taken so much time, she said, because with Germans she always behaved stupidly. She did not understand what they said, and then she would give stupid answers. Then she turned on him and said it was his business to listen for people coming – she had enough to do. He (foolishly) said something about the car engine being quieter, and then she really went for him. However they came they could kill them, she said – he could not be such a fool as not to understand that. Germans in cars could be more dangerous – officers, people who gave the orders. If he could not take the trouble to listen, he had the choice of spending all his time in the cellar where he would be utterly useless and nothing but trouble for her. For the rest of the day she neither spoke to nor looked at him, made loud noises with pans, set a bowl of soup on the table for him but did not eat herself, and muttered imprecations to the kid that he felt were meant for him. That was the blackest day since the morning he discovered that the destroyer had sailed without him. In the evening, when she called him down from his room, he saw a bottle of Calvados and two glasses on the table. She had washed herself and her hair was coiled neatly on top of her head (she had pulled it down when the Germans came so that it looked thoroughly unkempt). She asked if he would like a drink and he said, yes, very much. When it was poured and she had pushed the packet of Gauloises to him, having taken one herself, and he had lit them, he said that he had been thinking, and had decided that he should not stay. Where would he go? He should try to get a boat from Concarneau. He would not get a boat. It had been discovered that someone had left in that way and now all boats were checked by the Germans before leaving the harbour. He would not get a boat. There had been a short silence. Then he had said that boat or no boat, he ought to leave. Why? Because it simply was not fair on *her*. If he were not here she would be perfectly safe, would not have this constant anxiety. It was too much to ask of anyone, let alone a – he remembered floundering here – perfect stranger.

She had stared at him for a moment with an expression he could not fathom. A stranger, she had repeated eventually. You have lived here for four months – with a stranger! No, he hadn't meant that exactly. Just that he did not feel that he had the right to jeopardise her safety.

She ignored that; she supposed it was because he was English that he felt her to be such a stranger. The cold English, people had always said, but she had not known any English person until now. They were facing each other across the table. She pulled her black woollen shawl more closely to her and folded her arms. In any case, she said, if he *did* leave, he would not get far. His French was not good enough for him to pass as a Frenchman, he had no papers and also it was known that he had some association with her – or it would be if he were caught. He did not understand this, but when he questioned her, she said that, although nobody spoke of it, something was known. Also, there was a record about her after Jean-Paul had been killed. The Germans kept excellent records of such things. So! she finished. So! She shrugged and poured more Calvados. He felt both challenged and at a loss – uncomfortably powerless. It occurred to him then that although he was deeply beholden to her, he did not like her. There was a bitterness, a smouldering resentment about her that was alienating. My bloody ankle, he thought. If that hadn't happened, I'd have been away from here, might be home by now. And then something strange, that afterwards he could not in any way account for, happened. For a second – he *became* her: at least his own feelings, responses, needs, anxieties dissolved to be replaced by hers. Alone, having nursed her parents to their deaths, her man taken brutally from her and with him her future of marriage and children gone by a murder where justice had no power, she had been left to do a man's as well as a woman's job in this remote place.

Lone women were raped by the enemy: it was common knowledge. Every single time they came, that possibility – likelihood – was there. Today she had been through the fear of that. She had got Pipette away, she had harboured himself: in neither case was there the smallest advantage to her. Her outburst about it being his business to listen for vehicles approaching the farm was perfectly reasonable. He had grown careless, and then to say that he must go, and call her a perfect stranger was both chilling and offensive.

'I'm sorry I called you a stranger. I'm sorry you find that my French is so bad. I'm sorry I suggested going without thinking of the consequences for you—'

He had taken her hand and she now put it over his mouth. 'Enough! You have said enough,' she said. She was smiling – he could not remember seeing her smile before and her dark eyes had an expression that was both cynical and tender. They had become different people.

That night after supper – a stew of rabbit cooked with apple and onions – after they had bolted the doors and fed the kid they had gone upstairs and when they reached the door of her room she took his hand and drew him in. He had put his arms round her and kissed her small red mouth. 'Much garlic,' she had said and he had answered that he was not a bloody German, just a cold English. She had smiled again. 'I will warm you,' she said.

For months he had seen her in her voluminous black skirt – often with an apron added to it, her heavy fisherman's jersey, her thick cotton blouses, her shawl – naked, she took his breath away. High, separated breasts, an unexpectedly slender waist, below which there was the generous curve of her hips, her limbs muscular and rounded, wrists and ankles delicately articulate – the revelation was a marvellous shock.

Even now, in the dusty train, he could feel his body responding to the memory of that initial sight of her.

After that first night they were no longer *Monsieur* and *Madame*, no longer addressed each other as *vous*, although it was some months before either recognised what was happening to them.

Here he had to stop – some way beyond that was the beginning of pain, the knowledge that there could not be a future with her, that one day this amazing isolation with her would come to an end, and the closer that they became the more completely they would have to part. He had thought, at the beginning of their parting, on the boat and the first few difficult days after it, that he must, he should, banish all thoughts of her; now he knew just how difficult it was to do that for more than a few hours at a time. It was not made easier by his relationship with Zoë, which had, he thought now, all the anxious courtesy of two people trapped between two floors in a lift – a kind of wary limbo that neither seemed able to overcome.

Perhaps, he thought, he would feel better if he talked to someone about it: his thoughts would become clearer, he would be more able to deal with the situation. And the obvious person to talk to would be Archie.

THE GIRLS

August 1945

'I really wish we hadn't asked him. He'll eat up all our food and keep on wanting to go to the cinema. And he'll probably be no good at all at painting.'

'We can give him the easy bits to do.'

'He actually asked me if we were going to pay him for working. My own brother!'

'Oh, Clary! He was only joking. Are the sausages done?'

'They must be. They've been in the pan for ages.'

'If you'll have a go at the potatoes, I'll test them.' Her arms were aching and the potatoes were still lumpy.

'Poll, I think you're meant to put butter and milk into mashed potatoes.'

'We can't. We've finished the butter, and we'll need the marge tomorrow for sandwiches for Neville as well as us. And there's only half a pint of milk left. We'll have to stop having Grape Nuts for breakfast.'

'And have black toast and bright yellow marge.'

'It doesn't have to be black if you watch the grill all the time.'

'It seems to me,' Clary said, when they'd doled out the sausages and lumpy mash and were sitting at the little kitchen table, 'that cooking only works if it's the *only* thing you do. Like Mrs Cripps.'

'I expect we'll get better at it as the years go by. And there'll be more food to get good with.'

'Not for ages. There are thousands of starving Germans.'

'Noël says that masses of food that might have come to us has to go to them, and so rationing will get worse, not better. He says that bread will be rationed any minute.'

'Oh dear.' The pronouncements of Noël, Clary's employer, relayed as gospel by Clary, were invariably gloomy. 'Anyway, we have got our own house.'

'Yes. Do you think it will stop smelling so queer, or shall we just get used to it?'

'We'll get rid of the smell. The whole place will be wonderful when we've finished with it.'

The 'house' was, in fact, six rooms, two on each floor, of a small eighteenth-century house off Baker Street. On the ground floor was a grocer's shop and in the basement an unknown region where the Green Brothers, who owned the shop, plucked and cleaned poultry. The feathers drifted up to the first floor of their part of the building together with a smell of singeing that added a dimension to the general odour of the place, a damp, rotting sort of smell. It had been in an appalling state when they took it, with plaster crumbling and old paint blistering off the window bars. Someone had written wild messages in pencil on various bits of walls and doors. 'Hole house rotting,' said one; 'Hopeless place,' another. 'Damp and durty,' and so on. All true in a way, but six rooms for a hundred and fifty pounds a year seemed a bargain and what they could afford. The family was helping. Polly's father was giving them coconut matting for the three flights of stairs and the Duchy had donated a large quantity of old carpet from Chester Terrace that was to be cut and fitted for their rooms. Clary had the first floor to herself, Polly the second, and the top floor was to be the kitchen and dining room. There had been a lavatory in a kind of passage built out at the back, in which it had proved just possible to put a very small bath. This had been done, and a sink installed in the kitchen. They had bought a second-hand gas cooker, and three second-hand gas fires for their sitting rooms and the dining room. They had paid to have some replastering done and the most damaged walls relined. There remained the decoration. Polly, who now worked for a small, rather grand interior-decorating firm, said they must have wall-papers, and that she could get them slightly cheaper. Clary, who had no faith at all in her own taste, let Polly decide such things. But before the papering there was all the painting, and this they had to do for themselves. It was a warm August Friday evening, and they sat each side of the table with the crooked sash window open to let in the brown dusty air from the street.

'Is there anything else to eat?'

'Some sort of stewed apple. I peeled them and chopped them up and put them in the pan with quite a lot of water so they didn't burn – like last time.'

Polly cleared the sausage plates and doled out the apple into their breakfast cereal bowls.

'Is it all right?'

'OK. A bit sour.' Clary didn't mention what seemed like fingernails, but Polly said she was sorry, getting the cores out and leaving any apple was much harder than you'd think. 'Louise's house had an apple corer,' she said. 'I suppose we should get one.'

'We seem to have got worse at cooking.'

'I don't think so. I think it's just that we have to *do* it all the time. And I don't suppose we'll ever have a cook.

Noël says that the whole of society will never be the same.'

'As before the war? In my job it looks as though it's going to be *exactly* the same. I'm constantly being sent to enormous houses where people are putting their kitchens on to the ground floor so that it won't be far for the servants to walk.'

'But only rich and grand people *have* interior decorators. Thousands of people are going to be living in prefabs because of all the bombing.'

'Oh, well,' Polly said peaceably. 'Perhaps Noël is right about most of society. Perhaps it will be the same for my little lot – a minority, I do agree – and better for everybody else.'

'He doesn't say anything is going to be *better*. He never thinks that anything is going to be that!'

There was a pause while Polly, who found Noël's opinions and Clary's preoccupation with them irritating, tried to think of some way of deflecting her.

'Let's not do any more painting tonight. Let's choose our wallpapers. I've brought back some lovely books of Cole's who are easily the best.'

They did the washing-up first, but anything they did in the kitchen depressed them. There were no shelves or cupboards – nearly everything had to be kept on the floor. The sink did not yet have even a draining board, and their two drying-up cloths seemed always to be damp. They kept a list nailed to the wall on which they wrote their needs. It was already hopelessly long. The room was always hot because the boiler, a second-hand Potterton, was installed in it and the window, as all windows in the narrow little house, faced south.

'Let's go to your room,' Clary said. 'It's far the nicest.'

This was not only because Polly had already painted and lined its walls, but, Clary felt, because she had a knack of making places feel comfortable and lived in. It wasn't just the patchwork quilt on the bed, the fern in a pot on the mantelpiece, the gleaming white paint and the thick brown paper she had taped to the floor; there was the feeling that it was already neat and clean, that the odours of damp and singeing feathers would not dare to penetrate such a place. A door connected this room with the other, small one. This also was clean and painted, with Polly's clothes hanging neatly on a dress rail.

'Are you going to make this your bedroom?'

'No. I'm going to keep my clothes in it and work things, and I'm going to see if I can have a basin put in there. Then I'll just have this room with the divan and chairs and things. What about you?'

'I don't know. I thought, as I'm not nearly as tidy as you, that I'd better make the small room a bedroom and have my desk and things in the big room.' And never, she thought, let anyone into my bedroom because it will always be such a mess.

'It's important to decide before we choose the papers.'

'I don't think it matters what I choose.'

'Oh, Clary! Don't be so humble. It's what *you* want that matters.'

They sat on Polly's bed, side by side with their backs to the wall and the enormous wallpaper book on both their laps.

'I like red,' Clary said after a bit. 'But I don't want people on horses and harps and things all over it as well.'

'Our rooms aren't big enough for that sort of thing.'

After a bit, the harps gave way to stripes of various dimensions, and Clary seized upon a narrow one in two reds. 'That's what I want! Just like the Opera House at Covent Garden. All the passages are covered with it.'

'I didn't know you liked opera.'

'I don't especially – well, I don't know whether I do, but Noël is taking me to it as part of my education. He says opera is nothing like it used to be, but, still, I ought to know the obvious ones. They nearly always make me cry – they're so full of doom.'

'Red is a bit hot for a room that faces south.'

'You told me to choose. Red is what I like.'

'And stripes will be difficult on these walls – they're so bulgy.'

'What's the point of telling me to choose if you're going against whatever it is?'

'I was only trying to guide you.'

'Either *tell* me, or let me choose for myself. I hate being guided.'

In the end she chose the red stripes for her smaller room and let Polly advise a pale yellow paper covered with small gold stars for the larger one.

But, she thought, as she lay in bed later, I'm always being guided by someone. Then she thought again, and knew that she meant the Formans – mostly Noël, but Fenella a bit as well, though not nearly as much. This was partly because everything about them was so completely different from anything she knew about other people that when she was with them she kept having to have things explained to her. Fenella had explained quite a lot about Noël to her. He was, or had been, an only child (his parents were dead and when alive they had not been in the least interested in him). He had been brought up in a small house in Barnet, but from the age of three he had been expected to fend for himself. He had learned to read

The Times when he was four and subsequently all the books in the house, had got his own meals (how on earth had he managed that?), had been sent to a day school in Highgate but had never made any friends since his parents would not let him have them home. In any case, he did not really like men much, Fenella said, only women – he adored the company of women. He had gone to the theatre, the cinema and to concerts by himself from the age of eight (how did he get the money, she had wondered, but she had not liked to ask). He had grown up without any love or care, had been treated as a not particularly desirable third adult in the household. His father had been an unsuccessful architect who had lived largely on a small inheritance, the remains of which had gone to Noël when he died. His mother had made periodic forays into various societies and sects – the Oxford Movement, Gurdjieff, and an Indian with a Japanese wife who gave talks in a house in Bayswater – but none of them lasted, and in between she lay on the sofa reading novels and eating cakes. Then one day she left – simply disappeared, so far as Noël was concerned. His father informed him of this at breakfast one morning, adding that he did not wish to pursue the subject. Her departure did not seem to make much difference to the solitary and separate lives of her husband and son. Somebody who cleaned the house twice a week did some shopping. Noël lived on school lunches and bread and butter and lamb chops in the evenings. A dreadful childhood, Fenella said. One could not treat Noël as one might treat anyone else.

She had to agree. His parents sounded like monsters: she could not imagine the awfulness of being abandoned by a live mother – hers, after all, had died when Neville was born, which was completely different, and she could

66

not begin to imagine having a father who did not talk to her. It made her understand Noël's contempt for family life, his dislike of parents, of children, of the institution of marriage even. When she asked Fenella why, since he so much disapproved of the last, he had married her, she said simply that he was a conscientious objector, and it had been to prevent her being called up. 'I've been reading the papers,' he had said one morning, 'and I think I'd better marry you.' This seemed to Clary to be the most incredibly sophisticated proposal she had ever heard of, and she received the account of it in respectful silence. How had they met? she had asked at last. He had advertised for a secretary for the literary agency, and she had replied to it, gone to see him, and been engaged. He had rented a top-floor flat in Bedford Square, where he lived and worked, and shortly afterwards Fenella had moved in with him. It was hard to see, Clary thought, how he had ever managed without her. She not only did all his typing, she cooked, washed his shirts, cleaned the house (he did not like the idea of anyone coming in to clean it), but she accompanied him on his vast walks about London or the countryside, read aloud with him until well after midnight every night and then made his last meal of the day – yoghurt, bread and butter and a glass of hot milk – which he usually took in bed, where he stayed for breakfast the next morning. He liked to breakfast early, Fenella said, and to read the papers in bed before he got up. This meant, Clary knew, that Fenella did not get much sleep, and indeed she had admitted once that on the occasions when Noël took women friends to the theatre or opera, she usually went to bed early and slept until his return. Unlike Noël, who was small and wirily thin with very thick gold-rimmed spectacles, Fenella was large, with big bones, a matronly figure and huge hazel eyes – her best feature – that sparkled with intelligence. Noël, she had told Clary, was the most remarkable and interesting man she had ever met. If this was true for Fenella, who was middle-aged, at least thirty-five and probably more, *obviously* it must be true for her. Her life was now split into two distinct halves: life with Noël and Fenella, and life with Polly and the family; and sometimes she felt as though she was becoming two different people – the old Clary, who was playing house with her best friend and cousin, who had had the magic joy of Dad's return from France and who had now got used to it enough to start worrying that he seemed changed and, and, she felt, was not happy, and the new Clary who was being educated in a thorough, serious manner about practically everything. Each day with the Formans opened up new vistas of her ignorance. Information, about the arts, the paranormal, transport, history, disease – Noël seemed to know what any famous people mentioned had died of – the state of footpaths, canals, railways in England, the cost of Elizabethan sweetmeats, how coracles were constructed, the dying words of an astonishing variety of famous men, the eccentricities of others – Nietzsche and his cream buns, Savarin and his oysters, a millionaire in the Isle of Man who played cargo ships with a map of the world and real ships that he owned . . . Facts, extraordinary, improbable (though she did not question them) streamed from him in an apparently ceaseless flow. He seemed to know perhaps not all but something about everything, and, of course, as she lived with him, Fenella was pretty knowledgeable as well. But what was so wonderful was that, although she knew so little, they treated her absolutely as an equal, a serious adult like themselves – in fact, they often evinced an amused surprise when she said that she did not know what Blue John was or who had founded St George's Hospital or on whose novel *La traviata* was based. All that part of it was exciting, and she enjoyed Noël dictating letters to her as she typed, using amazing words she'd never heard of, like desuetude or flume. At twelve thirty they would send her to the post office for stamps, or the bank with the firm's paying-in book, and when she returned Fenella would have lunch ready, nut cutlets – deeply unpopular with Noël so she and Clary had them rather often and he ate Fenella's meat ration, a chop or cutlet of a more desirable kind, with huge mounds of mashed potato and cabbage or carrots, followed by rice pudding, of which he was extremely fond, and then a cup of rather weak grey coffee. This meal was eaten on the top floor in an attic that must once have been a servant's bedroom. It was the nicest room in the flat, as the room below it had to serve as an office as well as the sitting room. There was a small room at the back of the office in which Noël and Fenella slept, but she never saw it. The lavatory and small, dark bathroom were on a half landing below – a bath, for Noël, was a rare and rather menacing event, mentioned several days beforehand as a date that pre-empted much else happening on that day. It was interesting to know somebody who hardly ever bathed, but when she told Polly this, her reaction was sickeningly predictable.

'No, he doesn't!' she had retorted. 'That's the whole point. He's just as clean as anyone else.'

'What about Fenella, then?' Polly had asked.

'I don't know about her.'

She didn't, she realised; she knew hardly anything.

Fenella, when she was alone with Clary – which was not often – talked only of Noël. She seemed to have no family, no discernible background. When Clary asked her what she had done before she met Noël, she had answered vaguely that she had been a private secretary to a more or less retired playwright. But she couldn't have been *born* doing that, Clary thought, she must have had parents and gone to school and lived somewhere . . . She asked Noël one day about this. 'Fen's parents? They weren't much cop. Her father died of drink and her mother committed suicide. You know what parents are. A mere biological necessity, if you ask me.'

She had remembered then that when her father had come back from France and she had presented them with this amazing news, they had been only politely interested, and after lunch Fenella had said that talking about France depressed Noël and so it was better to avoid the subject. 'It's because he wants to go to America, you see,' she had (hardly) explained. And Clary, who felt that she ought to understand what was meant and didn't, shut up after that.

Noël's sensibilities were as numerous as they were extreme, and this meant that conversation was fraught with traps. His favourite theme was how much better everything used to be, and they could be comfortably and nostalgically ensconced in the nineteenth century and he would be advising her to read Lytton Strachey's *Eminent Victorians* when Cardinal Newman – one of the subjects – would pop into his mind, his face would cloud over and he would fall utterly silent. Anything to do with religion was dangerous, she discovered, because he was afraid that there might, after all, be a God, some vengeful deity who would certainly consign him to Hell. Then Fenella would coax him, would go out and buy teacakes, would, after Clary had been sent home early, settle down to some soothing read of Bertrand Russell, or Mencken, or Erich Fromm.

Noël had been most helpful when she and Polly had been looking for somewhere to live – well, he had not actually been helpful in the end, but he had made some interesting suggestions of a romantic nature such as choosing a street with a name that she liked: Shelley, he said, had chosen Poland Street for that reason; or they might look into the possibility of taking one of the towers of Tower Bridge – think of the amazing view from its windows. But it had turned out that the towers were full of the machinery for lifting the bridge, and, anyway, it seemed to be miles from anywhere and Polly didn't think she would like it. She had chosen Floral Street in Covent Garden as a desirable name; there was nothing going there, but the agents in Covent Garden turned out to have this house on their books so perhaps he had been helpful in an oblique way.

The best thing about the Formans was that they took her writing seriously. She had shown Noël a half-written story about two people who met as children, and then had separate lives until they were grown up when they were to meet again and fall in love. It was Noël who pointed out to her that she would not be able to deal interestingly with this idea in a short story but that in the space afforded by a novel she could make all kinds of interesting things happen. 'For instance,' he had said, 'both of them being in the same place at the same time but not knowing it. Turning out to have shared an experience – like some great performance, say – that affects them differently.' He had also given her a fierce and detailed lesson on her misuse of the pluperfect, and discouraged her use of exclamation marks, quoting Cleopatra to her in the process. This had made her want to call her novel *The Visiting Moon*, but he had said finish it and then see what it is called. She had been struggling on with it in evenings and at weekends, but it had not gone at all well until Dad came back, which had somehow released some block in her and for the last two months she had written nearly half the book. In fact, Noël had been rather disapproving at her sudden output: he spent hours himself battling with abstruse critical pieces for highbrow magazines or, and more surprisingly, semi-amateur specialist publications – he was extremely fond of trams, for instance, and wrote an impassioned piece on their superior merits. He would take one or two weeks to produce a piece and she learned not to boast of having written ten pages in a weekend as Fenella said it depressed him. She spent an evening with Dad every week. He and Zoë were going to move back to London in the autumn and meanwhile he was staying with Archie, so she only ever saw Archie on his own at weekends when she didn't go home, and even that was tricky, because she worried about Polly still being in love with him. Polly had said that she never wanted to talk about it, a wish that had to be respected, but it also showed, she thought, that Polly still felt pretty shaky. If she was still minding about Archie, it would be far better if she talked about it – but there we go again, she thought, this family is rotten about saying things that matter to them and I suppose Polly's caught the habit. Still, if they weren't like that, I probably wouldn't have thought of making one of my main people like my family in that way, and the other one not. After that, she thought about the novel until she fell asleep.

Neville arrived just after ten the next morning saying that he'd come to breakfast.

'You can't have! You're far too late. I bet you had some at home before you left,' she added.

'Only a snack. Just four bits of toast.'

'*We* only had toast, and we didn't have four bits.'

'Mrs Cripps gave me these for you.' It was a box containing six eggs. 'I've brought them all the way up, so surely I could have one of them now,' he said when they had exclaimed over them.

'Give him one,' Polly said. 'Journeys do make people hungry.'

'It is hard for me to think of anything,' Neville said, 'that doesn't make me hungry. Of course some things are worse than others.'

'You can't be hungry just after a meal.'

'After an hour I am,' he said simply. 'It's hardly surprising. Do you know what we're *supposed* to have each week? One egg, two pints of milk, half a pound of any meat, four ounces of bacon, two ounces of tea, four ounces of sugar, four ounces of sausage, two ounces of butter, two ounces of lard, four ounces of margarine, three ounces of cheese and a small amount of offal. And at school we don't even get that. I got some scales and did a controlled experiment for a week. The meat was Irish stew and one and a half ounces of it was bones, the sausages are nearly all bread and some foul-tasting herb, the egg tasted of prayer books. I had to go without sugar all the week in order to weigh it up and of course it was nothing like four ounces—'

'They would have been cooking with some of your ration,' Polly interrupted, 'and you aren't counting the things you can get on points. Who would be eating your rations anyway?'

'The masters. Mr Fothergill, particularly. He's unspeakably fat and his sister sends him homemade sweets as well as him reeking of drink. Sometimes.'

'Here's your egg.'

'Jolly good. Much better than the dried ones.'

From this careless remark they discovered that he had had breakfast on the train.

'Honestly, Neville! You are a cheat! *Two* breakfasts already.'

'There is a worryingly dishonest streak in you,' Clary added.

'There is not. I simply didn't mention it. I forgot until now. The point *is* that I'm extremely hungry. If you want me to work for you the least you can do is keep me from starving to death.'

In fact, he painted rather surprisingly well and undercoated all of Clary's larger room so they didn't grudge him two enormous bacon sandwiches at lunch-time plus two iced buns that Polly had got from the baker. The sandwiches used up all their bacon for the week, but Polly sometimes got extra bits from Mr Southey who kept the shop below. The buns had been meant for tea so they had to go and get more of them for that. 'He's grown so terrifically in the last year, we can't grudge him,' Polly said. In the evening they took him to *A Night at the Circus*, which was on at a cinema in Notting Hill Gate, and then they had macaroni cheese and cocoa. The whole house now smelled of paint, which made a change from poultry and burnt feathers. On Sunday he said he was going to see Archie, so he'd only be able to paint in the morning. 'But I might easily be back for supper.'

He loomed over them – a head taller than Clary now – nearly knocking things over, asking for things: 'I forgot my toothpaste,' 'Can I borrow that scarf, then I needn't wear a tie?' and so on.

'It's amazing that you *clean* your teeth,' Clary said, as he squeezed two inches of toothpaste in a double row on his battered brush.

'I used simply to eat it. But ever since I saw Mr Fothergill's teeth I've cleaned them like mad. He never cleans them. They're like those very old yellowy almonds you get on fruit cakes.' His voice no longer veered about between squeaking and rumbling. When he raised his head to sloosh his mouth out, she saw that his Adam's apple was just like Dad's. He was still in his pyjamas. The jacket had no buttons left on it and his bony elbows stuck out from holes in the sleeves. All of his clothes looked a bit like that: the grey flannel trousers he had arrived in had turn-ups that were well above his ankles, which were flimsily covered by a matted network of much-darned socks that in turn were encased in huge blackish shoes. These last he wore as little as possible, removing them on arrival and only wedging his feet back into them to go to the cinema. 'The laces broke ages ago, you see, so I can't undo them. It honestly doesn't *matter*,' he said, sensing their disapproval.

He top-coated both Polly's windows still in his pyjamas and then disappeared to dress. When he had gone, they discussed him.

'He's just like Simon was,' Polly said.

'I think he's worse.' Clary was thinking of his hopelessly frivolous answers to their questions about what he was going to do when he'd finished school. 'I'd quite like to own a nightclub,' he had said. 'Stay up all night and make tons of money.'

'Is that *all* you want to do?'

'Not quite all. I want to enjoy myself, of course. I might own a theatre, or be a conductor of an orchestra just for fun.'

'Don't you want to do anything for other people?' As soon as she had said that, she realised how priggish it sounded. Too late. He had looked at her for a moment and then said blandly, 'I don't want to do good to people; I want to be done good *to*.'

'It's our fault,' Polly said. 'We've started having the sort of conversations with him that boring old grown-ups used to have with us.'

'He does love Archie, though.' Another thing she wished she hadn't said.

But Polly, who was struggling to open a tin of Spam, simply said, 'Well, Archie sort of became his father, didn't he? While Uncle Rupert was away.'

When Neville reappeared, wanting the scarf he'd borrowed from Polly properly tied round his neck, they both became bossy and maternal with him: Clary tried to get him to polish his shoes a bit, and Polly made an effort to comb his extremely thick hair which stood up in tufts round his double crown – useless: the comb broke almost at once and teeth from it and from some alien comb, since they were a different colour, emerged.

'Your hair is absolutely revolting! What on earth have you been doing to it?'

'Or *not* doing to it,' Clary added: she had been watching.

'I don't *do* things to it. They cut it sometimes. And I

76

put Brylcreem on it when someone lends me some. There's no point in trying to comb it. As long as it looks shiny, they don't make you wash it. We tried that oil you get in a little can for stopping things squeaking but it tends to stink. Brylcreem's much better. There's no point in you rolling your eyes at each other – it's *my* hair.'

He went after that, but all the rest of that day, while they finished the top-coating of Clary's room, took it in turns to have baths and had boiled eggs and Spam in the hot kitchen, from whose window they watched two men fighting each other with knives in the hot, dusty street below, the thought of Archie lay, unmentioned, between them.

'I think we ought to call the police,' Clary said. A small crowd had gathered. One of the men had blood on his shirt.

'There *is* a policeman – look.'

But each time he walked past the men, they threw their arms round each other in a warm embrace; the knives were nowhere to be seen. Eventually, since the policeman did not go away, the men gave up and wandered off in opposite directions.

'I think they were Cypriot,' Clary said.

'How do you know?'

'Well, there *are* Cypriots about, and English people don't fight with knives. But it's quite an interesting street to live in, isn't it?'

'Mm. I wish we could see a tree from the house, though.'

'Can't we?'

'Oh, Clary, haven't you noticed? There's nothing green to be seen out of any window.'

Neville didn't come back that night – he didn't even

ring to say that he wouldn't. They finished the Spam with some tomatoes. The bread was rather stale so they toasted it.

'We'll have to have Grape Nuts for breakfast.'

'There's no milk left.'

'Oh, *God*! How do people manage to keep on having meals?'

'If Neville was right about the rations, I can't think.'

'Why isn't it better now the war's over?'

'I told you what Noël said.'

'At work,' Polly said pensively, 'Caspar always seems to have smoked salmon sandwiches for lunch. Or a small pot of caviar.'

'Does he give you any?'

'Occasionally. When Gervase is out on a job he does. But often then Caspar goes out to lunch himself and I have to mind the shop. I have a sandwich and he gives me a bunch of invoices to do. They take ages because I'm not allowed to type them – they all have to be written with a relief pen and brown ink on frightfully heavy white paper. When he comes back, he goes through them for mistakes.'

'Sounds boring.'

'Yes, but the other parts of the job are all right.'

'You mean going to houses to see clients?'

'Yes. The clients are usually awful, but sometimes the houses are terrific.' She fell silent and her dark blue eyes became dull and slate-coloured, which Clary knew meant some kind of sadness.

'Poll?'

'I don't know. The state of the world, I suppose. I mean, we so looked forward to the end of the war as though life would be quite different and marvellous and

78

it isn't, is it? We so wanted the peace but it doesn't seem to have made anyone happier. And it isn't just us. Our fathers don't seem to be happy – at least I know mine isn't, and you've said you're worried about yours – and Simon is loathing the idea of doing National Service. Everything seems to be so drab and difficult and nothing wonderful that one thought might happen is going to happen now.'

She picked up her sewing and stared blindly at it before letting it drop again. 'The thing is,' she said unsteadily, 'that I can't seem *not* to love Archie. It somehow was the point of my life. It doesn't seem to *stop*. Before I told him I used to imagine things – you know, the rest of my life with him – but afterwards when I told him and it was no good, I lost the imagining part. Or I can't bear to. Yes, I think that's what it is – that I can't bear to.'

She was confounded. Polly had not said a word about Archie since she had said that she never wanted to talk about it, and somehow she had thought that although Poll was still, as she had put it to herself, a bit shaky, she had no idea that she was actually miserable. She longed to comfort her, to distract her from her pain, to produce some wise and kindly maxim that would shed a new, more hopeful light on the matter, but she could think of nothing.

'I don't know about being in love,' she said at last. 'I'm no help to you. I wish I was.'

'It's a relief just to tell you. I thought it might stop if I never talked about it, but it doesn't seem to.'

Much later she said, 'You don't think that I'll feel like this for the rest of my life, do you? It will stop some time, won't it?'

'I'm sure it will,' she answered, but she didn't feel at all sure. 'You'll tell me when it does, won't you?'

'Course I will.'

She felt a kind of respectful anxiety for Polly after that – respect because she was so good about it, going through every day feeling so sad, and anxiety because she had a secret fear that once you were possessed by some strong feeling you would have it for life.

∞ ∞ ∞

Louise sat under the blasting roar of a hair-dryer. It was six thirty in the morning, and her second day at Ealing Film Studios where she was being an extra in a film about Ancient Rome – a comedy with Tommy Trinder and Frances Day. Of course she would have liked a proper part, but she felt pretty lucky to be in a film at all. The metal rollers in which they had wound her long hair had become so hot that in places they seemed to burn the skin on her head. They washed everyone's hair every morning – she had discovered this on her second day. When they decided that your hair was dry, you queued for Make-up – an amazingly elaborate process that made everybody look older but far less distinguishable in other ways. When her turn came, she lay back in a chair in front of a wall of mirrors bordered by strong, naked lightbulbs while Patsy or Beryl sponged and rubbed the foundation (entitled Caramel Peach) all over her face and neck. Eyebrows were arched and darkened and then eyeshadow the colour of carbon paper followed. Then she had to shut her eyes to be thoroughly powdered. After this they painted her mouth – a huge Cupid's bow with a dark outline, filled in with vermilion lipstick applied with a brush. The last, and to her most alarming, part was when they stuck the false eyelashes to her upper lids, covered the gummed strip with eyeliner and then brushed on coats of blue mascara. This made her feel like a moth whose wings were too heavy for flying – it was an effort to open her eyes.

'Lick your lips. There you are. If you'd like to pop along to Wardrobe.'

The first morning she had looked in the mirror: below the rollers and hairnet was this flawless expanse of Caramel Peach in which she recognised her own eyes that seemed now to be surrounded with barbed wire. Her lips – improbably voluptuous – gleamed like a pair of satiny cushions. Glamour, she thought – she had never felt so glamorous in her life.

In Wardrobe they strapped her into a brassière top, so hugely padded that she could not see her feet. A minute skirt – split on one side – completed the costume, which was made of yellow velvet edged with a gold fringe. Her midriff was daringly bare, but she and eleven others, identically dressed, were supposed to be slave girls and she imagined that scanty clothing was meant to denote their abject status.

Finally, it was back to Hairdressing where the rollers were undone and her hair dressed high on her head to one side with a great switch of artificial ringlets that were draped tastefully over her right shoulder. Then she repaired to her dressing room, shared with five other girls, to wait until called. Yesterday they hadn't been called: had sat all day with flimsy dressing gowns round their shoulders smoking, drinking cups of tea and talking about the jobs they had nearly got instead of this one. The only moment of excitement had been when someone called Gordon had turned up to inspect them and said what about their feet? Wardrobe was sent for and said that nobody had mentioned feet to *her*. Thereafter an assortment of people were called in for their views. The Period Adviser sent to say that sandals were the thing; the Art Director said they were slave girls so why not bare feet? The Assistant Producer, who arrived last, said nonsense, this wasn't an Art film, it was a comedy fit for all the family and all girls' legs looked better in high heels. 'I don't mind what colour they are so long as they're nice high courts.' The Art Director said that high-heeled courts really didn't seem to him *right* with the rest of the costume. The Period Adviser said wearily that *nothing* would be right with that and what he was doing on this picture he really didn't know. Wardrobe suggested that if the girls were to wear courts, they really should be white satin dyed to match. Gordon said that the best thing would be to take some of the girls on to the set to see what Cyril thought. Louise was delighted to be one of them: she was longing to see a real film set.

So she followed Jeanette and Marlene, who were following Gordon, down a long passage and out through a door that opened upon a narrow concrete path to what looked like an enormously high shed with a door over which a red light shone.

'Why are we waiting?' she asked Marlene, after they had stood outside the door for a bit.

'They're shooting, dear.'

'Oh.'

Two very small men staggered up the path with what looked like a vast shallow stone urn thickly ornamented with dolphins and a small naked boy standing in the middle playing some sort of pipe. It smelt strongly of fresh paint. They set it down and one of them searched for and found a cigarette butt behind his ear which he lit.

Gordon looked at the urn with distaste. 'What you been doing with that, then?'

'It had to go back – wasn't sufficiently distressed.'

The red light went off, and Gordon opened the door. 'Right, girls, follow me.'

They walked through the comparative gloom, over the concrete floor that was intermittently beset with thick cables, upright canvas chairs, a make-up trolley, men standing at the bottom of ladders, saying, 'Are you all right, Bill?' or nothing, men with earphones standing over large black machines, into the blazing light of the set which consisted of an oval pool filled with some milky liquid, a marbled surround and at one end a marble seat or throne, on which a lady with ash-blond hair, wearing a pleated pink chiffon dress bare on one shoulder, a diamanté strap on the other, was sitting while a thin man in his shirt-sleeves crouched on his haunches at her feet agreeing with everything she said.

'I *know* you ain't, darling. That's the problem,' he was saying, as they got within earshot.

'I mean, she wouldn't, would she? Not in this dress.'

'You couldn't be more right. She wouldn't.'

'*I* don't see why I have to get into the pool.'

'Darling, asses' milk!'

'Sod the asses' milk. It'll be freezing.'

'Darling, it won't be. Brian has promised.'

'It was absolutely *icy* just now.'

'That was only a rehearsal. When we come to shoot I promise you it'll be *warm*.'

He became aware of Gordon. 'What now?' he said, in an entirely different voice.

83

Gordon explained.

Louise watched as his eyes swept casually over her body; he did not look at her face.

'Camera won't be close on her feet,' he said. 'We're way over budget anyhow. Just paint their toenails – gold, or something.'

So that was that. Nothing else happened that day.

In the evening, after most of her make-up had been removed – she was given some cold cream and cotton wool, but it took her ages – she had gone home on the Underground to Notting Hill Gate and then taken a taxi back to Edwardes Square where she now lived with Michael (on leave before joining a new destroyer which he was to command in the Pacific) and Sebastian and Nannie and someone whom Mrs Lines had described as a cook-general – a Mrs Alsop – and her small boy. Mrs Alsop and Nannie did not get on: Nannie had somehow discovered that Mrs Alsop was not Mrs at all, but simply and disgracefully the mother of David, who was small, white-faced and terrified of her. The feud was kept in check by both ladies wishing to make a good impression on Michael, who was blithely unaware of any tension, but Louise dreaded the future when, for an unknown amount of time, she was going to have to cope on her own with it.

Michael had come out of the Navy in order to stand as a Conservative candidate in the election, and he had been assigned what was thought to be a fairly safe seat in a suburb of London. Every day for three weeks Louise had accompanied him: sat beside him on platforms while he made rousing speeches about education and housing and small businesses, and then separated from him for the afternoon while the chairman of the local Conservatives' wife took her round to meet other wives. Often she would have to have three or four elaborate teas with cakes from cake baskets with ladies in hats with gloves and handbags to match who asked her about her baby and said how relieved she must be to have her husband home. She managed by pretending she was in a play: for three weeks she threw herself into the part of devoted wife of war-hero and young mother. Zee got several high-ranking Conservatives – including two members of the Cabinet – to come and speak for Michael, and they must have been favourably impressed by her performance, as Michael told her that they had passed on to Zee how well she was doing. This pleased a small part of her, but only a part. She seemed to herself to be made up of small pieces that bore very little relation to one another – as though, she once thought in a rare, clearer moment, she was a sheet of glass that had been hit with a hammer or bombed, leaving jagged fragments that did not fit together because so many bits had been shivered to smithereens. Every time she looked at a piece and saw some reflection of herself she felt uncomfortable and sometimes actually ashamed. She wanted approval, for instance, even from people she did not like. She wanted people to find her quite different from how she knew that she was. The acting of parts came in here and even this capacity divided her. She was astounded at how easy she found it, and appalled at her dishonesty. She supposed it was so easy because she did not feel anything very much – beyond mild discomforts, irritation at domestic strife or boredom if she had to do something that she knew was going to be dull. She managed hardly ever to go to bed with Michael, who had sulked for a bit, and now, she was fairly sure, had found consolation elsewhere since he had more or less stopped saying anything about another baby or the means to one.

She did not mind this very much, and when Michael lost his election by three hundred and forty-two votes to the Labour candidate, he immediately took steps to go back to the Navy, who seemed prepared to have him. This would mean the destroyer and the Pacific. 'For how long?' she had asked. 'Not more than two years,' he had said. The thought of this absence was a kind of relief. She felt that she could not make any decision about her marriage until he was really home and out of the war, and the thought of having to consider such a step as leaving him frightened her so much that she was glad to have what seemed to be a right reason for not having to think about it. She told him that she was going to try to get back to acting, and he had not objected. 'I should love a famous wife,' he had said, only half jokingly. But after strenuous efforts all she had managed to get was this part as an extra in what promised to be a pretty awful film. Then on the first evening that she had returned from the studios she found that everything had changed again.

'The Americans have dropped an atomic bomb on Japan.'

'I know,' she answered. It had been mentioned in passing that morning after Make-up and while she was being strapped into her padded top.

'Whatever will they do next?' Marlene had said after the lunch-break, but nobody had come up with an answer.

'If anyone mentions the word bomb to me again I shall throw a fit,' someone called Goldie said.

Nobody did.

'. . . darling, don't you realise? It could mean the end of the war.'

'Goodness!' she had answered. She didn't believe him for a moment. He simply liked talking about the war.

At the end of the second day at the studios they had the Cargills to dinner and she told them about how she had come upon Tommy Trinder in a corner of the set. He had been wearing a very short, pleated white kilt and he was all by himself doing a little dance, flicking up the kilt with both hands and intoning, 'Now you see it! Now you don't!'

It wasn't a success. Patricia Cargill said, 'Good gracious!', and her husband, to be Number One in Michael's destroyer, gave an uneasy smile and said, 'How awfully funny,' before he turned back to Michael who said, 'Take Patricia upstairs, darling, and leave the gentlemen to their port.' There wasn't any port actually; it was just a way of getting rid of her – of them.

She took Patricia Cargill upstairs to the pretty L-shaped drawing room. She had painted the walls white and hung curtains made of mattress ticking – grey and white stripes with yellow corded ties. She was pleased with this room, although there wasn't much furniture – a sofa and two chairs and a beautiful mirror that she and Hugo had found together. 'Thirty bob if you can take it home,' the man had said, and Hugo had said, 'Done!' He'd even persuaded a taxi driver to put it on his roof. Now it reflected the two main windows that looked on to the square. She knew, whenever she looked at it, that it still had an aura of happiness, and she could not look at it if she was alone. After the first misery of knowing that Hugo was dead, that she would never see him again and

87

that his only letter to her had been destroyed, she had to shut out all thoughts of him. In her frozen state the memory scorched her; it seemed easier to feel nothing at all.

She set about being a hostess. 'Do you want to powder your nose or anything?'

'No, thanks.'

'I'm afraid the coffee will have gone into the dining room but I could get you some, if you like?'

'No, thanks. I don't sleep a wink if I have coffee in the evenings.' Patricia gave an apologetic little laugh and fingered the graded pearl necklace that lay unevenly over the salt cellars at the bottom of her neck. 'Your little boy is two, isn't he? You must have been married awfully young.'

'I was nineteen.'

'We had to wait until Johnny got his second stripe. He wouldn't marry me on a sub-lieutenant's pay. We were lucky. He got promotion sooner because of the war. We married in 'thirty-eight – Johnny was in the Med and I spent a glorious month in Gib. We had such fun! Dances, and parties on board ship, and treasure hunts and picnics. Then Johnny got moved and I had to come home. I was pregnant by then, with the twins.' She gave her apologetic laugh again. 'I mustn't bore you with all that. You must have been awfully disappointed when your husband didn't get into Parliament.'

'Oh, well, I wouldn't have been much good at political life. And I don't think he minded. He'd much rather have his destroyer.'

'But that's rather what I meant. I mean, he'll be away for such a long time. Just when you must have thought you'd got him home for good.'

'It's the same for you, isn't it?'

'Not really. Johnny's regular so, of course, I'm used to it. It's you Wavy Navy wives I feel sorry for.' Her rather protuberant faded blue eyes rested on Louise's face with a look of kindly speculation. She leaned forward. 'If you don't think me impertinent, I *could* give you a little tip.'

Louise waited, wondering what on earth it could be.

'If I were you, I'd do my *damnedest* to start another baby. You'll be amazed how the time will fly if you do. And you can get through all the unattractive part while your husband is away.'

'Is that what you're going to do?'

'Oh, my dear, would that we were! But we've got four, and I don't honestly think we could *afford* another. I should simply love to because, after all, I think that that is what marriage is for. Some of it,' her pale face became mildly suffused, 'is rather over-rated, if you know what I mean.'

There was a short silence during which Louise wondered why she seemed to be the only person in the world who didn't want her to have another child. Nannie kept mentioning it: 'Sebastian keeps wondering when he is going to have a little sister, Mummy,' was one of the ghastly ways she would put it. To change the subject, she said, 'You don't think this bomb will stop the war?'

'Oh, my dear, I wish I did. But you know the Japanese!'

'I suppose not, then.' She had never met a single Japanese person and knew nothing about them. One of the things she had discovered about her marriage was that she didn't know anything about a whole lot of things that she didn't want to know anything about.

But two days later another bomb was dropped, and within a week of that the Japanese surrendered. Michael, after all, did not get his destroyer, and was to come out of the Navy and go back to portrait painting.

When she knew this, the decision about what on earth she was to do about her life loomed again and she was overcome with the apathy of terror. The film work was over – there had only been a week of it – and she was back to not being a good wife or mother. She had to talk to someone, and the only possible person was Stella, and she realised then, with guilty dismay, that she did not even know where Stella was or what she was doing. Michael had never taken to Stella, and although Stella had always maintained an enigmatic neutrality about Michael, Louise had felt uncomfortably that she did not like him much either. She rang Stella's parents and Mrs Rose answered.

'Ah! Louise! It is long since we met! Your son is well? And your husband? That is good. Stella? She is away. She is working on some little newspaper out of town – writing nonsense about what the bride is wearing at local weddings. Her father is not pleased with her – considers it a great waste of her education. Of course I have her number. Wait one minute – I'll find it. Please, if you see her, try to advise her to find a more sensible thing to do.'

They met for lunch in a pub in Bromley the following day.

'It won't be a good lunch,' Stella had said on the telephone, 'but it will be quiet if you want to talk.'

The place was empty. 'How did you know I wanted to talk?'

'Well, I didn't think you'd bother to come all this way simply to look at me.'

'It is good to see you, though. I'm sorry I seem to have lost touch.'

'We've not seen each other, but I don't think we've lost touch.' She picked up the menu. 'Let's get the food ordering over first. Now. You can have soup – tomato – or grapefruit. Both will be out of a tin. Different tins, you will be glad to hear. Then you have the choice between cottage pie or fillets of plaice. I advise the plaice. It will come with chips, which they have to make with real potatoes, whereas the pie will have that dreadful Pomme on top of it.'

'You choose, I don't honestly mind.'

For some reason that she could not understand, her eyes filled with tears. She blinked and saw her friend smiling with that familiar blend of cynicism and affection that Louise recognised as a family trait: her father's smile.

Stella ordered their meal and then pushed a packet of cigarettes across the table.

'I didn't know you'd taken to smoking.'

'I haven't. They're for you. Have one. The food will be ages. Tell me what you came to tell me.'

'I don't know where to begin.'

'Is it Michael?'

She nodded. 'It's no good. I'm no good at it. I should never have married him.'

'Are you in love with someone else, then?'

'No. At least, I was.'

'What happened?'

'He died. Got killed.'

'So now you're sort of stuck with him.'

'Michael?'

'The lover. It is very difficult to fall out of love with

someone when they die. I'm really sorry,' she added. 'I knew you didn't love Michael, though.'

'I thought I loved him.'

'I know you did. How much longer will he be in the Navy?'

Louise explained about all that.

The soup arrived while she was doing it and a plate with two pieces of rather grey bread.

'So you see, I thought I had two years to think about everything – to decide, I mean.'

'You could still have that, couldn't you?'

The idea startled her, and she rejected it.

'It wouldn't be at all the same. I mean, he's *there* nearly all the time. And we have to have dinner with his family at least once a week now that they're back in London. His mother hates me. He told her about the other person and so, of course, she hates me more than ever.'

'And what about the little boy?'

'He's fine. We've got a very good nannie. Zee adores *him*. He looks exactly like Michael did at that age – she says.' She felt Stella watching her – tried, and failed, to meet her eye.

The waitress brought their fish.

'Everything all right?' she said, as she cleared the plates full of soup.

'Yes, thanks. We were talking and it got cold.'

When she had gone, Stella said, 'If you did leave, what do you want to do?'

'I don't know. Try to get a job, I suppose. I haven't got any money, so I'd have to. And somewhere to live,' she added, after a pause.

'You don't sound exactly thrilled at the prospect.'

92

'I'm not. Why do you expect me to be thrilled at anything? My whole life's a mess.'

'Eat some lunch, Louise. One has to eat.'

She separated a piece of the fish from its black skin and put it in her mouth. 'They taste awful, don't they? Like thick, congealed water.'

'Plaice?'

'Nannie makes Sebastian have them for lunch. He hates it.' She picked up a chip and ate it in her fingers. 'Anyway. If you thought I shouldn't have married Michael, why didn't you tell me?'

'Oh, *Louise*! What good do you think that would have done? People don't take that sort of advice from anyone.'

'But here I am – asking you what you think I should do!'

'Are you?'

'Yes! Yes, I am.'

'Well. Since you *did* marry Michael, and you have a child, I think you should do everything you can before you are sure that you can't make a go of it. You couldn't do that if he was off in the Pacific, but you can if he's around.'

'He's sleeping with someone else. Or possibly several someones.'

Stella seemed unmoved. 'Have you been faithful to him?'

Louise felt her face getting hot. 'No. Well, I did have an affair – after Hugo died. But it didn't mean anything.'

'That's not really the point, is it?'

'What do you mean?'

'I mean that what you feel about something you've done doesn't alter the fact that you've done it.'

'No. I shouldn't have, of course.'

'I'm not blaming you—'

'Yes, you are.'

'No. Just wanting to get the facts clear. I think you need to talk to someone.'

'I'm talking to you.'

'No, I mean a professional. I think there must be many things you haven't told me. And some things you haven't even told yourself.'

'You think I'm *dotty* or something? You mean, I should talk to a *psychiatrist*?' She had never even *heard* of anyone who had had to do that. 'Do you honestly think I'm mad?'

'Don't be silly. Of course I don't think you're mad, but it's very plain that you are unhappy, and it seems to me that you keep doing things that make you more so. Perhaps you should find out why.'

'You mean that if I was told that it was all because I'm in love with my father – all that Freudian stuff – everything would be all right? All those people think that anything wrong with people is to do with sex or their parents, don't they?' She wanted a cigarette, but her hands were shaking and she didn't want Stella – she seemed to have turned into some sort of enemy – to see.

Stella reached across the table, took a cigarette out of the packet, stuck it in Louise's mouth and lit it for her. 'Whatever we are has something to do with our parents,' she said, 'and probably something to do with sex as well. I wouldn't know about that. But I *do* know something about unhappiness because of my aunt, Pappy's sister, the one who lives with us.'

'Why is *she* unhappy?'

'Uncle Louis was sent to Auschwitz. It took weeks to

94

find out. All we really know is that he was sent there in June 1944. Uncle Louis, and his very old parents and his sister. A friend saw them being taken away.'

Louise stared at her aghast, but Stella's grey-green eyes were quite tearless and steady as she said, 'I shouldn't think his parents survived the journey. Two days in a cattle truck without food or water or even enough air. I hope they didn't. Anyway, Aunt Anna *knows* about all that now. She has found out everything about it that she could, in spite of Pappy trying to shield her.'

There was a silence while Stella drank some water and she tried to imagine how one lot of people could do such awful things to other people and failed. 'She had a daughter, didn't she? You said that she had a grandchild that she'd never seen.'

'They were sent to another camp. Apparently that happened earlier. They did not live in the same place.'

'Oh – poor Aunt Anna! It's too much for one person!'

'Yes. She can think of nothing but herself and her losses.'

'How can you blame her for that?'

'I don't. I am trying to explain something to you about unhappiness. I'm not saying what people should or shouldn't do about it – just trying to tell you what happens.'

'I don't see how my sort of unhappiness can remotely compare with your aunt's.'

'That's not the point, Louise. The point is that when – I *think* this is true – when anyone becomes more than a certain amount unhappy they get cut off. They don't feel any comfort or concern or affection that comes from other people – all of that simply disappears inside some bottomless pit and when people realise that, they stop trying to be affectionate or comforting. Would you like some grey coffee, or some pink-brown tea?'

She chose coffee, and while Stella was ordering it she went to the lavatory. While there, she thought of Mrs Rose telling her to try to advise Stella to find a more sensible job. The idea seemed even more absurd than it had when suggested: Stella seemed in no need of any advice. Then she realised that she knew nothing about Stella's work or life, that the whole of the lunch had been spent on her problems, and that Stella's advice – that she should make sure that there was nothing she could do to mend her marriage – had not been hostile, was, in fact, nothing more than difficult good sense.

But when she returned to their table, which now contained only the three purple asters in a green glass vase and their cups of coffee, it was Stella who said, 'Sorry, Louise. I have been a bully. I'm afraid it runs in the family. Everybody at home is always telling everybody else what they ought to do. It's fatal to ask advice of a Rose – you get it with interest.'

'No, I asked you because I knew you'd be sensible. It just seemed rather frightening.' Then she added, 'I don't want to get like poor Aunt Anna.'

Stella shot her a sharp look. 'I know you don't, so you won't.'

'Tell me about you. I know nothing about your job or anything.'

'I'm learning to be a journalist.'

'Why here?'

'You have to start somewhere. The approved method is to get yourself on to some provincial paper where you report on absolutely any local activity that's going. I do weddings, amateur dramatics, sports, accidents, prize-givings, fêtes, bazaars, charity events – everything. Pappy is furious. He wouldn't mind if I was on the *Times Educational Supplement*, or even the plain *Times*, but he can't stand the idea of me scribbling on about the colour of bridesmaids' dresses or how much money a bring-and-buy stall made. He says I'm wasting all the money he spent on my education. I should be training to be a doctor or a lawyer, *he* says. And Mutti continues to dream of some splendid marriage for me to a very rich, very English man. I had to leave home because whenever they stopped getting at me, they started arguing with each other. And Aunt Anna thinks I should be working with the children who have been sent here from camps.'

'I didn't know there were children here.'

'There are several places in the country. Pappy offered to be a medical adviser, but he fell out with them because they were so strict about the food being kosher. He said in view of the state of the children *and* rationing it was idiotic to make it even harder to rehabilitate them. *I* had a row with him about that.'

'Why? You're not religious, and you're certainly practical. Surely you're on his side about that, at least?'

'It wasn't that I didn't agree with him personally, I just thought he should have been able to see the other point of view.'

'Well, what is it? I should have thought that the only thing that mattered was to get them well.'

'Their Jewishness mattered. They lost everything from being Jewish – their families, their country, their homes, their livelihood. All they have left is what they are. The older Jews did not want the children to forget or discount that, and religion *is* a core. But Pappy cannot get past his own disbelief. He always thinks people should think as he does. And, naturally, do what he says.' She smiled her cynical, affectionate smile. 'It's easier not to do what Pappy wants away from him.'

'So you have a flat here, or something?'

'Digs. I live as you did at Stratford. One day I shall graduate to a better newspaper – in London, or Manchester, or Glasgow. At least I'm ambitious. Pappy approves of that.'

She was silent for a moment, then she said abruptly, 'I did think of offering to go and help those children. Then, when it came to writing the letter, I couldn't face it.'

It was some confidence, confession, she was not sure what.

'It was such a *chance*, you see. Such a small, *little* chance. In the thirties, Pappy was a consultant at a big hospital in Vienna. He had evolved a new way to treat stomach ulcers and one morning he arrived at the hospital to discover that another doctor had cancelled his treatment. He had a violent row with the doctor, who called him a damn arrogant little Jew, so he walked out of the hospital and decided to come to England. He knew he would have to qualify all over again to practise here, but he was prepared to do that. We left Vienna the following week. I was thirteen then, and I minded leaving my friends and school and all my things. But if that man had not insulted Pappy that morning, he might not have come here.'

Louise stared at her, beginning to see what she meant.

'So. Sometimes the knowledge that one has escaped a certain fate makes one even more frightened of it.'

THE WIVES
October–December 1945

'*How* long did you say you've known this chap?'

'I didn't – but ages. He was a sort of friend of Angus's.'

'But he's married, you told me.'

'Yes, John, I did. But he wants to marry me.'

'That's no good if he's married already, though, is it? I mean, it's not quite the thing.'

She watched a thought strike him.

'Unless he's thinking of getting a divorce.'

She had forgotten, with all these years that he had been away, how slowly the penny dropped with her dear brother.

'Well, yes, he *is* thinking of that.'

She watched his face, once so florid and full of creases that denoted how much so many things puzzled him, now clear to the seamless vacuity that any small resolution afforded; but now his skin was the colour of yellowing paper, the ginger moustache was gone, his hair, once so thick and coppery, was dry and dull and receding – his whole body seemed to have shrunk inside his uniform.

'Can't help worrying about your happiness, Diana, old girl. You've had such a rotten time – Angus dying and all that.'

He had eaten all of the small bowl of potato crisps she had put out for him, but his whisky and soda was barely touched. He was younger than she by three years, but now he looked like a frail, middle-aged man. He had been in the Army before the war, had disappeared with the fall of Singapore and nothing had been heard of him for nearly two years after that. She had thought him dead, and then information had trickled back that he was in a prisoner-of-war camp. He had been repatriated a month ago after some weeks in a hospital in New York where, as he put it, they had fattened him up. God knows what he must have looked like before they had done that, she thought now. She was very fond of the old boy even when, as nearly always, he proved slow on the uptake.

'Darling, you're the one who has had a rotten time.'

She got up and poured some more crisps out of the packet into the little bowl beside him, and almost before she had finished pouring, he had started to eat them.

'Supposed to eat little and often,' he said with an apologetic laugh. 'I don't have much of a problem with the often side of it.'

'If you've been starving for years, I'm not surprised.'

'Bit of a greedy pig, I'm afraid.' He picked up the bowl. 'We used to get a bowl just about this size of rice each day.'

'Was that all?'

'Well, sometimes there were some vegetables, if we managed to grow any or if we had anything to barter for them. Mostly it was just rice. And the water it was boiled in. People used to try and grow things, you know, but quite often the Japs used to drive a jeep over them – plough them up. Used to wait sometimes, until the stuff was nearly ready to harvest, and then bingo!' He saw her face, and said, 'They didn't always do it. It was one of the punishments if they thought anyone overstepped the mark.' He reached into his pocket and took out a gleaming new pipe. 'Do you mind if I smoke?'

'Of course not, darling.'

While he was unwrapping his oilskin pouch and tweaking out the oily shreds of tobacco, stuffing the bowl of the pipe with unsteady fingers, the thought recurred that perhaps Edward might have some sort of job for him, and she prayed that they would get on with each other. The trouble would not be with Edward, it would almost certainly be with John. Her brother's ideas and opinions were hard to come by but, once acquired, he tended to stick to them. She had not dared to tell him that Edward had 'helped' her acquire the short lease on the mansion flat overlooking Regent's Park where she and Jamie and Susan now lived. And she certainly had not revealed Susan's parentage. She had explained all this to Edward, in case he dropped a brick of any kind. God! How she longed to feel free of all this hole-in-the-corner business, to have a proper house, large enough for all four children, with servants and possibly even her own car. Edward had still not told his wife of his intentions, and she would not feel safe until he had, although she knew that it was useless to push him. But she was also deeply worried about her brother, who seemed to have returned from four years of hell totally unequipped for peace-time life. He had always been in the Army, who now, after an extended leave, was chucking him out. In the weeks that he had been back, she had realised how poor his health was: attacks of malaria and some obscure stomach bug that came and went, periodically prostrating him. Although he was not very communicative, she sensed that he was lonely and utterly at sea. If only he was married! But he wasn't. The one or two girls she remembered him going out with before the war had never lasted, but with a mass of surplus women there must now be around per- haps she might find him a wife. He was not bright, but he was kind and honourable; he might bore the woman he married but he would look after her. She knew that as he was so lonely she ought to have invited him to stay in the flat, but that would mean that Edward would never be able to stay the night. Or – anything.

'Supposing his wife won't give him a divorce?' He thought for a moment, and then added, 'I mean, one couldn't blame her. Divorce is a bit *orf*, isn't it? Shouldn't care for it myself.'

'Oh, Johnnie, I don't know! Edward seems to think she will.'

The doorbell rang ('Good for him, he's remembered he hasn't got a key') and as she got up to answer it, she said, 'Don't let's talk about all that tonight. I just wanted you to meet him. He's going to take us out to a lovely dinner. Let's all just have a nice time.'

Edward was wonderful with him; when he wanted to be charming, there was nobody to beat him . . .

'Let's have a bottle of champagne as it's my birthday,' he had said when they got to The Ivy.

'Is it really? Many happy returns.'

'He always says it's his birthday when he wants champagne,' she had explained.

'You mean, they wouldn't serve it to you if it wasn't your birthday?'

'Oh, Johnnie, of course they would. It's just a joke.'

'A joke.' He thought for a bit. 'Awfully sorry. I seemed to have missed the point.'

'He feels he has to have an excuse,' she explained.

'And any excuse is better than none.'

'Ah.'

Edward ordered dinner: oysters for them, but John had smoked salmon; partridges – John had a plain grilled steak; and chocolate mousse – John did have that. When they reached the coffee and liqueurs stage, John asked if he might have a crème de menthe *frappé*. 'One of the things we used to talk about in the camp,' he said, 'you know, go round the hut and each of us say something we looked forward to when we got home.' He stirred the mixture with its straw. 'Partly the ice – it was so damned hot, it seemed like a marvellous luxury.'

'I know just what you mean,' Edward said. 'We used to talk about hot baths in the trenches.'

'Pretty difficult to have a hot bath in one of them—'

'No, I meant when we were in the trenches, we used to dream about hot baths. And linen sheets, you know, that sort of thing. Of course,' he added, 'it was different for me. I got leave from time to time. You poor beggars had to stick it out.'

'But more people died in your war, didn't they, darling?' she said.

'Dunno. I read that fifty-five million died in this one.'

'And they say that people are still dying from those terrible atom bombs,' she said.

John, who sat between them, had been turning his head from one to the other during this exchange – like someone watching tennis.

Now he said, 'Made the Japs surrender, though, didn't it? Don't know how many more people would have died if we hadn't.'

'But it does sound such a horrible way to die!'

She noticed that the two men looked fleetingly at each other and then away, but it was as though some unspoken, unspeakable message had passed between them. Then Edward said: 'Well, at least the war's *over*, thank God. We can turn our minds to something more cheerful – like the bloody dockers.'

Then, as John was beginning to wonder what was cheerful about – what was it? forty-three thousand of them on strike, Edward said, well, income tax. Who would have thought that a socialist government would reduce income tax, although heaven knew it was high time; one up to Mr Dalton, whom he'd met briefly when he'd been President of the Board of Trade – nice, unassuming bloke, he'd thought him. Then he'd turned almost affectionately to John and asked what were his plans.

'Haven't really thought. Been sort of getting used to normal life. Got six months' leave, then I'll have to find something.'

'You're not staying in the Army?'

'I'd like to, but they don't want me, I'm afraid.'

'I say, that's bad luck! Have another of those things?'

'No, thanks. One's enough for me.'

'Thanks very much for that wonderful dinner,' he said, when they dropped him at his club. 'Be in touch,' he said as he kissed her cheek, in tones that were uncertainly poised between a command and a plea.

'Of course,' she had said.

They watched him mount the steps, turn to wave at them and then go through the outer doors to be received by the hall porter.

'Poor old bloke,' he said.

'You were sweet to him.'

He put his hand on her knee. 'Isn't it a bit lonely – living in his club? Couldn't you put him up in one of the boys' rooms?'

She said at once, 'Oh, I think he'd rather be on his own – for a bit, anyway. He's told me that there are a lot of things to get used to.'

But she felt guilty (and angry) that her lack of generosity had been exposed – also depressed that he hadn't considered the implications. It was all very well for *him* to be generous with the flat . . . Then she thought that perhaps he *had* worked out that it would mean they could see less of each other and felt frightened. Of course, Edward had no idea of John's Victorian opinions about divorce, but they were the last thing she wished to expose him to at the moment.

'How's the house-hunting going?' she asked, when they were back in the flat and he was pouring them a nightcap.

'Pretty slow. The trouble is that so many houses are war-damaged that you have to have very careful surveys, and the bloke I've been advised to employ quite simply has too much on his plate. And, of course, one doesn't want to find another house while one is waiting for a survey. Villy found one she liked, but it turned out to be riddled with dry rot, which is rampaging because of spore being blown all over the place from bombed buildings.'

Which was a lengthy way of saying that nothing had changed. It was curious, these days, how they seemed to collude in conversations that were really sort of coded messages. She no longer dared to say, 'Have you told Villy? If not, why not?' And he was equally unable to say, 'I'm letting everything slide because I can't face telling her.' So she would ask about the house-hunting and he would tell her how difficult it was to find one. Occasionally the messages did become *en clair* – like the time when she had burst into tears and told him that she could not stand another winter in that cottage. He had been amazed: he seemed honestly to have had no idea how much she had endured there in terms of isolation and cold. Also it had been so awfully cramped when the older boys were home for the summer holidays that in the end she had had to capitulate and go to Angus's parents in Scotland for a week to leave Ian and Fergus – where they were, in fact, far happier – for the rest of the summer. But the outburst about the cottage had resulted in his helping her to lease this mansion flat, and this had meant that she had been able to afford Norma, a girl she had found in the country who was fond of the children and who longed to come to London. She still had to do the cooking, which she loathed, but the children ate simple nursery food and she, who seemed nowadays to put on weight at an alarming speed, tried to eat as little as possible except when she was with Edward.

'Bed?'

He put his arm heavily round her shoulders. 'You are my favourite woman,' he said.

'I do hope so, darling. It would be really worrying if I wasn't.'

They walked quietly down the long, narrow passage, past the children's rooms and the room where Norma slept: everyone was peacefully asleep. Norma knew that Edward stayed the night sometimes; she had been told that there was to be an eventual marriage, and the illicit romance clearly thrilled her. She adored Edward, who gave her stockings and often told her how they could not do without her.

Romance, Diana thought, as she was taking off her make-up while Edward was in the bathroom; *she* was romantic: she would never have dreamed of having an affair with anyone if she was not desperately in love with them. The trouble was that she had begun to ache increasingly for security, for knowing that the children would be all right, that bills could be paid, and romance and security did not seem to go easily together. Of course, if Edward was not married, she could have had the romance *and* the marriage. Then Johnnie could be staying with them – she refused to feel selfish about that because she was not really a selfish person, not deep down. Edward had once said that she was the most unselfish person that he had ever met, excepting his sister; she remembered how much she had minded there being an exception. Because the other thing that was happening to her was that she had to recognise that she was capable of jealousy, an emotion that she had always despised, thought unworthy of any really good person. Again, she knew that she did not *really* possess a jealous nature; it was the situation that was provoking these unwelcome feelings – for instance, Edward's apparent inability to tell Villy that he was leaving her must surely have something to do with feelings beyond moral compunction? And then there was his daughter, the older one that was married to Michael Hadleigh. He was very anxious that she should meet Louise, to whom, he said, he was devoted, and he'd told her that Louise had seen them, him and her, at the theatre one night and had been violently upset and that things had never been right between them since. 'If we could all three meet, I'm sure everything would be fine again,' he said. But he seemed nervous of actually making the plan. It was almost as though the meeting was to be a kind of *test*, and she felt that the idea of being judged as suitable or not for her father by a young girl – she was only twenty-two, for heaven's sake – was distinctly humiliating.

By now she had undressed and put on the midnight-blue satin nightgown that Edward had given her for her birthday. It had a low V neck out of which one breast or the other was constantly falling. They had not recovered their shape since feeding Susan. Edward had said that the blue was to go with her eyes, but actually it was more of a peacocky dark blue, whereas her eyes were hyacinth. *They* hadn't changed, at least, but in a way they only pointed up everything else that had. Her upper arms that were beginning to sag, the tiny broken veins in the middle of her cheeks that had to be covered with make-up, the slight, but perceptible slackening of the skin over her jawbone and her throat, which was no longer smooth and creamy as once it had been . . . How much more one missed things that one had taken for granted, she thought, and then, almost immediately, Will I ever feel that I have got what I wanted, or will what I want keep changing so that I can't? She wanted Edward and it was entirely his fault that she had not got him, so it was also his fault that her reasons for wanting him were changing. When she had been so much in love with him, her love and her unhappiness had in no way detracted from her view of herself or of him: he had seemed to her the most glamorous, desirable man she had ever met, and his simple and continuous capacity for enjoyment had charmed her. There was nothing ignoble in being so much enchanted by such a man, especially as all his attributes showed her so clearly what for years she had had to do without with her husband. Edward was not a snob, he was no spend-thrift; he spent money with delightful extravagance, but he had it in the first place – he did not use it to show off to people he wished to impress at the expense of paying the household bills. She had been disillusioned about Angus long before she met Edward. But now she had known him for over eight years – had been his mistress for nearly eight of them – had borne him at least one child, Susan, if not two, if Jamie was indeed his, although she noticed that Jamie had the Mackintosh nose, not something she drew to Edward's attention. She had also, inevitably, learned more about Edward, had recognised that his simplicity involved a lack of imagination where other people were concerned, and that his capacity for enjoyment had also a good deal of selfishness about it, that he also never seemed particularly aware of or interested in what happened to her in bed. These things she had been able, most of the time, to excuse, reason away or ignore. Men *were* selfish, and lack of imagination was perhaps something that the person suffering from it could not really help – there was nothing either deliberate or considered on their part. But the failing in Edward that she could not ignore was his lack of what she had to call moral courage. He seemed unwilling, perhaps actually unable to say anything to anyone that they might find uncomfortable. To begin with she had called this his kindness, but as this trait began to affect her own life it had ceased to seem kind. Sometimes, she was afraid that he would never bring himself to leave Villy unless she managed to force him to do so. With every week that passed now she felt her respect for him leaking away, which in turn made her desire to marry him less respectable. When he had told her in the summer, one of those last evenings at the cottage, that he was resolved to go ahead with informing Villy, she had felt a surge of such happiness and love for him that she had easily fallen in with the proviso that he must get Villy comfortably settled in a house in London first. But that was months ago, and nothing had happened or showed much sign of happening.

She got into bed and almost at once he joined her. She was not in the mood for being made love to, but after all the hints about Villy's unresponsiveness to sex she did, as usual, conceal this with a kind of breathless eagerness that she had discovered he liked. 'Darling!' he kept saying until he came. And then, as always, he asked her if it had been all right. Later, and full of amorous contentment, he said: 'I've been wondering whether we couldn't perhaps find something for your brother to do in the firm. It wouldn't be frightfully well paid, at least not to begin with, but it would be something.'

'Oh, darling, that would be wonderful! I know he'd be thrilled.'

'I'll have a word with Hugh. It might be at Southampton.'

'I'm sure he wouldn't mind *that*!'

'Don't say anything to him in case it falls through. Got to get the other side of the bloody dock strike first.'

'Of course not. Oh, darling, it would be kind!' She felt doubly grateful to him: for wanting to help her brother, and perhaps even more for being somebody whom she could admire as well as love.

A fortnight later, Edward announced that he had fixed the evening when she was to meet Louise. It was to be at his club, he said, because it was quieter and would she not come until eight fifteen, as he wanted to prepare Louise first. She was coming on her own, he added; he'd especially asked her to do that. 'I'm sure you'll love each other,' he said twice during the conversation, which made her realise that so far as he was concerned there was a great deal at stake.

While she was dressing for the evening, she remembered that he had once or twice alluded to Villy being hard on Louise. She had already discarded her hyacinth crêpe, caught on one shoulder, as being possibly too tarty, too much – to hostile eyes – redolent of the kept woman. Now she put aside the black *moiré* with a heart-shaped neckline (with which she had intended to wear Edward's amethyst necklace) – again it showed her cleavage which she felt struck the wrong note – and opted for her very old black wool with long tight sleeves and a high cowl neck. She was bored to death with it, but it was reasonably smart without being glamorous. For the same reason, she discarded her usual cyclamen lipstick, and used a duller, rose-coloured one. She was aiming at a well-groomed but slightly maternal appearance as the one that Louise would find most reassuring.

She had decided to save money and go on the bus – or, rather, two of them, as she would have to change at Marble Arch. But it was one of those still, raw, freezing evenings when the lack of a breeze simply made one dread fog. It was extremely cold waiting for the bus, but if she gave in and took a taxi she would arrive far too early. She must wait.

In the end, however, she had to take a taxi from Marble Arch, as after another freezing wait and no sign of a 73, she knew she would be late if she waited any longer.

She had only once before been to Edward's club – or at any rate this club of Edward's – and over the years she had been forced to recognise that, as mistress, she could not be seen on what was tacitly known to be family territory. It was a place where she knew he had taken Teddy for treats before or after school, where he went for a quiet evening with one of his brothers, where, of course, he took Villy. He would be known to most of the other members, and to be seen there with a woman not his wife or relative would cause talk. She understood this but, none the less, it had been another small resentment. She supposed that now Louise was acting as a kind of chaperone.

They were in the room where ladies were allowed to have drinks with members, off which was the dining room where they were allowed to dine with members. The heavy velvet curtains were drawn, and apart from a colossal chandelier, there were various little lamps with parchment shades that provided patches of mellower light. Edward and Louise were seated in cavernous armchairs in a far corner of the room that contained a number of other people having drinks.

Edward rose on seeing her. 'There you are, darling,' he said, as though she was late, but he absolutely wasn't going to blame her (she wasn't late – she had arrived just when he had told her to). He kissed her cheek. 'Louise, this is Diana.' He clicked his fingers and the waiter, serving drinks at the other end of the room, immediately responded. She exchanged wary smiles with Louise, who she had to admit was really rather beautiful, long, glossy hair hanging down each side of her face, eyes like Edward's but with heavier, darker brows and a mouth that turned up at the corners. She wore a black silk dress with a low, rounded neck. When she pushed her hair aside, Diana saw that she had enviably high cheekbones and that she was wearing opal and diamond earrings.

'We're drinking Martinis – would that suit you, darling?'

But she was so cold that she said she would prefer whisky. When the drinks were ordered, and she was seated in the third, enormous chair, Edward said, 'I've sort of been putting Louise in the picture. She's enormously understanding, as I knew she would be.'

Not knowing from this how far into the picture Louise had been put, Diana smiled again. Nor did she, during that evening, find out, so she concentrated on trying to get Louise to like her. To begin with, she appeared not to make much progress. Louise did not seem to want to talk about her famous husband, or her child, answering questions about either with a small, remote, dismissive smile which ensured silence and a fresh start. She admired Louise's dress – it was unusual, the skirt swathed tightly in front and gathered to a small bustle with a loose bowed sash. She was amazingly slender, with long, childish arms and pretty, long-fingered hands (her own were her worst feature, large and shapeless; she always noticed other women's hands).

'I had it made,' Louise said. 'Michael brought the silk back from Paris when he went there and I found this tailor in Soho called Mr Perfect. He can make anything – you just tell him what you want. He has an enormous wife who is corseted from just below her neck to just above her knees – she looks like a torpedo, but she is very nice as well. And Dad gave me these earrings. He simply loves buying jewellery, but I expect you know that.'

She suddenly remembered driving away from Lansdowne Road with him, and Villy's jewel box falling open on her knees and how sick with jealousy she had felt. This feeling was interrupted by Louise, who, with a far friendlier smile, offered to give her Mr Perfect's address and telephone number.

Edward looked at them fondly. 'My two favourite women,' he said.

What really broke the ice was talking about the theatre and asking Louise what plays she had acted in. Louise became animated and told her about the student rep, and the extraordinary house they had lived in and how they had all managed on one meal a day and had lain down in the road to get a hitch to the theatre in the mornings – it was three miles and if they couldn't afford the bus they had to walk it.

Edward said, good heavens, he'd no idea it was as spartan as that, and she had turned to him and said, 'But you never came to see. You were the only parents who never came, even when I was playing the lead in *Granite*,' and Diana saw that this hurt his feelings. He shifted in his chair and muttered something, but Louise went on, 'My mother thought I should be doing something to do with the war, you see, and of course Dad agreed with her. Well, you didn't *dis*agree, did you, Dad?'

From the way Louise said, 'My mother', Diana divined that there was a good deal of tension there. She said, 'One so *wants* one's children to fulfil themselves, to be happy and to do what they want. But so often they don't *know* what they want. I think it's wonderful that you were so sure.'

And Louise – she was really hardly more than a child, after all – positively glowed.

She went on to talk about the current theatre in London. Had she seen Coward's new play *Blithe Spirit*? It had a marvellous actress called Margaret Rutherford in it

114

as the medium, and Kay Hammond was delicious as the spirit. Edward said he really liked *her*: she'd been in a frightfully funny play called *French Without Tears*. She had 'oomph', he said, and Diana made a little conspiratorial face to Louise that meant men would confuse 'oomph' with acting ability. Edward said he'd take them to *Blithe Spirit* if they liked. He did not seem to mind, or notice, that she was ganging up on him with his daughter – seemed only delighted that they were getting on.

By the time they were having coffee and brandy, Louise was calling her Diana – at her request – and had accepted a second brandy. She had drunk a good deal before, during and after dinner, and Diana was surprised at her capacity. Wrongly, as it turned out. When Louise disappeared to go to the lavatory Edward congratulated her. 'Darling, she loves you. You hit just the right note with her. I can't talk to her about Shakespeare and performances and all that sort of thing.'

'What have you told her exactly?'

'Oh. That you are the only woman in the world for me – that kind of thing.'

'And about Susan?'

'Well – no. I haven't mentioned that. I did tell her that it had been going on for a long time. She asked if you had a husband, and I told her about that.' There was a slight pause, and then he said, 'You *do* like her, don't you, darling?'

'I think she's lovely. She looks very like you.'

'Nonsense,' he said, but he was clearly pleased. 'She thinks it would be better to get Villy into a house before I tell her.'

'Oh, does she?'

'Well, when I talked about it, she agreed.'

Which was not really the same thing, she thought, but did not say so.

The waiter came round for last orders for drinks – they were back in the ladies' room – and Louise was still absent. She said she would go and see if she was all right. She had to ask the way from the drinks waiter, who explained that it wouldn't be upstairs because only members were allowed to use them, and pointed out a passage at the back of the hall.

She found Louise hanging over a basin laving her face with cold water. She looked up as Diana came in; her face was white and glistening. 'I should never have tried lobster,' she said. 'I might have known it would make me sick.'

Diana handed her a towel. 'You poor girl!' but as Louise took it, she said, 'Oh, God! It's starting again!' and retired to the lavatory.

By the time she finally emerged, Diana had repaired her face, considered and rejected going to tell Edward that they might be some time.

'It's kind of you to wait. Sorry to be so revolting.'

'It's horrid for you. Bad luck.' She saw the reflection of Louise's wan face in the mirror above the basin – saw also, then, that her eyes had filled with tears.

'I used to *have* to eat lobster when I was pregnant,' she said, 'and I used to feel dreadfully sick then. It was silly of me to have it at all.'

Diana said nothing. It seemed a very unlikely story, but she also remembered that when young she had intensely resented the idea that she might have drunk too much.

'Oh dear, I seem to have gone a sort of greenish colour.'

'I've got some rouge if you'd like it.'

'Oh, thanks. Then I won't have to tell Dad. And then he won't ask me if I'm having another baby.'

It had just occurred to Diana that pregnancy rather than drink might be the trouble. 'Are you?'

'Oh *no*! I couldn't be. God forbid!'

She had finished with the rouge and was now dragging a comb through the damp strands of tangled hair. 'Do you love him?'

There was something so urgent, as well as unexpected about the question, that she was taken aback – found herself looking at the girl in the mirror whose eyes met hers with a direct curiosity that was irresistible.

'Yes,' she heard herself say, and then, relieved that she could say it, 'yes, I do. Very much.'

'Oh, well, then. You should go ahead. *Nothing* should keep you apart.'

Diana saw that there were still, or again, tears in her eyes.

When they rejoined Edward, he seemed neither to have noticed how long they had been nor that Louise looked ill. At Diana's insistence, he drove Louise to Edwardes Square before they went back to the flat.

∞ ∞ ∞

'You're not to worry about me. I shall be perfectly all right.'

But as the taxi drove away from the cottage and she turned in her seat to see her mother standing at the

117

garden gate waving, with a gesture that looked as though she was warding off flies, Zoë felt pretty sure that she would not be. Maud's death had been so sudden that her mother was clearly still in shock. She had gone to the island in response to the telegram – 'Maud passed away last night. Very sudden. Mummy.' She had set out immediately, having tried and failed to get through to her mother on the telephone. She had arrived at Cotter's End to find the door locked, but just as she was going in search of a telephone to see if she could ring the Lawrences or Fenwicks, the latter turned up, Miss Fenwick driving a battered old Vauxhall, the front of which was entirely full of Mrs Fenwick. In the back was Zoë's mother.

'There!' Miss Fenwick exclaimed. 'What did I tell you? I knew your daughter would turn up.'

'We just came back to see if things were all right,' she explained, as she helped Mrs Headford out of the car. 'But I had the strangest feeling that you might be here. Isn't that a wonderful piece of luck?' Her excruciating cheeriness changed sharply to a tragic undertone as she said to Zoë, 'It's been a terrible shock for her. I don't think she's been able to take it in. All right, Mother, I'm just coming. Mother didn't really want the outing before her lunch, but I couldn't leave her to herself.'

Her mother walked slowly round from the car. She wore her old camel-coloured coat and a black woolly turban that was not quite straight.

'Have you got your key, Cicely?' Miss Fenwick called from the car.

'I thought you had it.'

'I put it in your purse, dear. Have a look, just to make sure.'

Mrs Headford fumbled in her stiff, glossy handbag,

118

which opened suddenly. A bottle of pills, a pink comb, a small hand mirror and half of a fountain pen skidded across the frosty path between them. 'Oh dear!' Zoë, who had been going to kiss her mother, stooped to retrieve everything.

'Have you found it, dear?'

'What? Oh – the key.' She fumbled again and produced an imitation snakeskin purse with a zip fastener. The open bag hung drunkenly on her arm while she battled with the zip on the purse.

'Let me do it.' Zoë took it. The zip was stuck because its teeth had caught the lining, and she had to wrench it open. The purse contained a ten-shilling note and six-pences, but no key.

'I remember now. I put it in my coat pocket to be more handy.'

Zoë put all the things back into her mother's bag.

'I'll bring over your night things after Mother's had her rest,' Miss Fenwick called, and the car moved off with a convulsive leap.

'I should have told her there was no need. I have other night things and I don't want to be a burden.'

They had walked up the path to the front door, which her mother failed to unlock. 'Maud always had the key,' she said, as she stood aside for Zoë to do it.

'It opens anti-clockwise, Mummy, that's why you couldn't do it.'

The house had the dank, silent air of a place abandoned for far longer than twenty-four hours. It was extremely cold.

'I think we'd better light the fire, Mummy, before we have lunch.'

'Do you, dear? Maud used to leave it until after tea.'

'But isn't it rather cold?'

'Well, it *is* cold weather, dear, so it would be.'

They had gone down the passage to the small sitting room. Two glasses and a sherry decanter stood on the rickety table by the window, whose curtains were drawn. Zoë opened them and the increased light seemed mostly to reveal a kind of ashy dust everywhere. Her mother's crochet lay splayed on her usual armchair. The fireplace was full of ash; a vase of dead chrysanthemums stood on the mantelpiece, which had Christmas cards leaning against the china rabbits and bottles of striped and coloured sand.

'I think we'd better both have a glass of sherry.' Her mother went to the glass-fronted cupboard that contained glasses and teacups. 'It was good of you to come,' she said, and her eyes, which were puffy from crying, filled with tears. Zoë put her arms round the soft, stiff body and her mother broke into convulsive, wailing little sobs. 'She was quite all right yesterday morning. At breakfast we had a little piece of fried bread because somebody had given Maud a tin of mushrooms and we were finishing them up as they were too rich for one meal. She was going shopping after – she always went on Tuesdays – and she was going to change my library book, but I'd left it upstairs. She *would* go – she wouldn't let me fetch it. I heard a crash and I thought she'd fallen down, and I went out and there she was – just lying there!'

For a moment she was speechless, and covered her face with the handkerchief Zoë gave her. 'I thought she'd fainted and I went to get a glass of water, but you know how it is when something unexpected happens – I couldn't find a clean glass and then I had to let the tap run because the pipes are funny here and she always said

120

let the tap run. When I went back to her, I realised – I realised that she wasn't breathing. I went and rang the doctor and then I went back and sat on the stairs with her. Oh, Zoë! It was such a dreadful shock!'

Zoë settled her in her chair and poured out the sherry. 'Then what happened?' She felt it was good for her mother to tell the whole story.

'I took off her hat.' She looked at her daughter as though appealing for approval. 'It seemed wrong for her to be lying there in her hat.'

'Drink some sherry, Mummy, it will do you good.'

During the rest of the sherry – there was enough left for two drinks each – she had learned that the doctor had come and said that Maud had had a heart attack. He had arranged for her to be taken away, and he had rung Miss Fenwick who had come and fetched *her*: 'They didn't think I should be alone, you see. Everyone was very kind – very thoughtful.' She had come back this morning to collect some clothes and to see if the cat was all right. 'I sent you the telegram, because I thought you ought to know.'

She had lit the fire and then gone to the kitchen to find something for them to eat. They had lunched off a small tin of baked beans with toast.

During the next few days before the funeral she had learned: from the doctor that, in fact, Maud's heart had been in what he described as a dicky state, 'But she never wanted it mentioned or known because she didn't want to worry your mother'; from a lawyer in Ryde, who came out to see them, that Maud had left the cottage and its contents to her mother, together with what he said would amount to a few thousand pounds, 'Her pension, of course, stops at her death'; and from her mother that she had every intention of staying on in the cottage. Zoë had suggested that she might like to return to London, but her mother had said, 'No, dear. I have *friends* here. Cotter's End is my *home*. And, after all, I'm used to being on my own.'

But years with Maud had softened her up. It had been Maud who had shopped and cooked for them both, who had made the decisions, who drove the car – her mother had never driven. It had been Maud who had paid their bills, who had got repairs to the cottage done, had taken things to be mended, had collected her mother's prescriptions.

The days before the funeral had been spent in helping her mother clear out poor Maud's clothes, all bought to be serviceable and most having done more than could be expected of them. The vicar said that they could go to the bring-and-buy stall for the Christmas bazaar and her mother seemed to think this was what Maud would have wished. Presumptions about her friend's desires loomed large during those days, and chief among these was the notion that Maud would have wished her to remain in the cottage. 'I'm sure that's why she left it to me,' she kept saying. After the funeral, friends had crowded into the small sitting room for tea and sandwiches and sherry, kindly donated by Colonel Lawrence, whose dog ate most of the sandwiches – potted meat and Maud's marrow and ginger jam.

Zoë had a talk with the doctor about her mother's health, which he said was considerably better than Maud's had been. The Lawrences and Miss Fenwick said that they would take turns to take her mother to town to shop. Doris Patterson, who had been coming in once a week to do the rough for them at the cottage, offered to come twice, which Zoë felt her mother could afford. Everybody had been kind and helpful, but Zoë, who had noticed how her mother stood by while she struggled with meals and washing-up, was still worried. She suggested that perhaps some of Maud's money (possibly all of it) might be spent on putting in central heating in the cottage, but her mother was dead against the idea: she was certain that Maud would not have wished it. 'She always said that central heating was death to good furniture.' The good furniture consisted of the glass-fronted corner cupboard and a chest of drawers in Maud's bedroom, but there was no point in arguing.

So here she was a week later, jolting along in the local taxi cab to catch the train for the ferry and then the train to London.

In the London train, crowded because it was nearing Christmas, she was assailed by the memory of her meeting with Jack. She had thought then that she was unhappy enough – guilty about her mother, despairing about Rupert's still being alive . . . and then, out of the blue, had come Jack to transform her life, it had seemed at the time.

Now, although the quality of her unhappiness had changed – the only familiar part of it being her guilt about her mother – she felt that nothing could come from anywhere that could possibly transform it. The difference, she thought – she felt too weary to read – was that before Jack she had had some kind of *right* to her unhappiness, with a husband missing and presumed (at least by her) to be dead. Now it was Jack who was missing; his death, and the manner of it, was something that she was still, after all these months, unable to contain in her consciousness for more than a few seconds. Every time she thought of him – a dozen times a day or night – the same shocked

123

imagination of his last bleak day replayed itself, his efforts to write to her and his abandonment of them in favour of writing to Archie (what would have happened if she had not taken him to see Archie that evening which now seemed so long ago, who else could he have written to, and, if nobody, how would she even have known of his death?), his driving back from some airfield to the terrible camp and finding some place where he would be alone for those last minutes of his life before he put an end to it, an act that implied courage and despair on a scale that she could not bear to consider.

She had gone back to the studio to clear out her clothes before she returned the key to the agent. It had been something she had dreaded – had nearly not done – but in the end she had felt it was necessary. She had trudged up the dark, dusty stairs with her empty suitcase, resolving to spend as little time there as possible, to pack up and leave. But when she opened the door she realised that he had stayed there since their last time together: the bed was unmade and an ashtray full of stubs lay on the table beside it. She walked through to the tiny kitchen to open a window and there was a jug with coffee grounds in it and an upturned mug on the draining board. His dressing gown hung on the back of the bathroom door and there was a used razor blade in the soap dish of the basin, which had a high-water mark of greyish dried soap foam. She touched this with a finger and could see the dark bristles from his shave. All these things continued to exist.

As she went back to the studio, the loss of him struck her like a heavy cold tide that threatened to drown or suffocate her, and unable to stand, she collapsed upon the rickety divan. The pillow was still dented. She put her face where his head had lain and actually screamed.

Some time later, when she had cried herself out, she sat up and set about the packing up. In his dressing gown pocket was the usual packet of Lucky Strikes. She smoked one before throwing the rest away, but even the familiar smell of the burnt caramel taste in her mouth evoked nothing. She had felt light and empty – as dry as a dead leaf. She had finished the packing, washed up the coffee jug and the ashtrays, cleaned the basin and folded the bed linen into a neat pile, had left the place which had contained their life together and taken the key back to the agents.

After that, the fact that he was dead was no longer a shock, but the manner of his dying continued to haunt her, and she could neither understand, nor accept, nor come to terms with it. Sometimes it seemed to her that his giving of his life was an heroic gesture of courageous love; sometimes it seemed that his taking of his life was an utter rejection of her with no love in it. Always the *difficulty* of the act terrified and appalled her: how could anyone make such a decision and live through the hours before carrying it out?

And then, an ordinary afternoon with Juliet determined to get her own way – the fruitless argument about going back through the woods or not – she had turned her head and there was Rupert walking towards her. She had thought he was an apparition, a ghost, had put out her hand to touch him, to ward him off, but when he spoke a different kind of fear invaded her and she took refuge in Juliet, had watched *their* meeting, so simple, she felt, compared to hers with him. Juliet had eased things between them: they had played her game with her; it was only when he helped her off the tree trunk that she saw that he felt as shy, as nervous as she. She had chattered about the family all the way home, faltering only when she came to Archie as she remembered how kind he had been about Jack, and she had fallen momentarily silent . . . They had not really been alone together until after dinner. She had sat trying to sew Juliet's frock while he talked about Pipette and her mother. Then he had tried to say something about his being away and what it must have been like for her and she was overwhelmed with confusion and guilt – wanted to flee and then was ashamed that she was not welcoming him, brushed it off with the excuse that his sudden appearance had been a shock (this, at least, was true).

She had undressed in the bathroom and it was while she was unpinning her hair that the turquoise heart, lying in the hollow of her throat, caught her eye. Jack's present to Juliet. She had been keeping it for when Juliet was older, but after Archie had come to tell her that he was dead, she had slung it on an old chain and worn it ever since, as a kind of talisman, or mourning, she was not sure which. She unfastened it and put it out of sight. She had got into bed and lain rigidly waiting for him. But when he had simply kissed the side of her face and turned out the light she had had the sudden and most violent urge to turn to him, to tell him all that had happened with Jack, to weep in his arms (for Jack) and to be absolved by him. But she did not. Once, she thought, she would have been so selfish, so absorbed in her own pain that she would have been unable to consider what he might feel. Much later – not that night – she knew she *had* to recognise that telling him about Jack would put him further in the past than she was ready for. Rupert's reappearance had not only interrupted her grief, it had made her feel guilty about it.

Sometimes, in the weeks that followed, she wondered whether Rupert sensed something. Certainly he seemed different – withdrawn, tentative, almost apologetic. He was tired, he said, and there was a lot to get used to again – life was so different, although he was uncommunicative about what it was different from.

At the Duchy's suggestion, they had gone away for a weekend in Brighton. This had been after Rupert was officially out of the Navy, in August. She was never very clear why Brighton had been chosen: the Duchy had suggested it, and Rupert had looked at her and said, 'Would that be OK for you?' She had answered that it would. There had been a lack of enthusiasm about the venture that had unnerved her; her own part in this made her feel guilty (the least she could do was to agree to whatever was suggested), but when she realised that, for reasons unknown to her, Rupert felt much the same, she felt frightened. What should they do? she wondered. What should they talk about? And then there was the business of going to bed together with the uncertainty about whether he would make love, or try to make love to her – both these things had happened at widely spaced intervals, and the occasions had been like meeting someone you hardly knew wearing no clothes at a party and pretending there was nothing unusual about it. Pretence certainly came into it. She pretended to feel what she thought he wanted her to feel; in a curious way, she felt responsible for their lovemaking, which had never happened in the old days, but she also felt *responsible* to Jack – going through the motions was not betraying him, but getting pleasure from it would be, in some way, despicable. Once, she had imagined someone telling the story of her and Jack – one man telling another – and when the teller reached the point of Jack's death, the listener, after the appropriate pause, would ask, 'And what became of the girl?' 'Oh, her! *She* simply went back to the husband as though nothing had happened.' Smiles of worldly contempt for such a vapid, unfeeling creature.

But Jack in his letter to Archie had said, 'Maybe that husband of hers will come back to her?' so he must have envisaged that as a kind of solution. And there he was, sitting opposite her in the train to Brighton, a kind and gentle man, looking much older, more gaunt – indeed, as though he had been through a good deal during those interminable four years. But now he no longer seemed so much older than she, as he had done when she married him, then in her early twenties. He would always be twelve years older, but now, at thirty, she felt as old as anyone – too old for that age gap to have any significance.

He looked up from his paper, caught her eye. 'Your hair looks very pretty.'

She remembered how – in the early years of their marriage, when she had been jealous of the time he spent with his children, and their mother, the dead Isobel, had seemed an even worse threat because he never talked about her – he would coax or reassure her by admiration for her appearance, homage that she would only notice if it was absent, and how she had longed to be admired for other things, her intelligence, her character, aspects of her that now, she felt, had not been worthy of remark.

She smiled at him, and said nothing.

Their hotel was enormous – mahogany and dark red carpets, ancient porters with waistcoats like wasps, endless corridors dimly lit. Eventually, at the end of one, the old man carrying their cases stopped in front of a door that was next to the fire escape, wheezed and fumbled with the key, and displayed their room. It had a small double bed, she noticed at once, and net curtains that did not conceal that their view consisted of another wall of hotel bedroom windows.

Rupert said, 'I asked for a room with a sea view.'

'I wouldn't know about that, sir. You could ring down to reception.'

He did, and after some argument was offered a room two floors up. They would send up a boy to meet them at the lift with the new key.

When they got to the new room, it proved to have twin beds. Rupert did not seem to have noticed this. He had given the porter half a crown and gone straight to the window. 'That's better, isn't it, darling?'

She joined him to look at the sea heaving on to the stony beach like molten lead in the sunset, with black breakwaters and the pier on its spidery stilts. The sky was streaked with narrow clouds of apricot and violet.

He put an arm round her. 'We'll have a nice time,' he said. 'You jolly well deserve a hol. Shall we have a bottle of champagne up here?'

Yes, she had said, that would be lovely.

He turned to the telephone and saw the twin beds. 'Oh, Lord! They never said – shall I have another go at them?'

But she said, don't. They could push the beds together – she couldn't face another move. She thought, but was not sure, that he was relieved, and she remembered with some shame how she had used to make minor scenes if things were not absolutely to her liking. She said she would unpack and have a bath and he said fine, he would go for a walk by the sea and come back with the champagne in half an hour.

That first evening, during which they both drank a lot – a bottle of burgundy after the champagne and then brandy with the grey-looking hotel coffee – he said: 'Zoë. We really ought to talk.'

Terror, and somewhere at the back of it relief – something like it – invaded her. He knew about Jack. Or knew something – or *wanted* to know? At any rate if he *asked*, she would have to tell him and having to tell was different from choosing to tell him – it felt like the difference between honesty and the wilful infliction of pain. She finished her brandy and reached for one of his cigarettes.

'You never used to smoke!'

'Oh, occasionally. I'm not really a smoker.' Nor really unfaithful, she thought. You can't be unfaithful to someone whom you thought was dead. She meant him, but then she realised that this could equally apply to Jack.

He lit her cigarette for her, and one for himself. 'I mean, the house, for instance. Do you think we want to keep it, or would you rather we looked for one that was nearer a park? Or we could get a flat. I don't think poor old Ellen is up to all the stairs in Brook Green. Edward wants me to go and run Southampton. I've told him I don't feel remotely up to it, but if you wanted to live in the country, I'm willing to have a go. And Hugh – I want you to have all the options – did say that if we wanted to share his house, we would be more than welcome. I think he was partly thinking of Wills, and how it would be nice for him to go on being under the same roof as Ellen. I don't expect you would like that, but I thought you ought to know it was on offer.'

Another relief, this time coupled with the kind of irritation that accompanies being given a fright and the consequent expenditure of needless courage. There was nothing to be brave about; she fell back upon being accommodating. 'What would you prefer?'

But, of course, he didn't know: decisions had never been his strong suit. She knew that if she had advocated any one plan, he would have fallen in with it, but she could only think of what she didn't want. She didn't want to lose Ellen, she didn't want to go back to the house in Brook Green that had always struck her as dreary, and in any case had once belonged to Isobel, but after that . . .

They spent the rest of the evening in polite and fruitless discussion.

In the night she woke and it came to her that perhaps Rupert was so indecisive because *he* didn't want any of it. Perhaps, now, he should go back to painting and/or teaching, and their having less money would mean that she might find some sort of job that would fill her life. Perhaps they could go and live in France with Archie. A completely new life – in the night it seemed to be the answer.

But when she had suggested this to him, he seemed appalled. 'Oh, no! I don't think so. I think it's a bit late to be thinking of that sort of thing.'

'But you often said how much you love France—'

'France? What's France got to do with it?'

'I thought you specially liked painting there—'

But he interrupted her, coldly. 'I haven't the slightest desire to live in France.'

There was an almost sullen silence.

'Is it – is it because you had such an awful time there?'

'No. Well – partly. I just wouldn't want to.'

They had been walking along the beach – the shingle hurt her feet and they had sat down with their backs to the breakwater. When he fell silent again, she turned to look at him. He was staring at the sea, preoccupied, withdrawn. He swallowed as though to rid himself of something painful, but he didn't look at her.

'Wouldn't it help to tell me about it?'

'Tell you what?'

'What happened to you. What it was *like*. I mean – why couldn't you come home some time after D-Day? Why did it take so long? Were you kept as some kind of *prisoner*?'

'No – not exactly. Well, yes, in a way. It was a very remote place – the farm . . .' There was a pause, then he said rapidly: 'They'd sheltered me for so long, looked after me when it was dangerous for them and there was a fearful shortage of able-bodied men. I felt I had to stay on a bit to help – you know, the harvest and so on.'

After a moment, she said, 'But harvests are in the autumn!'

'For God's sake, Zoë, stop trying to *trap* me! I made a promise to stay as long as I did. Will that do?'

Resentment, anger that she had not known was there, possessed her. 'No, it won't. You could at least have sent a message, written. What do you think it was like for your mother? For Clary? For me? Not hearing *anything* after the Allied landing meant that we thought you *must* be dead. You made everybody suffer when there was no need. Don't you see how incredibly selfish that was?'

132

He didn't answer – simply put his head in his hands with one racking sob. Before she could do anything, he took his hands from his face and looked at her. 'I *do* see. I *do* realise. There's nothing I can do about it now. I can't excuse it – it was just another life, different problems, difficulties. I can only say that, mad though it may seem to you, it seemed the right thing to do at the time. I don't expect you to understand that. But I am sorry – ashamed to have caused you so much distress.'

He was trying to smile; there were tears in his eyes. To put her arms round him, to kiss his face was not difficult. The rest of the weekend was spent in a kind of emotional calm: they were kind to each other; they finished their walk, had lunch in a bad restaurant, went to a cinema, browsed in second-hand bookshops, dined in the hotel, decided to give up the house in Brook Green, but got no further. 'You know what I'm like about decisions,' he had said. 'One is quite enough.' Through it all they were careful of each other. She was relieved both that he seemed to want no more from her than that, and also for those random hours in the day – in the bookshop where he found her a first edition of Katherine Mansfield that she was delighted to have, and during a long talk about whether Juliet should be allowed to have a puppy, currently her dearest wish – when she discovered that time had passed when she had not been thinking of Jack.

On Monday they had gone back to London; he had stayed there and she had returned to Home Place.

The Duchy had welcomed her affectionately. 'You look as though you have had *some* rest,' she said, and then Juliet and Wills, clattering down the stairs, had intervened.

'Mummy! While you were away Wills sleepwalked!

He sleepwalked down the stairs into the dining room! They put him back to bed and in the morning he said he didn't know he had sleepwalked at all! The next night I sleepwalked only I nearly fell down 'cos you can't sleep-walk downstairs at all well with your eyes shut and they put me back into bed and I can perfectly remember it. And Wills said I can't really have sleepwalked 'cos when you sleepwalk your eyes are open! They can't be, can they? Anyway, when *I* sleepwalk I sleepwalk with my eyes shut. I do it like this.'

'She only pretends,' Wills said. 'She doesn't do it properly – she's too young for that sort of thing.'

'I'm not too young for anything! I may not look it, but inside I'm older than I look. Like you, Mummy. Ellen says you're older than you look.'

'Ha, ha, *ha*,' Wills said, very slowly indeed. 'Would you like to see my tooth?'

'She wouldn't. I saw it and it was quite boring. Do you know what the Duchy told us? When her teeth were loose when she was a child they used to tie a piece of string to it and the other end to the door handle and slam the door and the tooth just jumped out at them and then she got a penny for being brave.'

'I'd charge a lot more to let people do that to me,' Wills said, and she said she agreed with him.

'Oh, Mummy! Don't agree with *Wills*, agree with *me*! She's *my* mother!' And she flung her arms round Zoë's legs and glared challengingly at Wills, whose face, Zoë saw, became suddenly blank.

'I'll carry your case, Aunt Zoë,' he said.

A few days later, she found herself alone with the Duchy. They had finished picking the sweet peas – a job that needed doing every two or three days – and were sitting on the seat by the tennis court. The Duchy took a cigarette out of her shagreen case and was returning it to the pocket of her cardigan.

'Could I have one?'

'My dear, of course. I didn't realise that you were a smoker.'

'I'm not really. At least, every now and then I have one.'

Silence, because she could not think how to start. She looked at the calm, frank face of her mother-in-law. One was supposed to find that relationship difficult, but she felt nothing but a profound gratitude for the Duchy's steady, perceptive kindness, right from the beginning when Rupert had brought her into this family, a spoiled, self-regarding girl, through the guilt and depression after that first baby's death, and then all the war years when Rupert was missing. It had been the Duchy who had encouraged her to go and work in the convalescent home at Mill Farm, the Duchy who had never criticised her inability to deal with Clary and Neville. But, above all, although she was sure that the Duchy had been aware that she went to London so much because she had a lover, and then, when he turned up, that it was Jack, she had neither confronted her with it nor betrayed her afterwards. She found herself trying to say some of this now. 'You have always been so good to me, even at the beginning, when I must have seemed incredibly selfish and irresponsible.'

'My dear, you were simply very young. You were only a year older when you married than I had been when I did.' After a pause, she said, 'I found it difficult enough adapting my romantic attitude to reality. Husbands do not spend their lives constantly on their knees before one,

135

offering bunches of flowers, but girls in my day had silly notions of the kind put into their heads – one read novels that contained a good deal of that kind of thing, and, of course, one's parents never *told* one what marriage and parenthood were really like. People did not consider it necessary or desirable to inform the young of anything that lay ahead.'

When the Duchy shifted so that she was facing her, Zoë had a sudden fear that, at last, here was coming an indictment, the forfeit of her mother-in-law's good opinion, but it wasn't that.

'I've always thought that you had a difficult time – inheriting two children, particularly Clary, who missed her own mother so much. And then the grief about the first baby – and, most of all, Rupert's long absence with all the miserable uncertainty attached to it. I think you've done well – very well indeed.'

At the mention of grief about the first baby, she felt herself beginning to blush. A brief affair with her mother's doctor, its humiliating dénouement and dreaded consequence was something that she had managed almost to expunge from conscious memory. Now she knew that it lay there, like an iceberg in the centre of her conscience, and at that moment it came to her that although she felt she could never bring herself to confess about Philip, she might, perhaps, manage to tell Rupert about Jack. And here was the Duchy, wise, kind, unexpectedly understanding – the best person for advice on such an explosive and delicate matter.

She did ask her.

'Oh, no, my dear! No, no! You must understand that I do not blame you for anything to do with that poor young man, but part of your responsibility now is to bear that experience by yourself. Do not burden your husband with it.'

She felt her hands being taken, pressed, but the Duchy had met her eye and held it.

'But if—' She struggled, uncertain of how much she should say. '*He* – Rupert – isn't happy. He feels – I think he feels bad about not telling us he was alive when he could have. He didn't want to talk about it, but if I told him things first, he might find it easier—'

Afterwards, she was never sure but it had seemed to her that the steady gaze had faltered, the sincerity shadowed by something else, but it was gone before she was even sure that it had been there. 'I think,' the Duchy said, 'that you should not try to get him to tell you about France. Leave it to him. If he wants to talk about it, he will.' She reached down and picked up her basket of sweet peas. 'You have a great deal of future before you both. My advice to you is that you should pay attention to that.' She took her arm and gave it a little squeeze. 'You did *ask* me.'

She had asked, that had been the advice, and she had taken it.

In the autumn, the house at Brook Green had been put on the market, but London was full of houses for sale in various states of disrepair, and as they could not buy anywhere else until it did sell, they moved in with Hugh, who was delighted to have them.

On the whole, the arrangement worked very well, although whether this was because it was acknowledged to be temporary, or whether she was so used to living with the family that it was easier to continue like that, she didn't know. The children seemed pleased: Wills, because it postponed his going to a preparatory boarding school, and Juliet, because she loved her morning school and quickly developed a full social life with endless tea and birthday parties with friends she made there. Ellen, installed in a back basement room that Hugh furnished for her, took over most of the cooking, and seemed relieved not to have to keep climbing stairs all day. The children had their nursery meals in the kitchen; Ellen still washed, ironed and mended their clothes, but Zoë got them up in the mornings and supervised their baths after their supper. Hugh had insisted upon giving up his bedroom to her and Rupert, and also spent two nights a week in his club so that they should have some evenings to themselves. Mrs Downs, a large, sad lady who described herself, to Rupert's delight, as bulky but fragile, now came four mornings a week to clean the house. She was one of those people who habitually looked on the black side of everything with a cheerfulness that bordered upon the macabre. When the war came to an end, Hugh had reported that she had said: 'Well! We've got the next one to look forward to, I suppose. You can't have every-thing in this life.' And when General Patton was paralysed from his frightful collision with a truck in Frankfurt and subsequently died, she had remarked that it came to all of us in the end – 'You've only got to wait for it.' Rupert had started reading out pieces of news in the morning paper and adding Mrs Downs's comments. During family life, at meals and so forth, Rupert was slowly becoming more like his old self; it was when they were alone together that he was constrained. He was unfailingly nice to her, consulting and considering her wishes about everything they did together, what plays and films they saw, which restaurants they went to afterwards, asking her if she liked what she had chosen to eat, wanted later in the evenings to go dancing (she never wanted to do that). In bed they had achieved a kind of conspiratorial calm: when they spoke it was in hushed voices, as though each was afraid of being overheard, as though they were trespassing on unknown territory. Their speech was mostly questioning about each other's pleasure, or courteous re-assurances. She tried to please him and he said that she did; he asked her if things had been good for her, and she said, or implied, small, protective lies.

When the telegram from her mother arrived, he had said, 'If you think it would be a good thing for your mother to come and live with us, you know I should be glad to have her. I know you find her difficult, darling, but if she can't manage on her own, I'm sure we could work something out.'

Well, she thought, as she queued on the icy station for a taxi, at least it didn't look as though they would have to have her mother at the moment, which was a good thing because, apart from anything else, there simply wasn't room for her in Hugh's house.

In the taxi just as she was thinking that, after all, her mother was only fifty-five or so, it struck her that in twenty-five years' time that would be *her* age. Would she simply become someone who irritated and bored her daughter? Was that all that life was *for*? She was thirty, and she had done nothing except marry Rupert, have his child and fall in love with someone else. It was not enough. She was going to have to search for and find something that she could do or become that had more to it, that had a life of its own, that would engage her. She could not imagine what that could be, and wondered –

139

there was a certain excitement in the speculation – whether she could search for something quite unknown to her.

∞ ∞ ∞

'You always said you liked houses that faced east and west.'

'I know, but the garden side will be sunny.'

'Yes, but at least half the house won't be. It's due north this side.'

Just as Villy was beginning to wish that she hadn't asked Jessica to look at houses with her (she seemed in a bad mood, but it *was* fiendishly cold) the agent appeared. 'So sorry, Mrs – Cazalet, isn't it? My car wouldn't start.' He fumbled in the pockets of his Army surplus overcoat and brought out an enormous bunch of keys with dirty labels attached to them. He had a heavy cold. 'Here we are.' He fitted a key into the mock Gothic door, which opened to reveal an unexpectedly large, dark hall. The agent turned on a light – a naked bulb that hung from a cord in the middle of a pargeted ceiling revealed a number of doors much like the one they had come through.

'It's a house full of features,' the agent said. 'Did you bring the particulars with you, Mrs Cazalet? If not, I have a spare copy.' He sneezed and wiped his nose on an overworked handkerchief.

'I have got them, but I'd rather just look round first.'

'Of course. Well, I'll just take you round and then I'll leave you to poke about on your own.' He walked across the hall to the furthest door. 'This is the main lounge. As you will appreciate,' he said, before they had a chance of doing so, 'this room faces due south with attractive Gothic

140

windows on to the garden, and a French window that opens directly into it. There is also an open fireplace with tile surround and parquet flooring.'

The room was quite large, she thought; she remarked on this to Jessica who thought it seemed larger than it was because the ceiling was so low.

The agent said would they mind if he just quickly showed them the rest of the house and then left them to spend as much time as they liked in it. He had another appointment, a house in Belsize Park, an awkward distance without his car. 'I'm sure I could leave you ladies to lock up and pop the key in to us afterwards.'

The rest of the house consisted of one equally large but dark room, a small kitchen on the ground floor, and four bedrooms, two large and two small, plus a bathroom on the floor above.

She said that she wanted to see the garden, and before he went, the agent produced another key.

'You can see the garden from the house,' Jessica said.

'I want to see the house from the garden.'

They shuffled across the small square lawn, thick with rotting leaves, and turned to stare at the house. Like the front, it was faced with roughcast, now a dirty grey from neglect. The slated roof had a pointed gable, which looked as though the upper rooms would be attics, but they weren't. The whole thing had a kind of rustic, romantic air; she thought that was most unusual in London houses, and she knew that she wanted to live in it. She felt resentful at Jessica's lack of enthusiasm.

'Why don't you like it?'

'It's just that I simply can't imagine Edward wanting to live in it. It's a kind of glorified *quaint*' – she made the word sound really horrid – '*cottage!*'

'That's what I like about it. Think how easy to manage! No ghastly basement, hardly any stairs. And this garden could be *made* nice.'

'But where will you keep the servants?'

'Oh, darling, don't be so out of date. I shan't have any living in. I shall get a really good daily, and do the cooking myself. After all, *you* used to do that.'

'I had to, but you don't. Seriously, Villy, you don't want to saddle yourself with all the cooking.'

'Why not? I shall have Roly to look after because Ellen will go with Rupert and Zoë, so I'd be fairly tied to the house anyway. I shall enjoy having something useful to do.'

'Well,' Jessica said, as they were going back in a taxi to her house in Paradise Walk, 'I still cannot see Edward wanting to live here. He likes lots of room for dinner parties.'

'He told me to choose exactly what I wanted. And he's going to get a yacht for sailing at weekends. And we'll still go to Home Place for the children's holidays.'

Two days later she took him to see the little house. He didn't say much except that weren't the front rooms rather dark, but he said that if she liked it, he would get it if the survey was all right. He was also very sweet, she thought, about her plan to have Miss Milliment to live with them. 'She won't be dining with us, darling. I'll make her a bed-sitting room in that large downstairs front room and she can have her other meals with me and Roly.' He had smiled and said that would be fine. The survey was set in motion and, in the meantime, there was Christmas.

Although the war was over, it felt like the last

Christmas of the war and in some ways it wasn't very different. Food was no easier, although Archie managed to bring two sides of smoked salmon, but with twenty people (Simon brought a friend from university, who seemed completely speechless except on the subject of Mozart) even that didn't go very far. Everybody was there, except Louise who had gone to Hatton, and Teddy and his bride, who were not yet back from America. The older children overflowed into Mill Farm, presided over by Rachel and Sid, but everybody converged upon Home Place for meals except for breakfast.

Everybody, she thought, was how they had always been, only more so. The Brig had become unexpectedly tyrannical about things that he had never minded before. 'I will *not* have a tree dying in my house,' he had said, when she had staggered into the hall with the Christmas tree she had bought in Battle.

'It's no good, darling,' the Duchy had said. 'That will have to disappear and McAlpine will have to dig one out of the nursery.' She thought of saying that he wouldn't be able to see it, but one look at the Duchy's face and she knew that any such subterfuge was out of the question, so she gave the tree away to someone in the village. Then there was some altercation about who merited Christmas stockings. She had thought that the children, from Lydia downwards, should be the recipients; when she announced this at tea-time, the children thought otherwise.

'I've been *banking* on my stocking for months,' Neville said. 'If I don't have one, people will give me stocking presents instead of real ones. I'm simply not prepared to put up with that sort of lowering of my standards.'

Clary looked at him with scorn. 'People who want

stockings years after they've known that Father Christmas is a myth are simply wedded to the material things in life. It's avaricious to want things so much.'

'*Is* it? Don't you want things? I seem to have noticed that you're pretty keen on some things.'

'Of course I want *some things*. I'm just not so dead set on getting them.'

Neville pretended to consider this. 'No,' he said at last. 'That just doesn't work. What on earth's the point of wanting things if you don't mind whether you get them or not?'

'I see his point,' Lydia said. 'It's one of the things we do at school. Have debates on things and try to see the other person's point of view. Miss Smedley says that's tremendously important.'

'When your father was a little boy,' the Duchy said, 'he was so greedy about his stocking that one Christmas he hung up a pillow-case thinking that Father Christmas would put more into it.'

Wills looked up with sudden interest. 'What happened?'

'In the morning he found it full of coal. Not a single present.'

This shocked everyone.

'Oh! Poor Dad!'

'What did he do with the coal?' Wills asked.

'That's not the point. There was nothing he could do about the coal.'

'Yes, there was,' Neville said at once. 'If it had been me, I would have sold it to poor freezing people who would pay pounds for it. Or I would have wrapped up each separate piece and given them as Christmas presents. That would teach people. And please don't see what I mean,' he said to Lydia just as she was going to. 'It's *my* point of view; I don't want *you* to see it.'

'Did it do Uncle Edward's character any good?' Wills asked.

'Well, he never hung up a pillow-case again.'

Then Archie, who had been listening to all this, suggested that perhaps people who were being struck off the stocking list should be given a year's notice, and this was considered a generally popular idea and adopted.

Throughout that Christmas – it still felt like the last one to her – while she coped with the various needs of the family whose ages ranged from Great-aunt Dolly, now approaching eighty-one and whose memory was shakily ensconced in the 1880s when she had been a young girl, and Juliet, now five, who lived firmly in the future when *she* would be grown up – 'I shall have twelve children and keep them in bed and just take them out one at a time to keep them *clean*!', etc. – she realised that she was actually excited at the prospect of having her own house again, where she could choose what happened, and where there would be opportunities for the indulgence of some solitude. It was years since she had had any sort of holiday; when Edward got the yacht they would be able to have a couple of weeks in her. Zoë had said that she would have Roly and she was sure that Miss Milliment could manage on her own, provided she got a decent daily. She broached this idea to Edward on Christmas Eve when they were undressing for bed.

'I don't know,' he said. 'I haven't got the boat yet – probably I'll wait till spring. This isn't the time of year for yachting anyway.'

He did not sound at all like his usual good-tempered self.

'Oh, well,' she said, 'there'll be masses to do to the house. I've decided to do all the painting inside myself. Do you think it would be nice to have the drawing room a sort of duck-egg blue?'

'Oh, Lord, *I* don't know – it's no good asking me things like that.'

She realised suddenly that whenever he talked about the house he seemed to become irritable and the awful thought occurred to her that perhaps, in spite of his saying that he liked the house and that she must choose, he was dreading it. Jessica's remarks came back to her.

'Darling,' she said, 'I have a feeling that perhaps you're not happy about the new house, that you're just being sort of kind about it. You really mustn't be. It's far too important a decision for there to be any disagreement at all about it. I would be quite happy to look at more houses, I really would.'

There was a pause, long enough for her to fear that she was right. Then he said: 'Nonsense. I think it's a very good choice. Not too large and all that. Hadn't we better go on Father Christmas's rounds?'

So, in their dressing gowns, they crept round the bedrooms that contained the small children, with the bulging, creaking golf stockings that Hugh and Edward donated for the occasion, ending with Lydia who lay with her eyes theatrically shut.

'She wasn't asleep.'

'I know. Better to pretend that she was, though.'

As she got into bed, she said, 'Does it feel like a last Christmas to you? It does to me.'

'What do you mean?'

'Well, we've all been living here for six years now – well, more actually – and now, quite suddenly, we'll all be going our own ways. I know we'll all come back for holidays, but it won't be the same.'

'It isn't all that sudden,' he said – rather defensively she thought. 'I mean, Teddy and Louise are both married, Lydia's at boarding school. There's really only Roly, isn't there? Things *do* change, whether we like it or not.'

'Oh, but I'm looking forward to that. When Roly starts school I think I'll try and find some sort of job. I don't want to go back to my pre-war life at all. I'd like to have some real work to do, and proper holidays. Oh, darling, I'm so looking forward to us having a boat! Do you remember our first sailing holiday in Cornwall? That very hot summer – catching mackerel and eating them that same evening? And the ants! Do you remember that extraordinary time when we saw them on the steps going up to that little hotel? When they were carrying things down and when they got to the edge of the step they just tipped the crumb or whatever it was over and then went down the step to collect it at the bottom? The Mannerings were with us. I remember you thought that Enid was frightfully attractive and I felt quite jealous.'

'Nonsense,' he said. 'Funny – I don't remember the ants. I remember that awful bumpy tennis court we played on, and how bad Rory was at bridge.'

He had joined her in bed by now.

'You took to sailing like a duck to water,' he said, put one arm round her and with his other hand, pulled up her nightdress.

She went to sleep, pleased that he had done what he wanted and relieved that it had taken less time than usual.

THE OUTSIDERS
January–April 1946

If anyone during the seemingly endless six years of war
had suggested that he would actually *miss* it when it
stopped, he would have been affronted and thought they
were simply trying to provoke him. Now, however, living
aimlessly in the toy house that Jessica thought was so
convenient, he had to admit that he *did* miss it – in more
ways than one. The first crunch had been in the autumn,
when he had gone back to see what was going on in his
house at Frensham. Of course, he had been delighted
when Nora and Richard had gone to live there after their
marriage: it had stopped the house being requisitioned,
because of Nora's intention to run it as a home for disabled ex-servicemen. But this he had seen as simply
a wartime project: he had always imagined himself re-
installed there – the squire of the village, living, for the
first time in his life, in the way to which he felt himself
suited. Jessica had warned him that he might find the
place changed, but he had not taken her seriously. In the
train, he had begun to form plans to make some sort of
flat in the house for Nora and Richard (Jessica had also
said that it would be very hard on Nora to turn them out).

He had sat in the train on the familiar journey
thinking fondly of Aunt Lena whose house it had been,
and of how often he'd taken this particular train – the
three thirty-five – when he had been sent there for a week

of his holidays. He had loved those visits: Aunt Lena had spoiled him – she was childless. He would be met at the station by Parkin, who had called him Master Raymond and agreed with everything he said. When he arrived, he would go and kiss his aunt's pillowy cheek. There would be a large coal fire at all times of the year and, within ten minutes, the maid would start bringing in an enormous, wonderful tea. Egg sandwiches, scones with strawberry jam and delicious butter that had beads of water in it when you cut it, mustard and cress sandwiches, gingerbread, fairy cakes, and to crown all, apart from a seed or a cherry cake, a wonderful iced affair that said, 'Welcome to Raymond' in contrasting piped icing. The cups were very shallow with dragons on them. Aunt Lena always said she was not hungry, but she usually ate some of everything, and he was encouraged to do the same. After tea, when the maid had cleared everything away, Aunt Lena would read to him from *The Water Babies* or a thin battered book about the exploits of a brownie, a kind of mischievous but well-meaning fairy. When he was older they played draughts, and Halma and Letterbags. There was an enamelled clock on the chimney piece that struck the quarter hours with delicate silvery chimes, and at six o'clock Aunt Lena would ring for Barker, the lady's maid, who would come to fetch him for his bath, after which he was conducted to what was unaccountably called the schoolroom where a bowl of bread and milk and brown sugar and a boiled egg awaited him. When he was in bed, Aunt Lena would come and say goodnight to him. She would have changed into black silk with a white cashmere shawl and long, elaborate, seed-pearl earrings that were shaped like baskets of flowers. She would make him say his prayers and kiss his forehead, and sometimes send for

149

Barker again: 'The boy's hair is damp from his bath – it should be dried – see to it, will you, Barker?' And then he would hear her painful, uneven retreat and the tap of her stick as she descended the stairs. Thus would begin a halcyon seven days of being petted, the centre of attention both with Aunt Lena and her servants for whom his visit provided a minute but welcome change from the stultifying regularity of their lives. He was given his favourite food, taken out for little treats, the best being a journey to Guildford with Aunt Lena to choose his Christmas and birthday presents, but most of all he enjoyed being the centre of utterly uncritical attention. Everything he did was clever and good; he was 'such a good child', he would hear Aunt Lena telling everyone, and he revelled in living up to this entrancing reputation. It had been utterly unlike home, where his father ruminated publicly and at length on his dimness – his mediocre reports from school, his paralysing inability to come up with the right answers to terrifying questions headed as 'elementary' general knowledge that were his father's favourite lunch-time conversational ploys. 'Can't think what they teach you,' he'd end up by saying. 'Never known such an ignoramus in me life.' His mother did not criticise him, she simply took as little notice of him as possible. Her interest was entirely centred upon his older brother, Robert – the one who was killed in the war. Robert had once accompanied him on a visit to Aunt Lena, but had professed himself bored; he had also been exceedingly naughty in some unspeakable way (at least he could never get anybody to speak of it). 'Not, I am afraid, a *good* child,' Aunt Lena had said the evening after he had been sent home in disgrace (he, Raymond, had been allowed to stay).

Thereafter he had the monopoly of Frensham and Aunt Lena and, bless her heart, she had left him everything when she died: the house that he had become so fond of, that had, in fact, felt like his real home, all its contents and what had seemed at the time to be a staggering number of most conservatively invested shares. He, who had never succeeded in making any money to speak of, was suddenly comparatively rich. But before he could really settle down in the house to enjoy everything, the war had come, he had felt bound to offer his services and the job he had got precluded his living at home. He had been banished, as it were, to Woodstock, and subsequently Oxford for the duration. As Jessica did not want to live at Frensham on her own, the house had been shut until Nora's marriage to that poor chap Richard, and when she had suggested running a sort of nursing home for paraplegics it had seemed the answer. All very well, but now that the war was over he wanted to get back to normal. He was perfectly prepared to convert the stables and coach house into a home for Nora and Richard, but he wanted his house back, whatever Jessica thought or said about it. *She* wanted to keep that doll's house in Paradise Walk, which, as he had pointed out to her, was barely big enough for the two of them, and impossible when Judy came home for the holidays. And giving Angela any decent sort of send-off there was out of the question.

At the thought of Angela he sighed – audibly, he realised, since the passenger opposite him looked up suddenly from his book, and, embarrassed, he averted his gaze to the window. Angela's impending marriage had been a shock to him as well as to Jessica, but in quite different ways. She had objected to her fiancé's being

nearly twenty years older than Angela; this did not seem
to Raymond a bad thing – Angela needed looking after.
She objected to the fact that he had been married before –
he partly agreed with that, but pointed out that if Major,
or Dr Black as he presumably now was, had reached the
age of forty-five without being married there might be
other things to be said against him. She had also said that
he was far from glamorous (Black had gone back to the
States before Raymond had the chance of meeting him),
and remembering bitterly her liaison with that slimy little
worm Clutterworth, he thought she was a fine one to talk
about *that*. Black being a psychiatrist was certainly a bad
mark: he had a profound distrust for head doctors and all
that mental stuff, but still he *was* a doctor – and had been
a major in the American Army, which was respectable. He
had certainly felt upset when he discovered that the
wedding would not take place here, either in London or
at Frensham which, of course, was how it should be. It
was not even that Dr Black was unwilling to come over
for the wedding, it was Angela who insisted that she did
not want a big wedding – a family do – she wanted to go
over to New York and be married quietly there without
any fuss, as she put it. So, in a couple of weeks' time, she
would be sailing in the *Aquitania* – entirely on her own –
sailing away to a life which probably meant, he felt, that
he would never see her again. That was what shocked
him. It meant that there would now never be any chance
of his repairing their awkward, uncomfortable relationship, something that he had craved ever since that disas-
trous lunch at Lyons' Corner House – five, no, six years
ago, that last time he had been alone with her. After it, he
had been so discouraged by her indifference and boredom; he had made two or three attempts to see her and

been put off – immediately, or worse, at the last minute – until he had lost his nerve. He had never had the opportunity to explain that he understood that she was grown up, that he was no longer simply a parent, but that he wanted to be her friend, an equal in some sort, that all he asked was affection and trust, that he could not bear being treated as a stranger who, he felt, *she* felt, she would dislike if she knew him any better. But this was how it was with them – or had become. He remembered now when the full realisation of his failure with Angela had flooded upon him: it had been the summer of '43, the evening after he had had that awful lunch with Villy to try – hopelessly, as it turned out – to get some help from her about Jessica's perfidy. The shame and misery he had endured when he had first discovered that his wife was having an affair! It would have been awful whoever it had been, but her choice of that dreadful little man had been the utmost humiliation. His Jessica *lying* to him – not once, but repeatedly – for months, for the best part of a *year*. The fool she must have thought him, the terrible fear that she could never have cared two straws for him, that he had imagined her love, that she had simply countenanced his adoration, had merely endured his love without returning it. He had descended then to a black pit of despair and isolation; his bluster, his rage at her when he was alone did not for one moment sustain him. He felt his failure as a husband and then, immediately, as a parent as well, and what on earth else was he if he was neither of these?

He had got off the train at Oxford and sat the whole hot, airless evening in a pub that he had never been to before, that he rightly assumed would not be frequented by his colleagues. He had sat there nursing the two small whiskies that was all the landlord was prepared to sell to a stranger, until his newly acquired ulcer caused him such pain that he knew he must go somewhere to eat.

The weeks that followed were the worst in his life. He had arranged the luncheon with Villy because he simply had to talk to someone, to share some of his rage and shock and the only possible person had seemed to be Villy, who he was sure would be as outraged at her sister's behaviour as he. Then, on his way to meet her, the dreadful thought had occurred to him that she already knew, and from there it was a short step to the nightmare possibility – likelihood – that *everybody* knew, that not only Jessica but the world was laughing at him behind his back. But she clearly *hadn't* known; seemed suitably, mercifully shocked. Then, as he was telling her what he felt about it all, he had the idea that perhaps he could get Villy to talk to her, something that he shrank from doing. But after lunch with Villy, and that first, awful evening in the pub, he had rung her the next day and asked her after all to say nothing. 'It may all blow over,' he had said, trying to sound hearty and optimistic. She had agreed to silence (he was pretty sure that she would have been silent anyway), and that was that. Of course, he played endless scenes to himself when *he* confronted Jessica, told her exactly what he thought of her monstrous behaviour. But here, always, after the first flush of exhilaration that the idea of doing this induced, he came up against her unknown response. Supposing she was in *love* with this frightful cad? Supposing she wanted to have a divorce – *leave* him and go off with Clutterworth? The thought paralysed him: the idea of Jessica leaving him was quite simply more than he could bear. Divorce would be a public humiliation that he felt he could never recover from, but beyond that, his private anguished contemplation of his life without Jessica made him too terrified not only to confront her but to give her the slightest inkling that he knew.

He took to giving Jessica as much notice as possible of his coming to London, and claimed that Wednesdays were the only day he could get off – and that not every week. The visits caused him a different kind of pain from that which he endured the rest of the time. He took her to the theatre and to restaurants – the latter with other people if possible – in order that they should not be alone. Once, when he stayed the night, he had tried to make love to her and failed. He had claimed that he had drunk too much because he'd felt he was catching some sort of bug and she had seemed to believe him – been extraordinarily nice about it. Afterwards he had turned away from her, had lain, tense and miserable in the dark; tears had run down his face until his neck was cold with them. After that, he made excuses about having to catch the last train back to work, and started having spasmodic pains in his stomach that the doctor diagnosed as a threatened ulcer. He was supposed to lay off drink and to smoke less, but he was so miserable that he did neither of these things and the ulcer got worse. He was irritable at work, aware that none of his colleagues liked him, but he hardly cared about that. Work became his best solace – he plunged himself into it with, unexpectedly, some success. He discovered that he had a capacity to think about and explore certain problems that promoted, and in one case achieved, their solution. Crumbs of self-respect occurred but they seemed only to emphasise his otherwise vast and despairing sense of failure.

And then, out of the blue, something happened that began to make a difference.

One morning he received a memo so badly typed that it was almost without sense. It was not for the first time that week, and he blew up, went in search of the perpetrator to bawl him or her out.

It was a girl. She sat in the semi-basement, in what must once have been a scullery, which now looked like a cell with its heavily barred windows and stone floor. She was hunched over her typewriter and she was crying. She looked up as he stormed into the room, but anything he was about to say left his mind at the sight of her. Her face was blotched and shiny with crying, and one side of it was swollen like someone with mumps. She looked revolting.

'What on earth is the matter with you?'

She had toothache, she said, really awful toothache.

'Better go to the dentist, hadn't you?'

She'd made an appointment, but in the end she hadn't gone.

'Why on earth not?'

She hadn't been able to face it.

'Better ring him up and tell him you're sorry you're late but you're on your way.'

That was last Monday.

'Do you mean you've had toothache for' – he calculated – 'over a *week*?'

She'd kept hoping it would go away. A fresh burst of tears. 'I know I'm an awful coward, but I just can't bring myself to go. I sort of know I must – and I can't!' She tried to blow her nose on a sopping handkerchief, and winced. She touched the bad side of her face and gave a little moan.

He asked her where her dentist was and she said Oxford.

'I'll take you,' he said. 'I'll borrow a car and take you.'

And that was what he did. Ordinarily he would have found it embarrassing and difficult to ask anyone for the use of their car – petrol was short and he had no allowance himself as Jessica had their car – but now he found himself powerfully resolute: the wretched girl had to be got to the dentist and he was organising it. He rang the deputy head of his department and said that one of the secretaries had been taken ill and he was taking her to a doctor, went and got the keys and returned to collect her. She was still sitting at her desk.

'Got your pass?'

She nodded. 'In my bag.' She was shivering. In the car, she said, 'It's awfully kind of you.' Then a moment later: 'You won't leave me there, will you? You'll stay with me?'

'Of course I will.'

'It's really most awfully kind of you.'

'What's your name?'

'Veronica. Veronica Watson.'

The dentist was off the Headington Road in North Oxford. They had to wait for some time, as the disapproving receptionist said that Mr McFarlane had a patient with him, and another patient at two thirty and before that he would be having his lunch hour. At this point, Veronica asked if she might go to the lavatory, and in her absence he managed to soften up the receptionist with an assurance that secretly amazed him.

The indirect result of this was that when the time came he was allowed by the dentist to accompany Veronica into the surgery and subsequently to sit holding her hand while the offending tooth was extracted. 'You have a whopping great abscess. You should have come last week, you know. Then we might have been able to save the tooth.' When he had finished, and was washing his hands, he remarked, 'You're a lucky young woman to have your father come with you.'

Raymond saw her about to deny this and put his finger on his lips; together they both looked towards Mr McFarlane – his back was turned and he was drying his hands on a towel.

In the street, she said, 'I'm sorry he thought that. I hope you didn't mind.'

'Not at all. After all, I'm old enough to be your father.'

'You're not in the least like him, though.'

'Feel better?'

'Golly, yes! It's a bit sore, but it's stopped throbbing.'

He drove her home. She couldn't possibly go back to work, he said, she should take a couple of aspirin and go to bed, and she said, all right, she would.

Her room turned out to be in the same building as his.

'I'm so awfully grateful to you,' she said as she got out of the car. 'I don't know how to thank you.'

'My dear, it was nothing.'

'Oh, but it was!' She had turned back to him, her small velvety eyes glowing. 'It feels as though you've saved my life!'

Driving back to Woodstock he felt happier than he had for weeks – for months, really. He was *not* simply a brain; he was somebody who, faced with a sudden emergency, could deal with it, could do a right good turn for somebody else with verve and assurance. Remembering those glowing eyes in her pear-shaped face, *he* glowed; it had not been that she was *pretty*, that his help had come out of some second-rate reason like being *attracted* to her, it had been pure kindness. The poor little thing had needed someone to take charge and he had done so. Her father, indeed!

Two days later he found a parcel on his desk. It was a box of Meltis Newberry Fruits with a card attached. 'I didn't know how to thank you for your kindness, but hope you will like these. Yours ever, Veronica.'

Really! There was something touching about the present and the card that had a little blue bird sitting on a twig in the right-hand top corner. She had large, rounded, rather childish writing. He opened the box, selected a green berry and ate it: gooseberry – it was actually rather good. He decided to go and thank her.

That had been the beginning of their friendship, which on her part, with a rapidity that slightly unnerved him, became a great deal more. In short, she fell madly in love with him, and he was touched, and quite soon more than touched. She was so *young*: it was flattering to be adored by someone so young – and really not bad-looking. Her face, when it subsided, proved to be rather round with rosy cheeks. She had dark curly hair that she wore short with a wavy fringe, and a small, full mouth that seemed always a little pursed. Her eyes were her best feature; their habitual expression was one of anxiety, but when she was with him they melted to adoration. She was like a small dark velvet pansy, a little spaniel, he told her when they reached the delightful stage of discussing themselves.

To begin with, he thought of her almost as a daughter: she gave him a kind of affectionate trust, looked up to

him in the way that he had always hoped Angela would
grow up to do. But when it dawned on him that she was
actually in love with him, of course he told her that he
was married – *he* wasn't a cheap little cad like some he
could mention. 'I thought you must be,' was all that she
said, but he sensed that it was a shock to her all the same.
He thought then that he should have told her before, but
it hadn't come up somehow. It changed things, whether
for the better or not he really couldn't say. It added
a dimension to her attitude towards him: she was no
longer assuaging his sense of failure as a father, she was
beginning to affect how he felt as a husband, as a man. It
was immensely comforting to be regarded as a romantic
figure: it shifted Jessica to the middle distance of his consciousness and his miserable jealousy receded, leaving
him with more distaste than despair. He told Veronica
how fond of her he was, how much he enjoyed her
company (they were now spending practically every
evening together, going for walks by the canal, spending
hours in various pub gardens, drinking cocoa in her
room). At work there was the delicious game of pretending hardly to know one another, of being formal, using a
code to arrange their meetings. His ulcer troubled him far
less, and in the end not at all. She had a birthday, her
twenty-first, and he gave her a Jacqmar scarf, yellow with
red hammers and sickles printed all over it – Russian
motifs were fashionable – and a silver bracelet with
'Veronica' engraved upon it. She had been thrilled; only
sad that she had to go home to her parents for the
celebration. She asked him to come too, but he declined.
She had returned with a car, a bright red MG that her
parents had given her. This had been wonderful: he
managed to wangle petrol, and it meant that they could

get further away from Oxford or Woodstock to places where they would be safe from meeting anyone they knew.

He had taken the opportunity while she was with her family to go to London, and there, because for once he had not given notice of his visit, he had come face to face with Clutterworth. He was apparently simply having tea with Jessica, but he suspected that a good deal had gone on before that. He was shocked by how dreadful this made him feel: he had found himself almost unable to speak, to utter more than a few words to the effect that he had simply come back to collect some important papers he'd left before. He had stumped upstairs, gone into the room in which he slept and noisily opened and shut drawers there. Her room was at the end of the landing. The door was open, the bed immaculate. Obviously tea came *first*. He went down the stairs and out of the house and left them to it. He walked to the Tube and took the first train that came in for Piccadilly, went to a news theatre and sat in it for two repeats of its programme. Then he went to the nearest restaurant he could find and ordered a meal; food made him feel sick, but he drank a bottle of wine and a glass of Spanish brandy. By the time he got to Paddington to catch the last train he felt feverish and drunk. Back at his digs there was a message: 'Your wife rang. Please would you ring her.' Would he hell! He went to bed and woke a couple of hours later with his mouth like a sandpit, stomach cramps and a pounding head. For the rest of the night, as he tramped back and forth from bedroom to lavatory, and after an abortive search for aspirin, he lay with fragments of dialogue repeating: 'Do you think he suspected anything?' 'Oh, good heavens, no! He hasn't the faintest idea!' 'Are you *sure*? Sure he won't come back?' 'Honestly, dear Raymond, he isn't very bright about that kind of thing.' And then weary smiles or sniggering laughter at his lack of brightness . . .

Veronica returned in the evening of the following day, was waiting at the bus stop in her car when he got back from work. 'It's mine,' she said, 'my twenty-first birthday present. Isn't it marvellous? I'm going to take you for a drive *now* – we could go to the Three Pigeons and have a drink there. Oh, I'm so glad to be back, though – What's the matter?' By now he was in the car. 'You look *awful*!'

'Not here,' he said. 'Let's get out of town.'

But when they had reached a secluded piece of lane, and she had turned to him again and asked with real anxiety what *was* the matter, and he started to try to tell her, he couldn't – he simply broke down. All his anger and hatred, of himself as well as of them, and his despair came uncontrollably out. He put his hands over his face and sobbed and couldn't say anything at all.

She was so sweet! So gentle and concerned, so much on his side. For he *did* tell her – the whole thing in the end; it was such an enormous relief to tell someone who cared about him, who seemed as utterly shocked as he. 'How simply awful for you! How could anyone do that to *you*?' were two of the things she said.

'I'm sorry to burden you with all this,' he said later, but he wasn't sorry at all, just incredibly relieved to have got it off his chest, and to relax in the balmy atmosphere of her concern and devotion. For this was when he recognised that she really did love him. 'Poor darling! I do love you so much. I'd do anything to make you happier. I think you're the most marvellous person I've ever met in my life.'

'Do you? Do you really?'

'Of course I do. Oh, darling, no wonder you're shattered. Anyone as brave and sensitive as you would be.'

Brave, sensitive. Nobody had ever called him either of these things. But he *had* been brave – years ago, in France, in the trenches, when that mad major had spent six weeks trying to get him killed. He'd done every single sortie that that dotty shell-shocked bugger had commanded him to do and he'd survived. And he was sensitive, really; it was just that none of his family seemed to notice the fact. But *she* did. This very young girl had the perception to see him as he was. He put his arms round her. 'I love you too,' he said. 'I don't know what I should have done without you.'

It had been a turning point in their relationship, although he hadn't realised it at the time. When, after leaving several messages at his digs, Jessica finally reached him at the office, he found it easy to say that he had had a train to catch and he thought he'd explained that.

That autumn had been a kind of halcyon renaissance for him. His times with her were entirely pleasant, angst-free; he basked in her reflected excitement at being in love. She wasn't beautiful like Jessica, or desirable in remotely the same way, but he liked her: she was sweet and attractive, always good-natured and eager to please him – this last an experience that was quite new to him. With Jessica, he had been the supplicant, suing for her admiration and respect; with Veronica it was the other way round. Remembering what it was like to be the most vulnerable, he was very careful with her; he was determined to be both responsible and kind. This entailed not actually going to bed with her. To begin with, he had not found this very difficult: he kissed and petted her and enjoyed it, and throughout the autumn he had thought that this state of affairs suited her as well as him. But when she came to him one day with the tale of someone breaking into her room – at night, when she was about to go to bed – and admitted that this was not the first time she had been so harassed, he decided to take action and found them digs out of Keble, where most of the staff lived, a flat on the other side of Oxford. She had been thrilled. The flat, the upper floor of a small terrace house, consisted of two bedrooms, a bathroom and a small sitting room with a kitchenette tacked on to it. It was furnished with bare and drab essentials. Money had to be put into meters for the gas fires and hot water; the beds were the sort to be found in boarding schools, narrow, made of iron and wire and horsehair, with blankets that had a rigid feltiness that did not promise warmth. The carpets were dirty and worn and most of the chairs were of the kind that made it unwise to sit on them without thought.

Veronica seemed unaware of any of these disadvantages. 'I'll be able to cook meals for us!' she had exclaimed when she saw the Baby Belling and the small cracked sink. 'Oh, I do think it's wonderful of you to have found somewhere so cosy!'

That first evening they had unpacked, and eaten a picnic meal of Scotch eggs and beetroot salad, procured from a pub that they frequented, which they ate in the sitting room before the gas fire. He occupied the battered armchair, she sat on the floor beside him and they were both slightly intoxicated by the sense of adventure and whisky, and he with the feeling that he had rescued her, and she was prattling on about how she had never dreamed that he would find such a solution to her problems so quickly . . .

She had fallen suddenly silent.

After a moment, he put his hand on her dark, curly hair. 'And?'

'Nothing – really.'

'Now, now,' he said, gently reproving. 'You don't have secrets from me. You were just about to say *something* – I know you.' He put his hand round the side of her head and tilted her face towards him.

'What I was *thinking*,' she said, as though this had in no way entailed her saying it, 'was that now we are really alone.' Her eyes were fixed upon his, and she began to blush. 'I mean, now it would be perfectly all right for you to sleep with me. Nobody would know.'

Somewhere, at the back of his consciousness, a warning bell sounded: commitment, total responsibility, divorce, another family, losing Jessica entirely . . .

'Now, my pet, it's time we had a serious talk.'

It was serious indeed. He told her that as he was married – never mind the circumstances – he could not possibly take advantage of her, it would be unkind, utterly wrong, since she was so much younger than he, with her whole life before her (he was beginning to believe himself, gathering strength and argument). His wife would never divorce him, he said, and therefore he could not dream of them becoming lovers when there could be no future to it. It was *not* (her eyes were full of tears now) that he didn't love her – she must understand that (she nodded, and the tears trickled down her face); there were some things that people such as himself did not do. However much they wanted to, he added, however hard it was for *him* . . .

She knelt upright and flung her arms round him. 'Oh, Raymond, darling! I didn't mean to make it harder for *you*! You're so good – and *sincere*. One of the reasons I love you is that I admire your character so much. It's not just a question of sex with you, like it is with so many men. You're different, I know you are.'

While he was mopping up her face with his handkerchief, she said, 'I'm lucky to have you at all!'

They must both be strong, he said. He felt an immense relief.

But there was no doubt that a darker note had been introduced that, in one way or another, changed everything. Not completely, of course, and by no means all the time; it was more as though territory had been laid round their hitherto innocent playground that was a kind of no man's land. They still met for lunch most days and – it was winter by then – went to the cinema and to pubs and occasionally out to dinner in between the quiet domestic evenings when she cooked stodgy meals and they played bezique or Racing Demon, or he listened to the radio, or wrote letters, while she did the ironing and mended her stockings. But now when he kissed and touched her small pointed breasts that were, he knew from more carefree times, of an engaging whiteness, she would become unnaturally still, and if he went on, would start to tremble and further persistence resulted in tears. Then she would apologise, protest her love and say how much she respected his self-control. There was now some of that to respect, since once he had decided that he must not have her he found her more desirable. In a way, he was grateful for this: it was somehow better than having to employ gestures and language simply to protect her pride. None the less, a kind of theatrical streak had crept into their behaviour with one another, a scene of dialogue between them about what they wanted if only things were different, and what they could have as they were not, that became worn and to him irritatingly familiar with its frequent use. It was irritating, because she never seemed to tire of it; could hardly allow more than a day or two without reverting to the hopeless anguish of their situation. He discovered two ways to stall these scenes. One was to make love to her by talking rather than touching, and if, as on one or two occasions, this simply inflamed her into taking the initiative – flinging herself into his arms, taking his head in her hands and pressing her fresh red pouting mouth upon his – he could become, in his turn, agonised and beg her to refrain before it all became too much for him.

When he returned from one of his visits to London – requested by Jessica – with the news that Nora was to be married, she had seemed quite sulky and uninterested. 'Oh, *that* was all she wanted you for,' was one of the things that she said. She did not ask anything about the engagement and altogether behaved in an uncharacteristic manner, refusing to meet his eye and disappearing into the kitchen where she made rather a lot of noise with pots and pans. He supposed she was getting her period – she sometimes had a bad time of it – but by the time he had changed out of his suit into the corduroys and thick polo-necked sweater that helped to keep him warm – the gas fire was too small for the room with its ingenious draughts – she returned from the kitchen and apologised. 'I thought, you see, that she might have asked you to come up for something quite different.'

'Did you? What?'

'Well, you know – about the marriage.'

'But that's what it was about.'

'I didn't mean Nora's. I meant yours.' She had gone rather pink. 'Silly of me. I just sort of *hoped*—'

'Oh, darling, I've told you, she'll never do that.' He put his arms round her and gave her a hug. Whenever he made the future impossible for her, he found he could be indulgent about the present.

She had made a large, rather watery rabbit stew, and while they ate it, he told her about Nora's fiancé.

'Does that mean that they won't be able to have any children?'

'I'm afraid so. It apparently means that they won't be able to have anything.'

'Do you mean he won't be able to sleep with her?'

'That's about it.'

'Oh, how *awful* for her!' She thought for a moment. 'She must be an amazing person.' After that she enquired tenderly after Nora and was intensely interested in her wedding.

During the following year, he became aware somehow that Jessica's affair had waned and eventually finished. His feelings about her were confused. There was an immense relief when one day she referred with perceptible disparagement to 'poor Mercedes', Clutterworth's wife. What was poor about her? he had asked. Oh, she seemed constantly to have to put up with students and girls in choirs falling in love with her husband. 'It must be a frightful bore for her.'

168

Aha, he thought. He's deserted her. It was a moment of triumph. But the triumph did not last or, rather, it quickly became adulterated with other, less celebratory feelings. If Jessica had been left, as from her listless manner he thought most probable, ought he not to re-establish himself with her? But if he did that, what was he to do about Veronica? Supposing he left Veronica and resumed married life with Jessica who then found *someone else*? Or supposing she didn't get anyone else and he tried to live with her and, well, it turned out like the last time? What would he do then? She would most certainly despise him if he proved impotent. In the end, he decided to do nothing, except to go to London more often to keep an eye on things up there.

Some months later, Jessica had announced that she and Villy had decided to sell the Rydal house in St John's Wood, and that she was going to rent a much smaller one with her share of the proceeds. She had found one, she said, in Chelsea.

Life with Veronica in Oxford continued ostensibly to be the same, but as his confidence gradually came back about Jessica, he found less pleasure in Veronica's adulation – sometimes it was even slightly irritating. She was so *young*! he thought, but the inference of this had become different. Whereas it had been balm to his vanity that someone so youthful should find him attractive, now he found her youth something that required his patience. She was so predictable! It was as though he knew what she thought and felt and was going to say about everything, which made everything not quite worth talking about. Poor little thing! She could not help any of it; she was slipping back into being his daughter.

Throughout that year, he consoled himself with the

idea that the end of the war would bring about every kind of change – for the better. His job would come to an end, which would mean a natural severance from his Oxford life. He would go home and Jessica would be unable to stray because he would always be there. Indeed, he would take her back to Frensham and they would settle down to a stable and sedate country life . . .

None of this had come to pass. He was, in fact, moved to London by the War Office, a curious job that took place, rather surprisingly, in Wormwood Scrubs. This entailed, of course, some unhappy scenes with Veronica. 'Couldn't you come back at weekends?' 'Couldn't you ask for *me* to be moved?' But he could not, or would not, do either of these things. It was time to say goodbye, he felt, and set about it as carefully and kindly as he was able. Of course she wept; he had known she would do that. (He spent one sleepless night holding her in his arms on her narrow bed while she sobbed and slept and woke again to cry.) He explained, again and again, that he could not leave his wife. He would always love her – Veronica – but as there was no future for them, it was essential that she start her own life when she would, he was sure, find someone and be very happy with them.

A few days later, when he returned from a night in London, where he had told Jessica about his new work, with the intention of packing up his things to move from the Oxford flat, he found Veronica lying in a pool of blood on the kitchen floor, unconscious. She had cut the veins in both wrists, but had not, most fortunately, been efficient about it. None the less, he experienced moments of panic and horror on a scale that reminded him of the First World War. She lay face downwards, and at first he thought she was dead, but when he managed to lower

170

himself on to one knee (his other refused to bend) and, pulled at her shoulder until he had turned her over, he realised that she was still breathing. Her face was a frightening grey-white colour; one wrist was clotted with drying blood, but from the other it was still weakly pumping out. He bound the wrist tightly with his handkerchief and rang for an ambulance. Then he fetched a couple of blankets from her bed and waited. He felt like a murderer: if she died he would be responsible. Those minutes, until the ambulance men arrived, were the worst in his life.

They were wonderfully professional and reassuring. In no time at all they had put her on a stretcher, had undone his bandage and fixed a tourniquet. 'She'll be all right, sir. She hasn't lost all that much blood. It always looks more than it is. You can come along with us, if you like.' He went. In the ambulance they said that they would have to inform the police, who would want a statement from him. 'She's your wife, is she?' He said no.

In the hospital she was wheeled away and he was put in a small room where he sat and worried about what on earth the police would ask him. Of course it would all come out, that he had been living with her. They would discover that he was married and they would assume that she was his mistress. Her parents would have to be told, Jessica would find out and he would probably be sacked from his job. Had she *meant* him to find her? Of course she must have meant that, but whether she knew that he would find her in time was uncertain. He always returned from London on the same morning train, and almost always went first to the flat before going in to work. He began to think that she had simply meant to give him an awful fright, had not meant actually to kill herself. He began to feel a dull anger with her. By one stupid, irresponsible act she had mucked everything up. Then the really awful thought occurred that, if she hadn't meant him to find her in time, she might do it all over again. This made him feel utterly trapped, and unable to think at all clearly.

The police came, and he made his statement. He stuck to the truth about the facts connected with finding her. What else could he do? But when he was asked if he could think of any reasons why she might do such a thing, he became ingenious. They went away with the idea, if not the actual knowledge, that she was highly strung and impressionable, had conceived feelings for him that he had been unable to reciprocate, but that in view of the disparity in their ages, he had tried to be paternal and patient with her. He had had absolutely no idea that she would do such a thing. 'She always knew that I was married,' he had said. He explained that the War Office was moving him to London, and added that he supposed that this had upset her more than he had realised. He implied, as delicately and in as many ways as he could think of, that she was not and never had been his mistress, but he wasn't sure they believed him.

They finally let him go home. She was sleeping, quite comfortable, they said. He could see her later in the evening if he liked.

He got back to the flat with its bloodstained floor and a six-page letter she had written to him laid upon his bed. He had a stiff whisky and spent half an hour mopping up the blasted lino before he read it.

But even after reading the letter twice, he was no clearer about what her intentions had been. You could say that she wouldn't have written it if she hadn't meant to kill herself; on the other hand, if she had simply meant to frighten, or *blackmail* him into doing what she wanted, she would still have written a letter because she would have wanted him to think she was serious. Well, in either case, it hadn't worked, he thought grimly. All he wanted now was *out*. His feelings for her, whatever they had once been, had now diminished to a sense of angry responsibility. He poured himself another whisky. The shock had worn off, and what he described to himself as enlightened self-interest took over.

He took her car and went to work, where he requested an interview with his boss to whom he gave a brief – and, he felt, fair – description of the situation. Anstruther was a man with an incisive mind and a distaste for emotion of any kind. He was briskly sympathetic. 'Nasty situation. Hysteria, I suppose. Bit unwise to set up with her, wasn't it? Have you got hold of her parents? I should advise that, because the police or the hospital are likely to and it might be better if you got there first.'

'I hadn't thought of that. Yes, I'd better.'

'Not pregnant or anything, is she?'

'No. Nothing like that.' He explained again, without delicacy, why she couldn't be.

At this, Anstruther became incredulously impatient, said that he had no wish to go into details, and would take Raymond's word for it.

'I'll arrange for Miss Watson to have extended leave, and perhaps you would arrange for her parents to fetch her. We don't want any more trouble. When do you start in London? Next week? Well, you'd better take a few days yourself.'

He said something about not wanting to upset his wife.

'Naturally not.'

'Thank you, sir.'

He rang the parents, got the mother, and told her the most emollient version he could muster. Veronica had been overworking; he was afraid she had become a little too fond of him, in spite of her knowing that he was married with four children, and when she had learned that he was being sent elsewhere for work, she had done this foolish and unfortunate thing. She was going to be perfectly all right, he repeated (he had begun the conversation by saying that), but her boss thought it best if she had a long leave at home. Would they come and fetch her as soon as possible?

Mrs Watson seemed unable to take things in. 'I can't understand it,' she kept saying. 'Veronica's such a *sensible* girl. *Cut* herself. With a knife? I can't understand it!'

He said how sorry he was, and repeated Anstruther's verdict of hysteria. Mrs Watson said that they would both come to Oxford the next day. That was that.

He went back to the flat in her car and packed up. He decided to leave no trace of his having lived there so this took some time. He dismantled his bed, leaving it with its bare striped mattress, took his socks and shirt off the washing line in the kitchen, leaving her pink fluffy jumper that always got up his nose hanging on the line. He even went through her chest of drawers, discovering a small bundle of notes he had written to her. These he burned, together with her letter. By now he was feeling quite fugitive: the thought of going to see her in hospital unnerved him. He was afraid of what she might say – of what people might hear her say. 'After all, I never went

174

to *bed* with her,' he kept saying to himself. By the time he had packed and called a cab, the whole thing was beginning to feel hardly his fault.

He didn't go and see her.

Thereafter, when he thought of 'the episode', as he came to call it, he was subject to unease, a certain amount of guilt which he became adept at rationalising. A large number of the staff at Woodstock had engaged in extra-marital activities – there were rumours of pregnancies, abortions, even an eventual remarriage or two. He had not behaved differently from any of them, except that he had behaved better. It had been just his bad luck to land up with someone who had refused to take him at face value, who had insisted upon reading more into the affair than was ever there. He heard on the grapevine that she had gone home and had not returned, had been discharged. He went back to London and to Jessica with whom he resumed an (almost) chaste marriage. Sex with each other did not seem rewarding or to enliven either of them. He decided that it was because of his job, which took a lot out of him, and the awful little house that she had insisted upon them living in: a doll's house, no room to turn round. It would be different – and better – when the war came to an end and they got back to Frensham.

The war did come to an end, but the visit to Frensham had been discouraging, to put it mildly. Nora had sent John, the old man who had always worked in the garden – a gardener's boy in Aunt Lena's day – to meet him at the station. He seemed to have aged about twenty years since Raymond had last seen him, and now shuffled in a rheumaticky way and seemed not to hear much that was said to him. 'You'll find the place changed,' he remarked more than once during the short journey.

He did indeed. From the moment they arrived on the gravel sweep before the house, it was clear that changes had occurred. The lawn below was now a tract of frozen mud, punctuated by the shabby spikes of Brussels sprouts. The Virginia creeper that had so charmingly clothed the front façade was gone, and the mellow brick had been covered with some frightful yellow paint. The stained glass in the waisted front door had gone, and in its place was some white opaque stuff commonly used, he thought, in bathrooms.

Inside was worse. He stood in the hall staring at the dark green linoleum that now covered the floor and the bright yellow painted walls where Aunt Lena's Morris willow-pattern paper had always been. Odours of Jeyes fluid, Irish stew, carbolic soap and paraffin reached him.

Nora appeared. She wore a dark blue overall and tennis shoes with ankle socks; her sturdy legs were otherwise bare. 'Hello, Dad. I do hope you aren't expecting tea because it's over. But supper is at half past six so you haven't got long to wait. We have it all together, because it takes a long time to get some of the chaps to bed. I'll take you up to your room, and then you can come and talk to Richard.'

'I can find my way to my room.'

'Can you? Oh, fine. It's at the very top, the little attic on the right.'

Wordlessly, he picked up his case and limped upstairs. *Attic*? Why on earth did he have to sleep in an attic? It was where the servants had slept, two in a room. A large chromium-plated stair rail had been installed on the wall side of the staircase. Nora had certainly been taking liberties with the place; he would wait till they were having drinks and then find out what on earth she thought she'd been up to.

His attic contained the maid's furniture. A small battered chest of drawers, an iron bedstead and the old blackout blinds that had not been removed. It was icy cold up there – next to the roof, it would be. He had imagined tea in front of the drawing-room fire with Nora and Richard. This did not seem unreasonable at half past four. He left his suitcase on the bed and limped downstairs in search of the bathroom. This, too, had been substantially altered, with a heightened seat for the lavatory and steps into the bath that also contained a seat. A row of bedpans filled with some milky substance were ranged on the window shelf.

Nora was standing in the hall. 'I was afraid you'd got lost.'

How could he get lost in his own house, he thought testily, but he decided to wait until they were settled with a drink before tackling her.

This proved far more difficult than he thought. She didn't settle anywhere; she rushed about the place either because someone came and asked for her or simply, he thought, because she imagined herself wanted. For half an hour before dinner he sat with Richard in what had been the morning room, now described by Nora as 'our own little haven'. The room was stuffy, and smelled strongly of the paraffin stove that flickered sulkily, emitting the minimum of warmth.

'Why don't you have a fire? There's a perfectly good fireplace.'

'Nora says it's too much for the staff. It's awfully difficult to get people at all. She says.'

Richard sat in his wheelchair. He wore an open-necked flannel shirt with a heavy cardigan, the empty sleeves pinned neatly to the sides. A tray placed over the arms of his chair contained a Bakelite mug with a straw in it. Every now and then he bent his head to suck his gin and tonic. 'Sorry there's no ice,' he said. 'Still, a gin and tonic is something of a treat, I can tell you.'

'Is it still difficult to get gin in the country?'

'I don't think it's *difficult*. I think it is considered not to be affordable.'

'Oh.'

'While you're up' – he wasn't – 'I wonder if you'd give me a refill? Before the boss gets back?'

He did as he was asked, and refreshed his own glass.

'If I was in control,' Richard said, when he'd had another suck, 'there'd be unlimited gin. But there you are. I'm not known for my control. Over anything.'

A silence, while Raymond felt ripples of uncomfortable pity that somehow pre-empted his being able to think of anything to say.

'Still,' Richard said, 'I suppose we're a good deal luckier than the other poor blighters. Don't mention the gin to them. Because, unless their relatives visit them, they don't get a drop.'

There was another short silence.

'I wonder whether you'd be so good as to get the packet of fags which you should find behind that dictionary behind you on the bookshelf and light me one? Have one yourself if you feel inclined. Only be quick about it, before she gets back.'

He found the nearly empty packet and a box of matches beside it and lit the cigarette, which he placed between Richard's lips. He inhaled deeply twice and then indicated that he wanted it taken out.

'Sorry, if you pulled your chair over to me, you wouldn't have to stand up to do this. Shove it in again. Do have one yourself, and put the packet back, if you wouldn't mind.'

Nora returned before the cigarette was over.

'Poor Leonard! He'd fallen out of his chair and Myra couldn't get him up off the floor on her own. I thought I heard a thump so it was a good thing – Darling! *Where* did you get that cigarette?'

'Raymond gave it to me.'

'Oh. He's not supposed to have them, Daddy. I thought you knew that.'

'Might as well finish it,' Richard said, his eyes fixed upon Raymond with such determination that Raymond put the fag back between his lips. Richard inhaled again and started to cough.

'I told you, darling!' She twitched it away and stubbed it out. 'It only makes you cough. He has to be careful of his lungs because they don't get enough exercise.'

'And as you can see, it's vital to keep me in good nick.'

There was no mistaking the irony. Raymond watched Nora mistake it. 'Of course we must,' she said cheerfully. She picked up his mug and shook it. 'Goodness! You haven't even finished your drink.'

'For God's sake, don't take *that* away.'

'You know I wouldn't dream of it,' Nora said gently, 'but drink it up, darling, because supper is ready.'

Supper took place in the old dining room, now

furnished with a long trestle table round which the five
wheelchairs could be placed, interspersed with ordinary
chairs for the helpers – there were two besides Nora.
Nobody was so incapacitated as Richard, Raymond
noticed: mostly they were able to feed themselves, though
two of them used a spoon. Nora helped everybody to
Irish stew, from which, she said, the bones had been
removed, and fed Richard. The carpet had been removed
from the floor, which was just as well because a good deal
of food got dropped on it. Conversation was constrained
and spasmodic. The patients did not talk much to one
another, and did not seem to find anything that anybody
else said of much interest. They concentrated upon the
food: the stew was followed by a weighty treacle sponge.

It was not until some time after the meal that he was
able to get Nora to himself. The patients had been
installed in the old drawing room: another room that had
been stripped of its Victorian contents and now had very
lurid, he thought, posters drawing-pinned to the walls
('the paper was so dingy, we had to do something'), and a
linoleum-covered floor spattered with small, baize-topped
tables so that cards and board games could be played
alongside the wireless, which seemed to be permanently
switched on. After he had been shown all this and Richard
had said that he would stay to listen to the nine o'clock
news, Nora consented to return to the 'haven' so that he
could, as he had told her he wanted to, talk to her.

The outcome of the talk was deeply depressing to
him. He discovered that Nora had been led to believe
by Jessica that she could continue in the house, running it
as a home for the present inmates. 'Mummy said you
wouldn't *want* to live here now we're all grown up –

except for Judy, of course, and she'll soon be on her way. She thought it was a marvellous idea for me to run this. And it does do a lot of good. If it wasn't for this, my patients would be in a large institution and here we do try to make it more like family life.' It transpired that she had raised a considerable sum of money for what she described as the 'improvements' to the house. 'It really wasn't at all suitable for them as it was. But of course I got the money on the understanding that we were staying here.'

He said he couldn't *understand* why she hadn't consulted him first.

'I was so afraid you'd say no,' she said. She had gone rather pink. 'The thing is, Daddy, that when one feels really *called* to do something, one must not let anything stand in the way. Of course you could always come and *stay* here. Absolutely whenever you liked. It depresses Mummy, but that's because she has got a bit of a selfish side. I don't think she stops to think what it's like to be in Richard's position – or any of them. Richard is my life now. It's my job to look after him. And I do feel that it's good for him to have other people around who are more or less in the same position as he is. It gives him a sense of proportion about things.' These were some of the things she said. Then she had to go and put Richard to bed.

When she returned from that, he asked if there was any whisky.

'There might be a bit left. I keep it for very special occasions.' She found a nearly empty half-bottle, poured an extremely small drink into his before-dinner gin glass, and handed it to him with a jug of water.

'After all, we are paying a rent for here,' she said.

'I didn't know that.'

'Well, I've been paying it to Mummy. It isn't much, I know, but it's what we can afford.'

The water had dust on it.

'And Mummy's bought a house in London anyway. And she says you have lots of money to buy another one if you want. I've put all the furniture and stuff in the coach house. If you don't mind, I must go to bed now. I have to get up for Richard in the night.'

He asked what time breakfast was.

'Well, I have it at six, because of getting it for everyone else. They have it in their rooms.'

'We've really got to talk a bit more about all this.'

'I can't tomorrow because I'm taking Albert to the dentist quite early. Anyway, Dad, I don't think I've much more to say. I think you ought to talk to Mummy, she knows all about it. Would you put out the lights when you go up?'

That was it. She took his breath away. She seemed completely unaware of the outrageousness of the situation. He gulped down the whisky and gave himself another. He'd buy her another bottle, but he needed a proper drink to calm his nerves. He limped up the two flights of stairs (how on earth did she get the poor chaps up even one flight?) to bed in his freezing room. It was so cold that he wore his pyjamas on top of his vest and pants. He lay awake for most of the night with angry, circular thoughts. It seemed to him that he was facing a well-planned conspiracy to deprive him of his house and home. Jessica's part in it enraged him, but it also made him feel frightened. If she really refused to leave London, how could he live here? He couldn't contemplate it on his own.

He left as soon as he could the next morning, and on the train rehearsed various ways of tackling Jessica and her perfidy. Although Nora's calm assurance that she almost had a *right* to the house had rendered him at the time almost speechless, he could not altogether blame her. It was clear to him that Jessica was largely responsible. He alternated between wanting to vent his rage upon her, 'to put her in her place', and wondering rather tremulously how he could coax and prevail upon her to *want* to live in the country. For, he now realised, she had in various ways intimated to him that she wanted to stay in London. He hadn't taken a great deal of notice of the hints, casual remarks, that had been thrown out. Frensham was their home and of course they were going back there. But now he saw that she had always, in fact, been decided, and was afraid of her determination.

'You might have told me what was going on,' was what he did manage to say.

'Oh, darling, I knew you had a lot on your mind. I was really trying to make things easier for you.'

'The things she's done to the house!'

'Only things that were necessary for the poor patients.'

'She's taken the Virginia creeper right off the front. That can't have made much difference to them.'

'There was appalling damp, darling. The walls had to be rendered with some damp-proof stuff.'

'But I did have a good idea,' she said some minutes later.

'What was that?'

'*I* thought why not convert the coach house into a little weekend retreat? Don't you think that would be rather fun? It could be quite small and cosy and easy to run.'

'I don't want to live somewhere small and cosy and easy to run.'

'Raymond, I *do*. I've spent most of my life struggling with places and having to do everything, and now, just when I might have expected to stop doing that and have some servants to do things, there aren't going to be any. So I do think you might look at things from my point of view.'

That was the only way he was going to be allowed to consider them, he thought resentfully. He was silenced, while she told him that *he* wasn't going to do the house-work *or* the cooking, and that she was absolutely sick of doing that. 'I want to have things as simple as possible, so that at least there's some time for other things.'

When, some weeks later, he said what a pity it was that they couldn't have Angela's going-away party at Frensham, she retorted, 'That would have been out of the question even if we had been living there. We couldn't begin to put enough people up for the night. It would always have had to be London.'

She used not to be like this, he thought. Before that little worm Clutterworth had come along she had always tried to fit in. Now she had joined the Bach Choir and was also having singing lessons.

'Where *does* Angela want her party to be?'

'She doesn't mind. I thought Claridge's would be nice.'

'How many people does she want?'

'She's going to make a list. About twelve, she thinks – not counting the family, of course. I should think we shall be about fifty, counting the children. And then just a few of us for supper afterwards.'

'Shouldn't we give them all supper?'

'It would be awfully expensive.'

'Never mind that. I'd like to give her a really good send-off.'

'All right, darling. Whatever you say.'

∞ ∞ ∞

She leaned forward to allow the servant to put her pillows into a sitting position – Mamma had always said one must try to make servants' lives easier for them in every way possible – and waited until her breakfast tray was placed on the bed table in front of her. She was so excited.

'Did you know I'm going to India, Harrison?'

'No, darling, I didn't. Who with?'

It wasn't Harrison; it was Kitty's little daughter, what was her name, Beryl? Barbara? It began with a B, she was sure . . . Rachel, that was it. How she had grown! Shot up, as Papa used to say, to quite an unbecoming height for a girl. She looked at the tray again. 'They have coddled my egg, haven't they? Coddled eggs are far more digestible than boiled. I must make a good breakfast because . . .' But she could not remember why she should, although she knew there was a very good reason.

'Lady Tregowan!' she cried triumphantly. It was all coming back to her. 'Mamma's friend, Lady Tregowan, is chaperoning me. I really think, you know, that I should have more than one egg before such a journey.'

'Darling, we haven't got many eggs. I know the war is over, but it's still difficult.'

War? What could war have to do with eggs? Sometimes, she felt, people fobbed her off with the flimsiest of excuses. However, it did not do to make a fuss. In this spirit, she allowed her niece to help her into her bedjacket and to tie a napkin round her neck.

'Actually, we're going to London, Aunt Dolly. Don't you remember?'

She smiled to conceal her irritation. '*First*. My dear, I am not so foolish as to suppose one could board a ship – any ship – *here*. Naturally we are going to London first. Then we may well go to Liverpool or' – she searched for other places by the sea – 'or *Brighton*, possibly. That is something I do not know. Because nobody has told me!'

'Shall I butter your toast for you?'

'That would be most kind.' She accepted a thin triangle with the crusts cut off – very little butter, she noticed, but when she mentioned this, ever so tactfully, Rachel made some incomprehensible excuse about rations. Perhaps Mamma was worrying about her figure. Ah! Give her time and she should solve any mystery.

'Maud Ingleby is a very good sort of girl, but Papa described her as plain as a pikestaff. Between you and me, I think it most unlikely that she will marry well – even in India.' Seeing that her niece looked mystified, she explained, 'Maud is Lady Tregowan's daughter.' She had picked the shell off the top of her egg and was cutting the faintly translucent white dome. It was one of those eggs with a very small yolk, you could see.

'Flo is very cross, you know, not to be coming too. But Lady Tregowan would only take one of us and Papa said it should be me. "With Kitty getting married, you will be holding the fort," I said to her, but I fear hers is not a happy nature as she shows no sign of making the best of it.' She put down her spoon. 'You know, I am afraid something has *happened* to Flo.' She looked searchingly at Rachel to see whether she was concealing anything. 'She seems to be avoiding me.'

There was a silence. Rachel had gone to the window, and was drawing the curtains. 'Rather a dreary day, I'm afraid,' she said. 'Don't forget to drink your tea, darling, before it gets cold,' she said, as she left the room.

When she was alone, her mind filled suddenly with disturbing thoughts. Something was not right; she knew it. She was not at home: this was not Stanmore – she was somewhere quite else. Staying with Kitty! That was it. But where *was* Flo? She remembered someone – a man she most certainly did not know – saying something about Flo having gone to her father, but what on earth could that mean, and who *was* he? Everybody had listened to him – you could have heard a pin drop. Flo's father was *her* father, of course. Anyway, Flo could not have gone to him because he was dead; he died in the winter and she was not able to go to India after all – she had to stay at home with Flo and help look after poor Mamma. It was still a fearful muddle. If she had not been able to go to India then she couldn't be going to India now . . . The bubbling excitement had all died away and she felt nothing but disappointment and dread. 'It was the worst disappointment of your life,' she told herself. But at least that meant that Flo had no reason to sulk, to keep away in this cruel manner; she would get Mamma to speak to her about it. But that was no good because she could now remember as clearly as anything that Mamma was dead too.

The trouble was not that she could not remember

things – she had too much to remember, more than most, she supposed, and this made it difficult to sort out their order. For instance, she was perfectly certain that when she had stayed here before, with Kitty, Flo had slept in a bed over there – by the window, because she had always had a passion for fresh air. Mamma had died from getting a chill, so perhaps it ran in the family. It had been quite a small funeral, she remembered, only Flo and Kitty and herself, the family doctor and his wife and, of course, the servants. She had been to much larger funerals in her day – she could *not* remember when it was; in one way it seemed to have happened a long time ago, and in another it felt as though it had happened yesterday. Yesterday must be nonsense, because yesterday she had been packing, sorting things out and packing. So – and this was what was so confusing – one did not pack things unless one was going away.

Her egg had got cold but she persisted in eating it because to go on a journey without a proper breakfast was, as Papa used to say, sheer folly. I have my common sense, she thought, as she scraped the inside of the shell for remaining scraps of white. Perhaps she was simply *ending* her visit with Kitty, and going home. And perhaps Flo had gone ahead of her to get the house ready. She was the one with common sense, but Flo had always been the practical one, and who knew what those wretched Zeppelins might have done to the house? Of *course*! That was what little Rachel (only she wasn't so little nowadays, more of a beanstalk, one might say) meant when she was chattering about a shortage of eggs, although what eggs had to do with Zeppelins, she really couldn't think. 'I really cannot *think*!' she repeated to herself, glad to have found something so absurd to account for this loss. But things were falling into place. There had been a terrible war (this *was* a terrible war? she wasn't quite clear about that) and so many gallant young men had been killed that no odium could any longer attach to being unmarried: there were simply not enough men to go round. In any case, she had always thought that whereas she would rather enjoy being *engaged* to someone, marriage might be rather—

'I suppose Flo has simply gone before me?' she said to Rachel when she came to collect the tray.

Rachel stooped and kissed her. 'Yes,' she said. 'I think that's it.'

∞ ∞ ∞

'Just look at me for a moment, would you? No, don't move your head – just your eyes. That's perfect.' He smiled admiringly. Lady Alathea stifled a yawn and smiled back.

Her eyes were small, pale blue, but mercifully fairly far apart. He could make something of them. He had made them darker, of course, and larger, and he had substituted their vacancy with an alert, enquiring expression – as though Lady Alathea was about to ask an intelligent question. The trick was a likeness, but a flattering likeness. She had a rather pudgy nose, and he had sharpened it – he had even managed to give her face some shape by heightening the colour high up under the eyes. But her mouth defeated him. It was small and thin, more like a slit in her face with a narrow edging than a mouth, and this tricky state was compounded by her painting quite another mouth in dark red lipstick round it. During the sittings, she usually licked most of the lipstick off, which was the case now. It was midday, and he was due to lunch with his mother.

'I think you've had enough for today,' he said. 'I know how tiring it is sitting.'

'I'm afraid I'm not a very good sitter,' she said as, hitching her pale blue satin skirts, she climbed down from the dais. 'May I come and look?'

'If you like. It isn't finished yet.'

'Goodness! My dress looks wonderful. And you've painted Mummy's necklace marvellously. I should think diamonds are quite difficult to paint, aren't they?'

'You're very modest,' he said. 'What about *you*? Do you think it's a good likeness of you?'

She looked again at the picture. He could see that she was fascinated by it. 'Oh, I don't know,' she said. 'I don't know that sort of thing. I should think my parents will be pleased.'

Which is the main thing, he thought, while she was changing in a curtained-off end of the studio. He was charging two hundred guineas, and for that it was necessary to please. There were three daughters and so far only the pretty one had married. He had hopes of painting the other two. Mummy had helped him buy the house in Edwardes Square on the understanding that he paid her back, but the household cost quite a lot: Sebastian's nannie and a cook and the daily woman, not to speak of the girl he employed to act as a part-time secretary, coffee-maker and general factotum at the studio, which he rented. And, until recently, there had been the fees to pay to the psychiatrist Louise had been going to. But only last week she had stopped, said it was pointless, and she was never going to him again. He sighed. She was actually being quite difficult and he was afraid that Mummy was begin-

190

ning to notice this and would ask awkward questions about her.

Lady Alathea emerged in her twinset and flannel skirt. He was glad that he had not been called upon to paint her legs, he thought, as he put her into a taxi, kissing her hand and saying, 'By the way, you're a *wonderful* sitter,' as the right kind of parting shot.

Outside it was freezing and dirty snow lay in ruts and ridges on the pavement. It had been filthy weather, either fog or rain or frost, and keeping the studio warm enough for sitters had cost a fortune. The stove that he had had installed was virtually useless since it was impossible to get enough coal for it. At least he'd get a better lunch with Mummy than at home. Mrs Alsop was a dreadful cook – the meals were all grey mince and boiled cabbage and potatoes filled with intractable grey lumps. Louise didn't seem to care. Oh, well, he supposed it was good for his figure as he had an unfortunate tendency to put on weight far too easily.

His mother was lying on her usual sofa by the window that looked on to the small formal garden. She was wearing what she called her Russian jacket – dark red velvet with black fur round the high collar and cuffs of the loose sleeves. 'How nice!' she exclaimed, as he leaned down to kiss her. 'What a lovely treat to have you all to myself! Give yourself a drink, darling, and then come and tell me what you've been up to.'

There were decanters of sherry and gin on the table with a small silver jug of water. He helped himself to a gin and pulled up a stool near her sofa. 'I've spent the morning painting Alathea Creighton-Green,' he said. 'Rather hard going.'

His mother smiled with sympathy. 'Poor Ione! To

have *three* daughters and *no* son! And only one daughter was presentable. Is Alathea so very plain?'

'Yes. So very.'

They smiled at each other. Occasionally, he went to bed with his sitters; somehow, he knew that she knew this although it was never mentioned. Her enquiry about Alathea's plainness was her way of asking about that and his answer the denial.

'Any minute now, one of us will say that beauty is not everything.'

He sensed that this was the most delicate probe towards discussing Louise and headed her off. 'How's the Judge?'

'Embroiled in his committees. And as if they were not enough, in other people's committees. Horder came to dinner last week. The British Medical Council want to launch a fund to fight the proposed National Health Bill. They want Peter to back them. And there's another committee that wants MPs' salaries to be increased to a thousand a year. Quite a step up from four hundred. Perhaps you should think again, darling. I'm sure I could get you a nice safe seat to nurse.'

'Luncheon is served, my lady.'

'Good morning, Sarah.'

He smiled at the solemn old parlourmaid, who smiled discreetly back. 'Good morning, sir.'

As he helped his mother off the sofa, she said, 'One thing I can promise you: we are not having squirrel pie.'

'Squirrel *pie*?'

'Darling! Do you never read the newspapers? The Ministry of Food has decreed that we should eat squirrels and to this end has issued a recipe for squirrel pie. Doesn't it sound horrid?'

192

During their cheese soufflé she asked him about his future commissions for portraits and what arrangements he was making for an exhibition, and he felt himself expanding, basking in her lively, detailed interest, her assumption that he was a highly gifted painter with an important future ahead of him. Outside, enormous white flakes fell slowly from a darkened sky, but in the dining room she created another climate, both cosy and exciting; her obvious pride in him, her certainty of his worth, rekindled his assurance – he caught self-satisfaction from her like a delightful fever.

She had provided a bottle of hock for him, although she drank only barley water, and by the time they reached the pudding, he discovered that he had drunk most of it. It was arranged that she should come to his studio to help him pick the pictures for a show, or in some cases to look at photographs of them. 'It doesn't matter if up to a quarter of the pictures are already sold,' she said. 'The point of the show is to get more commissions.'

'We shall have to offer the gallery a cut on *them*.'

'We shall have to negotiate that. Now for a treat!' Sarah had cleared the plates and returned with a silver platter on which something mysterious steamed.

'It smells of bananas!'

'It *is* bananas. Our very first. I kept them for you. And Peter was given a lemon from the Admiralty.' She said this as though that was where one would naturally acquire such a thing.

'Darling Bubbles James gave it to him. Wasn't that sweet? So we have fried bananas with *brown* sugar and lemon!'

They were delicious. She ate very little, which meant that there were two helpings for him.

193

But when they returned to the drawing room for coffee before the fire and she was installed again upon her sofa, the atmosphere changed. She began by asking about her grandson, 'whom I have not seen for far too long'.

'Sebastian? He's fine. Talking quite a lot now. Which I suppose he should be – he's nearly three. Shall I get Nannie to bring him to tea with you?'

'Do, darling.' She picked up her embroidery. After a moment, she asked lightly, 'And how is Louise?'

'She's all right. She read some poetry for the BBC last week, which thrilled her.'

'And what else is she doing?'

'How do you mean, darling?'

'Well, I don't imagine that reading some poems on a single occasion can have occupied her entire time for the last two months. I haven't set eyes on her since Christmas.'

'You frighten her, you know.'

'I do *not* know. Oh no! I don't frighten her, she dislikes me.' And before he could protest, she added. 'She dislikes me because I can see through her.'

'Mummy darling, what do you mean by that?'

She put down her sewing and looked at him steadily. 'I have been trying to make up my mind whether to talk to you about this or not. But we have never had any secrets from each other, have we?'

'Of course not,' he said untruthfully, and with haste.

'Of course not.' The only secrets she had had about him had been concealed entirely for his own good.

There was another silence crowded with things unsaid.

'I'm afraid – how can I put this? – that Louise has been a very naughty little girl.'

'Oh, Mummy, I know you don't think she's a good mother, but she's still very young—'

'Old enough to behave unforgivably.'

'What are you trying to say?'

So then it all came out. Louise had been unfaithful to him. When he protested that he was certain that she had not been to bed with poor Hugo – his death had somehow softened the anger that he had felt about that affair – she said no, no, it was *after* Hugo, when he had taken her to Holyhead, some naval officer she had encountered there and subsequently met in London. She mentioned his name and he recognised it.

'But how do you know that she—'

'Had an affair with him? My dearest boy, they were seen going into a flat late one evening and then leaving it – separately – the following morning.'

Then she said, 'For all I know, it may still be going on.'

'I know that isn't so. Rory got married about eight months ago. We were asked to the wedding.' But she had shaken him badly. It was another shock – something that he had thought would never happen after the miserable business with Hugo.

'Oh, darling. I can see it's a shock to you. I am so very sorry. And angry as well. What have *you* done to deserve it?'

'God knows. *I* don't.'

She put out her hand and he grasped it. Memories of Louise's unresponsiveness in bed, something he had never really thought about before, were filling his mind. 'It's over anyway, whatever it was,' he said, with difficulty and at last.

'What is over?' There was a sharpness in her tone that made him look at her.

195

'That – affair. With Rory. They've gone to live in Cornwall.'

'Ah.'

'What did you think I meant?'

'I thought you were talking about something else. Never mind.'

'She – she was going to this doctor. This psychiatrist chap.'

'Was? She's stopped?'

'Last week. I don't know why. But she says nothing would induce her to go back.'

'Why don't you have a word with him?'

'I can't see that that would do much good. I did meet him once and I must say I didn't take to him.' Something she had said earlier was worrying him. 'Mummy, how on earth did *you* hear about Rory – the flat and all that?'

'Oh, darling, someone told me. That doesn't matter now. What matters is your happiness, your well-being. *And* Sebastian's as well. I do worry about him. Louise isn't simply a bad mother, she isn't a mother at all.'

Then she suddenly burst out. 'Oh, Mikey darling! I blame myself. I feel I am greatly at fault.'

'Nonsense, Mummy. You didn't *make* me marry Louise, I wanted to.' But even as he said it, he realised that he had fallen into one of her little traps.

'No, but I encouraged you. And it is you who have to suffer. I thought she was simply young and malleable. How could I know that she would turn out to be so utterly selfish and self-absorbed?'

'Oh, come! It's not as bad as that. You must remember that we had a rotten start. I was away nearly all the time and completely taken up by my ship. I do see now that she had a rather thin time of it.'

'She had Sebastian.'

'Yes, well, she didn't want to have a baby quite so soon.'

'How extraordinary! You might have been killed, and she with no son!'

'Not everyone is a mother like you.'

The little carriage clock on the chimney piece struck a silvery three. 'God! I must go, darling. I've another appointment.'

He bent over to kiss her and she folded him in her arms. 'Mikey! I do want you to know one thing. Whatever you decide to do, I'll back you all the way. And if that includes Sebastian, so much the better.' She gazed at him with her penetrating eyes that he had once told her were the colour of aquamarines. 'You won't forget that, will you?'

'No, of course I won't.' Again he felt at that moment comfortingly enfolded by her love.

But in the car outside and during his journey across London, he felt dispirited and confused. There were a number of things he had *not* told his mother, such as the fact that Louise refused to go to bed with him, something which had caused him to sulk and her to pretend not to notice that he was sulking. He still found her immensely attractive – in fact, she had grown during the last four years from being a rather gawky, leggy, charming young girl into someone whose glamour was wildly noticeable. If not exactly a classical beauty, she was someone who made people's heads turn when she came into a room. She was an asset, and he felt aggrieved that she was not more, as he put it, on his side. If, for instance, he was invited to Sandringham, which was possibly on the cards (he had drawn one of the young princesses and had hopes of drawing their mother), she would not be simply thrilled and do everything in her power to help him, as most young women, he felt, would; she was just as likely to appear in the wrong clothes, say the wrong things and behave generally as though she was totally unaware of the importance of the occasion. And if he was to go there at all, he desperately wanted to make a success of it. Perhaps it would be better to go without her. He should have asked Mummy's advice about that. It would certainly be *easier*. Another thing he had not told Mummy was that Rowena was back in his life. They had met some months before in the King's Road, when he was coming out of his framers. She was walking along on the opposite side of the street, with a champagne-coloured poodle on a lead.

He called her name and she stopped. 'Michael!'

He dodged a bus and crossed the road to her. She was wearing a short fur jacket over a black skirt and a black velvet beret over her blond hair. She looked very pretty.

'How lovely to see you! What are you doing here?'

She blushed the palest pink. 'I live round the corner. In Carlyle Square.'

'It's really nice to see you.'

Her pale, wide-apart eyes regarded him, then she bent down to the dog who was straining on his leash. 'Shut up, Carlos! I saw you coming out of Green and Stone. I didn't think you'd see me.'

'I was leaving some pictures to be framed. I suppose you wouldn't invite me back for a cup of tea?'

She looked nervous. 'Oh! I don't think—'

'Oh, please do! It's such years. I'd really like to hear what's been happening to you.'

'Nothing very much. Oh – all right. Yes, do come.'

Her rather flat, girlish little voice, which did not alter whatever was happening to her or whatever she said about it, came back to him. Poor little Rowena, as Mummy called her. She had wanted to marry him so badly; he supposed now that perhaps he hadn't treated her very well. But, as Mummy had said, it wouldn't have done. 'A very amiable nonentity,' Mummy had called her, but that was all six or more years ago; she must have changed.

Her house was rather impressive: large and filled with good furniture. She put him in the drawing room and went away to make tea. When she had taken off her gloves, he saw her rings – a wedding ring and one with a large sapphire and diamonds. Of course, she had married – he vaguely remembered Mummy mentioning it.

'I married Ralph Fytton,' she said, when she had brought the tea tray and he had asked her.

'The scientist?'

She nodded. 'He died last year. He got all the way through the war and then he died of pneumonia.'

'I'm so sorry.'

'Yes, it was very sad for him.'

'But not for you?'

'Oh, yes, it was sad for me too. In a way. But it wasn't working out. As a marriage, I mean. I wanted children, you see, and he didn't.' She poured the tea and handed him a cup.

'How odd!' he exclaimed.

'I know. But he thought the world wasn't a fit place for children any more. He knew about the bomb, you see – long before it was used, I mean. He got awfully depressed. He used to say it was time for the human race to come to an end. I couldn't argue with him. I never

199

could argue with him about anything, he was so terribly clever.'

'It sounds rough on you.' He wanted to say, 'Why did you marry him?' but thought better of it. Instead, he said, 'He was a good deal older than you, wasn't he?'

And she answered in her flat little voice, 'Nearly thirty years.'

She was, he knew, thirty-five – only three years younger than him – and another argument that his mother had employed against his marrying her had been her age: too old, Zee had said.

'So,' she said, not looking at him, 'how are you? I saw that you nearly got into Parliament. That was bad luck.'

'Not really. I don't think it was what I really *wanted* to do.'

'And you have a little son! I saw that in *The Times*. How marvellous for you.' There was a slight pause, and then she said, 'Your mother very kindly asked me to your wedding. But it didn't feel right to go actually.'

He remembered their last walk, after the lunch at Hatton when eventually he had told her that he thought he was going to marry Louise, and how she had said at once, 'I know. I knew the moment I came into the room and saw her. She's very beautiful and I could see she's awfully clever.' And then she had wept. He had tried to put his arms round her but she had pulled away from him to lean against a tree and continue crying. All the while she was crying she kept apologising. 'I'm so sorry – be all right in a minute – sorry to be like this—' and he, embarrassed and uncomfortable, had said, 'I never said anything about – that I would—'

'I know,' she had said. 'I know you didn't. I just – sort of hoped . . .' Her flat, childish voice had died away at this point. He had offered her the cliché handkerchief then and she had mopped up and said she would go home now. He remembered telling her how fond of her he was, and saying what good times they had had. They had gone back to the house, and Rowena had thanked Zee for lunch, and he had taken her to her car. He had kissed her face and said how sorry he was. He had really not thought of her again. But now earlier memories of their times together flooded back: the first time she had taken off her clothes – God, what a lovely body she had! – and her always agreeable admiration; how, even in those times she was always beautifully dressed (she made her own clothes); the eager interest she took in everything he did . . .

He leaned forward and took her hands. 'We did have fun, didn't we?'

'Not fun,' she said. 'I never thought of it as fun.'

He did not see her for some weeks after that. Then he ran into her on his way to his gallery in Bond Street. It was then that he discovered that she worked three days a week in another gallery. He took her to the Ritz for a drink where they had two Martinis each, followed by a longish lunch. She said that she had to go back to work, was already late, and on an impulse, and because Louise was in Sussex seeing her family, he asked her to have dinner with him. 'And we might go dancing somewhere,' he added. She had always been a good dancer, could follow him on the floor whatever he did.

That had been the beginning of it. He had told her that things were not good between him and Louise; she had been unmaliciously sympathetic – she had always been good-natured; he could never recall her speaking ill of anyone. She bore him no resentment which, as their intimacy increased, he began to see she had the right to do. He *had* treated her badly. The moment on their last walk together at Hatton when he had tried to excuse himself by saying that he had never intended to marry her now made him feel ashamed and in the end he told her so. 'It was selfish and pompous and altogether *crass* of me,' he said, and she had answered: 'Oh, Mike! You always overdo that kind of thing, to make people disagree with you.'

The truth of this and the fact that she did not often say anything that surprised him by its perception made him feel – for a moment – just a little in love with her. And she *was* lovely. She had always been so with each feature perfectly in place, a broad forehead, large wide-apart eyes, which were neither grey nor blue nor green but, at different times, the palest version of those colours, a small nose and a wide mouth that drooped at the corners, like small commas, giving her expression a gravity that enhanced it and made incident in the broad sweeping planes of her face. He had explored all these things in his drawings when they had first become lovers; now he was rediscovering them with the minute changes wrought by time and her experience – both of which seemed to have added to her attraction. She had poise now and more animation, and she did not invariably agree with him.

They did not meet often: he was working very hard, and, as the daylight hours gradually increased, for longer, and most evenings he had engagements with Louise. But there were times when Louise announced that she was spending the evening with her cousins Polly and Clary or her friend Stella, whom he had never really taken to, or she wanted to go to some play that he knew he would not enjoy, and then he would ring Rowena from his studio and make a plan with her. She seemed always to be free, and when, on one of these occasions, he remarked upon this and said that surely she must have other friends, she had answered that she put them off. That was the evening when he first went to bed with her, and it was a great success. She had always been easy in bed and he was able to enjoy himself, as well as his effect upon her, with no trouble at all. She combined passivity with obvious sexual satisfaction – the perfect combination, he thought.

Afterwards they lay in her bed and had a serious (stock) conversation about the fact that he was married and did not want to rock the boat – the child and so forth – and she listened and accepted everything he said in just the right way. 'I'm so happy,' she said. 'I don't care about anything else. I'm here if you want me.'

His marriage seemed to be at an impasse. However, a gallery in New York who had shown some of his pictures before the war had written asking him whether he was interested in another show. He had discussed the matter with his mother, who thought it an excellent idea, although she had advised him to be firm about a date sufficiently far off for him to accumulate enough portraits. If this did come off, he decided to take Louise with him: a complete change of scene might also improve their marriage. It would get her away from her preoccupation with the theatre and give them a chance to be really alone together. Sebastian and Nannie could go to his mother at Hatton. It would be a kind of second honeymoon, and Louise, who had never been abroad in her life, must surely be excited at the prospect. Rowena did not come into these plans – how could she? – but the knowledge that she was there, in the background, gave him a new kind of assurance that he badly needed. The spring of '47, he thought, would be the right time to go to America, and he wrote to this effect.

∞ ∞ ∞

As Christopher tramped back down the cart track from the farm to his caravan he noticed with satisfaction that the wind had dropped, not completely, to that stillness that usually prefaced rain at this time of year, but to a kinder, more domestic breeze. Perhaps it would be a fine weekend – he passionately hoped so. He had had his weekly bath and supper with the Hursts, a day earlier because tomorrow Polly was coming to stay. She had never been before; indeed he had never had *anybody* to stay in the caravan with him and his excitement at the prospect was beginning to congeal into anxiety. Although it was dark, he didn't need a torch – knew the way blindfold. But Polly would need one. He must be sure the battery was working on the old one he had – come to that he must find it, must add that to his list. Lucky he'd asked for the day off tomorrow because there was a hell of a lot to do before Polly arrived.

He had asked her on the spur of the moment at the party given for his sister Angela before she left for America. After Nora's wedding he had decided that family parties were not for him; they only made him feel depressed and isolated, something which in his ordinary life he did not feel at all. But he was very fond of Ange; she was his sister and he felt he might never see her again. Mindful of the fiasco of the very old suit that he had tried to wear to Nora's wedding (his mother had made him borrow something from Uncle Hugh, which hadn't fitted

204

either but in a different way), he had bicycled into Hastings and bought himself a dark suit and a utility shirt. Then he remembered that he'd used his tie to bind the splint on the vixen's leg, and bought himself another: green with blue spots on it. It wasn't silk, which meant it wouldn't tie very well, but it didn't matter as he didn't expect to wear it much. Mrs Hurst had knitted him some socks for Christmas. He hadn't enough coupons left to buy shoes, so he would have to wear the awful old ones that were far too tight, or his boots. In the end he chose his boots. *He* didn't look at people's feet, so he didn't think they would be noticed. He'd have to stay in London on the night of the party, and he absolutely didn't want to have to stay with Mum and Dad, so although he hated the telephone, he rang up Ange at her house and asked if he could stay with her because she knew how he felt about Dad. She was nice about it, and said if he didn't mind the floor he could. 'Anyway, there's no room in their tiddly little house because Judy will be there,' she had said.

So that stormy Saturday he took Oliver over to the Hursts and bicycled against a violent headwind to the station. It was bitterly cold and hail fell with little stinging blows on to his face; he was glad of his oilskin jacket.

Journeys always made him anxious; the train was all right because all he had to do was to sit in it until it finally stopped in London. But then he had to find the right bus stop for the right bus that would take him to a stop by Lyons' Corner House in Tottenham Court Road, and then he had to walk on until a turning to the left, which was Percy Street where Ange lived. But it was nice when he finally got there. Ange seemed really pleased to see him and made him tea and toast. She had her hair in curlers and she was wearing her dressing gown, but the main thing was that she looked happy. This made her look so different that he realised that she must have been pretty unhappy before.

When they were sitting as near to the small electric fire as they could get and drinking the tea, he said, 'Do you remember when I met you in the drive at Mill Farm after we all knew there wasn't going to be the war and you were so unhappy and you couldn't tell me about it?'

'Yes. I could now. I thought I was in love with Rupert—'

'*Uncle* Rupert?'

'Yep, I thought it was the end of the world. I thought he loved me back, you see. Well – I suppose I sort of *imagined* he did. And, of course, he didn't.'

'Poor Ange!'

'Don't worry. It's completely over. Everybody has to have a first love and I expect they mostly go wrong.'

'Did good things happen after it?'

'Not much. I fell in love with someone else and that was far worse. *He* was married too.'

'Was that the person you nearly did marry?'

'Yes – no. It was the person Mummy thought I ought to marry. For the obvious reason.' She looked at him to see if he knew what she meant, and just as he was about to ask her why their mother thought she ought to marry someone who was married already, she said: 'I was pregnant.'

'Oh, Ange! Did you lose the baby?'

She hadn't answered at once, then she had said, gently, almost as though she was comforting him, 'I'm glad I didn't have it.'

She offered him a cigarette, but he didn't smoke.

'But now,' he said, 'you've got Lord Black, haven't you? I didn't know Americans had lords.'

'He's not a lord! That's his name. Earl. I shall be Mrs Earl C. Black. And live in New York. I can't wait.'

He could see she was happy, which was the point. But it did feel a long way away. She said she must get ready for the party – 'the probably awful party' – and told him where the bathroom was.

'Do you think I ought to shave again?'

She felt his face. 'Well. Did you shave this morning?'

'Yesterday. I only do it every other day usually.'

'You are a bit bristly. And you're bound to have to kiss people. Better.'

So he did, and managed not to cut himself.

The party was in a large room in a very grand hotel. All the family were there – well, it felt like all. *His* family, at any rate. Dad was wearing a dinner jacket and Mum had a long floaty blue dress. They put Angela between them to talk to everyone as they arrived. Judy had got rather fat and was wearing the bridesmaid's dress she'd worn for Nora's wedding. She rushed about the room eating things off the plates on the tables as well as things that were handed to her. He felt very proud of Angela who wore a red velvet dress that just reached her knees and marvellous stockings that she said Earl had sent her. Her hair was piled on top of her head and she had long red and gold earrings. 'You look absolutely terrific,' he had said before they left her home, and she kissed him. She smelt like a greenhouse full of flowers.

Nora arrived a bit late wheeling Richard, whom she placed beside her parents. 'So that he has a chance to see everyone as they come in,' she explained. Everybody who arrived was given a glass of champagne and Nora held

Richard's up to his mouth to give him little sips, but Christopher noticed that she did not do it very often.

He stood a little way off from his family and watched the Cazalets arrive. He had not seen any of them for three years – since Nora's marriage, in fact. First were Uncle Edward and Aunt Villy who looked as though she had shrunk inside her dress. They brought Lydia, who looked very elegant in a dark dress that made her waist look tiny (the opposite of Judy, he thought sadly), and Roland in grey flannel shorts with matching jacket and hair spiky from brilliantine, and Wills, dressed exactly the same. He saw Wills and Roland confer, and then descend upon Richard in his chair, whom thereafter they fed steadily with the little bits of food that were being handed round. Then Uncle Rupert and Aunt Zoë arrived and Aunt Zoë looked nearly as terrific as Ange in a dark green and white striped dress with dangling diamond earrings. He watched as Uncle Rupert kissed Ange, but she didn't seem to mind. Then the Duchy came with Aunt Rachel, both dressed as he always remembered them, in misty, bluebellish blues, but with long skirts. Uncle Rupert got the Duchy a chair and Aunt Rachel went at once to talk to Richard. Some other people arrived whom he didn't know – friends of Ange's, he supposed. Some of them knew each other, but they didn't seem to know the family. Then – and this was what changed the whole party for him – Clary arrived with Polly. Clary looked like he always remembered her, but Polly, although of *course* she was not unrecognisable, looked so extraordinarily beautiful that he felt he was seeing her for the first time in his life.

They came up to him at once. '*Chris*topher! Hello, Christopher,' was what they severally said. In a daze he allowed himself to be hugged by them. Polly's dress was the colour of autumn beech leaves; she smelt of some indefinably rich scent.

'You do smell extraordinary,' he found himself saying.

'It's a scent called Russian Leather,' Clary said, 'and I keep telling her she puts far too much of it on. She only wants to smell like *one* very expensive leather chair, not a whole row.' She added, 'It's French, actually. It's called Cuir de Russie in France.'

'If I had a scent, I'd choose one called Fried Bacon.' Someone very tall loomed behind the girls.

'Neville, you can't choose scents like that. You can only choose from what there is.'

'Not if I was a scent inventor, which might be a very good way of getting rich; they must have used up all the soppy flower smells by now. Also, sometimes people might like a scent that puts people off. Essence of Grass Snake would be good for that. Or Burglar's Sweat could be another – oh, hello, Christopher.'

Neville was now as tall as he.

'Don't be silly and disgusting,' Clary advised. 'This is a party. It's meant to be *fun* for people.'

She went with Polly to be greeted by Ange. Neville stayed.

'I must say I think parties are vastly overrated. You're not meant to have a proper conversation at them, but you *are* meant to kiss the most awful people and exchange platitudes with whoever is the most dull. Do you agree with that?'

'Well, I don't *go* to parties much. At all.'

'Really? How do you manage that?'

'There aren't parties where I live.' As he said that, he felt panic. He *did* live cut off from people: apart from the

Hursts and Tom, the other chap who worked for them, he didn't live with *people*. Of course, he saw people in shops, when he went to them, but otherwise he lived with Oliver, a half-wild cat who made use of him when she felt like it, and intermittently with other creatures whom he looked after when they were in the wars, like the vixen last autumn found in a horrible trap, various hedgehogs weak from fleas, birds that fell out of nests, and the young hare that Oliver brought him, one of whose eyes had been pecked out when it lay in a stupor – from some kind of poison he had suspected. But all these cousins, whom years ago he had spent holidays with, who had all once been part of his landscape, *they* all seemed to know one another, had continued to grow up together, while he had been cut off. Cut myself off, he admitted: in his intense determination to have as little to do with his father as possible he had isolated himself from everyone else. He looked at Neville, who had been choosing a sausage roll off a plate with great deliberation. He remembered him as a *boy*.

'How old are you?'

'Sixteen. And a half. But I'm working on being old for my age. It's largely a matter of vocabulary and never being surprised by anything.'

He bent his head to take a bite out of the roll, and a lock of reddish-brown hair fell across his bumpy white forehead, but at the crown, Christopher noticed, his hair grew upright in two tufts.

'Are Teddy and Simon coming?'

'Teddy's still in America, although he'll soon be back, with a girl called Bernadine who he's married. Simon's swotting for his finals.'

He didn't know whether he was sorry or glad about this.

At this point Christopher's father called for silence and made a fairly long, not always audible speech about Ange. He stopped listening to it almost at once because Polly came over to him and again her incredible beauty struck him so forcefully that the room seemed to contain only her. She *was* listening to his father's speech, so he was able to look at her – at her shining coppery hair that had been cut so that it stood out inches from the back of her slender white neck, and when his father made some sort of joke and there was laughter – not the real sort but polite – she turned to him and there was an eddy of the rich scent; she wrinkled her white nose, just like Aunt Rach used to do, he remembered, when she wanted to share something funny with anyone, and her dark blue eyes shone with conspiracy. What? That she knew that they both knew that his father was not funny? That she was simply pleased to see him?

Anyway, when his father had stopped speaking and there was applause, and before Ange began to say anything back, he took a deep breath and asked if she would come and stay a weekend in his caravan.

And now she was coming. He had *warned* her that he didn't have things like baths and electric light. He'd *said* it was only a caravan. But he hadn't said that there was only a sort of outdoor privy that he'd constructed just inside the wood, or that there was only a wooden bunk in the tiny bedroom at one end of the caravan. He'd put her in that, and he could sleep on the floor in the main part.

He spent the whole of the next day cleaning things and tidying up, and making a vegetable soup. Mrs Hurst, who had been extremely helpful, had made him a fruit cake and a baked custard with her own eggs and milk, so they would do for puddings. He decided upon a macaroni cheese for the main course, which he could cook in his little Dutch oven. He collected plenty of wood for the stove, cleaned the windows, which were always dim with woodsmoke and condensation, and his outdoor larder – a box with a zinc mesh door that was hung from the roof of the caravan. This was to house most of the food for the weekend. On one of his many borrowing trips, in this case for extra bedding, Mrs Hurst had suggested that his cousin might like to sleep at the farm, but he felt that it would spoil things. As the day drew on, however, and it was nearly time to go to the station to fetch Polly, he began to wonder whether he was wrong: perhaps she would prefer to sleep in a proper room in a proper bed.

He need not have worried. It was dusk when he met her on the platform. She was wearing trousers and a dark jacket and a scarf tied over her hair. They kissed in a family way and he took her small case.

'I didn't know you had a car!'

'It's not mine; it belongs to the farm I work for. He lent it to me to fetch you.'

'It's all pretty rough,' he warned her as he drove carefully out of Hastings – he didn't drive much and, anyway, felt he had to be extra careful with Polly: her face had felt like cool china when he kissed it.

'I know it will be lovely,' she said, with such a warm assurance that he began to feel that perhaps she *would* like it.

But when he had parked the car in the farmyard and begun to lead Polly up the track in the dark, all his anxiety surged back. He should have lit the oil lamp so that there was a welcoming glow ahead, he should have brought the torch . . . 'You'd better hold my hand,' he said, 'the track has rather deep ruts.' Her hand felt very soft and cold in his.

'You've still got Oliver, haven't you?'

'Oh, yes. I left him to guard things.'

She stood quietly in the dark while he fumbled with matches, and the soft yellow light bloomed.

'How pretty! What a lovely light!'

Oliver, who had been standing in the middle of the floor, went up to her and stared up at her with his rich brown eyes. While she was greeting him and his interest in her was speedily progressing from courtesy to affection and then towards passionate devotion, Christopher anxiously looked round his home, trying to see it with her eyes. The table looked nice with its red and white checked tablecloth with a jam jar of berries on it, but the piece of carpet in front of the stove, whose doors he went to open, looked worn and rather dirty, and the one comfortable basket chair – once painted white – looked rather grey and bristled with pieces of cane that had worked loose, and the cushion that concealed the hole in its seat was made of a balding plush of the colour that moss was not. The shelves he had made were littered with china – all odd pieces – and his books, and every hook or peg he had put up was covered with his clothes, all in a state of disrepair. The walls of the caravan and the partition that marked off the bedroom were, excepting for the four small windows, entirely choked up with stuff so that it seemed even smaller and more crowded than he felt it really was. Oliver's basket occupied a lot of space near the stove. He moved it now and pulled out a stool from under a shelf.

213

'Oh, Christopher, it's lovely! It's so *cosy*!' She was taking off the scarf and then her jacket; her hair looked like conkers just after they'd had their green spiky skins peeled off. He hung up her jacket and made her sit in the basket chair; he took her case into the tiny bedroom, came back and offered her tea, 'or there's some cider' (he'd forgotten about drink; she probably drank things like *cocktails*), but she said that tea would be perfect. Her presence in this place where, until now, he had always been alone, except for Oliver, elated him; her perfect loveliness filled him with excitement and joy, and beyond this, and perhaps best of all, she was not a stranger – she was somebody, one of the cousins, somebody he had known practically all his life. If he had not known her, he thought, as he pumped up the Primus to boil the kettle, he would never have dared to speak to her at Ange's party, and even if, by some amazing chance, *she* had spoken to *him*, had *asked* if she could come and stay with him, he would have been so intimidated by her radiance that he would not have been able to say a word.

They had tea, and some time after that the macaroni cheese.

She asked about a lavatory, and he escorted her, with the torch which he left with her.

'I heard an owl,' she said, when she returned. 'It is a lovely wild place, isn't it? A bit like your camp in the wood at Home Place, but much nicer.'

They had talked quite a bit about the family by then, and she'd told him about her job in what sounded like a very posh shop and about life with Clary in their flat. He asked her if she liked living in London.

'I think I do. When we were at Home Place in the war I used to long to live there, and have a job and my own place and all that. It's odd, but things always seem much more exciting when they're a long way away. I suppose that's why people like views so much. You know. Something that they can see a lot of but they're not *in* it,' she added.

He thought about that. 'No,' he said. 'I see what you mean, but I don't in the least feel like that.'

'You've always wanted to get away from things, haven't you?'

'Some things.' He felt guarded.

'Is it nice now that you have?'

'I haven't really thought about it. Shall I make us some hot chocolate? I get lots of milk.'

She said that would be lovely. He went out to fetch the milk and when he came back, she said, 'What about the washing-up? Can I do it if you tell me how?'

'I'll do it later.' He took the kettle for washing-up water off the Primus and began mixing the chocolate powder in a saucepan. He suddenly felt crowded with things he wanted to ask, to discuss, to talk about, to find out what she thought about them.

'Do you think one's meant to be happy in life?'

'What else do you think one should be?'

'Oh, *useful* – er – helpful to other people. Trying to make the world better, that kind of thing.'

'I think being happy *would* make the world better.'

'You have to be quite clever to be it, though, don't you? I mean, it's not as easy as it sounds.'

'No.' She sounded sad; then she suddenly laughed. 'I've just remembered Miss Milliment saying that when she was young there was a saying "Be good, sweet maid, and let who will be clever." It used to make her *furious*. She said even when she was ten, she couldn't see why

215

goodness should be an alternative to being clever. But it could be an alternative to happiness, couldn't it?'

'But if you had to choose,' he said doggedly. He saw her white forehead marked by little frowns that came and went as she searched for her truth. 'I was thinking of Nora,' he said. 'She's given her life to looking after Richard – and other people.'

'Well, hasn't that made her happy?'

'I don't know. I don't think she looks at things like that.'

'I suppose,' Polly said, 'that, in that case, what would matter was whether she was making things happier for the people she's giving her life for.'

There was a silence, and he remembered Richard sitting in his chair at the party. He had not looked happy; indeed, his face seemed closed to any feeling at all, excepting the glancing animation of (mild) greed when Wills or Roly put little pieces of food in his mouth.

'Of course,' he said, 'one could always fail at whatever it is – goodness or happiness or anything.'

'Not at our ages,' Polly said. 'I mean, if we get things wrong, we've still got time to try again.'

He searched for an unchipped mug for her chocolate, but he'd used it for her tea, so picked the next best one for her.

'Drink out of this side,' he said.

While they were drinking the chocolate, she asked him about his work on the farm. 'Tell me your whole day.'

'They aren't always the same. It depends on the time of year.'

'Well, now, then.'

'Now is tomato time,' he said. 'Tom Hurst has two large glasshouses for tomatoes and the thing is to get them fruiting as early as possible. I've been potting up seedlings for the last week – hundreds of them. Before that I was mixing the potting mixture. In winter, I mostly do repairing jobs – like the chickens' house – and then the cows are mostly in and have to have hay. We don't have a lot of stock, just a few of each thing, but that's mostly because he's always had that. He makes his living out of the tomatoes and soft fruit and some salad things we grow in spring and summer. He's got a few sheep – only about a dozen – but he hasn't got the land for growing cereals. He's getting on and they don't have any children – his only son was killed in Burma. In fact, that's one of my problems.'

'You've become his son?'

He nodded. He loved how quick she was. 'Yes. Marge, his wife, told me he wants to leave me the farm – the house and everything.'

'And you don't know whether you want it?'

'I don't. But if he *leaves* it to me, I'd feel awful if I just sold it and got out.'

'Have you talked to him about it?'

'God, no! I couldn't do that. I'm not supposed to know, you see. She just told me. She thought I'd be thrilled.'

He got up to put the kettle back on the Primus. He still felt he had so many things to say to her, but it had occurred to him that he might be boring her: people who were used to living with other people probably didn't talk to them so much – or, at least, not all the time as he seemed to be doing.

217

'Do read a book if you want to,' he said. 'I'm just going to put our supper things in a bowl – you needn't do anything.'

'Where do you get your water from?' She had watched him refilling the kettle from a tap over his small stone sink.

'I've got a cistern outside. It takes the run-off of rainwater from the roof but I top it up about once a fortnight with a hose from the farm. I have my baths there and Marge said you were welcome to have one any time you want.'

'She's very kind, isn't she?'

'She really is. That's what makes it so difficult to walk out.'

'But why do you want to walk out? You like animals and the country and growing things.'

'It's not just a question of what I like. It's – it's – more . . . Well, this business of copping out – of being against things. Like being a conscientious objector—' He looked to see whether she remembered Simon's word for his pacifism and she did. 'I realised in the end that it meant other people doing the things that they might be just as much against as I was – the dirty work – so then I felt I had to go back into the Army. As it turned out, they wouldn't have me, because of my being ill – that time when I couldn't remember anything at all. But at least I tried, and that felt right. But coming here was a kind of copping out as well. It was getting away from – well, mostly Dad, I suppose, and not having to live in London with the family. But then when I saw Richard and Nora I thought, perhaps I ought to offer to go and help her. She's got several other very disabled people as well, and she was saying it was really difficult to get staff and especially people strong enough to do all the lifting. What do you think, Poll? I really would value your opinion.'

There was a silence. Then she said, 'Do you *want* to go and help Nora?'

'It's not a question of what I want—'

'Oh, Christopher! It *must* be. In some way or other you have to *want* whatever it is or it simply wouldn't work. I mean, even if you simply wanted a horrible time – that's a kind of want. But you can't just decide on something just because you think it ought to happen, or someone ought to do it. You'd do it awfully badly for one thing.'

'Would I?'

'Your heart wouldn't be in it.'

'So what can I *do*? I don't – seem – to want – anything!' Something about the way he said this made her laugh. Oliver, however, got to his feet, came over and leaned his head so hard against Christopher's knee that he dropped the plate he was wiping and it broke.

'I think Oliver is pointing out that you want him. Or you ought to.'

He put his hand on Oliver's neck to scratch him gently behind his ear and Oliver gave a small moan of pleasure. 'It's mutual,' he said.

'Do you remember that day when Dad brought him?' Polly said. 'He was so frightened of everything. Excepting you.'

'He still can't stand a car backfiring or guns.'

They were back to reminiscence, and soon after finishing the chocolate, began preparations for the night. These took longer than when he was alone. He made Polly a hot-water bottle and explained her bedroom to her. 'There's a sleeping bag which you get into and then

219

the blankets to go on top.' He lit a night-light to put beside her bed, and offered her warm water poured into the large china basin for washing.

'Where are you going to sleep?'

'In here, in another sleeping bag in front of the stove. I'll be fine. I often sleep in here in winter anyway.' He gave her the torch for another trip to the privy.

'Goodness! It's lovely and cosy in here,' she exclaimed again when she came back.

He took Oliver out for his pee while she was washing. It was a clear night, frosty – a few stars and the moon, like a piece of mother-of-pearl high in the sky. It was lovely having her to stay, and this was only Friday night: there were nearly two full days more.

On Saturday they went for a long walk in the woods and along the narrow steep-banked lanes that surrounded the farm. The day began fine, the sun like a tomato in a thick grey sky, and frosted cobwebs decorating the hedges that still had some berries left. They talked a bit about Angela – now on her way to America with hundreds of GI brides. Polly said she thought it was very brave to set off for an unknown country, leaving all her family and friends behind, and he said that he thought she'd been so miserable for so long that she was happy to have a complete change.

'She's been in love twice, and both times were awfully unhappy,' he said.

'Poor her!' She said it in such a heartfelt manner, that he suddenly wanted to tell her about Ange and Uncle Rupert. 'That must have been *awful* for her.'

'It was. I found her being miserable one day and I didn't know what it was. Of course he didn't love her back. I think that must have made it worse – at the time.'

She didn't reply, so then he said. 'It was better in the long run. Because of his being married and all that. But, anyway, he was far too old for her – it was a hopeless idea, really.'

'I don't think he was too *old* for her at all. Less than twenty years – that's nothing!'

She said it so vehemently that he looked at her, surprised. She was striding along, with her hands plunged into the pockets of her jacket, her face set in what was for her, he thought, a quite fierce expression.

'Poll—'

'His being married, of course, does make it hopeless. But his *age* has nothing whatever to do with it.' After a pause, she said, so quietly that he could hardly hear her, 'His not loving her back is the worst thing. The saddest for her, I mean.'

He opened his mouth to say that, anyway, Ange had fallen in love with someone else quite soon after Uncle Rupert, but it didn't feel right to tell Polly that as she seemed unaccountably hostile, so instead he said, 'Well, anyway, that's all in the past. She's going to be all right now.'

'You never met him, did you?'

'No. But she showed me a picture of him.'

'What's he like?'

He thought. 'Rather *furry*. He looked kind. He's much older than her, too.' He hadn't thought of that before.

'You see? It doesn't matter. I told you.' But she seemed friendly again. Then she saw some spindle berries and wanted to pick them, and after that, she kept seeing things she wanted to pick. I don't know nearly enough about people, he thought, and wondered whether, when you didn't know, the thing was to ask, but then he was

221

afraid that that might make her angry again, and couldn't bear the idea.

They went back to the caravan and while he heated the soup she made a wonderful arrangement of the berries she had picked. He was afraid that she might be bored and asked her what she should like to do in the afternoon, and she said that she would like to go to Hastings. 'I haven't been there for ages.'

This meant borrowing the car again, but the Hursts didn't seem to mind. 'You enjoy yourself,' Mrs Hurst advised.

Polly said that she wanted to go to the old bit that had the antique and junk shops. 'I do love going round them. Is that all right with you?'

Anything was all right: he simply wanted to be with her, and look at her as much as possible when she wasn't noticing.

In the car he asked her about her job. He couldn't imagine what interior decorators did.

'Well, what we do is listen to people about their houses or flats or whatever, and we go and see them, and then we suggest things, and in the end they sort of choose things and then they pretend they did it all themselves.'

'What sort of things?'

'Wallpapers, or colours of paint for walls and doors, and carpets and curtains and loose-covers or upholstery for furniture – sometimes, even, all the furniture. Once we had to do every single thing for an extremely nasty house in Bishop's Avenue – that's sort of beyond Hampstead. I had to choose the china, a complete dinner service and candlesticks and little silver claws to hold place names. It was for some fantastically rich foreigner. I thought he couldn't be married if he wanted all these things chosen for him, but he was. His wife simply wasn't allowed to do anything about it. Gervase said that she was like a prisoner, hardly ever allowed out.'

'Who is Gervase?'

'He's my boss. Or, rather, one of them. There's Caspar as well. Caspar does the shop part, and Gervase does the designing – you know, curtain drapes or pelmets, and plasterwork and the layout for bathrooms and kitchens, that sort of thing.'

He didn't know. It seemed extraordinary to him that people did any of that, and even more that there would be people who paid to have it done for them. 'And what do you do?'

'Well, I'm sort of learning, which means really that I do the dullest things – anything I'm told.'

'Don't most houses *have* kitchens and bathrooms anyway?'

'Yes, but often they're hideous – or there simply aren't enough of them.'

She was very good at antique shops: found things, seemed to know about them, how old they were, sometimes, in mysterious cases, what they were for. She also bought some things: three silver forks, very plain and heavy. 'George III,' she said, although two pounds ten seemed a lot to him for three forks. Then she found four pairs of decorated brass hoops but with a bit open. She said they were curtain ties, ormolu, and that Caspar would be delighted to have them in the shop.

She found a small walnut desk she called a davenport that she said Caspar would also like. This was twenty pounds, and she said that she would telephone from London if the desk was wanted and would they keep it until Monday? Of course they would. She bought a small piece of green velvet that she said she would make into a table cover for her room. Then she absolutely fell in love with a tea service of pink and gold lustre with tiny green flowers on it. 'Oh, *look*, Christopher, a teapot – perfect – and seven cups and nine saucers and two cake plates! The prettiest set I've ever seen!'

It was nine pounds, nearly two weeks' wages, but he decided to give it to her. 'I'll buy that,' he said, and saw her face cloud and then clear as she said, 'Well, it *is* your turn,' and turned her attention to an array of mugs. She bought two.

While the china was being packed in yellowing newspaper by the proprietor, she wandered round the furniture. 'Look! A Regency supper table. Goodness, what an elegant sight! It's rosewood.' (Of course, she knew about wood because of her father.) 'And look at the declivities for each plate and its charming legs.'

He was amazed at how much she knew.

They carted everything into the car. It was dusk and it had begun to rain.

On the way home, she said, 'The last time I went to those shops was with Dad,' and fell silent and he sensed some sadness.

This time tomorrow, he thought, I shall be driving back along this road without her.

Over supper – baked potatoes and a wing of chicken for her that Mrs Hurst had cooked and some roast parsnips – she asked whether he still drew. He hadn't – for ages.

'You used to be jolly good at it.'

'So did you.'

'Nothing like you. I especially remember your owls, how good they were.'

'You were going to go to an art school.'

'I did. All it did was make me see I wasn't good enough. Do you mind if I eat my bone?'

'Of course not. I live with somebody who eats his bones.'

'If we were characters in a novel or a play,' she said sadly, 'one of us, at least, would turn out to be a frightfully good painter. And if it was a bad novel, both of us would. As it is . . .'

'I'm a sort of farmer—'

'And I work in a shop,' she finished. She put down her chicken bone and licked her fingers delicately – like a little cat, he thought. He took away their plates and laid two Crunchie bars on the table.

'Oh! How lovely! Is this our pudding?'

'I knew you liked them. Do you remember that day when you were sitting on a wall outside the kitchen garden and you gave me some of your bar?'

She thought for a moment, then shook her head. 'I don't, actually.'

'You wore a bright blue dress and a black velvet hairband, and you offered me some and I took too much, but then you let me have the rest of it because I'd missed tea.'

'Funny! I don't remember at all.'

'I hope you still like them.' He felt dashed that she'd forgotten.

'Love them.'

When he suggested making tea, she gave him the two mugs she had bought. 'One for you and one for your guests.'

'But I don't have any guests,' he said, when he had thanked her.

'*Never?*'

225

'You're the first one.'

'But don't you have – any *friends* here?'

'There are the Hursts, of course. And there's a boy who works with me, but he's not exactly a friend.'

'And you have Oliver,' she said.

She said it in a protective kind of way, which somehow made him feel worse (obviously she *expected* him to have friends and why hadn't he got any?). 'I suppose I do lead a rather solitary life,' he said.

'But you like it?'

'I hadn't really thought about it.' He did now, though. This time tomorrow she would be in London, and he would be eating supper and struggling with his Greek. He was trying to translate some fragments of Menander – Mr Milner, one of his teachers at school, had been particularly fond of Menander, and he was one of the few people Christopher had ever been able to talk to. He had never told anyone about the Greek because he was afraid it would be considered absurd, or pointless, and that then he would not want to do it any more. And if that happened, he would have nothing. But he was dreading Polly's departure – so much that he almost wished she had never come to stay at all. He went to sleep that night telling himself that it was stupid to wish any such thing.

In the morning he woke early, as usual, to hear the rain drumming down on the roof of the caravan, and wondered what he could do to entertain her. She had said that she wanted to see the farm, but it would be too wet for that to be much fun for her. The stove had gone out – too much rain down its chimney. He got up as quietly as possible, put on his boots and a mac and went to collect wood from the pile he kept under a tarpaulin outside.

When he came back with an armful she was up, wearing her trousers and dark blue jersey with a roll collar, her shining hair tied back with a piece of blue ribbon. He explained about the fire and she said if he would light the Primus she'd make the porridge while he relit it.

It hadn't gone out for some time, and badly needed cleaning. Clouds of wood ash rose in the air as he riddled and brushed the little grate inside. He got a bucketful of ash to take outside. Then he had to go to the farm to fetch the milk and Mrs Hurst most kindly gave him a small jug of cream. 'You're not getting the weather we could wish for and that's a fact,' she said. 'If you'd like to bring your cousin over to dinner you're welcome.' He thanked her and said he would see what Polly wanted to do and let her know after breakfast. He was divided between not wanting to waste the time with Polly, and worrying that scrambled eggs would not seem much of a Sunday lunch for her.

When he got back she was not in the van. Making a miserable wet trip to the privy, poor girl. He looked round his home, seeing it this morning with different, outside eyes. It really did look a dingy, drab little place, with last night's supper things still unwashed in the sink. She had taken the porridge off the Primus and put on the kettle.

When she returned, she looked really cold: her nose was pink and her hair was dark from the rain. But somehow, in spite of the cold, she managed to change the scene: it stopped being drab and dank, and became all right. They had the porridge and she said what a treat it was to have cream. Then, while they were doing the washing-up – the supper things and breakfast – she said:

'As it's raining, why don't we spend the morning cleaning your house? I'd love to – I love making everything tidy and neat.'

He began to protest – it was too boring for her, and he didn't mind doing it later – but she took his finger and wrote 'POLLY' in the dust on the shelf by the sink, and said, 'You see? It really needs doing.'

So that was how they spent the morning, and it turned out to be a good idea in every way. She was not only very good at cleaning things, she had brilliant ideas about arranging them. She took all his books off various shelves and arranged them all on one single shelf where they were not only easier to find, but looked far nicer. 'You have a lot of Greek books,' she said. 'I didn't know you could read Greek. What's this one?'

'It's the New Testament.'

'Gosh! Can you read that?'

'More or less. I was having a go at translating it. Just to see if it came out the same as it does, you know, in the English one we all have.'

'Does it?'

'Not always, but of course I'm not very good at it. Some Greek words have several meanings, you see, and it's a question of which one is what was meant. Sometimes it seems different to me from the published version.'

'I didn't know that about you,' she said. She seemed impressed, and he hastened to tell her that he was only a beginner and just did it for fun in the evenings.

She did other arrangements: with his china, and his kitchen things. She got him to put up hooks on the wall for hanging his saucepans and frying pan. He'd bought the hooks ages ago and never used them. She actually washed the walls before he put the hooks in – something he had never done – and the place looked lighter. He was kept busy getting water and boiling it, and finding her a rag and scrubbing brush, and going over to the farm to beg another bar of soap and to explain that they would not be able to make it for lunch. However, some time after one Mrs Hurst appeared with a basket in which were two covered plates of Sunday dinner.

'My! You have been working hard! Chris won't know himself, will you, Chris?' He could see she approved of Polly. She offered to take the piece of carpet, give it a good shampoo and dry it out in her kitchen. 'Don't let your dinners get cold.'

In the bottom of the basket was a small bottle that had obviously once contained medicine, but was now filled with a very dark red liquid and labelled 'Sloe Gin 1944'. She was always making drinks of this nature, but usually he was only given a whole bottle at Christmas.

They finished the cleaning and fetched a bowl of fresh water to wash in. Her face was smudged with grime, and when he told her so she wetted the drying-up cloth and asked him to clean her up. 'As you don't seem to have a looking glass anywhere.'

He took the cloth and rubbed the marks, at first so gently that he simply seemed to spread the dirt. Use soap, she said, and he rubbed his finger on the cake and massaged it into her delicate skin and then used the cloth again and she stood completely still with her eyes looking not at him, but straight ahead. In the middle of doing it, he had the most extraordinary feeling – that she was his dearest, oldest friend and the most mysterious, unknown creature he had ever encountered. His hand was trembling, he had to swallow to keep his heart down and to quell its knocking. In those few moments he changed and nothing was as it had been before he touched her.

They both tried the sloe gin; he didn't care for it, and he didn't think she did either. She said it was one of those drinks that she thought one was only supposed to have very little of 'which stops it being a drink really – it's more like having a very rich chocolate: they're not meant to quench one's hunger'.

They ate the Sunday lunch, which was by then cold: it was Yorkshire pudding and some roast beef with it for Polly; Mrs Hurst knew that he didn't eat meat, and always provided him with extra vegetables.

Then she mended one of the leather pads on the elbows of his jacket. He tried to stop her, but she insisted. He made some tea while she packed up her things; her departure loomed.

In the car, she asked him if he ever had holidays.

'Not really. I had one this weekend because you came.'

After a pause, she said, 'It might be nice for you to have a change sometimes. Perhaps if you went for a visit to Nora, you'd find out whether you wanted to work there.'

'I suppose I might.' He answered mechanically. He was so preoccupied with her – with the duality of his feelings about her – that he almost wished she wasn't there; when they talked she was his childhood friend – his cousin – when he looked at her, her beauty surprised, assaulted, overwhelmed him each time as though it was the first. Through lunch, and when she was saying good-bye to Oliver and then walking down the track to the farmyard, he had said things to the cousin; things like thanking her for helping him so much and sending his love to Clary and yes, he would thank Mrs Hurst for the lunch, but to this new beauty, this perfect stranger, he could find nothing to say.

They got to the station early (how much he wished afterwards that they hadn't, that there had only been time to carry her case and put it on the train for her). As it was, they stood for a few moments on the platform and then she suggested that they go into the waiting room where it would be warmer. 'Unless you want to go,' she said. 'You can perfectly well leave me.' Before he could stop it, he heard himself (as though he had nothing to do with it) saying, 'I don't ever want to do that.'

They went into the waiting room and sat down. There was a small coal fire that glowed in the grate in a subdued manner, and wooden benches against two walls. They sat on one of these in silence, and just as it was beginning to occur to him with a curious mixture of regret and relief that she had not heard him, she said, 'What did you mean just now?'

'We aren't really cousins,' he said. He wanted to be able to think, to choose his words with enormous, delicate care, but he couldn't actually *think* at all.

'Because you mean our parents aren't related to each other? Well, I don't think that matters. We've always *felt* like cousins.' She saw his face, and stopped. 'Sorry, go on.'

'We could be married,' he said. 'Do you think that you could, by any chance, consider that in some way or other? I mean, not immediately, but next year – or possibly in a few months? I'd have to think of the right place to live because I wouldn't let you put up with the caravan – it's nothing like good enough for you and you probably wouldn't want to be married to a farmer so I'd have to think of something else. But I would, I promise you. We could even live in London if that is what you wanted. I'd do anything. It is because I love you so much that I want us to be married, if possible,' he added, and then suddenly came to a stop.

'Oh, Christopher! Is that why you asked me to stay?'

'No! I only found out today – this morning – just before lunch. I would have told you.' He thought for a moment. 'At least, I suppose I would. But I didn't mean to tell you now – it just came out. I know I haven't put it very well, but I suppose it's the sort of thing that's so important that that wouldn't make much difference. Would it?' He turned to look at her.

'No.'

'Perhaps,' he said quickly before she could deny him, 'perhaps you don't feel like it because you haven't thought about it.'

'It's not that. I couldn't marry you but it's not because of *you*. I think you're one of the most interesting and good people I've known. And I think you're extremely brave – and kind – and . . .' Her voice tailed away; she couldn't think of anything else, he thought miserably.

She put her small white hand on one of his. 'Oh, Christopher! I don't want to make you feel miserable, but I am actually in love with someone else.'

He might have known. 'And you're going to marry them.'

'No! No, I'm not. They don't love me. So it will never be any good.'

'So do you think you will always love them?'

'I don't know. It feels as though I will.'

His eyes filled with tears at her prospect. 'Oh, Poll! I'm really sorry. I can't imagine *anyone* not loving you.'

The waiting-room door opened and a couple came in with a child in a perambulator. 'It's not worth it,' the man was saying, 'train'll be here in a minute.' He was heaving two suitcases that he dumped by the fire. The child wore a pixie hat and had a dummy in its mouth. The woman rocked the pram and the dummy fell out of the child's mouth on to the floor. It started to wail and the man picked up the dummy and crammed it back.

'Think of the germs!' the woman said. She rolled her eyes, including Christopher and Polly in her perfunctory dismay.

'If you want to be right in front of the train, I think we'd better start moving,' he said. Christopher couldn't bear his last few minutes with her to be shared with anyone else.

But in fact they had hardly walked the short way to the end of the platform before the train appeared and he had to put her into it.

She said she had had a lovely time, thanked him, kissed him rather uncertainly, and then he was out of the train and seeing her through the thick glass window that she tried to pull down, but could not. She made a little face, and with her dark blue eyes still anxious, blew him a small kiss. The whistle sounded, the guard got on to the train and it puffed slowly away, then gathered speed so quickly that he lost count of which was her window.

He waited until the train was out of sight, then walked slowly back to the station yard. The rain had stopped; a cold grey dusk had descended.

He drove back, parked the car, and trudged up the

track to the van. Oliver was waiting for him with his customary, courteous enthusiasm. He lit the lamp and opened the doors of the stove, then sat in the chair that had been hers. Everything – his books, his china – everything in the van had been touched by her, had been transformed, as she had transformed him from extreme joy to his despair. If only he had not *told* her, had not blurted it all out in that senseless manner simply because they were early for her train – if only he had not done that, he could have held on to his astonishing happiness, could have continued to feel the new and extraordinary sensation of love that might be returned. In the end, of course, he would have had to know that she loved some idiot who didn't love her back, but to know it so soon meant that his pure joy had lasted hardly at all whereas he could see no end to his present hopelessness. For what had he got to offer her? All he had been able to say was that he would change things – live somewhere else, *do* something else, vague, weak promises with no substance to them. He remembered her saying, 'But don't you have any *friends* here?' and realising when she mentioned Oliver that she knew he didn't. He hadn't been living a proper life; he'd simply run away from things he couldn't bear, and put very little in their place. How could anyone love that? He was twenty-three and he had done absolutely nothing with his life. He remembered her saying, 'You have to want whatever it is, or it simply won't work.' Well, all he wanted was Polly, to love her, all the time and for ever, to live his life for her. 'You can't decide to do something just because you think you ought to – your heart wouldn't be in it,' she had said. In a sense, he thought, she had given him his heart – the fact that it hurt so much was probably not the point.

He became aware of Oliver, standing on his hind legs with his front paws on the arm of the chair, licking the tears off his face. When his vision cleared, he saw the cardboard box, with the pink lustre tea-set that he had meant to give her, by the door of the van, perfectly obvious, but he had completely forgotten it. If he gave it now, would she think it a bribe or an attempt at one? Then he thought it didn't matter what she thought; he had bought it simply because she had loved it and he had wanted to give her something she loved. He would still give it. Oliver was sitting now, with his head resting heavily against him, brown eyes glowing with sentiment. People laughed at sentiment, always dubbed dogs as sentimental, but sentiment was simply a part of their love, he thought as, later, he eased himself into the sleeping bag that he had provided for her, and put his head on her pillow. Sentiment would be not good if that was all, but he knew now for himself, as well as from Oliver, that it was not.

Oliver waited until he had blown out the candle, and then settled himself in his usual position against his friend, back against his belly, head on shoulder, a bulwark against what would otherwise have been entire despair.

∞ ∞ ∞

All morning the removal men, wearing aprons, had tramped back and forth from their van with the furniture for the new maisonette and Sid had been helping Rachel with its disposal. By eleven o'clock all the larger pieces were in – one of the pianos, the grandfather clocks (two), the vast mahogany wardrobes (three), the Duchy's bureau, the Brig's huge kneehole desk, the beds, the dining-room table, the dressing tables, what seemed to her an incredible number of chairs, a sofa, the Duchy's sewing machine and gramophone, the Brig's glass-fronted bookcases of laurelwood. She wanted Rachel to sit and rest while the men drank tea and ate buns in their van, but Rachel wanted her to see the garden with a view to tidying it up a bit before the Duchy's arrival, so out they went into the bitingly cold wind. The garden was so small that she felt they could just as well have surveyed it from the house. It was a small rectangle; a square of lawn – now sodden, with high grass – edged by a weed-ridden gravel path, and with narrow black beds that contained the remains of Michaelmas daisies, blackened by winter frosts, a few ferns and an old pear tree. It was bounded by low black-brick walls, and there was a rotting shed crazily perched in the far corner.

'If we could just cut the grass before they come,' Rachel said. 'Do you think I could borrow your mower?'

'You could, but it wouldn't cut this. It needs scything first. Let's go in, darling, I can see that you're freezing. There are some daffodils – look!'

'The Duchy said they were King Alfred, and she hates them. Oh, darling, I do hope I've done the right thing! It does seem rather small now that the furniture is in. Still, it's lovely and near to you.' She tucked Sid's arm in hers with that smile that melted her heart.

The afternoon was spent unpacking the tea chests that arrived in such a fast, steady stream that Rachel was reduced to telling them to put them all in the sitting room. This meant that those containing linen and bedding had all to be carted upstairs in armfuls. The flat consisted of a large sitting room, a dining room, a study and a small kitchen and cloakroom on the ground floor, and two large and two small bedrooms and a bathroom on the floor above. Needless to say, Rachel had designated the two larger bedrooms for her mother and Aunt Dolly, the south-facing smaller room for the Brig, and had taken the smallest room (not more than a boxroom, Sid thought angrily) for herself. 'It's quite large enough for me,' she had said. 'I have too many clothes anyway, and they're all as old as the hills. It's high time I gave them to the Red Cross.'

They had unpacked the tea chests, kitchen stuff, china – 'Where *are* we going to put everything?' Rachel had said. 'I'm afraid the poor Duchy is going to feel dreadfully cramped' – until she could see that Rachel was absolutely 'done up', as she would put it.

'Darling. We must stop. I'm going to take you home and give you an enormous gin and then you can have a hot bath and supper in bed.'

And in spite of some protest, that is what they had done. Sid had cut up the pork pie she had bought and made a salad, but when she carried the tray up to Rachel's room, she found her lying in her dressing gown, flat on her back asleep. She put the tray on the dressing table, moved the armchair to where she could see Rachel, and sat down to wait.

When the idea of the older Cazalets moving back to London had first been mooted, she had had a sense of relief that at last and at least there would no longer be such a distance between them. She had even had the fantasy, as now she bitterly called it, of Rachel settling her parents somewhere and then coming to live with *her*. That was soon exploded: Rachel had explained at some length how she could not possibly leave the Duchy – no longer with the staff she was accustomed to – on her own with the blind Brig. So then it had been a question of where they would find a flat, and the house – or rather half of it – in Carlton Hill had seemed the perfect answer. Now, she wondered how much time, freedom and privacy this would really afford them. Its size precluded ever being alone with Rachel if she went there, which left Rachel coming to *her* at odd times and when she felt able to get away – the only alternative. And here was the dilemma. Ages ago – it must be nearly two *years* – she had resolved that if Thelma ever got in the way of her seeing Rachel, Thelma would have to go – for good. Somehow, however, this situation had never actually occurred; her meetings with Rachel had been so occasional, and always so much planned in advance, that there had never been the pressing need that would have precipitated such a decision. And Thelma? She was fairly sure that Thelma guessed or knew that there was someone else in her life, but it was never mentioned. Thelma had all the ingenious flexibility of a piece of ivy determined to conquer a tree or a wall; she clung unobtrusively, she encroached by minute degrees, and if Sid defeated any particular advance, she fell back upon a series of apparently innocuous excuses: she had only thought she would stay an extra night because she planned to wash all the paint on the stairs and to do this in one day meant a very early start; she was only staying that particular evening because she knew Sid got back late from Hampshire where she taught in a girls' school and would be too tired to cook for herself. Sid had ceased wanting very much to go to bed with her, but in a curious way, which she had not expected, this made it almost easier to do. The fact that she did not enjoy it in the way that she had at first made her feel less guilty. A piece of twisted morality, she now thought, as she gazed at Rachel's peaceful face. Asleep, she shed years: it was easy to see the beauty she had had as a young girl. Thelma would *have* to go.

The next day, she set about it.

'But I don't understand!'

'It's simply that our situation isn't right for me – any more. I'm very sorry about it, but I must tell you. I can't go on like this.'

The hot brown eyes peered at her with a look of hurt bewilderment. 'I still don't understand. What has happened to change things?'

How could she answer that? She simply no longer felt the same. In any case, it would be much better for Thelma to go. 'I can't give you all you want; you are quite young enough to go and find that with someone else.'

This, before it was out of her mouth, she knew to be a tactical error.

'But I would far, far rather have what little I do have with you than any life with anyone else! Surely you know that.' The eyes were brimming now and, from much past experience, she knew that they were in for a major scene.

'Thelma, I know it's very hard for you, but you've simply got to accept this.'

'That you don't love me any more?'

'That I don't love you.'

'But you *did* love me. Something *must* have happened.'

'Time has happened.'

Tears, sobs, violent crying – she managed not to touch her throughout all of it, to continue to stand by the piano repeating at intervals that she was sorry.

'You can't be very sorry, or you wouldn't do this to me! You couldn't be so unbelievably cruel to someone you cared for!'

She had no choice, she said. This was to be the end.

'You don't mean that I'm not to come here any more? I mean, even if you don't want – to spend nights with me – you surely can't banish me completely?'

A clean break, she said, was the only way.

But Thelma had the indomitable strength of the abject. She would only come once a week. She would clean the house and do the shopping. She would not expect payment for any of this. She would get herself another job that would keep her. She would not expect any more music lessons. She would not ever, *ever* turn up unexpectedly. She would be content if they simply had coffee together in the kitchen when she had finished cleaning.

Eventually, it got through to her that none of this was to happen, and it was almost with relief that Sid recognised resentment beginning to smoulder in the girl's eyes. She said she supposed she would be given time to pack up her things, or would Sid prefer her to return tomorrow for all that? Sid saw this attempt to clutch at a thin edge just in time to thwart it. No, she should pack everything now. She would pay for a cab. While Thelma disappeared upstairs to the spare room, Sid collected her music that lay on the piano and in the music stool and put it all into her music case. She was shaking with shame, the horrid discovery that apart from not loving Thelma she no longer even liked her, and the realisation that their natures – hers as well as Thelma's – combined to make it impossible for her to conduct this ending with any sort of kindness or delicacy. The inch would become an ell, the straw seized would become a rope with which she would certainly get hanged; a brutal, sudden and complete termination was all that she could manage.

She did contrive to give Thelma some money, and found her a second case (she turned out to have far more possessions than Sid had been aware of) and rang for a taxi cab while Thelma was filling it. She was anxious now that there should be no hiatus between Thelma being ready and her going.

The cab arrived and the considerable luggage was stowed in it. There was a final horrid moment when she had to ask Thelma for her latchkey; she had nearly forgotten to do this, and saw from the expression on Thelma's face as she fumbled in her bag for it that Thelma had been hoping she would forget. When Thelma – now tearless and white with anger – was finally ensconced in the cab and driven away, she almost tottered back to the house. To her dislike, she now admitted a certain fear; she had actually become afraid of this seemingly soft and clinging girl, feeling now, with more than a touch of hysteria, that had she retained the key, Thelma might easily have returned to burn the house down or effect some lesser destruction.

It had been early evening. She made herself a stiff drink. Part of her wished passionately that Rachel was in London, but another part felt so besmirched by what she had done that she felt unworthy. She decided to go out, to leave the house for the evening.

Two days later she received an eleven-page letter from Thelma, the ostensible reason for which was that she needed a reference. She supposed that Sid would not grudge her *that*, at least. It was not much to ask, considering the way in which her love and loyalty had been treated. The rest of the letter consisted of descriptions of this, together with her reactions to them. She had put up with being taken for granted, with being used when convenient with no thought for how *she* might feel. She had put up with slights, selfishness, a lack of consideration for any of her feelings, with being excluded from the rest of Sid's social life – she had never, for instance, even laid eyes on any of that family Sid went off and stayed with in Sussex. She felt that a good deal of the time she had been treated like a *servant*; it had been humiliating, considering the rest of their relationship. On and on it went, lamenting the cessation of a relationship that Thelma seemed to feel had been intolerable. She seemed to regard her love flourishing in such a climate as a particular triumph and could not now imagine how she was to get through the rest of her life, except that she knew that she would be unable ever to trust anyone again.

She had read the letter twice. It seemed extraordinary to her – even after only two days – that she had persisted in putting up with such a dishonest situation for so long after she had recognised it. She had felt responsible, angry and ashamed. She had liked to think of herself as honourable and straightforward, and decisive, and this proved her to be nothing of the kind.

She wrote a carefully generous reference and posted it to the house in Kilburn where Thelma had a room. This sort of thing, she thought, must never happen again. She would never love anyone but Rachel, and therefore had no right to go to bed with anyone else.

∞ ∞ ∞

'And this is your room, Miss Milliment. I thought you would not mind being on the ground floor as there is a little cloakroom with a basin next door, and you will only have to brave the staircase when you want a bath.'

'That is most thoughtful.' She had found stairs increasingly difficult lately, largely because she could not see where they were.

'Perhaps you'd like me to put your suitcases on your bed, then it will be easier for you to unpack them. Tea will be ready in about half an hour.' Viola heaved the cases on to the bed and left her.

Miss Milliment had come up by train that afternoon. It had seemed very strange to be leaving Home Place: it had been such a delightful refuge for so long. Naturally, she was extremely grateful to dear Viola for giving her a home, and had she not sometimes hankered for London and its galleries during those years of war? 'It is impossible to please you, Eleanor,' she admonished herself.

The room was rather dark, so she trotted to the door to switch on the ceiling light. Apart from the bed, there was a nice solid wardrobe in one corner, a chest of drawers, a writing table, one easy and two upright chairs. The walls were pale blue. There was a gas fire with a rug in front of it and a bedside table with a lamp on it. There was also a small open bookcase – she had not seen it at first, because it was on the far side of the wardrobe. She would be able to unpack her books at last, which she had never had room to do at Home Place. They had lain at the back of the garage in the same boxes that had contained them since Papa's death. She had so much to be thankful for! It was clear to her that the house was not very large, and that she had been given one of the greater rooms; a bed-sitting room was what it was meant to be, and she resolved to exercise the utmost tact about how often and how much she used the rest of the house. I must feel my way, she thought. I must never encroach upon dear Viola's family life. By which she knew she meant her life with Edward; she knew that, where Roly was concerned, she could still be useful – she was preparing him for prep school, and there was talk of Zoë bringing Juliet over for lessons. Lydia was to have her heart's desire and go to the boarding school where her cousin Judy was. And when the older Cazalets were settled in their flat – which, Viola said, was within walking distance – she would be able to continue to help the Brig with his book. She did not think he would ever finish the work since he so often changed his mind about the course it should take – they were now deeply involved in the historical geography of the forests, when originally the book had been meant as a survey of trees indigenous or imported into Great Britain. However, it gave him something to think and to talk about, and she found the subject, which was new to her, of great interest.

She was so occupied with these thoughts that she did not notice (until the drawer was so full that she was unable to shut it) that she had simply been putting everything from one case into one drawer. A pretty pickle! Now her stockings were all muddled up with her vests and drawers and even one jersey that needed washing. 'Really, Eleanor! You are not to be trusted with the simplest task.' But she decided to leave the drawer as it was for the moment and to unpack the second case. This seemed to contain a daunting miscellany. Summer clothes – her best yellow and brown outfit worn in the evenings, although she could not help noticing that the holes under the arms had, in spite of her cobbling them together, *enlarged* to a point where she doubted that much more could be done to repair them. Her cardigans – all three of them – were in need of attention; it scarcely seemed worth putting them away. The one with which she had had that unfortunate accident with the golden syrup seemed far stickier than the small mishap warranted and the nice heathery blue one that dear Polly had so kindly made for her, the sleeve of which had most tiresomely caught on some protuberance, had acquired a large rambling hole that she feared it would be impossible to mend. She sighed. Sometimes her uselessness appalled her. She could no longer see well enough to thread a needle, but honesty compelled her to admit that even when her eyes had been better, she was a poor sewer. And here was Viola proposing to do all the cooking for the household! Surely she must be able to help with that! She could peel potatoes, perhaps, she could surely learn to do that or – but here her imagination failed her. She really had little or no idea what one did with food. One presumably washed and chopped and mixed things and then boiled them or put them in the oven. The nearest she had ever come to preparing food was spreading the dripping on hot toast for her father, and, of course, making tea for him. After his death she had eaten in tea shops, or in lodgings until dear Viola had invited her to Home Place where, of course, there had always been delicious food prepared by Mrs Cripps. Viola was not used to cooking either: she had always had a cook and other servants. This move was going to be a very great change for her. Miss Milliment resolved to be as much help as possible and (although it seemed rather contrary) to keep out of the way as much as she could.

When Viola called her to tea, she left the room with some relief. It now seemed such a muddle that she was afraid she would never get it straight.

That evening, however, she was invited to dine with Viola and Edward. 'Our first night here, you must join us, Miss Milliment,' Viola had said. Roly and Lydia were absent, as Viola had wanted to get their rooms straight before they came, so it was just the three of them. Edward arrived rather late from the office – she heard Viola greeting him in the hall: 'Darling! Of course, you haven't even got a key to your own house yet! You *do* look fagged. Have you had an awful day?'

'Pretty bloody.'

Her door had been ajar for the hearing of this exchange; she must remember to keep it shut but, even so, the walls must have been quite thin because, after shutting it, she could still hear them in the kitchen.

She was bidden to join them in the drawing room for a glass of champagne that Edward had brought.

'Here's to the new house!' Viola had said, and they all drank.

It was a strange evening, however. Viola was the one who talked. In spite of her looking exhausted (she had not bothered to change, she said, as she was cooking), she hardly stopped talking throughout the meal. She had certainly worked very hard. A fire had been lit – which was comforting as it was one of those cold spring evenings – and before it she had laid a small round table with dinner. 'We'll probably eat in the kitchen on ordinary evenings,' she said, 'but I thought we ought to christen the drawing room tonight.'

Edward said, 'Good idea!'

In spite of his hearty agreement with Viola about all her plans and arrangements, there was something subdued about him – about the whole evening, she thought afterwards. But, then, she had become so used to a large table and at least a dozen of the family round it – on the occasions when she had dined with them – with all the noise of several conversations going on at once, that naturally it felt strange to be in such attenuated, intimate surroundings. She resolved to suggest to dear Viola that she dine in her room in future, in order to allow them time to themselves.

After dinner, a most acceptable stew with rice and an apple pudding, Viola cleared the table and put everything on a trolley to wheel into the kitchen. Left alone with Edward, she felt that this was an appropriate moment to thank him for his great kindness in housing her.

'Not at all, Miss Milliment. I know how fond Villy is of you, and you will be company for her.' Then he asked her what she thought of the League of Nations being dissolved, adding that he personally had never thought them much good. When she was beginning to say that she thought that some sort of international organisation might be desirable, Viola put her head round the door to ask if they would like coffee.

This seemed to be her cue for retiring, and she did so.

Her room was such a muddle that it took her some time to find a nightdress and she felt too tired to tidy things. She had not lit the gas fire so the room was cold, and the bulb in her bedside lamp was broken. She lay awake for a long time in the dark without her usual hot-water bottle, wondering why, considering how grateful she felt – and ought to feel – she also felt a vague sense of unease.

∞ ∞ ∞

She had stood by the gate onto the drive to see them all off. Frank had brought out the cases earlier, and they were now strapped on the back of the car. Then he had helped Mrs Cazalet Senior to get her sister into the back seat. Poor old Miss Barlow seemed rather confused: she kept stopping to talk, and then she wanted to pick the daffodils that grew under the monkey puzzle tree, but Mrs Senior was ever so patient with her, and in the end they somehow got her into the back of the car with Madam beside her and Frank was smoothing the old car rug over their knees.

'Goodbye, Mrs Tonbridge,' Mrs Cazalet said. 'I know I can leave everything about shutting up the house quite safely to you.' Which was no more than the truth. Then Frank went back to get Mr Cazalet and lead him to the front seat. Of course, he didn't know she was there so she couldn't expect *him* to say anything. When he was safely shut in, Frank gave her one of his little sideways nods and a wink. He was dressed in his best grey, with black gaiters and a cockade in his cap. He was to spend the night in London, and then come back for a week's holiday when they could really get down to making the cottage over the garage into a home. The wind was quite sharp, and she was glad when they left. She stood and waved until the car was out of sight, and then she went back into the house, locking the front door behind her. She wouldn't be using *that* again. Tomorrow Edie was coming up from the village to clear the beds, clean out the fireplaces and start the spring cleaning.

She stood for a moment in the hall; the house felt very queer with nobody in it. She couldn't ever remember it being completely empty of the family. All through the war they'd been there; poor Mrs Hugh had had William in her room upstairs; poor Miss Barlow's sister had died in the morning room; Mr Rupert had come walking in from the war after all those years . . . Of course, *Mrs* Rupert had had Juliet – a sweet little baby she was, always had been. She had only been with the family since the beginning of 1937, and she wouldn't be moving now. She'd been half afraid that Mrs Senior would want her to go with them to London, which she didn't fancy as London houses were all stairs and her legs were not up to them, but no, she'd wanted her to stay at Home Place and cook for them in the holidays.

The dining-room lunch would want clearing. A really beautiful rabbit pie she'd made for their last lunch – the rabbit in a nice white sauce with plenty of onion, and puff pastry to mark the occasion. She'd made a nice bread and butter pudding to follow. Edie had served lunch. Not so long ago she wouldn't have allowed that girl out of the kitchen, but times had certainly changed, and so far as she was concerned, she could not say that they'd changed for the better. She only had to look at the dining-room table to see that. Poor Eileen would have had a fit. No butter knives, only one glass for drinking and the places laid anyhow. Eileen had left last year: her mother was poorly and wanted her home. She'd had the proper training; you wouldn't get young girls nowadays who'd take the trouble to learn what was what. Dottie and Bertha had gone to London, but not into service – to work in a *shop*. That left Edie and Lizzie to help when the family came down for holidays. She had not liked to ask what Mrs Senior was doing for staff in London (because she had been afraid she might think she was volunteering to go), but Miss Rachel saying that she was going to do the cooking was clearly some kind of joke. She'd never so much as boiled an egg, which was as it should be seeing as how she was a lady. Frank would tell her what was going on up there when he got back.

She had started clearing the plates on to a tray: no

sense in leaving them until Edie came – the food would have dried on them and then they would be harder to clean. She piled them on to the trolley to wheel into the scullery.

When she had put the dishes to soak in the sink, she decided to make herself a nice cup of tea and have it with her feet up in the servants' hall: the small room with a nice coal fire where she and Frank had their middle mornings and tea, and sometimes supper.

The house already felt cold, and the room was the only snug place. She put the pot of tea on the table to draw and eased off her shoes – polished by Frank until you could almost see yourself in them. He wasn't exactly handy, but he was a good polisher. She kept her slippers, comfortingly large and shapeless, in this room, and now that she was married to him, she wore them in front of Frank.

Marriage, she reflected, had turned out to be very much what she had expected. It made some things easier, and some more difficult. On the one hand, she didn't have to *worry* any more – about Frank's intentions, or what would become of her when she got too old to work; on the other, there was the strain of having to keep up the position of being interested in world events and what Frank thought about them. She had thought that this sort of thing would stop when the war ended, but it hadn't – it hadn't at all. He went on about the League of Nations, and nationalisation and someone called Cripps (he made a joke about it being one of her relations) going to India to talk to Indian leaders about India (why-ever would he want to do *that*, she wondered), and how shocking it was to have women diplomats, whatever that might mean. On top of that, there was the nightly embarrassment of getting into bed. She simply wasn't used to taking off her clothes with another person in the room, and not merely a person, a *man*, and she had noticed that he seemed to find this difficult as well. They had evolved a method whereby they kept their backs to one another while the undressing went on, and she encouraged him – it was the only time that she did – to talk about the world as much as he liked. Last night it had been a lot about Hitler and Goering and them not knowing about the Final Solution. She knew about *them* – after all, they'd been in everyone's lives for years now – and he had explained to her about all the nasty murdering that had gone on with the Jews. They called it all kinds of other names, but what it was was murder, she made no mistake about that. Once he was safely in his pyjamas and she in her nightgown they could get into bed and turn off the light and things became all right. They would have a cuddle that would sometimes – not as often as she would like – turn into something more. But here again, things were not straightforward – far from it. He was so worked up, all his movements were a little nervy, darting stabs at her, like a small boy trying to steal a jam tart, she had once thought, but she had learned that the slightest hint of her playing any active part simply froze him up. She had to lie there, not quite as though nothing was happening, but certainly as though it was nothing to do with her, until, emboldened by her apparent indifference, he could do it to her. When it was successful, she felt downright motherly, but she knew that that was the last thing he wanted. He wanted to be the master, like men they saw at the pictures, and letting him feel that seemed right. She *was* fond of him, and she put down her boredom and occasional baffled exasperation at his idea of a good conversation to his being a man. Her idea of a good conversation was commenting on people, what they did and why they did it, and whether it was a good or a bad thing for them to do. She had used to have really nice chats of that kind with Eileen, and missed her.

She poured her tea and put her feet up on the other chair – Frank's – and felt the ache in her legs slowly recede, as it always did if she gave it the chance.

When she awoke it was dark, and the fire was nearly out. She hadn't even had her second cup – a wicked waste. She hoisted herself to her feet and poured the rest of the pot on to the aspidistra that Frank had given her. The house was quiet. No sounds of bath water running out, or children, or Mrs Senior playing her piano, or the master with his wireless. Nothing. She drew the curtains in the room, and made up the fire. She'd leave the remains of the rabbit pie for her and Frank tomorrow night, and have a nice poached egg on toast for her supper. She would have liked a bath, but she didn't fancy having one when she was alone in the house. And if I was retired and on my own, she thought, had remained single, every evening would be like this. The great fear that the mere thought of this induced was succeeded at once by a warm surging relief that tomorrow there would be Frank, with his little bandy legs and his scrawny arms and his nervous eyes, gazing at her bust and telling her what a good mind she had for a woman.

PART TWO

ARCHIE

May–June 1946

'I know it's terribly late but, Archie, I don't know what to
do! I feel as though I'm going out of my mind. I—'

'Where's Edward?'

'It's about Edward! He's left me! Gone! Just like that!
Without the slightest warning, he said that he was leaving
me and going to – going to—' Here, her voice failed her
and he could hear nothing but her desperate and unavailing efforts not to sob. He looked at his watch: it was past
two in the morning.

'You want me to come round.' It wasn't even a
question; he knew that she did.

In the taxi that he eventually procured he wondered
why she wanted him. Why not her own sister? Pointless
to ruminate. She had simply caught the Cazalet habit of
depending upon him for sympathy and going through the
forms of advice that people seek when they want support
for what they were going to do anyway. Archie, the arch
spectator, he thought, and then felt thoroughly ashamed
of himself. Poor Villy! Apart from anything else, it had
been clear from her voice that she'd had the most frightful
shock. There had been rumours about; Rupe had mentioned it, but only as something that he didn't think, when
it came to the point, Edward would have the heart, or
lack of it, to do, and he'd noticed that Hugh seldom spoke
to his brother when they were *en famille*. She must have

had some idea that all was not well. But to tell her on the evening of the party for Teddy and Bernadine did seem to him to be a bit much. He'd been to the party, but he'd left it fairly early as he'd felt he had a cold or something starting, and there had been so many people crowded into the sitting room of Villy's new house that he'd had to stand, which did his leg no good at all. Most of the family had been there to greet Teddy's bride, who was certainly spectacular. She arrived in full evening dress, clinging white crêpe with a slit high up the skirt, gold sandals and what looked like half a gold cracker in her elaborately upswept hair. But when he was introduced to her and she said how perfectly wonderful everyone was to her, he saw that she was well over ten years older than Teddy, who stood by her side glowing with pride. She wore thick pancake make-up as though she was on the stage, out of which her almost round, light grey eyes gleamed at him with a sexual appraisal that he felt was born of much repetitive experience. She wore long jangling ear-rings, a thick gold necklace and two charm bracelets, and her nails were long and painted bright red. She was ferociously animated and laughed after everything that she said. He thought all these things because he didn't like her, and found, during the evening, that Rupe felt much the same. 'A bit jungloid,' Rupe said, 'but, of course, you'd hear her coming for miles, so I suppose you could avoid the pounce.'

'Not Teddy,' he had said.

'Not Teddy.' And they both glanced across the room to Teddy, who now had a small moustache and was obviously and successfully trying to look like his father.

He noticed that Edward was charming to his new daughter-in-law and that she was charmed by him. If *he* thought her unsuitable, he did not let it show, and, as usual, he was being a very good host.

However, when Archie had felt he'd stayed a decent amount of time, he'd quietly left. He'd asked the girls if they wanted a lift home, and Polly had said yes, and Clary no. In the end, Polly changed her mind, and said she'd wait for Clary. So he'd limped out into the Abbey Road and picked up a cab, and gone home to have a hot bath and some whisky to try to ward off his cold or whatever it was. He'd just dropped off when Villy rang.

She opened the door to him as he reached it. It was dark in the hall. Without saying anything she led him into the drawing room, still littered with the remains of the party. There were piles of dirty plates and a tray of used wine glasses on the table where she had laid out the food, and overflowing ashtrays on the arms of chairs and small tables. The fire still burned – it had been recently made up – and the standard lamps, with their rather murky shades, cast random pools of buttery light over the debris.

She shut the door with a finger on her lips. 'Mustn't wake Miss Milliment,' she said, and then indicated that he should sit down – 'I know you hate standing' – and offered him first a drink and then a cigarette. When he refused both she said, 'It was very good of you to come.' She smiled, and he cringed. 'Did *you* know anything about this?' She had wandered to the table with the bottles on it and spoke over her shoulder.

'No.' He had decided in the taxi that from her point of view he couldn't know; he *didn't* know, after all. 'Don't you think it would be better if you sat down and told me about it?'

'I'm just getting your drink.'

She came back with a glass of whisky and a syphon. 'I expect you'd rather put in your own soda.' Another awful little artificial smile. She offered him a cigarette from a rosewood box, but he refused again.

Then she sat suddenly on a chair opposite him – almost as though she'd collapsed – and stared at him with agonised eyes. 'I can't believe it. It's like some ghastly bad dream – a nightmare! When everybody had gone, he said he wanted to talk to me about something. Little did I know!' She began a bitter laugh. With her white hair and dark eyebrows, and face uncharacteristically puffy and shapeless from crying, she looked like a small furious doll. He began to feel really sad for her, when the smile again twitched across her face as she said, 'My life in utter ruins. My marriage a farce!' – and his pity shrank before he could stop it.

'Why—?' he began, but she interrupted.

'Oh, some bloody gold-digging woman has got her claws into him and hasn't let go. A real destroyer – that's what I shall call her, the Destroyer! It's all been going on behind my back for years! Our whole marriage has been nothing but lies and deceit on his part! I imagine the whole of London knew before I did. The frightful humili-ation! There's never been anyone else in my life – I've given everything up for him – everything! I've run his house and brought up his children, and now he throws me away like an old broom. He bought this house simply to leave me in it. And now I shall be alone for the rest of my life . . .'

These were only some of the things she said, many of them several times. In between, she veered from the situation being utterly hopeless, to the determination that surely Edward could be got to change his mind. She did not know how she could forgive him, but of course she would have to. If only he would see that he could not desert her in this way. Perhaps somebody could persuade this awful woman that she simply could not behave like this. Diana something, she was called. She'd met her, once: Edward had brought her back to Lansdowne Road one evening when he had not expected her to be there. It made her sick to think how they must have laughed at the narrow escape. But what would suddenly make him do *this*? Could Archie think of any reason for it – any at all?

The reasons that occurred to him seemed best left unsaid, so he simply shook his head (he was beginning to be glad of the whisky). He was at a loss: he sensed her shock, but her anger, her bitterness were so overwhelming that there was no room for his sympathy or anything so simple as her own unhappiness. For what seemed like hours she raged back and forth over the situation until she was – temporarily – exhausted.

'I'm so sorry,' he said at last, as he leaned forward to light her fifth or sixth cigarette.

'The children,' she said. 'What on earth shall I tell them? Teddy and this frightful woman he has married. Lydia, thank God, is away at school. And Roly's far too young to understand. I don't suppose Louise will care, but poor little Roly without a father! Because he needn't think I shall let Roly near that woman!'

There was a short silence and a piece of coal fell out of the grate.

'I gave up my dancing for Edward,' she said, and for the first time she sounded simply sad. 'And it's no good wishing now that I hadn't, because I'd be too old anyway. Too late to do anything about *that*.'

259

She was fifty, he knew – there had been a birthday party in January at Hugh's house.

'What do you think I should do?'

'I think you should have a rest before you even think about that.'

'I couldn't bear to go up – to our room!'

What a relief it was to feel sorry for her – even for a second. He said, no, she needn't; she could lie on the sofa and he'd make up the fire and cover her with the shawl that lay on the piano. He'd make her a hot drink, he said – no, he was good at finding things . . . He got her on to the sofa; the puffiness had gone from her face, leaving it gaunt and haggard with fatigue. But as he settled her, she looked up at him and said, with a kind of jocular heroism that shrivelled him, 'Oh, well. It will all be the same a hundred years hence.' He said nothing. He tucked the shawl round her and got down on his knees to make up the fire – the room was becoming cold. She was quiet, and as he hauled himself to his feet and glanced at her, he thought that she had fallen asleep. Better do the tea anyway, he thought, and made quietly for the door. But as he was opening it, she said, 'Archie! You will talk to Edward, won't you? Try to get him to see . . .'

'I'll do what I can,' he had replied. What else could he say?

By the time he had made the tea and brought it into the room, she was asleep. He poured himself a cup and drank it gratefully. His head and his throat ached; he felt rotten. It was nearly six o'clock: just time, he thought, to get home, have a bath and shave and go to work. He wrote a note telling her this, and let himself out.

In the taxi it occurred to him that in all those hours, when she had been pouring out her shock, her rage, her humiliation, she had never once said anything about loving Edward. He wondered not so much about Edward leaving her as why he had married her in the first place. She had always seemed to him admirable, without being in the least endearing.

∞ ∞ ∞

'You should have rung me before, you really should.'

He opened his mouth to say that he had not rung her at all and the thermometer fell out.

'Steady the Buffs!' she said as she retrieved it. She put it back into his mouth and continued, 'If Marigold hadn't rung me I'd never have known. How long have you been like this?'

He removed the thermometer to say, 'Four days', and put it back again. She said that if she went out of the room he'd have to keep quiet, and went.

He took out the thermometer and looked at it. It registered just under a hundred and one. His temperature was coming down. The day after the vigil with Villy he'd gone to work feeling pretty frightful, but he'd got through the day on aspirins and cups of tea brought by a filing clerk who, over the years, had done him innumerable small favours. At about four, just when he thought he would pack it in, he was sent for. The fussy little man for whom he worked said that he'd been to a very important meeting that afternoon, and the upshot was that the forms currently in use for the processing of demobbed men were being changed which would, he said, have far-reaching consequences. He had waited in silence to hear what these might be, but he might have guessed. They reached no further than himself: he was to redo the last batch – a

261

fortnight's boring repetitive work down the drain. A minute was to be sent out to all relevant departments that evening and tomorrow; forms that had left the building would have to be cancelled and the new ones put to use as soon as the format had been passed by the deputy assistant head of the department. It was not clear precisely when this would be, but Archie was to hold himself in readiness for all systems go.

He had saluted himself out of the stuffy room and walked out of the building. It was raining. He couldn't face the bus and walk to his flat, and had taken a cab. The weather had been foul for May: dark grey skies, rain and thunderstorms – one started on his way home. By the time he had let himself into his flat he was shivering, and all he wanted to do was go to bed and get warm. The next day, after a miserable and feverish night, he rang to say he wouldn't be in to work and then unplugged the telephone. On the fourth day, his doorbell had rung and there was Nancy. He'd clean forgotten that he was supposed to meet her yesterday evening outside the Curzon cinema. She was a kind girl – or woman; she did not reproach him and seemed only anxious to help. She quickly discovered that there was nothing to eat in the house, and went shopping for him. She ran him a bath and changed his sheets while he had it. She returned now with a bowl of soup and some toast. He was ravenous and grateful.

'It's turtle,' she said. 'Supposed to be very nourishing. I bought another tin. I suppose you haven't had a doctor?'

'There's no point. It's only flu. I'm on the mend, anyway.'

'Your telephone doesn't seem to be working – I've reported it.'

'It wouldn't. I unplugged it.'

'Would you like me to – stay the night? I could sleep in the sitting room.'

'It's very kind of you, but I'd rather be alone.'

She looked disappointed, but unsurprised. 'All right. But do plug your phone in, so I can ring to find out how you are tomorrow.'

He spooned up the small jellyish square of turtle meat provided in every tin and ate it. 'Thanks awfully for being so kind.'

'Don't mention it. I'm really very fond of you.'

It was said carelessly, but it worried him. 'You honestly don't need to come tomorrow. You've got me enough provisions and you can tell them I'll be back in the jolly old Admiralty by Monday.'

'*If* your temperature's been down long enough.'

She removed the small tray from his lap. 'I'll just wash this up and then I'll be off.' She'd put on her mac, which concealed her knees hitherto exposed by her short dirndl skirt.

'I won't kiss you,' she said. It sounded like a concession. 'I'll be off, then,' she said for the third time, at the door, as she tied a silk scarf – royal blue with mustard-coloured treble clefs printed at random over it.

'Thank you so much. It was really sweet of you to come.'

'*De narther,*' she said.

'We'll have that film when I'm well,' he called after her.

'Fine.'

When she had gone, he imagined her walking to South Ken, taking the Circle to Notting Hill Gate, catching a 31 bus to Swiss Cottage, and then walking again down one of those streets lined with dark red-brick houses until she reached the one that contained her small flat. It would take her well over an hour.

He was still hungry. He got out of bed, and went to the kitchen where, feeling rather dizzy and weak, he boiled himself an egg and made more toast.

He'd cut off his telephone partly because he hadn't felt up to dealing with the family about Edward's defection. But he had also known that Nancy, if he'd told her he was ill, would be round in a flash. He hadn't thought, which was stupid of him, that she'd hear about it anyway, as she worked in the same building. They'd met nearly a year ago in the canteen after she'd been taking the minutes of a particularly pointless meeting he'd had to attend. They became united through a mutual hatred of his boss and an interest in old films. She belonged to the film society and invited him to go to the Scala Theatre on Sunday afternoons where a succession of classics were shown. Afterwards, he would take her out to a meal that was a cross between a serious tea or a light supper at Lyons' Corner House in Tottenham Court Road. Gradually he had come to know a bit about her: fiancé killed at El Alamein; brother taken prisoner in Burma and eventually returned a wreck. He quickly became an alcoholic, unable to hold any job down and always asking for money. She also had a Siamese cat called Moon to whom she was uncritically devoted. She asked for, and got, very little, it seemed to him, from life; she was unaffected, simple – and kind. She never said anything very silly, or very interesting, although he had initially been deceived by her enormous knowledge of the cinema into thinking her more sophisticated than she was. (In the same way, when she talked about Moon she was often rather funny, and he had at first thought she possessed a more general sense of humour.)

Moon died. He got out of the flat, disappeared for more than a week, and when he finally returned it was with a terrible wound that had become poisoned. When she told him about it tears streamed out of her eyes, as she spoke in a rapid monotone without heeding them. 'The wretched man who came to read the meters,' she said. 'He left the front door open although I asked him not to, and Moon was always looking for excitement. The vet said it was too late: he tried to clean up the wound – it was awful; Moon had an abscess but it kept on coming back and in the end he was so ill and in so much pain that the vet said the kindest thing was to put him down. So he did. I held him in my arms but he was past speaking at all. I haven't got a garden to bury him, so he hasn't even got a grave. It's so awful going back to the flat and knowing he won't be there discussing his food, shouting about where the hell I've been.'

That evening, he took her back to his place and she spent the night with him. 'I'm a bit out of practice,' she said as she climbed into bed. 'Haven't made love to anyone since Kevin died. But I expect I'll soon get the hang of it again.' She was awkward and affectionate and really rather sweet.

All the same, he thought, during his lonely, convalescent weekend, it can't go on like this because she will get to think that it can't go on like this. She'll imagine that I wouldn't have gone on seeing so much of her if I didn't want to see more of her in the end. And he didn't. Which meant that he ought to make his lack of intention clear. He always seemed to know what he *didn't* want, he thought irritably – he had reached that stage of convalescence when weakness allied to self-pity led to boredom and made for general discontent – but he seemed far less sure of what he did want. France, for instance: when he finally got out of his present job, did he really want to go back there? He would have to try to find out. For years there, he had been so used to wanting Rachel, and getting *over* wanting her that his entire life had been coloured by it. Well, now he was free of that and it had been supplanted by a most tender affection for her and for all of her family, who had almost become his own. If he went to France, he would see much less, or in some cases, nothing of them.

Early on Sunday evening, he went for a short walk to get some air. It was good to be out. The air was warmer, the pavements every now and then powdered with petals from flowering crabs and there were occasional wafts of lilac from people's back or front gardens. Cats sat on walls enjoying the end of the pale sunlight that also winked on high bedroom windows of the terraced houses, most of which were badly in need of a fresh coat of paint. But if you were faced with the building of twenty new towns to house a million people who presumably had nowhere to live, painting houses that were otherwise serviceable was hardly a priority. He wondered how long it would take for the outer consequences of war to disappear, for people to look well dressed, well fed and less tired. When he got back to the flat, he thought he really must pull himself together and ring. Villy. Or perhaps Rupe, to test the water. For all he knew, Edward might have changed his mind – no, he surely wouldn't have screwed himself up to telling Villy unless he had been sure of what he intended. And he would ring Nancy to make a date for the cinema with her, and after the film, he would explain that there was no future for her with him. I may be drifting, he thought, but it isn't fair to make her drift with me. Strengthened but depressed by these decisions, he walked slowly back.

He made a date with Nancy for the following Friday evening. Then, not feeling quite up to tackling Villy, he rang Rupert.

'Archie! Been trying to get you all weekend. Your telephone's been out of order. It's rather bad news, I'm afraid.'

'I know. I went to see her the night after the party.'

'See – who?'

'Villy.'

'Oh, *that*! No, it's not that. It's the Brig.' There was a pause and then he said, 'He died on Thursday.'

'Oh, Lord!'

'He'd had another of his bronchial attacks and it turned into pneumonia. They gave him M and B but it didn't work. They said his heart was a bit dicky as well. Anyway, the dear old boy passed away quite peacefully at three in the morning. We were all there. Rachel and the Duchy were with him, and he couldn't talk, but he knew them. He had a good innings, but it still feels pretty awful. Hard to believe. Rachel wanted me to tell you.'

'I've been having some kind of bug, and I unplugged my telephone. I'm so sorry. How are they?'

'The Duchy seems to be bearing up.'

'Rachel?'

'She's not so good. Of course, she did most of the nursing – especially at night – so I think she's simply worn out physically. She put her back out lifting him which hasn't helped.'

There was a short silence.

'Anything I can do? You know I would,' he said.

'I do know, old boy – you're practically family.' Then he said, 'Do come to the funeral. I'm afraid it's a cremation but he said he wanted that. Two thirty, Golders Green on Friday. I'm rather dreading all that – especially – with all the other stuff going on. Hugh's so angry with Edward, he won't speak to him. Between you and me, I'm just praying Villy won't want to come to the funeral. She's completely frantic, poor girl. She got Hugh to have a go at Edward and, of course, all that happened was that they had the most fearful row. Families. Sometimes I envy you. If this goes on, Zoë and I will have to get ourselves our own house. I can't face what goes on in the office all day *and* evenings as well.' Then he apologised. 'It's not your problem.'

'Let's have an evening. Just you and me.'

'I'd love to, old boy, but not this week. I'll give you a call after the funeral.'

Archie borrowed a car to go to Golders Green, arrived early, parked and sat watching small groups converging on the place. It was raining and windy, and people were having trouble with their umbrellas; even from the car he could detect the muted, uneasy friendliness that seems to pervade occasions of this nature. There seemed to be an awful lot of people, but he realised when he decided to join them that there were several funerals going on in different chapels.

There was a halt; they had to wait outside while the previous service finished. Most of the family seemed to have arrived (with the exception of the Duchy and Rachel – waiting in a car probably, he thought). A number of respectable-looking chaps in raincoats with black arm-bands had also arrived; from the office, he guessed. There were also some old – some remarkably ancient – men, members of his various clubs, and one or two middle-aged ladies – secretaries, mistresses, it was impossible to say. They wore black and one of them had a bunch of artificial violets pinned to the lapel of her overcoat.

The door opened and everyone filed slowly inside.

'Sit with us.' It was Clary, dressed entirely in black in clothes that he was certain she must have borrowed since she looked so awful in them. She'd got much thinner lately, and looked tired. Polly, on the other hand, looked most elegant in her very dark blue coat. She gave him a small, remote smile and looked away.

The chapel was not very large and was soon completely full. At the far end lay the coffin with a wreath of dark red roses upon it. It was sad, he thought, that the place had to look so ugly and depressing: a church, almost any church, would have been better than this oak and brass and dreary little stained-glass windows. It was not in bad taste; it was without taste of any kind. He tried to imagine an architect being commissioned. Something practical, he would be told: they must be able to conduct as many ceremonies as possible. So a series of chapels, non-denominational, so that all could be used for any sect; discreet, don't want the ovens to be obtrusive; nice peaceful grounds round the building; somewhere under cover for the people to admire the flowers afterwards. That's about it Mr Cubitt, Nash, Kent, Sir Christopher, whoever . . . And the customers, of course, only came because they had to, and stayed as short a time as possible – there was no indigenous population to inspire or criticise . . .

The Duchy, on Hugh's arm, followed by Rachel, came in. They were conducted to the front row in the left aisle.

Rachel's appearance shocked him: she looked grey and drawn, almost as though at any moment she might break down. He had taken a seat on the aisle because of his leg, and she passed by him so close that he could have touched her, but she did not see him; her eyes were fixed upon the coffin and she looked at no one.

The service began. A prayer was said by the tired clergyman; a hymn was sung. A psalm, the Lord's Prayer, another hymn during which the doors at the end of the chapel opened, and the coffin slid slowly away. Unable to take his eyes off Rachel, he saw her give a small, anguished gasp as it vanished. It was over. The fifteen minutes were up, another set of doors opened and, led by the Duchy, Hugh and Rachel, everybody left the chapel.

'Goodness!' Clary said. 'What a horrible little end. Poor Brig!' Her eyes were full of tears.

'I don't suppose he knows,' he said.

'How do you *know*?'

'I don't.'

She gave a loud sniff, and said, 'It's the usual thing, isn't it? Not believing in anything is not much fun.'

'Things at funerals aren't meant to be *fun*, Clary,' Polly said, but she hooked her arm into Clary's.

Outside people wandered about, looking at the wreaths and bunches laid upon the ground. He saw Edward, but no Villy. He wanted to speak to Rachel. As he approached her, he saw Sid go up to her and put a hand on her arm. Rachel moved; he saw her looking frantically for someone, then she noticed him and he heard her say, 'I'm going with Archie, but thanks.' And Sid turned away.

He took Rachel's arm. 'Do you want to go?'

She nodded. She seemed unable to speak.

270

She stumbled as they walked to the car.

'Your back hurting?'

'Mm.'

He put her in the car, and she said, 'Just drive – out of this place.'

He did. He drove up a road leading on to Hampstead Heath until he found a quiet place to stop. When he turned to her she was sitting rigidly, staring ahead. 'Darling Rachel, does your back hurt dreadfully?'

'Everything hurts.' Then she began to cry. She cried as though the act of crying was inexpressibly painful. Of course, it's her father as well, he thought. It's been quite sudden – a shock – and on top of that she's worn herself out nursing him.

'You looked after him so well. You couldn't have done more.' Then he realised that it was better to say nothing, to let her cry. He kept his arm round her – how easy it was to do that now! Once it would have caused him both ecstasy and anguish. After a time he sought for and gave her his handkerchief.

'Oh, Archie, you are a blessing. There's nothing like an old friend.' But for some reason this made her cry afresh.

'He did have a very happy and successful life, didn't he?' He felt now that some talk might steady her.

'Oh, *yes*! You should see the letters the Duchy has had! Some of the nicest are from the people who worked for him. And the day of the night before he died he told me that he'd been afraid he might die without knowing about Rupe. And he wasn't really ill for long . . .'

She continued in this vein for a while, assembling small, comforting facts, but somehow they were not comforting her. She had stopped crying; although he sensed that she had not reached the end, that there was something else, or more to come.

'Do you think that we should perhaps be getting on to Hugh's?' There was to be a gathering at his house with tea and drinks.

'I can't,' she said. 'I really can't face it.' It was said with an intensity that surprised him, and it occurred to him that she might be starting some kind of breakdown.

'I'll take you home, then,' he said, with all the calm and good cheer he could muster.

'Thank you, dear Archie. Do you mind if I smoke?'

'Course not.'

'You know,' he said, as they reached Hampstead, 'what I think you need is to send the Duchy and Dolly back to Home Place and have a good long holiday. Wouldn't Sid be able to take you somewhere restful and nice?'

'Oh no!' she began to say, but was prevented by a fresh flood of tears, of sobs that racked her and made her gasp with pain as she cried.

'Darling Rach. I'm just going to get you home and put you to bed.' A doctor, he thought: at least he might give her something for her back and she might sleep.

He reached the house, found the key in her bag and came round to her side to help her out of the car. This hurt very much. Somehow he got her up the steps to the front door and into the sitting room and thence to what looked like the most comfortable armchair – 'Upright is best.' She asked him to fetch her some aspirin from her dressing table upstairs. Her room was very cold and bare – a nun's cell, he thought. She asked him to ring Hugh and he did. He suggested ringing her doctor and she said no, what she needed was her osteopath: 'There hasn't been time to get to him – or even make an appointment.' He rang and, using all his powers of persuasion, managed to get Mr Goring to agree to see her at six that evening. 'I'll take you,' he said. He went to the kitchen and made some tea. She had started to worry about smaller things: was not six o'clock after people like Mr Goring stopped work and, if it was, wasn't this rather unfair on him? And what about the Duchy's supper? She liked to eat early, 'and I'm afraid it takes me ages to make anything'.

He rang Hugh again to explain about the osteopath and Hugh said he would look after the Duchy. 'Jolly good you're looking after Rach,' he had added.

He had tried to get Rachel to have a tot of whisky with her aspirin but she had absolutely refused: 'Whisky on an empty stomach and I'll arrive at poor Mr Goring roaring drunk.' Now he realised that with Rachel this meant that she had not only had no lunch, she had probably had no breakfast either. He questioned her; she was evasive, but in the end admitted to a cup of tea at breakfast, and not having felt like any lunch. She agreed to his lighting the gas fire and toasting some bread which she said she and the Duchy always did at tea-time.

Everything seemed to be getting calmer. She talked with affection and an only reasonable degree of emotion about the Brig and how funny he had been about her awful cooking, about the problems that Dolly, with her distinctly patchy grasp of reality, posed for all of them (she had had to be sent to stay with old Sister Crouchback – now retired – when the Brig became ill, but would, no doubt, be returning soon).

'But, darling Rach, can you really cope with the two old ladies and no living-in help? Ought you not to con- sider getting a cook?'

'Oh, no. It will do me good to do something for a change.'

'A woman to clean, perhaps?'

They had had a Mrs Jessup, but she had only stayed for a fortnight and then disappeared without trace.

'Sid must have someone, and even if they couldn't come to you they might know someone who could. Or you could put a card in the local newsagent's? That often works.'

'Oh, no!' He had been stooping to put the toasting fork back into its niche on the hearth but the sheer misery of this cry made him turn to her. She was frowning, biting her lips, rigid with the effort not to break down. When she met his eye, she said: 'I did. Put a card. Someone came . . .' Her voice died away and she started to shake. Then before he could reach her she put her face in her hands and began to weep – a soft, heartbroken sound that pierced him more than anything that had gone before.

He drew up his chair so that he could sit close to her. 'Rachel, tell me. You must tell someone what is making you so unhappy.'

'I think I must, I don't know how. Such horror – such dreadful things!'

In the end she did tell him. Or rather, from what she said, and what she left unsaid in a confused, circuitous account, he thought he came to understand what had happened.

A girl had come in response to the advertisement in the newsagent's. She had come in the afternoon; mercifully the Duchy and Dolly had both been having a rest and the Brig was out. Rachel was alone. At least she had been alone. She had seemed a nice, quiet, suitable girl, and also vaguely familiar. Then, after she had asked the appropri-

274

ate questions and received the right answers, *just* as she had been about to accept her for the job, the girl suddenly said that really she had come about something else. 'I had no idea what that could be, but for some reason I felt frightened.'

Then it had all come out. The girl knew Sid – hadn't Rachel *heard* about her? Of course, she'd met her once in Sid's house. She had been in Sid's life, oh – for *years*! 'She said something about knowing that I was a friend of Sid's but she had thought just a friend. I said that that was true; we had been friends for a very long time – since before the war.'

The girl had said that friends were one thing, but Sid had *lied* to her, had pretended that she – her name was Thelma – was the only love in her life. 'And then she said – she said – so *dreadful* – that the moment I came to London, she had been turned out of Sid's house, out of her life without any warning at all. I couldn't understand any of it, why she was so upset, and worse, what had made Sid be so unkind to her. But when I said that there must have been some reason – I didn't like her very much but I did feel sorry for her – she suddenly shouted at me, "*You!* You're the reason!"'

Then she had looked at him and he could see what it cost her to continue. 'She started to talk about herself and Sid, things they had done together . . .' A slow and painful blush suffused her. 'I can't speak of that. It was too horrible. I asked her to go, but she didn't go. I was sitting down and I was afraid to stand – I mean, I was afraid I wouldn't be able to stand if I got up . . .' Her voice died away and she was silent, swallowing as though nauseated. She kept swallowing as she stared down at her lap.

He wanted to say that he knew jealousy was a terrible

275

feeling, that he was sure Sid loved her, that the girl sounded a bitch and was also possibly a liar, or at least was exaggerating, but something warned him to say none of these things. Instead he asked: 'How *did* you get rid of her?'

'My mother called from upstairs. When the girl realised we were not alone in the house, she got up and said she had felt she had to tell me, to *warn* me – presumably I didn't want my life to be ruined by Sid as hers had been. She actually said' – and here her disgust was tinged with contempt – 'that she was *sorry* to have upset me. I don't think she was, at all. She said she would see herself out, but I went with her to the front door and I said, "Never come back," and shut it after her.' Her eyes filled again with tears. 'But you can see why I cannot see Sid – can't talk to her at all.'

Then it was time to take her to the osteopath.

In the car she said, 'Thank you for letting me tell you. I think it will be a relief to have told. But only you. Nobody else.'

'Of course.'

While she was with Mr Goring, he rang Nancy to tell her that he would not, after all, be able to keep their date. She was very nice about it.

While he sat in the drab waiting room – four upright chairs and a pile of old copies of *Punch* – he tried to imagine being either Sid or Rachel, and failed. He could not think what had induced Sid to betray Rachel over such a long period of time, and he could not think how, or why, Rachel had felt so utterly unable to confront her about it. He knew that Rachel had had a terrible shock; that she felt desperately humiliated by the inference of so much lying and deception on Sid's part. And, given Rachel's description of the girl, what on earth could Sid, loving Rachel, see in that creature? But he knew that this question was one that could never be answered. Rachel, he thought, was such a frank, whole-hearted and somehow innocent person that concealing her only love affair from everybody must have been a very great and continuous strain. And then, as soon as circumstances permitted the prospect of more time together (he was sure that Rachel must have had a hand in getting her parents to choose a house so near to Sid), to be betrayed, and to hear of it from a total stranger, was indeed shocking. No wonder she was so upset. It would have been bad at any time, but to have it practically coinciding with her father's death was really a bit much. Yet if Sid had sent the girl away, it must be because she loved Rachel, and if that was so, the only chance of a reconciliation lay with Rachel being prepared to talk to Sid, who, from her expression and behaviour at the funeral, clearly did not know what Thelma had done. He resolved that he would try, if he could, to help Rachel to see that talking to her lover was necessarily the best thing to do. 'I don't 'arf live vicariously,' he said to himself, acknowledging that kind of intimate contempt that had gone with much of his soliloquy.

He could see that the treatment had been a success. She walked differently and looked more relaxed.

'I have to go back in a week,' she said, 'but he's done marvels. I had put something out and he's popped it back.'

'Has the pain gone?'

'Quite a bit, but he says I've pinched a nerve and that

will take time to settle down. I just feel a bit sore, but *so* much better. Bless you, Archie, for making me go and taking me. I'd never have made it on my own.'

'Have you got anything to eat at home?'

'Oh, yes. Heaps. I've got quite good at baked eggs. And the Duchy likes them so that is what we shall have. Perhaps you'd like some supper?' She looked anxious, and he was fairly sure that there were only two eggs.

'I was thinking of taking you out,' he said, 'for a slightly squarer meal.'

She refused this on the grounds that she could not leave the Duchy alone, but when they got back to Carlton Hill, there was a red MG parked outside.

'Sid!' she exclaimed. 'She must have brought the Duchy back from Hugh's.' Her immediate level of distress was alarming. 'I can't! Archie, I really can't face her. Oh, what shall I do?'

He took her to the nearest restaurant he could find – a rather dubious little place it turned out to be – and rang the Duchy from there to say what he was doing. Then he added that Rachel was awfully tired after her treatment and didn't want to see anyone, wanted simply to have something to eat and then to go to bed. He had no idea what all this would mean to the Duchy – he never knew how much she knew of what was going on in the family – but he hoped that the message would somehow get through to Sid and that she would take the hint.

He managed to get two stiffish gins down her before they ate and he kept the conversation deliberately light and untaxing. She responded – ate nearly half of her boiled chicken and rice and all of a crème caramel – and some colour returned to her face.

It was not until he was waiting for the bill that he touched on what he knew had been in both their minds throughout the meal. 'I know it seems awfully difficult,' he said, 'but you might find it cleared things up a lot if you *could* talk to her. It won't get any better if you don't.'

'But what could I *say*?'

'You could ask her about it. Tell her you know, and that it has made you very unhappy. You might,' he added, discovering this, 'even find that it is not true, or not all the truth. The girl may have been exaggerating – from jealousy. Many people, even if they have only been to bed with somebody else once, feel that they have, or ought to have, a kind of ownership. I'm sure you can understand that.'

'But I don't—' she started. She clasped one hand over the other on the table in a vain effort to stop them trembling, as she began to blush again, and then, in a small, unsteady voice, she asked: 'Do many – most – people – does everybody – want to – to go to bed with people they love?'

'Darling Rachel, you must know that they do.'

She looked up into his face. The pain, the anguish in her eyes made him shut his own for a second. Not seeing her, he heard her say: 'I have never been to bed with Sid. Like that. Never.'

There was a silence, then she said: 'I must be the most selfish person in the world.'

He took her home. She wept silently all the way. Turning to her in the dark, he saw, by the intermittent street lights, that her face, pale again and white as bone, was streaked with tears.

The car had gone and the house was dark excepting

279

for one light in the hall. He helped her out of the car, took her up the steps. 'Will you be all right? Dear Rachel, shall I come in with you?'

She shook her head. 'Thank you, though.' She tried to smile. 'I really do thank you.' She let herself into the house and shut the door quietly.

During the journey home, the long whisky that he gave himself, the bath that he thought might calm him, the hours that he lay awake, he thought about both of them – Sid, now, as well as Rachel. The months, even years, in France when he had longed for Rachel and known that he could never have her came back to him. He had endured and survived, and eventually overcome that loss, but he had removed himself from her; he had arranged his life so that he would never see her. But Sid's situation was infinitely more painful. Rachel had never loved him, but it was clear that she did love Sid, and so there had been no reason for them to part; Sid had spent all these years loving Rachel and not being essentially requited. He could understand how an affair with someone else could come about; he felt nothing but pity for Sid about that. That astonishing, astonishingly naïve, question of Rachel's – did most people, everybody, want to go to bed with people they love? – now cast a light upon that relationship that he could hardly bear, on Sid's behalf, to contemplate. And then – and these three things that Rachel had said to him repeated themselves again and again – she had said that she had never been to bed with Sid, followed by her indictment of herself: 'I must be the most selfish person in the world.' Rachel, whose life had always seemed to him the epitome of self-abnegation, whose creed had, ever since he could remember her, been to put other people's comfort and happiness before her own, had now to live with the knowledge that she had withheld what the person she loved most had most wanted, needed. Had they never talked about this? Clearly not. *Why* not? He could only suppose that Sid, understanding Rachel's attitude, nature, had been afraid to risk what she had. But *why* did Rachel feel, or not feel, as she did? When he had gone first to Home Place to see all of the family again, and he had seen Rachel, with whom he had once been so much in love, with Sid, he had thought that all was clear to him: she loved women rather than men. Now, he could only imagine that Rachel in her incurable innocence had assumed that love with a member of your own sex meant love without it.

He couldn't sleep. What would she do now – now that she knew how Sid must have suffered (although she couldn't really know that, since she neither valued nor understood that particular deprivation)? She did love Sid; she had not been wittingly selfish – although he doubted whether she would give herself the benefit of that. But how could Sid accept, supposing it was offered, any gesture that arose from mere apology or sheer unselfishness? There might be – indeed there were – men who could manage that, he thought, as he remembered wardroom tales of single-minded and relatively heartless debauchery, but Sid, apart from her sex, did not come into that category at all.

He got up and made a pot of tea, sat in his kitchen to drink it. I must go away for a bit, he thought. Getting stale. I need some life of my own – something more than this keeping-my-head-above-water existence. He decided that he must straighten things out with Nancy, go back – for a holiday, at least – to his flat in France, have a change.

As he settled in bed for the second time, he thought

that he might perhaps take Polly and Clary with him. Neither of them had been abroad in their lives – it would be fun to introduce them to the delights of Provence.

The next day he met Nancy in the canteen and they ate lunch together. He explained why he had let her down the previous night, and she said that she quite understood. She asked how old the widow was and he said seventy-nine. 'The poor lady!' she said. 'It must be awful to be widowed when you are very old.'

He realised then that he had been so taken up by Rachel that he had hardly thought about the Duchy.

'Did she have a happy marriage?'

'I really don't know,' he said. He knew nothing about that marriage, he discovered, and remembered now that he had hardly ever heard them talk to each other. They had seemed to have little in common beyond their children and descendants. Their interests had hardly coincided: she loved gardening; he was passionate about forestry; she adored music which left him unmoved; he had loved to ride and shoot, to go to his club, to entertain all kinds of people, to eat and to drink – particularly good burgundy and port; she had no other outdoor interests beyond her garden, hardly ever left either of her houses except to go to a concert or to deal with a difficulty about housekeeping; she seemed to have no friends outside the family, condemned nearly all food as too rich and drank nothing. Ever since he had known them, they had slept in separate rooms. On the face of it, it would hardly seem to have been either a very close or happy arrangement. And yet, perhaps preserved by Victorian veils of a discretion that almost amounted to secrecy, it had not been *un*happy. There had never seemed to be that uncomfortable, airless vacuum in which mysterious tensions could suspend themselves that he associated with unhappy or difficult marriages. The household had jogged along with that pair at its head and he felt sure that, like himself, nobody in it had ever questioned how the couple who had instigated it had got on with one another.

'You are lucky to have such a large family.'

'They aren't my family. They sort of took me in, in the war. Before that I was at art school with one of the sons and we became friends.'

'I never knew you went to an art school!'

He shrugged and then felt ashamed of himself because it showed that he didn't particularly care what she didn't know about him. 'Well,' he said, 'I have to be *somewhere*.'

He knew that he needed to talk to her seriously and that the canteen at lunch-time was hardly the place, but meanwhile he was finding it difficult to talk to her about anything.

'She must have been extremely beautiful,' he said.

'So I expect she minds, anyway, about being so old.'

'Don't think so. She's never cared in the least about her appearance.'

'Anyway, you said she has a daughter. That must be a comfort to her.'

He agreed.

After they had parted, having made an arrangement for the film they were to see together, and he had gone back to his office, he wondered whether, perhaps, the Brig and the Duchy's marriage had sustained itself at Rachel's expense. It had seemed taken for granted that she should do everything for her father – even things that one might have expected his wife to do for him.

He had a meeting with his boss mid-afternoon and

found him in a state of indignation, fulminating, as usual, against the government.

'Attlee must be *mad*! If we withdraw our forces from Egypt, those wogs will take the canal from under our noses. And then where will we all be?'

'I suppose it *is* their canal, sir,' he ventured, but was shot down at once.

'Nonsense! Nothing of the sort! Do you know how much money the Egyptian government put into the building of it? *Ten thousand pounds*! How much canal do you think that would pay for?' He glared at Archie with his burning blue eyes.

'They say that they're leaving adequate defence of the canal, sir.'

Commander Carstairs snorted. 'We all know what that means. Just enough personnel to call for help after the balloon's gone up. You mark my words, this government's hell-bent on giving everything away. Empire will go to pieces – look at India! These bloody socialists will see to it that we shall emerge in the next ten years as a second-class power, but they won't care a damn. Five years of them and we shall be back where we were in 1937, without enough of an army or navy to say boo to a goose.' (He did not like the RAF, Archie knew, so it usually got left out of his calculations.)

The trouble with men like him was that they had been trained to go to sea, to command in a ship, and when they were reduced to sitting in an office and paperwork, they became crusty and hidebound from frustration.

He let Carstairs rumble on until he reached the every-man-in-the-country-will-have-a-suit-and-own-a-bloody-little-car stage, when it became possible to raise the matter that he had come for in the first place.

This is what happens, he told himself, if you do something you don't like every day simply in order to earn enough money to go on doing it, and it's what I'm doing, and it's got to stop.

France. France meant painting – he felt a nervous frisson at the word. He had become so used to regular money, to not experiencing that anxiety and excitement that trying to do something difficult with a fair chance of failing used always to induce. With painting you started something and anything could be there. And as he worked, the gap between what he had seen and what he could show of what he'd seen widened inexorably, and sometimes to such a degree that the picture was abandoned. Sometimes it seemed worth struggling on, and the result would most often be neither the original vision nor the simple failure of it, but a kind of crafty compromise. Then, occasionally and without warning, he pulled something off . . . I must get back to it, he thought, wandering restlessly to his balcony window to look, as it did, on to the square.

It was a windy evening. Blossom was being tossed off the trees to join the browning petals on the ground – it had rained earlier. A small child was listlessly kicking a large rubber ball down one of the straight gravel paths. Square gardens, he thought, were an adult's view of a nice place for children. They had the appearance of being verdant – grass, lawns, shrubs, trees and a few flowers – but they were so ordered and confined that they contained no sense of adventure, of mystery; it was hard to enjoy something if you could see all of it at once. He had a sudden yearning for those two views from the windows, for the ordered ranks of olives and apricots set in the ruddy earth, the narrow fields of sunflowers or maize, and the greater, more spectacular view from the other side of the house, the valley and the hills beyond with the distant, terraced vines below which the river lay, unseen, but whose course was marked by poplars that grew on its banks. But it was the light he thirsted for – that clear, translucent brightness that slaked the eye and, perhaps best of all, that one could take for granted, day after day. Painting landscape in England, he had quickly discovered, was a nightmare of false starts and procrastination, since the light was hardly ever the same for two days running and, moreover, could change from hour to hour during those days.

Yes, he would go back, for a short holiday to start with. And he would invite the girls to come with him.

∞ ∞ ∞

'It's very kind of you, Archie, but I don't think I will. I don't know about Clary – at least, I sort of *do* know, but you'd better ask her yourself. She'll be back any minute.'

She was ironing some piece of sewing and a lock of her chestnut hair had fallen over the side of her face so that he could not see it. She wore a long black cotton skirt below which her feet were bare: they looked as white as alabaster.

She had made her room astonishingly pretty: the walls were the pale blue of a robin's egg, the paint was white and the floor was covered with yellow haircord. Her curtains were made of mattress ticking, pale grey and white stripes, and edged with a yellow woollen fringe. Over the mantelpiece she had hung a painting of Rupe's that he had given her for her twenty-first birthday. It was flanked by two large blue and white Delft china candlesticks, rather cracked, that she had bought when she was a child, reputedly for sixpence.

'You have made this room nice. How are Clary's quarters getting on?'

'She insisted on red striped paper so they're rather cross and hot. She's lost interest in them anyway, so I should think they'll stay as they are.'

She finished her ironing, laid it on the divan and began folding up the board.

'I'm sad you don't want to come to France.'

'Are you?'

He began to say that of course he was but she interrupted him. 'We don't see you for weeks, and then you turn up here, without the slightest warning – you don't even ring up – and then you calmly suggest that I should go to France with you! As though – as though I have absolutely no feelings! Or if I have, they simply don't count! How am I *ever*—' The front door slammed loudly downstairs. 'That's Clary. You'd better go down and ask *her*.' She picked up the ironing board and tramped out of the room with it.

He was stunned. He'd never seen her so angry, or indeed, seen her angry at all. What was all that about? he started to ask himself, but he knew, and felt ashamed of his crassness. He tore a leaf out of his pocket diary and wrote: 'Really sorry, Poll. Please forgive' and propped it on the mantelpiece. Then he went downstairs to find Clary.

Her door was open and she was on her knees before a chest of drawers; she had cut her hair as short as a boy's, he noticed.

'It's me. May I come in?'

She turned round, and he saw that she had made

other changes. Her face was covered with some sort of white make-up, her eyes were sooty with mascara and she wore a lipstick so dark that it was almost black.

'Oh, Archie! Yes, do. Find somewhere to sit if you can. Take those clothes off that chair.' She got to her feet and there was a splitting sound. 'Oh, damn! That's my skirt. It's always doing it.'

She wore a tight black skirt, black stockings like a hospital nurse, and a man's shirt with collar and black tie. It was not a becoming outfit, he thought. He put her pyjamas on to the unmade bed and sat on the chair.

'The trouble is that Poll's sewing machine only does chain-stitch, so every time I split it, the whole thing comes undone. I've got some trousers somewhere. Won't be a sec.'

She disappeared through the communicating door that led to her smaller room.

While he waited for her, he reflected that he had really got rather out of touch with both girls. When they had first moved into their flat, he had come round quite often, taken them out to dinner and to films, but he realised now that, although they had gone out as a threesome and he had occasionally taken Clary by herself, he had not once spent an evening alone with Polly.

Clary returned, wearing black rather baggy trousers in which, he thought, she looked rather like a clown.

'Are all your clothes black these days?'

'The ones I wear. Have you seen Poll? She usually gets back before me.'

'I have. I came to see whether you would both like to come to France with me – just for a holiday.'

'What did she say?'

'She doesn't want to. I'm afraid I rather dropped a

brick there. I thought – well, water under the bridge, you know.'

'No. She wouldn't. Have you got a cigarette?'

'Didn't know you'd taken to smoking.'

'Oh, well – it helps.' The mascara made her eyes look enormous. When he had lit it for her, she sat on the floor opposite him and pushed a large pottery ashtray between them.

'I'm afraid she still thinks she's in love with you. So seeing you is purely masochistic.'

'Oh dear. What about you?'

'*What* about me?'

'Well – everything what. Why do you wear those funny clothes? How's your job? How *are* you? I feel really out of touch. Oh, and how about France?'

'I'm afraid I couldn't come to France for the same reason.'

He stared at her in dismay. 'Oh, God, Clary! *You* aren't secretly in love with me.'

This made her laugh. 'Oh, really, Archie,' she said, in the middle of laughing. 'What an idiotic idea! As if I would be! It's a bit conceited of you even to *think* that, isn't it?'

'It was you who said you couldn't come for the same reason.'

'Yes. I can't, because I'm in love – with someone else. It's funny that shouldn't have occurred to you.'

'I suppose it is,' he said. He felt dashed: of course it was. 'Tell me about him, Clary. What does he do? How did you meet him?'

She told him. It was the man she worked for. He was called Noël and he was married.

'Oh dear.'

'That doesn't matter. I don't believe in marriage anyway. Nor does he. He only married Fenella for practical reasons. She's a marvellous person. She quite understands about Noël and me. In fact, he needs *both* of us. He's desperately unhappy, you see. He hates everything about the modern world. He's the most extraordinary, intelligent, gifted person I've ever met in my life. He knows the most incredible amount about everything. He's sort of trying to educate me. He has the most amazing energy – after you've been with him for even *two days*, you feel exhausted. That's not just me. Fenella feels like it as well. He hardly needs any sleep, you see, and when he's awake things are always happening. So I sort of share him with her.'

'Doesn't he have any other friends?'

'Not many. He doesn't like men much, you see. He says women are far nicer and more sensitive and intelligent.'

'It all sounds rather serious and gloomy.'

'Well, life *is* gloomy. Despairing, really. One just has to make the best of it.'

'Any jokes?' he asked hopelessly – he was pretty sure that there wouldn't be.

'Noël says that wit is one thing – he's all for wit, like Oscar Wilde, for instance. But silly jokes, he says, are just a way of covering things up. Like my family does all the time.'

'Not all the time, Clary.'

'I mean, a way of not facing things. Look at Uncle Edward and Aunt Villy! That's a perfect example of the futility of marriage and not facing things.'

'I think there might be other reasons for that.'

'Well, sex, of course. Noël says that sex is fearfully

important, but it doesn't ever last. He says romantic people understand this. You have to be prepared for everything to go wrong. Noël's a romantic. He says you can't have a serious relationship with someone *and* have children and be financially dependent – all that. You have to be prepared to risk things – and suffer if you have to.'

'Gosh!' Everything she said so appalled him that he recognised the need for extreme caution.

'Are you – happy with him?'

'Not happy!' she replied with scorn. 'Not merely happy! I'm simply completely, utterly in love with him. It's the most wonderful thing that has ever happened to me.'

'Darling Clary. I'm glad you've told me. Do you think that as about the thirty-second best thing that could happen to you, you would have dinner with me?'

She said she would. She'd just go and tell Poll and see if she wanted to come as well. Do, he replied.

Polly wouldn't come. He took Clary to a small Cypriot place near Piccadilly.

'We came here on VE night, do you remember?'

'So we did.'

'You told me a bit about Noël then.'

'Did I?'

All the black lipstick was gone by the time she had finished her kebab. She ate a lot and was glowing with the pleasure of having told him. With her short hair and her white face and black-rimmed eyes, she looked like a marmoset, he told her. She had beautiful eyes, he added, in case she thought likeness to a marmoset was frivolous – currently her most damning word.

'I've got thinner as well,' she said.

'You certainly have. Thin enough, I think.'

'I eat a lot. But Noël likes to go for tremendously long walks, and then he likes to read aloud until quite late at night. He dictates letters all the morning – he and Fenella run a literary agency and I'm being the secretary. And then we have lunch, which Fenella cooks, and we work all the afternoon. Every other weekend I go away with him . . . Sometimes I get a bit sleepy and tired. But Fen does too,' she added defensively. 'That's why it's sensible for us to share.'

'What about your writing? How's that going?'

'Not awfully fast. The days I'm not working, I seem not to feel like it. And Noël has been over my book and he says a lot of it is no good so I had to start again. The trouble is that I only have the weekends I'm not with him for proper writing, and there always seems such a lot to do – you know, washing my clothes, and cleaning up the house with Poll. And if I do get going then it's Monday again and I'm back at work. Noël finds writing frightfully difficult too. He's told me to write in the night, but then I just get too sleepy.'

'What does your father think about all this?'

'Dad? I haven't told him. Please don't you. Poll knows, of course, but nobody else. I don't think anyone would understand.'

'I see.'

'Do you?'

'I'm not sure,' he said cautiously. 'I want you to be happy. Are you?'

'Happy!' she said with contempt. 'That isn't at all the point. He isn't happy, so how can I be? He's afraid of going mad, you see. And the only thing that keeps him from that is me. And Fenella too, of course. He *needs* me. That's the point.'

As he was taking her home, he said casually, 'Could I meet him? I should like to.'

'Afraid not. He's said he doesn't want to meet any of my family.'

'I'm not family, Clary, I'm your friend.'

'It comes to the same thing. He simply doesn't want anything about the rest of my life to come between us.'

He was silent. Nothing that he wanted to say seemed sayable.

'I can feel you disapproving, Archie. I wish you wouldn't.'

'I don't approve of these awful clothes you're wearing. Collars and ties? I suppose he wants you to wear them.'

'He prefers women dressed like that. So we do.'

'You and Fenella.'

'Me and Fenella.'

'Well,' he said, as he said goodnight to her. 'Just one thing. I'm really honoured that you've told me. So will you go on telling me? I mean, whatever happens, will you keep in touch about it?'

She thought for a moment. 'All right. I will.'

'That's a promise.'

She gave him a perfunctory hug. 'I said I would.'

ARCHIE

July–August 1946

The water was amber-coloured in the sunlight as he stepped into it on the sandy gravel. The bank shelved steeply and he was soon up to his neck in the river. It was clear and wonderfully cool after the burning sun, and it moved unhurriedly past and round him. Bright weed streamed out below, like long green hair being endlessly brushed out. Some of the river was dangerous with currents, but this was a safe place where he had always come to bathe. He swam out and then turned on his back to float and drift gently. In the middle, the water reflected nothing but the sky, a delicate bleached blue, but near the far bank, where the trees overhung it, it was dappled with dark and oily greens. Beyond the trees, the terraces of vines shimmered, trembled in the white light. He turned to swim back to the opposite shore, which was decorated with pale grey rocks set in the stony ground.

He had taken to coming here in the mornings, had borrowed Marcel's bicycle which he furnished with his knapsack filled with lunch and painting materials. He found a great need to get out of his rooms which, for reasons that he did not fathom, depressed him.

It had been strange, amazing, to find it all there: dusty, ill-kempt, but still with his furniture, his pots and pans, his easel, his paints and books and even some old clothes. We knew you would return, they said. There had

294

been a welcome; the first night and day there he had felt heady with the reunion, had shaken hands, kissed cheeks, consumed quantities of *pastis* and coffee, asked after the health of children now grown, but then a kind of lethargy descended upon him and he began to feel alone. He had begun to sense that he was regarded as an outsider almost at once – when they were drinking in the café and he had asked what it had been like while he had been away. There had been a short, defensive silence – shrugs. Pierre, who kept the *épicerie*, seemed about to speak, but his father, who had always ruled the family and made his wife and sons work while he sat on a hard wooden chair outside the shop, grunted and he was silenced.

Early the next morning he had gone to collect his bread from Madame Gigot and she had remarked upon his limp. He had told her how he'd got it, and she had said, ah, yes, the war. The war had been terrible for all. But when he had asked after her family, she had closed up. Yvette, he had pressed, pretty Yvette, she must have made a good marriage by now. It had not been possible, she said. Her eyes, black as sloes, had regarded him without expression. Where was she? She had gone north, to Lyon. It had been necessary – many things had become necessary. She would not be returning. It was better not to speak of her in the village. Then she had sighed, slapped his baguette on the counter and wished him a good holiday. She knew, as everyone in the village seemed to, that he was only there for a short stay.

Then when he had gone to ask Marcel if he could hire a bicycle and asked whether Jean-Jacques, who had worked in the garage and was a cousin of Marcel's, might know of one, Marcel had said that he was not in the village any more. He had been taken away – they had taken him in 1944 to work in Germany. He had not returned, and nothing was known of him. These were the only two pieces of information he elicited, and he quickly learned not to ask for more. There was a constraint: relationships had changed between people, and between him and them. So he felt lonely, isolated, sensing that the discretion came out of some shame, which in turn bred a passive hostility that he could neither fully understand nor overcome. Agathe, who used to clean his house for him and do his laundry, had died, Marcel's wife had told him that first evening when he was dining in the little restaurant at the back of the café. She had had something wrong with her insides, had needed an operation, but by the time they had got her to Avignon to the hospital it was too late. He had cleaned up the place a bit, enough to be able to live in it, but then he had found that he did not want to be there, and so he had taken to these long days by the river, bicycling back when the sun had begun to sink.

This feeling of alienation, which he had not at all expected, drove him to think all the time of the people he had left. Of Nancy, with whom he had spent a last miserable evening. She had been stoic. 'Thanks for telling me,' she had said. 'I suppose I sort of knew when you kept putting me off.' It was useless, unkind even, to say that that had not been the reason; it had seemed useless and not particularly kind to say anything. And yet things had to be said. He had tried to protect her pride, only to find that she had none. 'Yes, I did hope we'd come to something,' she had said, rubbing the tears from her eyes, 'but I do see that it was rather silly of me. You're far more intelligent and interesting than I am.'

When he asked whether he might keep in touch with

her, or whether she would prefer him not to, she had said, 'Not to begin with. I've got to get over it, haven't I? And I know people do.' Well, he had said, write to him if and when she felt like it. 'All right.' They had parted in the street. He had seen her on to her bus – saw her standing on the platform, looking back at him before it moved off, and she began to climb to the top deck.

The next Saturday morning he had gone to Harrods and bought her a kitten. The pet shop there was noisy with the trills and whistles and squawks of captive birds. There were hutches full of smooth, secretive rabbits and smaller cages of mice, hamsters, a white rat, tortoises, and two pens with kittens. A litter of Persians, and one of blue Burmese. He chose one of the blue Burmese, a female – a queen, they said. While they were putting it in a cat basket, he wrote a note. 'It's time you had another friend. Love, Archie.' Then he took it in a taxi to her flat. It protested loudly throughout the journey. He asked the driver to ring the bell and deliver the cat, and made him park a few doors away. He did not want to confound her with his presence, but he wanted to make sure she was in. 'Don't say you're a cab driver,' he said. 'Just say you've been told to deliver the cat.' From the back window he saw her open the door, the delivery made, and her look of astonishment and delight. She took the basket, the door shut and the man returned. 'That went down a bit of all right,' he had said.

That had been one good thing. She had sent him a postcard saying simply: 'Thank you so much. She's quite lovely.'

But other things . . .

He thought of Villy and her bitterness and wondered whether her hapless dependants – Roly and Lydia and

Miss Milliment – would galvanise her into feeling that she had something to live for, or whether her hurt pride and her misery would simply infect them all with despair. Lydia was out of the worst of it – her boarding school would provide her with some other life – but Roly and Miss Milliment were trapped. He remembered Rupert once saying to him that the trouble with Villy was that she had always behaved as though her life was a secret tragedy understood by none. The tragedy, if that's what it was, was no longer secret. Edward had always done more or less what he wanted, but knowing – because Rupert had told him – that this new woman had one, if not two children by him might have trapped him. What was the moral choice? To stay with Villy and let Diana what'shername fend for herself? To pay his way out of that, if he could afford to? Or to ditch Villy and take on his new responsibilities? He'd still have to pay for Villy, but that might be easier. Whatever he did, whatever he wanted, he must feel guilt. At least Rupert had made a clean break from that affair in France. When Rupe had told him about that, he had felt really sorry for him, for all three of them, because Zoë had Jack's death to endure – and not just a death, but a suicide, surely harder to bear. He remembered that evening in his flat when Rupert had poured out his unhappiness and all the while he had kept thinking of Zoë and the look of extreme pain that had come and gone on her face when he had told her that Jack had loved her and thanked her for it. It had wrenched his heart: her saying that she expected he would think it very bad of her to fall in love, and then saying that she did not believe that Rupert would ever come back. On the evening with Rupert he had thought of their emotional symmetry and how it would save them both: they had only to tell each other these things that they had separately told him for all to be well. But such a solution proved too simple, and too dangerous for either to attempt it. Of course, he had urged Rupert, but Rupert had said that he could not possibly tell Zoë until he was honestly not in love with Michèle. And he *was* still in love with her. He could keep away from her, but he could not order his feelings about her.

He'd been drying off on the bank in the steady, burning sun. It was time for a drink and lunch. He fetched the bottle cooling between the two rocks in the river and drew the cork. It was a rosé of the region, light and refreshing. He unpacked his bread and cheese and the peaches. In the old days, he would have been looking at the scene before him as he ate, considering, planning what he would draw. Now he did not look; his mind's eye was crammed.

Much later last year, at Home Place, he had gone for a walk with Zoë. It had been just before they had moved to London, to live in Hugh's house, and he had asked her if that was what she wanted. She had said, 'I think it will be *easier* – in some ways. Someone else about the place, you know.'

'*Is* that easier?'

'It does seem to be.'

'Dear Zoë. Are you still grieving about him?'

'I shall always do that. Not about Jack – but *for* him.' Then, seeing that he did not understand her, she said, 'I mean, I know now that he came back to be sure that I could manage without him, and he was right, I could. I do. But he didn't *lose* his life, he gave it, and I grieve that he should have felt he had to do that. He was a very loving person, you see.' She was silent a moment, and then – and he could hardly hear her – she said: 'Probably the most loving person I shall ever know.'

He took her arm, and they walked on until he felt he could say, 'Don't you think it might be a good thing to tell Rupe about it?'

But she had recoiled from him at once. 'Archie, no! I couldn't. He wouldn't understand! He'd be so hurt. And everything is so . . . fragile between us. I mean, *everything* – you know. It's my fault. I don't delight him, we don't get lost together – we seem separately lost to start with—' and she had stopped, trying not to cry.

He had put an arm round her then, and when she had recovered somewhat, had reiterated as steadily and gently as he could, 'I still think you should try. I think it might surprise you – not be as you imagine.'

But she had said almost angrily, 'You don't understand, Archie! I know you think you do, but you don't. Everything would be in smithereens.'

He had had to give up. He'd had another go at Rupert, to no avail, and then, hopelessly and thoroughly frustrated, he had left it. It wasn't his business, he told himself, people could not be made to do even what was sensible and right. But, then, who was he to decide what was either of those things? The trouble about being outside any situation was that you couldn't see the trees for the wood. Interference, for whatever reason, was simply a vicarious way of living.

At least I didn't try to interfere about Clary, he thought, as he poured the last of the wine into his glass and found a Gauloise. God! He had wanted to! The more Clary had extolled his virtues, the more paranoid, selfish and manipulative Noël had seemed. And Mrs Forman too. At least there *was* a Mrs Forman – he was fairly sure

300

Clary's views on marriage stemmed from them. If Noël
had been single, he would probably have trapped Clary
as he had trapped his wife. Like a bomber, he seemed to
need a serious crew on the ground to keep him operative.
He had hated to see Clary so tired, made up like some
twenties film actress and all the fun knocked out of her.
And having her writing got at, so that she was losing her
way about it. *He* found it difficult to write, so he made
sure that Clary would do the same. If that was true, and
he betted it bloody well *was*, it was unforgivable. But he
didn't feel inclined to forgive that little creep *anything*.
It was just Clary's luck to come up against someone
like that in her first job. She was such a whole-hearted
creature, had always been so extreme in her feelings, that
once she had decided she loved somebody, she would
stick to them through any amount of thin. She was nearly
twenty-two now – her birthday was this month and this
was the first time for her. Of course she must be going
to bed with him. The idea filled him with distaste, and
something more than that. She had not *said* she was, but
he was sure this was so. Those ghastly weekends she
spent with him! She had told him a bit about that. Noël
had his parents' house in Barnet, a small detached house
with a derelict garden. It sounded awful: nobody had
lived in it since his father had died, but he had kept it just
as it had always been – thick now with dust, Clary had
said, a bit like Miss Havisham. She had said it was cold
there – 'But we wear our overcoats' – and everything was
rather damp. He had asked what they did, and she had
replied that they went for walks and Noël played bits of
opera on his gramophone – had he heard of Rosa Ponselle
and Martinelli? – and she cooked chops and there was
spinach in the garden. Noël read to her until two in the

morning. He didn't want the house cleaned because he didn't want anyone to come to it. There was no hot water, but there was a gas fire in the sitting room. Clary clearly found it all romantic and exciting. She was, after all, very *young* – and young for her years, he thought, almost unfortunately so. He tried to remember exactly how he had felt at twenty-two and couldn't honestly remember. He had been falling in love with Rachel and he had been both happy and very unhappy. He could not wish that for Clary, an unrequited, hopeless love. He remembered how she had laughed when he had made the foolish assumption that she didn't want to go to France with him for the same reason as Polly. It was a bit much the way she seemed to think he was too old for anyone to be in love with him. That was extreme youth again. Anyone over forty was past it, poor old thing. He had asked how old Noël was – just to see – and she had said he was thirty-eight, but that he was one of those people who simply didn't age. I see, he had said, before he could stop himself, he doesn't age, he simply matures. She had looked at him with those amazing eyes in that absurd make-up and said, 'Archie, don't be sarcastic, everybody loves you. The whole family. You know that! Of course including me.'

It felt simply like a consolation.

Must get to work. A punt had come in view, or a boat that looked like a punt, with an old man in it fishing. He got out his pad and a piece of charcoal and began to draw. He drew a man fishing in a boat with the poplars behind him – it turned out a dogged, explicit little drawing. He had a go at the vine terraces; their ranks and faintly undulating lines were well known to him. He was looking, but without any spirit. Got to get my hand in, he

302

thought. Just a bit rusty. But drawing required constant practice and it was years now since he had really practised. What that meant was that one fell into all the early traps. Like a beginner one got something wrong and tried to manipulate it into being right and in that process the life went out of whatever it was. The first sight of something that made him want to draw it got lost; he had not the capacity to hang on to it. He had almost forgotten what this felt like – this feeling one's way into work after a break. He'd been back a week now and he was still struggling. But he also realised that he was only intermittently struggling; he wasn't trying often or long or hard enough to break through because he only had one more week before he had to go back to England.

By the time he packed up the sun was sinking and parts of the river had become dark. As he bicycled back along the narrow straight road edged by plane trees that arched over it, he decided that he would give up his white-collar work. He could have got out months ago if he'd really wanted, but a combination of indolence and preoccupation with the family had intervened.

When he got back to the silent, empty flat, had climbed the steep stairs, unpacked his knapsack and poured himself a *pastis*, he thought that perhaps there had been some fear as well. He was no longer good at living alone, or disposed to find some casual female company as occasional solace. He felt aimless and afraid to be so. In spite of the fact that his money was getting low – fifty pounds was all he'd been allowed to bring over, and what he'd left in the bank had simply paid his back rent and taxes – he decided to dine in the restaurant. The *prix fixe* was not expensive and included a carafe of wine. He took a novel by someone called Arthur Koestler to read while he ate. He'd bought it on the railway station in Paris and had not opened it.

Marcel's wife brought him his hors d'oeuvres: thin slices of sausage, juicy black olives, tomatoes strewn with basil and rich green oil, and a basket with slices of bread. The food, after England and the war, was delectable.

'Did you find your telegram, Monsieur?'

'No?'

'The boy put it through the door – I saw with my own eyes.'

'I must have missed it, then.'

He got up and went outside the restaurant to his door. When he opened it he found the little buff envelope that had slid sideways so that it was propped against the wall on the ground.

'Please ring after six. Trouble, Polly.'

It took him nearly an hour to get through, and then the line was awful. He could hardly hear her.

'It's Clary,' she said. 'Clary's in trouble. She's . . .' and then he couldn't hear *what* was said.

'What's happened to her? Polly? Are you there?'

There was a lot of crackling and then he heard her, very faint. 'So could you possibly come back, Archie? I can't think of anyone . . .' And then her voice faded away again and he was cut off.

So he didn't stay his second week. He didn't even finish his dinner. Madame made him a sandwich while he packed up, shut the flat, and arranged for a taxi to take him to Avignon. There was a night train to Paris and he spent his last francs on a taxi to the Gare du Nord. All the way across on the ferry he tried to imagine what had befallen Clary. She had eloped; Fenella had tried to murder her; she had become suddenly and dangerously ill . . .

At Newhaven, he took the Pullman: he was tired from sitting up all night and had gone without breakfast. He was served an execrable lunch by the impeccable steward who behaved like an old family retainer.

'Nice to see you, sir. I hope you had a good holiday,' he said, as he tenderly placed a plate of brown Windsor soup before Archie. He drank the soup and ate some of the rugged little fillets of plaice that followed, but then he gave up and fell asleep.

The steward waited until they were drawing into Victoria before giving him his bill. 'Didn't like to wake you, sir.'

He had debated whether to go home first and telephone from there, but he didn't. He took a cab straight to Blandford Street. It was just under eighteen hours since he had got the telegram. He rang the bell, waited, rang again, and eventually, she came down to let him in.

'I thought you were in France!'

'I was. Let me in, Clary.'

She had been standing, indeterminate in the gloom.

'Oh – all right.'

She led the way upstairs to her room, which was in its usual state of chaos. The relief he had felt at seeing her, at her being there, ebbed to a different anxiety. She looked dreadful. Her face, devoid of the absurd make-up in which he had last seen her, was puffy and grey with bruising circles under her eyes. She was wearing a ragged, peach-coloured kimono that he recollected Zoë had used to wear. Something to do with Noël, he thought. She would take that very hard.

'I was in bed, actually,' she said. Her voice was lifeless and carefully non-committal. All the same, some relief returned.

'What made you come back?'

'Poll sent me a telegram. She said you were in trouble.'

'Did she say what kind?'

'The line was too bad. I couldn't hear.'

'You said a telegram.'

'Yes, and as a result of it I rang up.'

'Oh.'

There was a silence. She stood facing him, and he saw that she was trembling.

'What's up?'

'I might as well tell you. It seems that I'm pregnant. Pretty corny of me, isn't it?'

'You know that you are?'

'Yep. I'd been worrying a bit – and I found out for sure last week.'

It was the last thing he had expected.

'Nobody else knows,' she said, 'except Poll.' After a pause, she added in the same lifeless voice, 'And Noël, of course. And Fenella.' She frowned, as though she was trying to hold her face together. 'Oh, Archie! They're so *angry* about it! As though I *meant* to be! It was just an awful mistake – I really don't know how it happened at all. I don't!' And she collapsed onto the floor hugging her knees and began a painful, dry sobbing.

He knelt beside her and she clung to him. He stroked her head, put his arms round her and let her sob. There were no tears.

'I can't even cry properly any more,' she said. ' I seem to have used up all the usual ways of doing it.'

'Darling Clary. Of course it's not your fault. Of course it isn't.' After a bit, he said, 'Why is Noël so angry?'

'Because he *hates* the idea of children. He says it would drive him mad. And *she* says – Fenella says – that it's true. He made her promise never to have one and she did, and she says I've betrayed them both. I didn't *mean* to! It was just an awful accident!'

'Do *you* want to have it?'

'How can I? He would never speak to me again – or see me. I love him and I couldn't be so selfish and wicked as that.' A moment later, she said, 'It's all over anyway. They told me yesterday – at least *she* did. He can't even bear to see me. Oh, Archie, I don't know what to do! I don't know how to – how to – have an abortion, and anyway, they cost hundreds of pounds.'

'If he doesn't want you to have it, he might ante up for that.'

But she looked at him with speechless denial. Then she said, 'I thought he loved me. I really believed that. Sorry, Archie, I've got to go and be sick.'

While she was gone, he removed books, papers and some clothes from the only easy chair for her return. A sheet of writing paper floated to the floor. He picked it up. 'My darling Noël,' he read, and read no more. The line between what was his business and what was not had suddenly become very tenuous. It *was* his business to help her now. He must not lose his temper in front of her about that bastard; indeed, he hoped that Noël would stick to severing all connection with her, as it might shorten her misery about him. He must be careful to say nothing that would provoke her into defending him.

She came back and he made her sit in the chair, drew up a kitchen stool and sat by her.

'Better?'

'I jolly well hope so. That's the third time today. It usually stops by now.'

'Do you want a cup of tea or anything?'

She shook her head. 'I don't particularly *want* one, but I'd better have a water biscuit. They're supposed to be a good thing, Polly says. She's been finding out things like that.'

'What does Poll think about it all?'

'It's difficult, because she didn't like Noël the one time she saw him. I don't know why, she just didn't, and I asked her and, of course, she told me. She's extremely truthful, so she had to say.'

There was a pause, and then she added, 'It was mutual, actually. Noël thought she was shallow.'

'You don't agree with *that*.'

'No,' she said wearily. 'I sometimes don't agree with him about things.'

'Where are your water biscuits?'

'I think under my bed – I think they must have got there.'

'Did you have any lunch?'

'There wasn't much point. I usually have dinner. That seems to be OK.'

'You mean you can fancy it *and* keep it down?'

It was an old family joke. She nearly smiled then. 'That was one of Dad's chars, wasn't it? Dad did seem to have the most remarkable collection of them.'

'Do you think it might be a good thing to tell him about this?'

'Not if I can help it. I suppose if I *have* the baby, he'd have to know – everyone would . . .'

'Well,' he said, 'you don't have to think about that

now, *or* make any decision. I think it might be a good idea if you had a little sleep. I can stay upstairs in Poll's rooms and then I'll take you out to dinner. Would that suit?'

'What will you do?'

'I'll read, or I might have a short kip myself. Didn't sleep much on the train.'

She agreed to this, although she said she wasn't sleepy. 'But I have got rather a headache.'

He got her some aspirin from the cupboard in the tiny little bathroom and a glass of water. When he returned, she'd got into bed. 'Goodness! London water tastes so horrible! I've only just started noticing it.'

He drew her curtains. 'I'll be upstairs if you want me.'

'Yes, you will. Archie! Did you come back specially for me?'

'Yup. I'm very much attached to you, you know.'

'I'm attached to you,' she responded – more like the old Clary, he thought.

He waited fifteen minutes before going down to look at her: she was deeply asleep.

∞ ∞ ∞

Away from her, he was able to think more clearly. She had three options: to have the baby and get it adopted, to have it and bring it up herself, or not to have it. It was essential that she should make this decision without his or anyone else's influence. He knew nothing about abortion except that it was illegal, which must in turn mean that it might be difficult to find somebody who would do it, and even more difficult to check up on them. It occurred to him that Teresa, Louis Kutchinsky's partner, might know somebody, and she had met Clary once when he had taken her to dinner there about three years ago. He rang them and made a plan to go and see them the following day. If she wanted that, he could pay for it, and he resolved upon telling her so that that would not be an influence, but there was no point in an option that she thought was practically impossible. If she decided to have it, then Rupert would have to be told; he wondered why she had not told him already. But, then, Clary would not have told him, Archie, if Poll hadn't got him back. What on earth would have happened if Poll hadn't sent the telegram – if he hadn't come back? Supposing Teresa *didn't* know of anyone, how would he set about finding them? On the other hand, how could Clary have a baby and a job? He was too tired to contemplate these problems. He wrote a note to Polly saying that he was upstairs in her room and that Clary was asleep, and went down to put it on the stairs by the front door. Then he went back to Polly's room and cast himself upon her divan.

When he woke Polly was putting a tea tray on her table. 'Thought you might like some.'

'Thanks. I would.'

'You did get back fast. I couldn't hear you properly on the telephone so I wasn't sure if you'd come.'

'I hope you didn't mind me passing out on your bed.'

'Of course not. You've got very *brown*.'

'It was hot.'

He sat up and she gave him some tea.

'It's pretty awful, isn't it?' she said.

'Yes. Poor Clary. He does sound a perfect swine.'

'He sounds like he *is*.'

'She said you didn't like him. What's he actually like?'

310

He saw her small frowns come and go on her forehead – something that always happened when she was thinking hard.

'Everything he *is*,' she said slowly, 'is about *himself*. He only came here once – for tea. Clary awfully wanted me to meet him. But he didn't want to come, and he sat sort of slightly sneering if we talked, and otherwise he talked to Clary, mostly about things he wanted her to do for him. He won't go into shops, for instance, so everything has to be bought for him. He was telling her how to get to some ghastly place in the East End to get him some kind of special socks because his feet are so sensitive and he does so much walking. It was going to take her a whole afternoon. Not one when she was working for him – she was to do it on her free Saturday. Clary keeps on about his having had such a frightful childhood, but it seems to me that he's never stopped having one. Only now, he's a completely *spoilt* child, getting the grown-ups to make it up to him all the time. Fenella – that's his wife – doesn't eat meat at all now, because she thinks he needs her meat ration for his energy. His blasted energy! He wears poor Clary out. Apart from what he's done to her now.' She looked at him, wrinkling her nose in disgust. 'The thought of poor Clary having a ghastly miniature Noël is more than I can bear. You must stop her, Archie. Somehow.'

This last thought, he realised, was one that he had been suppressing all the afternoon.

'That must be her choice,' he said. 'Although, if you really feel it would be such a disaster, I suppose there would be no harm in your saying so.'

'I hoped you would be the person to do that.' Then she added, 'You must be right. It must be wrong to try and influence her, or we wouldn't each be trying to get the other one to do it.'

Poll was different, he thought. She looked, as usual, elegant, wearing a grass-green sleeveless dress and bright blue sandals, with her hair tied back by a ribbon of the same colour. It was not her appearance that had changed, but her manner: she seemed more poised, more assured, and he realised then that she had never treated him as an equal before. It was over two months since he had seen her. She seemed cooler, and at the same time more open. Just as he was beginning to wonder whether she no longer thought she was in love with him, she said, 'Archie. I feel I ought to tell you. I've got over you at last. Oh dear, it sounds rather rude, doesn't it? But I mean you needn't worry any more. Naturally, I'm extremely *fond* of you. But I do realise that the difference in our ages made the whole thing silly.' She smiled charmingly.

'There now,' he said. 'I'm glad you told me. Did it happen suddenly?'

'I think it happened extremely slowly, but I *noticed* it suddenly. But I'm sorry about it. One of the things I discovered is that it must have been pretty awful for you. I thought it was only awful for me.'

'No, no,' he said. 'In a way it was a good thing you started with a nice safe old buffer like me instead of some frightful cad.'

'You're not an old buffer! You know, Archie, I honestly think you should get married to someone. It's what I keep telling Dad. I mean, there must be thousands of middle-aged ladies whose husbands were killed in the war who'd love to marry either of you.'

'Oh, Poll!' A queue of middle-aged women in black cardigans, all looking as though marriage was the least he could do for them, shuffled through his mind. 'You really mustn't patronise me. It will probably surprise you to know that I, too, have been hopelessly in love so I do know what it feels like, and although I'm over that now, I still have romantic notions of being thoroughly in love before I would think of marrying anyone. And I'm about seven years *younger* than your father. Not,' he added, feeling this last to be rather petulant, 'that that actually makes much difference. I expect your father feels much as I do.'

She had been confounded, had gone a dark pink with tears of chagrin in her eyes, as she apologised again and again. 'It's so difficult to see people one has known when one was young as *people*,' she had said. 'Particularly with parents. But you aren't a parent, Archie, you've always been our friend, so there's no excuse with you. Well,' she had finished bravely, 'I hope you find someone who you become terrifically in love with – if that is what you want. And not if you don't, of course.'

Much later, long after he had got home from the evening with Clary, which, although it had had its ups and downs, he felt on balance had been a good thing, and when he had read his letters, unpacked and had a bath, he wondered briefly whether he ever *would* find anyone, or whether, in spite of what he had said to Polly, there was a kind of watershed that he had reached after which everything that he had taken for granted that he believed in and wanted was no longer possible. Lying in the dark he was able to acknowledge that he did not want to be alone for the rest of his life and wondered uneasily whether that might in the end make him settle – as he imagined poor Hugh might – for someone who would at least reliably be *there*.

PART THREE

EDWARD

1946

He sat in what he still thought of as the Brig's office. He had not changed it at all: it still contained the vast desk, the laurelwood drinks cabinet stocked with beautiful decanters and cut-glass tumblers, the rows of yellowing framed photographs – various members of the firm standing beside vast logs, the earliest lorries, even one of a horse-drawn wagon that had carried timber, of various giant aged trees that had taken the Brig's fancy at Kew or on some estate or arboretum, or himself mounted upon a variety of horses, and then the ones of the family, particularly two that Edward kept looking at of himself and Hugh in uniform taken just before they had gone to France in 1914. One of the many awful things about that war had been worrying whether Hugh was all right. He remembered that extraordinary meeting, after they had both been in France for months without being in touch at all, when their horses had neighed in recognition as they rode towards one another on that road into Amiens. And then, when he had heard that Hugh had copped it, was in hospital, he'd managed somehow to wangle the time to get there and see the poor old boy. He'd been so shocked at the sight of him – his head and arm bandaged, his face drawn and white, and how even when he smiled the haunted expression in his eyes did not change. He'd felt such a surge of love for him that when he knew he had to

317

go and, after all, might not see him again, he'd kissed the old boy. They'd neither of them mentioned then, or ever afterwards, what hell it was out there, but the knowledge that they both knew had been yet another private bond between them.

And now there was this awful rift. Hugh's disapproval of his leaving Villy and going off with Diana made him angry; there seemed nothing he, Edward, could do about it. He wasn't just angry, he was deeply hurt. He and Hugh had always stuck together; they had argued sometimes – Hugh was an obstinate old devil – but they had always come to some agreement. They had worked together, had holidays together, spent much time together playing chess and golf and squash. Hugh was, he now thought, probably the person he'd been closest to in his life.

He'd rung him a few minutes ago on the intercom, but they said he'd left, and Edward remembered that there was a party for Miss Pearson. He decided not to go to it. He won't want me there, he thought miserably. Just as he got up from his desk there was a knock on the door and Teddy appeared. He was so pleased to see him that he suggested a drink. 'Just a quick one, and then I must be on my way.'

Teddy said that would be fine.

While he was getting the whisky out he thought how extraordinarily like himself as a young man Teddy had become: the same crinkly, curly hair, the same blue eyes, even the same moustache. The boy looked tired, though, but he supposed that the combination of a long hard day's work (he had told Hartley to put Teddy through it – not only not to spare him, but to work him harder than employees not called Cazalet) plus a wife whom he

318

suspected of being pretty insatiable in bed was fairly taxing. He'd taken them both out to dinner with Diana the previous week: they'd gone dancing, and it had been clear to him, dancing with Bernadine, that she was fairly keen on men.

'All well at home?'

'Yes, thanks.'

'And work? Getting on all right with the new boss?' Hartley had left for Southampton that week.

'I think so. But that's what I wanted to talk to you about.'

'Oh. Yes?' He felt instantly wary.

'The thing is – I was wondering when I was going to be paid a bit more . . .' There was a short silence, during which Teddy met his eye, and then looked away.

'My dear boy, you've only been working for us for – what is it – three months!'

'I know. That's just it. The electricity and gas bills have just come in and I simply can't pay them.'

'You realise you're being paid far more than most people who are starting in a new job about which they know nothing. Far more than many people get paid in their entire working life.'

'I know, Dad. At least, I sort of know.'

'You're getting more than those footballers were threatening to strike for. They wanted seven pounds a week, didn't they? Well, if I remember rightly, you're getting nine. You really ought to be able to manage on that, Teddy, old chap.'

'I thought I was. I'd forgotten about those bills. The trouble is, you see, that Bernie doesn't understand about money much. And she's used to a warm climate so she keeps the fire on all the time – even in August, she did.

And she always leaves all the lights on because she says the flat is so dark.'

'It sounds as though you're going to have to talk to her about that sort of thing . . .'

'I have tried. But I don't like to go on about it; it's not much fun for her with me out all day. She's pretty bored, actually.'

Oh, Lord! he thought. He has got himself into a mess. Aloud, he said, 'How much are these bills?'

Teddy felt in his jacket pockets and brought out a small sheaf held together by a paper clip. 'They're all red notices,' he said, 'threatening to cut us off if we don't pay. That's the trouble.'

'Let's have a look at them.'

The gas bill was twenty-eight pounds – a staggering amount for three months in a small flat. The electricity was twelve, and the telephone, which hadn't been mentioned, was thirty. 'She was calling the States. I have explained to her that we can't afford to do that.'

'This comes to seventy pounds.'

'I know. I know it does.'

'Anything else?'

'Well, there's going to be the next month's rent any minute. That's six pounds.'

'Teddy, you must put money by for these things. Every week.'

'If I do that how on earth am I to pay for everything else?'

'You mean food?'

'I mean food, and my fares to work, and you know, things that Bernie needs. Not to mention going out once a week, which doesn't seem much, and cigarettes and the odd meal in our local restaurant. Bernie hasn't done much cooking in her life, and she finds the rations impossible. They just don't last. So we have to go out sometimes.'

In the end Edward said he would pay off these bills, but that Teddy would have to make a proper budget and live within his income. 'I can't possibly pay you more now,' he said. 'It would be favouritism. Other people working for us don't have fathers to bail them out. You chose to get married. This is something you should have thought about. You're going to have to cut down your expenses.' He looked across the desk at Teddy, twisting the empty whisky tumbler in his hands; his expression, which had been grateful, was becoming sulky.

'I'll try,' he said, 'but it's not as easy as you think.' He got to his feet. 'I'd better be going back.'

'Hang on a minute. I'll give you a cheque. But mind you use it to pay the bills.'

'Thanks for bailing me out,' he said, when he was given the cheque. 'Of course I'll pay the bills with it.'

'Why don't you suggest to Bernie that she gets some help about housekeeping from your mother?'

'I might.' He sounded as though this was a hopeless idea.

He gave Teddy a lift to Tufnell Park, which made him late for Diana.

After he had dropped Teddy, he remembered that Bernadine had apparently had two children by her first marriage, whom she seemed to have abandoned. Nothing had ever been said about them. Perhaps that meant she didn't like children or want any more. Which would be a good thing, he thought rather grimly.

It wasn't a good evening to be late, because he wasn't taking home the news that he knew Diana wanted to hear. He'd thought that leaving Villy and setting up with Diana

321

would make one of them happy at last, but it hadn't, or at least hadn't anything like as much as he'd expected. Of course, she'd been thrilled when he told her and had moved into the house that she'd found for them some months back. It was a large, rather modern house, built in the thirties – not his kind of house really, but she loved it because she said it would be so easy to keep. It had three floors – the top, she said, would be perfect for a house-keeper's flat, and she had at once engaged a Mrs Green-acre, a widow, who did the shopping and cooking. She had also found a daily for the housework. Jamie had been sent to a prep school, so there was only Susan, but Diana had also engaged a daily girl to look after her every day from nine until four. Quite a household, he thought, and then there was Villy to pay for. He had started using some of his capital. But once in the house, Diana had begun worrying about when he was going to be divorced. To begin with she had assumed that this had been agreed upon, and he hadn't the heart to tell her that, actually, it hadn't. He'd sort of supposed that Villy would want to divorce him, but in various oblique ways during the last months it had become clear to him that she wouldn't – or, at any rate, wasn't going to initiate it. And last week Diana had confronted him about it. They had been undressing after a dinner party – friends of hers – and he had noticed that she was rather silent.

'Tired, sweetie?'

'A bit.'

'I did like your friends.'

'Paddy and Jill? Yes. I was sorry the Carews didn't come, though.'

'Oh, yes. Why didn't they?'

'I think they don't relish the idea of unmarried couples.'

'How foolish of them.' He went into the bathroom to take out his teeth and clean them – something that, unlike with Villy, he did not do in front of Diana. When he came back she was still sitting in front of her dressing table.

'Edward! What is happening?'

'About what?'

'About the divorce.'

He had said that it was far too late to start talking about that, but she had said, no, it wasn't, she really wanted to know. 'I mean, I understand that the whole thing will take some time, but I'd at least like to know that it had started. And it hasn't, has it?'

'Not formally.'

'You mean not at all, don't you? Have you discussed it with lawyers? Or with her?'

'If you must know, no, I haven't.'

'But if you don't, nothing will ever happen.'

'There's always the chance that she will start things off.'

'Do you seriously mean just to wait for that?'

He didn't answer.

'Supposing she doesn't?'

'I don't know! Honestly, how the hell am I supposed to know?'

He felt cornered: it seemed to him that everyone – even she – conspired to make him feel in the wrong. And she was supposed to be on his side, dammit! Just as he was beginning to feel that he couldn't take any more, she changed: got up and went to him and put her arms round him. 'Poor darling! I know how hard it has been for you.

323

You've been so marvellous facing up to everything . . .'
She had said a lot more of that kind of thing and he began
to feel better. They went to bed and he made love to her
and she seemed keener than usual on him which was
enjoyable, and afterwards as they lay with his arm round
her, he said that he would make an arrangement to see
Villy to talk about divorce.

So he'd lunched with her. He'd picked a restaurant
that he didn't usually go to in Soho: he didn't want to
meet friends or have devoted waiters distracting him.
He'd rung her up and simply said that he'd wanted to
discuss things and she'd sounded guarded, but she'd
agreed.

She was waiting at the table for him, dressed in her
navy blue suit and wearing rather a lot of cyclamen
lipstick. He greeted her heartily and ordered Martinis for
both of them.

But it had been a difficult lunch. Conversation had
veered unpredictably between carefully chosen subjects
(he did the choosing) and her sudden, bitter asides, conducted in a tone of voice that he described to himself
as stagey, but which, none the less, made him feel very
uncomfortable. He had, for instance, been asking about
her recent summer holiday with the Duchy and Rachel –
she had taken the children to Home Place – when she
almost interrupted him by saying: 'I suppose I shall have
to live on charity with people being sorry for me for the
rest of my life!' That first time, he had made the mistake
of asking her what on earth she meant, and she had
looked at him with that awful heroic smile, which, he
realised now, had always irritated him, and said: 'Mean?
I mean that beggars can't be choosers.' There had been a
frightful silence while she had watched him being at a

loss. Later, when he told her about Teddy and his financial troubles and added that he didn't think that Bernadine was proving much of a wife, she had said: 'Oh, well, we know what predominates in this family, don't we? Lust!' She made the word sound so disgusting that he felt himself going red. All in all, it wasn't a good climate for broaching the idea of a divorce. However, he'd promised Diana that he would, so he did.

The idea appalled her, she said. Nobody in her family had ever gone through such a disgraceful procedure. She could see no reason why she should be the first, simply to satisfy the predatory instincts of a woman who had, after all, ruined her life. He said he thought it would make things tidier, easier for the children than the present rather ambiguous situation, to which she had replied that it would be easier for the children if there was no situation at all.

Would she at least think about it? he asked.

'What I simply cannot understand', she said, after nobody had said anything for some time, 'is what induced you to let me think we were choosing a house together, when all the time you had no intention of living in it.'

'I thought you would feel more secure if you had a house.'

'But if I'd known what was going on behind my back, I might have wanted to live somewhere quite different – away from it all.'

'If you want to, you could do that. I'm making the house over to you, so it will be yours to sell.'

'Oh – it really doesn't matter where I live!' she exclaimed.

'It wasn't my idea. Louise thought you'd be happier if you had somewhere to live.'

'Louise? Do you mean you discussed me with Louise?'

Oh, Lord, he thought, what a damn silly thing to have said. 'I was trying to get things right. I was trying to do it the best possible way.'

'There isn't a "best possible way" to do what you've done to me. But you could at least have refrained from going behind my back with my own daughter. Don't you see how terribly humiliating that is for me?'

'Yes, yes, I do now. I'm most awfully sorry. I honestly wanted not to upset you—'

'Not to upset me! Oh, my dear Edward!' She gave a bitter laugh, drank some coffee and began to choke. She was given to the occasional choking fit, and they usually seemed to occur in a restaurant or some other public place. He had ceased to feel embarrassed by them years ago, and now, having poured her a glass of water, and timed a few judicious thumps on her back, he handed her his handkerchief ready for the fit of sneezing that would ensue when the choking was over. He smiled encouragingly at her now, as she blew her nose, sneezed, mopped her eyes – her make-up had gone into orangey streaks – sneezed twice more, apologised, blew her nose and sneezed again. She looked awful, familiar, totally undesirable and somehow touching. For the first time since he had left her, he recognised the immense importance to her of her pride.

'I always admire the way you deal with your chokes,' he said.

'I've had plenty of practice.' But she sounded calmer. She got out her powder compact and, with small clucks of dismay, tried to repair the streaks.

He was at a loss now for things to say to her. Any mention of Roly would be unwise: she had earlier announced her intention of refusing to allow him ever to go to the new house or meet that woman. In the end, he offered her a car and she seemed pleased at the idea. 'It would make visiting Lydia at school much easier,' she said.

That was that. He paid the bill and they said goodbye in the street without touching; he lifted his hat to her as he would to a stranger.

That afternoon in the office he asked Rupert if he would bring Zoë to dinner at Ranulf Road, saw that he was about to refuse and said, 'Do, old boy. It would make things so much easier,' and Rupert said fine, all right, he would.

At least that would please Diana, he thought as he drove back after dropping Teddy. It would help about the other bit, which wasn't so good.

She was wearing a new dress, a dark blue and emerald-green affair, and luckily he noticed it before she told him it was new. She had made a large shaker of Martini – he would rather have gone on with whisky after the drink with Teddy, but hadn't the heart to say so.

'It was so funny,' she said. 'I found this dress in one of those awful little boutiques in Finchley Road. I took Jamie with me, before he went back to school, and the shop lady said, "Won't your daddy be pleased with Mummy in her lovely new dress?" And Jamie said, "He's not my daddy. He's the man my mummy lives with." '

'Oh, God!'

'The poor woman didn't know where to look!'

'I've asked Rupert and Zoë to dinner,' he said.

'Oh, good! I do so want to meet them. Give me the other half, darling.' He poured it. 'And how did lunch go?'

'Not too bad.' He felt her waiting. 'She'll think it over,' he said. 'There really isn't anything else I can do. I can't divorce her.'

'Did you tell her about Susan?'

'No. No, I didn't. She's pretty bitter, you know. There's no point in making things worse.'

There was another silence. This isn't the kind of evening I want to have, he thought.

'It doesn't sound very promising.'

He got up from the chair where he had been sitting. 'I must wash,' he said. He wanted to get away from her before they had an argument, or something approaching it.

He had a dressing room adjoining their bedroom with a bathroom leading off it. He had a pee, laved his face in cold water, and washed his hands, then brushed his hair with his pair of silver-backed brushes. He was beginning to go bald. He felt curiously dispirited, something he wasn't used to feeling. Usually he didn't think about how he felt, he simply felt it, but today – the board meeting, with Hugh standing out against him and the consequent compromise; the interview with the bank when the loan he had negotiated had been on surprisingly harsh terms; his decision to take another ten thousand out of his own money to finance things (two more lots of boarding-school fees for Lydia and Jamie, plus getting Villy's allowance organised, and now buying her a car) and then Teddy wanting more money – it had really been the sort of day that made him notice that he felt tired and kind of driven and hemmed in to uncomfortable and hitherto foreign corners. He realised now that he had left out the lunch with Villy, which in its way had been one of the worst things because, although he couldn't possibly discuss it with Diana, he did feel bloody awful about her – he had been married to her for damn nearly twenty-six years, after all, so it must be a frightful blow for her suddenly to be left. Of course, she'd never liked sex or any of that sort of thing, but she had obviously liked being married; women did – look how keen Diana was on the idea; he didn't think he'd really care for the sort of woman who didn't think that marriage was important . . . although it was not something that a man particularly wanted – he, for instance, would be perfectly happy if the situation with Diana stayed as it was. The point was that he was in love with her, in a way that he knew he had never been in love with Villy. He thought of Villy: his first sight of her in the restaurant, wearing make-up, which she used only to wear in the evenings for parties; the sharp lipstick had made her mouth look thin and bitter, and the brown powder had emphasised the deep lines that ran from each side of her nose to below her mouth. When young, she had seemed rather delightfully boyish, but this was not a quality that aged well: now she looked merely unfeminine and, after the choking, pathetic. Again, when they had been standing in the street outside the restaurant, neither of them knowing how to finish their meeting, and she had looked at him with a smile that was not a smile – a kind of grimace that smouldered with resentment damped down by self-pity . . . He was amazed now to realise that he had seen all this because he had not acknowledged any of it at the time. What had gone through his mind had been, I can't kiss her, it might make her break down; I can't shake hands with her, she would think I was being unkind – what the hell do I do? And he'd raised his hat, returning her smile, and walked away. He wondered now whether she had ever loved him. He'd never thought about that before.

Diana calling him to come down for dinner was a welcome relief from these thoughts. The dining room looked festive with silver candlesticks and a silver bowl and white and yellow chrysanthemums and white linen and his favourite decanter full of burgundy, and Mrs Greenacre cooked good English food well, roast lamb, angels on horseback – he was known to prefer savouries – and then there was some decent Stilton, but he discovered that he wasn't hungry at all, and in spite of eating only a token amount, he had quite severe indigestion even before the meal was finished. Diana was sweet to him, got him some bicarbonate – filthy stuff to drink but it did the trick so well that he felt like a brandy with her in the drawing room before they went to bed. He made love to her more seriously than usual, to make it up to her about not getting the divorce thing settled, and because he needed her to be, as he put it to himself, on his side, and she was: she seemed thrilled and appreciative and happy and she fell asleep immediately afterwards. But he – and this was not at all like him – found that he could not sleep; his indigestion returned and, after lying miserably awake for some time, he got up to go in search of bicarb.

RUPERT

November 1946

'What did you think of her?'

'She seemed friendly.' She thought for a moment, and then said, 'She had very ugly hands. And those rings Edward's given her make one notice them more.'

'Oh, Zoë! I never noticed them.'

'You asked me.'

'I meant a bit more generally than that, I suppose.'

They were driving down West End Lane; it was late, and rather foggy.

'She's very much the opposite of Villy, isn't she? To look at, I mean.'

'Amazing eyes,' he said, 'sort of bluebell-coloured. Well, you wouldn't expect her to be like Villy, surely.'

'I don't know. I thought men usually went for the same type. And there were some things that were the same about her.'

'What?'

'Well, she was a bit dramatic, a bit what the Duchy would call theatrical.'

'I can't see that at all—' he began, but she interrupted.

'Yes! She was theatrical about being sincere. She kept saying how much she believed in people saying what they thought, being straightforward, that sort of thing.'

'You didn't like her, then.'

'Well, I didn't dislike her.'

'Oh, well. We don't have to be enormous friends with her. Edward wanted us to meet her, and we have.'

'We'll have to have them back, though, and we'll have to shut up to Villy about having met her.'

'And Hugh,' he said. 'Oh, damn!'

They had almost reached the bottom of the lane and, without warning, were surrounded by dense fog. Rupert slowed down at once as he narrowly missed hitting a parked car.

'It's like the fogs before the war!'

'Can you watch out for the left-hand kerb – and any more parked cars. Wind your window down.'

She did, and the acrid smell filled the car. 'I can only see about three or four feet ahead,' she said, 'so do slow down.'

The occasional street-lights had become dull yellow blurs against which the fog writhed and swirled as though it was being blown upon them, although there seemed to be no wind. After a few minutes, he pulled up against the kerb. 'I want a fag,' he said. 'And also, I've got to think what would be the best route. It's going to take us hours to get home.'

'We may come out of it. Can I have one?'

'Of course. Wind the window up, darling, while we're thinking – there's no point in you getting cold.'

'I suppose we could try to get to the Duchy's,' he said, when he had lit their cigarettes. 'It's far nearer. We haven't got a torch, by any chance, have we?'

'I'm afraid I let Jules have it for Torchlight Ogres.'

'Or we could get down to Edgware Road and then straight to Marble Arch and along Bayswater Road. That's all main roads. There'll be more light and there won't be parked cars.'

'Won't the fog be worse by the park?'

'Probably. Well, we could go via Carlton Hill and see if—'

At this moment there was a thud behind them. The car rocked.

'Oh, Lord! Stay put, darling.'

He got out of the car and a woman's voice said, 'I'm most terribly sorry. I was trying to follow the kerb and I simply didn't see you.' She sounded old and frightened.

'It can't be helped,' he said. 'Better have a look at the damage, though.'

'I've got a torch.'

She went back to her car and returned with it. His tail-lights were both smashed, which meant, he thought gloomily, that more people than ever would run into him.

'I really am so sorry,' the woman was saying. From the flickering torch he saw that she had white hair and was wearing evening dress. 'If you'll wait a second. I'll give you my name and address.'

He followed her to the open door of her car and saw that she had a passenger, a man who seemed to be deeply asleep but, as the woman reached for her handbag, he lifted his chin from his chest and, enunciating with exaggerated care, said, 'Bloody women drivers!' and seemed instantly to resume sleep.

'My husband has slightly overdone it,' the woman said – apologies seemed her strong suit. She handed him the scrap of paper on which she had been writing.

'Have you got far to go?' He had begun to feel sorry for her.

'Oh, no, not far, thank goodness. We've got a flat in Abbey Road. The night porter will help with him. What about you?'

'We'll be all right.' He did not want to journey in tandem with her and, to his relief, this feeling seemed mutual.

'I shall be on my way,' she said. 'But please get in touch with me in the morning about the damage.'

It wasn't until she'd got into her car, manoeuvred round him and driven slowly off that he realised he still had her torch.

Zoë was shivering. 'Let's go on. I keep feeling that more people will hit us.'

He said that they'd better find a side road, park the car and walk.

'All the way home?'

'No, to the Duchy's. Or Villy's, I suppose – she's even nearer.'

'Wouldn't it be better to drive, if it's not far?'

He explained about the lack of tail-lights. 'If people do hit us it'll be our fault. And it's more likely to happen.'

They set off.

'Was she on her own, poor woman?'

'No. She had a drunken husband.'

'I'm glad you're not drunk.'

'So am I.'

The fog seemed, if anything, worse.

'Why don't I get out with the torch and walk in front of you?'

'We could try it. For God's sake don't go too far ahead of me. We're looking for any left-hand turning. OK?'

It was no good. He kept losing her and then being afraid that he'd run into her or into something else while he was concentrating on trying to see where she was. He stopped the car and lost her. He hooted, and after a bit she came back to him. 'It's no go. I keep losing you.'

So she got back into the car and they crawled on.

'There must be a turning soon.'

Eventually, of course, there was. He turned, drove a few yards down and stopped. The silence, when he stopped the engine, was eerie.

'Right. You've got awful shoes for walking, poor girl.'

'It's all right if you don't go too fast.'

'No chance of that. Thank God for the lady's torch.'

'What good will it do? It's very faint – the battery's nearly dead.'

'It means we can read the street names if we can find them.' He linked his arm in hers. 'Keep with me.'

They struck off for the opposite side of the road, and when they found the wall of someone's front garden, turned right. 'The name will be somewhere on the corner. We'll keep the torch just for that. Priory Road. That's something.'

'How far have we got to go?'

'I should think not more than half a mile. But at least we'll know where the car is tomorrow.'

By now they were both cold: the air was raw and they could not walk fast enough to get warm. It took them over an hour to reach the corner of Clifton Hill.

'What's the time?'

'It's – twenty past one. I think it had better be Villy. She's nearer.'

They crossed Abbey Road, and then couldn't find the road.

'It's a crossroads. It must be here!'

'We think we walk straight, and we don't. That's the trouble.'

After some fumbling to and fro they found it. 'Villy is on the left-hand side about half-way up.'

'It's not like the other houses, so it shouldn't be too difficult.'

'We can't see the other houses so I don't see how that helps.'

They did find it in the end, got up the path and rang the bell. At the second ring, they saw a light come on upstairs and then heard Villy's voice from an open window above. 'Who is it?'

She was very good about it. Got them hot toddies and made Zoë take off her shoes and ruined stockings and got her some slippers. She gave them her bed and said she would sleep in Lydia's room. 'I hope your dinner party was worth it,' she said at one point, and Zoë said, oh, no, it had been rather dull. She gave Zoë a nightgown, and apologised, her voice alive with meaning, about not having any pyjamas.

Villy's bedroom was very cold and bare – a comfortless place – but they climbed into bed with relief. He thought how difficult Zoë would once have been throughout the evening's ordeal, and how good she was now and, feeling a surge of affection for her, pulled her towards him. Instantly he felt her twitch away. 'Just affection,' he said. He felt suddenly hopeless.

'It's my heels. You touched them and I've got enormous blisters on both of them. Well, not even blisters – they're raw.'

'Oh, darling! And you never once complained. You are a good, brave girl.'

'I don't think I'm good, but I was a bit brave. I couldn't have walked much further.' She put her head on his shoulder and moved so that he could get his arm under her. 'It's over now, anyway.' Then she said, 'I suppose that it's what adventures in real life usually are, isn't it? Nerve-racking and dull at the same time—'

'And better to look back on afterwards,' he finished. There was a silence while he thought that that wasn't true, that sometimes the opposite was the case.

She said, 'I don't know. I don't think that that is always true.'

'Nothing is.'

'Is what?'

'Always true. End of conversation. Go to sleep now.'

She gave a little high-pitched yawn and turned on her side and, minutes later, he knew that she slept.

Things are getting better, he thought.

The next morning the fog, though it had by no means lifted, was far less dense; buses were running, cars had their headlights on and people wore scarves over their mouths. He sent Zoë home in a taxi, retrieved the car and plodded through his day, which consisted of a visit to the dentist, a meeting with two architects, who did not agree with one another, a visit to the garage to get his tail-lights replaced, and lunch with two brothers who ran one of the largest building firms in the country. The brothers said 'we' the whole time, and never disagreed with one another. Unlike us, he thought grimly. It wasn't that he didn't get on with Edward and Hugh. It was Edward and Hugh with each other. And they kept on asking him what he thought but, really, each of them simply wanted him to agree with them.

When he eventually got to the office – late because of the car – he found that his secretary had flu. After the meeting with the architects he really needed to dictate a report while the facts were fresh in his mind, so he rang through to Hugh to see if he could borrow his. He could, in half an hour.

Rupert had taken over Edward's old office; he had done nothing about it but, then, there had been nothing very personal to move from his last one. It was almost as though he wasn't admitting to himself that this was his permanent place of work. But it would be, of course: he had Jules to educate – not to mention Neville, who might be going to university. And there was Zoë, of course. He wondered briefly whether all life consisted of parents having to sacrifice any notion of doing what they wanted in order to bring up children, who would bring up children and sacrifice any notion of doing what they wanted. By the time he'd retired with a pension, he would be too old for painting to be anything but a hobby. He envied Archie, who was so free of obligation and who didn't seem to know how lucky he was. He knew that these thoughts surfaced largely from lack of sleep, and it was not the kind of day to think about Archie anyway because he knew that whatever he thought would make him even more uncomfortable with him when they next met than he was already.

He was quite glad when there was a soft knock on his door and Hugh's secretary arrived. She was small, so small that it must be the first thing anyone ever noticed about her. Her hair was very pale, absolutely straight and cut with a fringe, which made her look like a page boy. She said good morning in a subdued way, as though she was not sure whether she was meant to speak. He asked her name.

'Jemima Leaf.'

'Right, Miss Leaf. Perhaps you'd sit on that chair and then, if you want to, you can use the desk.'

The session went easily. He sensed that she was nervous, so he said stop him if he dictated too fast for her and she said thank you, she would. When he had finished, she said, 'I hope it's all right to ask, but how do you spell' – she searched her notes – 'pinkerdo?'

'P-y-i-n-k-a-d-o.'

'Thank you. And Jarrah is J-a-r-r-a-h?'

'That's right.'

'Will it be all right if I type this in the afternoon?'

'Fine. It's very good of you to help me out.'

She got to her feet, which he noticed were shod in leather brogues, polished till they looked like brown bottle glass. 'Is there anything else you want?'

'I don't think so. If Miss Marriott goes on being ill, it might be a help to have you do my letters tomorrow.'

'As long as your brother doesn't want me.'

'Don't worry, Miss Leaf, I'll ask him first.'

'Actually, I'm Mrs Leaf.'

'I'm so sorry.'

Her very pale face went slightly pink. 'It doesn't really matter,' she said. 'I'm a widow.'

She was gone before he could say anything.

He got through lunch in plenty of time for the dentist. Mr Yapp had looked after the family's teeth for many years. He was getting on now, and Rupert hoped that he would soon retire and leave the way clear for someone younger, as Mr Yapp was of the old school who equated hurting patients with being thorough.

'Two of your fillings are leaking badly,' he said, in a tone that implied Rupert had been careless with them.

'Oh dear.'

'But we can put that straight. We'll just gouge out the infected matter and replace it. Pity about your father.'

'Yes.'

'Still, we can't all live for ever.' This time the implication was that he intended to, which added to Rupert's
general apprehension. 'Just a little injection.'

Mr Yapp's injections nearly always hurt so much
that anything after them seemed trivial. Today proved an
unfortunate exception. The injection made him want to
shy like a horse, but it was nothing to what followed.
After much drilling and picking with a sharp little hook,
Mr Yapp said that things had gone further than he had
thought and that quite a bit of decay had set in. Rupert
tried hard not to look anguished in case that provoked
another injection, but he got one just the same. 'That
ought to hit the spot,' Mr Yapp said, 'I always forget what
a low threshold for pain you seem to have,' as he started
drilling again.

An hour later Rupert left, feeling sweaty with a face
that felt like a rubber ball, resolving for the hundredth
time never to go back to Mr Yapp. By the time he got
back to the office, the injections were wearing off, replaced
by a throbbing jaw and the beginnings of a headache.
When Mrs Leaf arrived with the typing, he asked her if
she could get him a cup of tea.

'Yes, of course. There are two or three messages
for you. I've put them on your desk.' He considered
asking her for some of his brother's headache dope,
but Hugh was touchy about people knowing he took it,
and Mrs Leaf was new and might not yet know about
Hugh's headaches. However, when she brought the tea,
there were two aspirins sitting in the saucer. When he
thanked her she said, 'I thought you might need them.
Someone rang to check the time of an appointment with

you tomorrow, and I saw in your diary that you were at the dentist.'

'Jolly thoughtful.'

At least, he thought when he was alone again, he had his teeth – unlike poor old Edward – although they had got into a pretty poor state after all that time in France, when going to a dentist had been out of the question. Once, when he'd had a really frightful toothache for nearly a week, Miche had pulled out the tooth with pliers. God, it had hurt! She'd been really tough with him about it. Looking back on it, he recognised her courage and physical strength and, above all, her determination. Once she had decided that something must be done, she immediately set about doing it. She had made him sit with his head against a high-backed chair, and then she had fastened a bandage round his forehead and tied it behind the chairback, had told him to grip the arms and keep still. In two goes she had it out, root and all. He realised that he was able now to think about this without the surges of painful longing for her that once had accompanied any thought about her. Perhaps he was letting go – casting her off? He felt regret – and relief.

He remembered that evening in July, a year and a half ago, when he had taken the train back to London from Southampton and gone to have dinner with Archie, and told him about Miche and how he felt. They were sitting in a small restaurant near Archie's flat; it called itself French, but it produced a poor imitation of French food. Archie had remained silent while he told him all about it, how hard the parting had been, and how much harder it was now than he thought it would be.

'That's why you stayed on,' he had said at last.

341

'Yes. It was probably the wrong thing to do, but I felt I had to do it. I owed my life to her, you see, and she had risked so much for me. It was the only thing she ever asked.'

'Yes. Hard on everybody else, though. Hard on Clary.'

'Harder on Zoë, I should have thought.'

'Have you told her?'

'Nothing. I don't know how to.'

Archie looked at him thoughtfully; he was filling his pipe. 'I suppose you would start at the beginning and go on from there.'

Rupert stared at him to detect any sarcasm or other critical response, but Archie looked calmly back. 'How are things with Zoë?' he asked.

'Sort of constricted. Of course, it's not easy for her.'

'Why do you say that?'

'I don't know. I suppose I mean that I've been away so long . . . She told me she had thought I was dead.'

'You can't blame her for that.'

'I'm not blaming her for anything. It's just – well, if I told her it seems like a kind of betrayal of Miche. Also, if I did, she would ask me – Zoë, I mean – if I still loved Miche and the answer would be yes.'

'Are you in touch with Miche?'

'Absolutely not. When I left her, it was the end.'

> '. . . It's cruel to be kind,
>> So leave my body now
>> As you will leave my mind.'

'What's that?'

Archie had shrugged. 'Something I read somewhere.

Can't even remember the beginning of it. But if you really leave someone – go away and never see them – they do eventually leave your mind. I mean, you cease to think of them – or think of them in a different way.'

'You're thinking of Rachel.'

'Yes.'

'I've got some idea now of what it must have been like for you.'

'That's well over, you see.'

As they were walking back to Archie's flat, he remembered telling Archie how the Duchy had once said to him that part of bearing the responsibility for one's actions entailed not unburdening them to other people and making them unhappy also. 'Oho!' Archie had said with distinct irony. 'So that's where the Cazalet withholding syndrome stems from! I did wonder.'

'You don't agree with it?'

'No. I can see why she thinks that, but I think that not telling people things is a cop-out.'

They had spent the rest of the evening telling each other that they really ought to make time for painting.

Just before they retired for the night, Archie said, 'Have you read Clary's journal?'

'Not yet.'

'Not yet? She spent hours writing that for you – for years.'

'Well, she's decided she doesn't want to show it to me. So I can't, can I?'

'I think you might be meant to beg for it a bit. You know what writers are.'

'I don't. Never known one, unless you count the Brig. Do you think she's got it in her?'

'I rather think she might.'

343

'You were awfully good to her while I was away. She told me.'

'I'm very fond of her.'

There was a tap on his door, and Rupert started guiltily. He had simply been sitting there, drinking tea, not making his telephone calls, not reading his messages . . .

'Come in.'

John Cresswell put his head round the door, and his heart sank. He knew now that Cresswell was Diana's brother, recently booted out of the Army on grounds of ill health. Edward had got him a sort of clerical job; nobody was very sure what he was meant to be doing but he sat in a small office battling with figures which, it became quickly clear, he did not understand. He was currently engaged upon checking the previous month's tallies of softwood delivered to the London wharf. He came to Rupert when in difficulty, largely, he thought, because he was more patient with him than anybody else would be.

'Terribly sorry to bother you,' he began, as he always did, and laid a piece of paper covered with shaky figures on the desk, 'but when I'd done all this, it struck me that possibly what had been wanted was the actual profit to be made on softwoods, rather than what it cost us to buy them. But I'm not absolutely sure. I did make a start on the latter here,' he laid a tobacco-stained finger half-way down the page, 'but then it struck me that when we sell very large quantities the price is different, and I wasn't absolutely sure whether you wanted me to average it out. Or what.'

He was shaking, Rupert noticed, and looked distinctly ill. 'You feeling all right?'

'Touch of malaria. It's not what I call one of my really ace attacks – the old brain still functions. Up to a point.'

It took an hour to understand what Cresswell's problem was, what he had been asked to do and what he had done, and by the time he'd more or less got to the bottom of it, it was time to go home.

There was still enough fog about to remind him that he had done nothing about the tail-lights. He stopped at a garage, but they said there was damage to the bulb sockets. In the end he left the car with them and waited for a bus.

An average day, he supposed it had been, composed of a collection of very small pluses and minuses; in most cases, the pluses were merely palliative, like collecting the car from Priory Road and finding it without further damage, the aspirins Mrs Leaf had brought him that relieved his headache, the fog being better, working at those architects so that their disagreement with one another at least did not mean that the Cazalet brothers lost the contract – a delicate balance that had been, of seeing both points of view with equal charm and enthusiasm, trying to sound what Juliet called 'strickerly fair'. . . The only plus about Mr Yapp was that he'd done it, and need never do it again. The Brig, who had had splendid teeth, thought that dentists should hurt one, it meant that they were doing their job properly, so tradition had it that all the family had gone to Mr Yapp. They had all been held in thrall by the dear old Brig, he thought, in many ways that they mostly didn't even notice. Home Place, for instance. Eventually it was going to be one third his financial responsibility. He had gone into the firm originally largely for Zoë's sake. Then there had been the war and that short interim in the Navy before he'd become a

345

fugitive. Then he'd returned to the fold, this time largely because the Brig expected him to . . . He realised now that he'd made the provision (to himself) that when the Brig died he would review the situation. But he hadn't. The expansion of the firm to Southampton, his brothers' disagreements, and his own emotional conflict had kept him running to stay in the same place. He had always found decisions frightening: nothing ever seemed either black or white enough to make any choice easy. The family teased him about this, making an eccentricity of what was, in reality, a fault. I'm a weak character, he thought – it seemed to account for his dissatisfaction. Last night had been a perfect example. He'd agreed to take Zoë to meet Diana and they'd gone through an evening when everybody tried too hard: Edward to show how happy he was, Diana to show what an admirable character she had, and he and Zoë to show how much they appreciated both these things. And then, the other end of the evening, the night in Villy's house, a bleak place that reeked of bitter despair. He wondered how Miss Milliment coped with that, poor old lady; it was impossible to believe that she did not notice the atmosphere, as it was clear that the little boy did. He was unnaturally quiet and eager to please his mother; breakfast had been full of unease. Rupert had had a foot in both camps – had taken no side, unlike Hugh.

'But you can't take sides about something like this!' Zoë said, when they were mulling over the previous evening. 'I mean, you might have an opinion about it, but it's done now, and nothing any of us say will change things.'

He'd got home – it was beginning to rain so he arrived fairly wet – and had seen Jules, who gave him

a blow-by-blow description of her day, and then thank-
fully subsided with a drink in their – still new to him –
large, high-ceilinged sitting room that smelled of paint
because Zoë had been painting the new fitted book-
shelves that ran along the walls of each side of the
fireplace.

'You sound as though you've had an awful day.'

'Ordinary, I think. I just started it tired.'

'Rupe, how would you feel if I got some sort of job?'

'I'd feel fine about it, if it's what you want. What do
you want to do?'

'That's it. I don't know what I could do.'

During dinner they talked about what she might do,
but came to no conclusion; it seemed that the jobs she
might get were too dull, and that interesting ones all
required some sort of training. 'I can't even type or do
shorthand,' she said, as though providing him with new
and unwelcome information. 'It takes years to train for
something. A doctor, for instance. Seven years!'

'Do you want to be a doctor?'

'No. I was just giving you an example. If I did, I'd be
too old, I should think, by the time I qualified. I'm
probably too old for most things.' She spooned up some
coffee sugar and crunched it morosely.

The old Zoë, he thought. She used always to say
things like that, and it used to irritate him. Now he found
it endearing; she was only thirty-one, after all, and was
still young enough to feel that that was terribly old. He
was just about to embark upon a whole lot of sensible
advice to the effect that she should think carefully about
what she really wanted to do, and then they could discuss
how she could set about getting the qualifications to do
it, when the telephone rang.

'I'll answer it,' he said. After a few moments he said, 'It's for you. Someone called Miss Fenwick.'

'Oh, Lord! It'll be to do with Mummy.'

The telephone was in the passage outside the dining room; they had gone to the expense of having two instruments, one on each floor. He could not hear what she said, but the thought occurred that her mother had died. How would she feel about that? Guilty, he supposed: she had always felt guilty about her mother.

'That was one of Mummy's neighbours. She found Mummy in a faint on the floor – she says she's not feeding herself properly. I knew she wouldn't! I said I'd go down first thing tomorrow.'

He said he'd take her to Waterloo on his way to work, then remembered that he hadn't got the car.

Then, instead of going peaceably to bed, they had a quarrel about Goering. Goering! Afterwards it seemed utterly absurd. He'd picked up some magazine that lay on the table her side of the bed. It was open at an account of the execution of ten Nazi war criminals the previous month. It described how each of them behaved before being hanged, and there was a picture of Goering taken after his suicide. 'Rather grim reading,' he said, when she returned from the bathroom. 'What on earth makes you want to read that?'

'It interests me,' she answered. 'But it doesn't say how that brute managed to keep a cyanide pill on him. He must have been searched. It seems extraordinary that they didn't find it.'

'It doesn't matter now, does it? He's dead, and I should think it's better to take a pill than be hanged.'

'I don't want it to be better for him!' she exclaimed. 'I

should have liked him to be hanged – to go through all the fear and humiliation in front of people!'

'Zoë!'

'Now that we know what those people did, hanging seems to me too good for them!'

He was shocked. 'Darling, you sound like one of those frightful women who knitted by the guillotine. Anyway, I should think committing suicide is pretty awful when it comes to the point. A coward's way out, I agree, but not easy.'

'Not necessarily a coward's way out at all. It depends on the reason. He was simply doing it for himself.'

'I shouldn't think people who kill themselves do it for anyone else—' he began, mildly enough, he thought, but she turned on him at once.

'You don't know what you're talking about!' Her voice contained so much anger that he was nonplussed. There was a short rather frightening silence. Then she said more quietly but with intense feeling, 'He was one of the most wicked and horrible men who ever lived. He should have had a horrible death. They all should – every single one of them.' And he saw that she was crying. She was sitting on the edge of the bed, but before he could reach her she had got up and run into the bathroom; he heard her bolt the door.

He felt completely at a loss. This was a side of her that he had not encountered; in all the years of marriage to her, she'd had her tantrums, but he'd always known what they had been about. Jealousy of Clary and Neville; wanting things that, when he was a schoolmaster, he had not been able to afford, and her first pregnancy when she had certainly been very difficult. But all that had been during the early years; she had grown up, and since his return, there had been nothing of the kind. Bad time of the month? No – that had been last week. Then he remembered her mother. Supposing the poor old girl couldn't manage on her own and hadn't got enough money for a nursing home or whatever, she would have to live with them, a prospect that he knew had always terrified Zoë; she had always resisted any offer he had made to have her mother even to stay. But she must be worried stiff now that this might be the only possible course. He knew better than to solicit her through the locked bathroom door. He got into bed and turned off the light on his side, and waited.

He waited until she had come almost noiselessly out of the bathroom and got into bed and turned off her light before saying, 'Darling! I'm so sorry. I know what all that was really about and I do entirely understand.' He put out his hand and touched her: she was as taut as piano wire.

After a moment, she said, 'How do you know?'

'I haven't lived with you all these years without knowing *some* things about you. I know how you feel about her. I know how difficult you will find it. But if that seems the best thing, of course she must come and live with us and I'll do everything I can to make her feel welcome and help you about it.' He put his arms round her and she did not resist. He moved strands of her hair from her face to kiss it; she was making a sound that was between laughing and crying, he could not tell which, and then she was clinging to him repeating his name and he felt the frenzy of her relief.

He saw her off the next morning. 'Good luck, darling.' The combination of a railway station, the raw cold and

350

her romantic fur hat reminded him of *Anna Karenina*. He told her this thinking it would please her, but to his surprise her eyes filled with tears. 'It'll be all right. I'll ring you this evening to see how things are.'

She nodded and withdrew from the window as the train began to move.

That's that, he thought, as he walked back down the platform; he was conscious of that mixture of freedom and desolation that seeing someone off on a journey seemed always to induce. He was pretty sure that Mrs Headford would be coming to live with them and, in spite of making light of it to Zoë, the prospect was an imprisoning one. Her presence, apart from Zoë's feelings about it, would undoubtedly circumscribe their lives. He decided to make the most of his immediate freedom: he would ring Archie and see whether they could have an evening together and put things right. Archie had been away a good deal since the summer; he had recently given up his job at the Admiralty and had rather slipped from view. But he seemed to spend some time in his flat, although on the one or two occasions when Rupert had tried to arrange something with him it hadn't come off. He'd have one more go, ring him when he got to the office, and if he was in London, explain that he, Rupert, really wanted to see him. He did: apart from anything else he felt he owed Archie an apology. Even now, when he thought of that evening in August – he had not seen him since – he felt a deep embarrassment, amounting to shame.

It had been at the end of August while Zoë and Juliet were still at Home Place; Ellen had gone with them and they had taken Wills for the month. He and Hugh had been keeping house, but on that particular evening, he knew that Hugh had some engagement and, on the spur of the moment, he'd decided to call on Archie on his way back from the office. It had been one of those stifling days when people kept telling each other that a good thunderstorm would clear the air. Archie's flat, with its large window and balcony looking onto the square, would be wonderfully cool after the office, which had been relentlessly baking and airless. Someone was going in at the outer door to the flats and let him in. He had walked up the stairs – two flights (poor Archie, he thought not for the first time, his leg had never got right) – and rung the flat bell. Just as he was thinking that Archie couldn't be back yet, the door opened – and there was Clary.

'Dad!'

'I didn't expect to see you,' he said, as he bent to kiss her.

'Nor me you,' she answered.

'I haven't seen you for such a long time. Did you have a good holiday?' She'd told him she was going away with friends – she wanted a change from always going to Home Place.

'It was all right.' She had led the way into the sitting room. On the table was an enormous jig-saw puzzle. 'I was just doing it to pass the time,' she said. 'Archie's gone out to do some shopping. He'll be back any minute.'

He felt a curious constraint between them. 'Are you having dinner with him?' He knew that she sometimes did this.

'Yes. Yes, I am.'

She wasn't exactly dressed for going out to dinner, he thought. She was wearing a pair of cotton trousers that were very baggy on her, and one of her usual collarless men's shirts. The sleeves of the shirt and the bottoms of her trousers were both rolled up and her feet were bare. She had become very thin, particularly her face. 'Have you found a new job?' Even the information that she had left the last one had come via Hugh from Polly. He'd been really bad about keeping in touch.

'Nope.' She had wandered back to the table and her jig-saw.

He had sat in the large armchair by the fireplace and lit a cigarette. For some reason, he felt nervous. 'Clary. One thing I've been wanting to ask you for some time now is about your journal you wrote for me. I should so very much like to see it.'

'I'm afraid you're too late. I got rid of it. Burned it, actually.'

'Why on earth did you do that?'

'It was childish stuff. Noël said—' She stopped and he saw her bite her lip. 'It was something I'd utterly outgrown. I didn't want anyone to see it. So I burned it.' She looked at him and he felt she was challenging him. The old Clary: doing something that would make him pay attention – mind.

'I'm really sad about that,' he said, after a moment. 'And I feel it's my fault. I've been out of touch with you and I don't like it.'

'Don't you?'

They both heard the key in the lock, and a second later Archie walked into the room. 'Well, well,' he said. 'Fancy seeing you here!' In some way he did not sound enthusiastic.

'I was on my way home, and I just thought it would be nice to see you.'

'I expect you'd like a drink. Have we got any ice, Clary?'

353

'I expect so. I'll go and get it.'

'Clary doesn't look well,' Rupert said.

And Archie replied, 'She's been a bit under the weather.'

'She says she hasn't found another job yet.'

'Time enough for that.' He was busy with the drinks cupboard. 'Like a gin and tonic?'

'That would be lovely.'

The French window on to the balcony was open and Rupert went towards it. 'How was France?'

'It was the same and not the same, if you know what I mean. I didn't stay long.' He went to the open door of the sitting room. 'Clary! I think there's a lemon some-where about. Could you bring it? And a knife?' He took off his jacket and threw it on the sofa. 'God, it's hot out!'

'Is your office as hot as mine?'

'It's not so much hot as completely airless. Their lordships don't believe in windows that actually open.' He went to his shopping bag, which he'd put by the door when he'd come in. 'I'm afraid the tonic will be distinctly tepid.'

Clary came back with a bowl of ice in one hand and a lemon and knife in the other. She gave these things to Archie and then went and sat in front of her jig-saw puzzle. Archie made the drinks and asked after Zoë. He said she was still at Home Place with Juliet and Wills, but that when she got back they would start house-hunting, as it looked as though they had a buyer for Brook Green at last. 'And how's Poll?' he said – to Clary.

'All right as far as I know.'

The feeling of unease prevailed. When Archie offered him one for the road, he suggested taking them both out to dinner, but Clary instantly said: 'I don't feel like going out.'

Archie said that he had bought a pork pie and a lettuce, and he could share that with them if he liked, and he accepted, feeling rather desperately that if he spent more time with them, things would get back to normal, and also because he thought then that he would drive Clary home and find out what was the matter with her. Something was, he was sure, and Archie knew what it was.

At supper he and Archie talked about impersonal things, chiefly the situation in India – there had been three days of bloody fighting in Calcutta and they had a prolonged but not very heartfelt argument about whether there would be less of a bloody mess if the Muslims had their own state in Pakistan, which branched out to a division between him and Archie about British power, casting off the Empire, and generally taking a back seat from the point of view of international politics. He thought this was a mistake; Archie thought it right. Clary, who did not eat her dinner, nibbled a lettuce leaf and said nothing.

'We're boring you,' he said.

'Well, you aren't, actually, because I wasn't listening.'

'Why aren't you eating?'

'I'm not hungry.'

'You've got awfully thin.'

'I expect that's because I'm not hungry.' She was blocking him and he felt defeated by her.

'Look here,' he said, when Archie went to the kitchen to make coffee, 'I feel I'm spoiling your evening.'

When she did not reply, he said, 'Clary! What's up?

If you're angry with me, I wish you'd say why. When we've had our coffee, I'll drive you home and perhaps I could come in and we could have a proper talk.'

'I'm not going home,' she said. 'I'm staying here. At present.'

He stared at her and she stared back. 'Why?' he said at last. 'What's been going on?' Looking into her eyes, which now seemed so enormous in her uncharacteristically white and bony face, he saw that for a moment they came alive – with a shocking misery. Then they clouded again to the deadness that he realised he had seen at intervals all the evening. She had gravitated back to her jig-saw; he pulled a chair opposite her at the table. 'My darling girl, what is it? I know you're very unhappy. I love you and you always used to tell me things. What is it? What can I do?'

'You can't do anything.' She looked up from the puzzle. 'I will tell you if you like. I fell in love with someone and I got pregnant. And then I had an abortion – killed the baby. But Archie's seen me all the way through it.'

Archie! Suddenly, everything – all the things that had seemed so odd and uneasy all the evening – became horribly clear. Her being in the flat, her staying there, Archie's defensiveness when he had remarked on her looking ill, his attempt to get rid of him, 'one for the road' – good God, and he was old enough to be her father, only a year younger than himself! It was monstrous! Trusting, loving young Clary – his beloved daughter, being betrayed by his best friend. He wanted to kill him – murder him . . . He got to his feet with an inarticulate cry of rage and turned to see Archie leaning against the door frame. 'You bastard! You – bloody – bastard!' For the first time in his life he knew what seeing red meant. As he launched himself across the room, Archie's form became obscured in a red haze.

'Steady on! If you're leaping at me I'm the wrong conclusion.'

At the same moment there was Clary, grabbing his arm. 'Dad! Dad – for goodness' sake!'

It took him minutes to believe them, but, of course, he had to believe them: Clary seemed to think it was almost funny – absurd, anyway; he didn't know what Archie thought but he sensed that he was deeply angry or hurt or both. In his confusion and embarrassment, he thought he had said a number of foolish things. He knew that he said he was sorry – more than once – and that he also tried to make them see how easy it was to make such a mistake. He knew that he had asked Clary why she hadn't told him, to which she had replied that she had simply thought he would be angry with her. Archie said almost nothing; most of the time he stood on his balcony with his back to them.

'I suppose it was the man you were working for.' He didn't make a question of it.

'It doesn't matter who it was,' she said. 'It's happened now. I'm all right, Dad.'

'You don't look it.'

'I am. I'm over twenty-one, Dad – I'm not a child.'

He floundered a bit more in this manner, feeling worse and worse about the whole thing – that this should have happened to her, that he had jumped to crass conclusions, that she had turned to Archie rather than to him, there seemed no end to it. He said he thought he'd better go, and Archie, speaking for the first time, said, 'I rather think that would be a good thing.'

357

Clary came to the door of the flat with him.

'Are you all right for money?' he said hopelessly. At least he supposed he would be allowed to do that. But she said, yes, she was. He wanted to hug her and bear her off. She allowed him to kiss her cold little face, but then she stepped backward, eluding his grasp. Attended by Archie, he went. Down the stairs, through the outer door to the street where his car was. It was almost dark. It felt like the worst evening of his life.

The next day he had rung Archie at work to apologise and was told that he'd gone on leave. He rang the flat at intervals during the day and in the evening, but there was no reply. Since then, his efforts to see Archie had failed – messages left saying that he would really like to see him got no answer – and when he rang the girls' flat, Polly, when eventually he got hold of her, said that Clary had gone to stay with friends. 'I think she wants to have a good shot at writing her novel,' she said, 'but if she rings me I'll tell her you called, Uncle Rupe.'

His own life had overwhelmed him after the problems with his brothers, house-hunting, the move, all that had intervened. Now, however, he would make one last throw to see Archie. By himself, he thought. He was conscious of an uncomfortable jealousy – that Archie should clearly have so much more of Clary's confidence than he did. And I won't just turn up, he thought. He knew that he couldn't cope with them together.

He got Archie, at his flat, first go. He sounded guarded, but agreed to meet him at the Savile Club to which they both belonged.

The prospect made him feel nervous, but was also a kind of relief.

POLLY

September–December 1946

Afterwards, many times in the ensuing months, she had thought how very nearly she hadn't met him. She had almost decided not to go to yet another of the drinks parties that Caspar and Gervase regularly gave and to which they always asked her. But when, on this particular occasion – in September – they had informed her of the next one and she had started to say that she didn't think she could (would) come, Caspar had said, 'You must, darling, you really and truly must. I think, my dear one, that you must regard your attendance as part of the job.' And he had run his hand through his silvery hair and regarded her, head a little on one side with the dispassionate brightness of a bird. He combined a romantic appearance with a shrewd expression that people who did not know him often mistook for sympathy.

'A woman's touch,' Gervase chimed in. He said it as though it were a distasteful necessity. He had just returned from his bi-annual visit to Tring, where starvation and massage had temporarily reduced his paunch, and he was perpetually sidling towards mirrors to regard the improved profile of his belly. 'You're really part of our interior decoration. Mr Beswick has hung the new tobacco-silk paper, chosen with you in mind. Do wear white, darling, when you come.' They were always redoing their flat, removing to Claridge's while the work was being done and getting nearly everything off expenses.

'I haven't got anything white,' she said. She'd given in. She'd gone in her old lemon-peel-coloured dress that she'd first worn for VE-Day and dinner with Dad, but it felt different because she'd added a collar of large, pea-cock paste stones that Dad had bought for her from Cameo Corner. And there she was in the large room of the Belgravia mews (two mews made into one, in fact) that was now a symphony of blue and brown, the tobacco walls enhanced by a carpet of gentian blue '*à la* Bakst', as Caspar said, with thirty or forty people, a few of whom she knew by sight. Part of the deal was that she should hand round dishes of canapés sent in from Searcy – they hired a waiter to deal with the champagne. When she was introduced by Gervase or Caspar it was as 'our wonder-ful Polly who looks after us in the shop'. This seemed somehow to stop anyone from wanting to talk to her: they would ask the sort of questions that royalty employed, where courtesy and lack of interest cancelled each other out. As usual, she was even more bored than she remem-bered being when she wasn't at the parties. She'd been handing things round for nearly an hour and been subject to increasingly dismissive smiles from the company, who didn't want to eat any more. She'd just put down the dish and was looking for the waiter to give her a glass of champagne when one of the elderly blue-haired crêpe-de-Chined ladies tapped one of her bare arms. 'I know who you are because Hermione Knebworth told me. I wonder if you'd take pity on my nephew? He's over there. He's lamentably shy and he doesn't know anybody.' Without waiting for an answer she took Polly's arm and steered her to the far corner of the room where a man stood by the window seat, clutching a glass and staring at the ground. 'Gerald! This is Polly Cazalet who works for Caspar come to talk to you. Mind you talk back.' And she withdrew.

They looked at each other, and he blushed from his cheekbones to his forehead, but he was wearing a very old tweed coat in which she thought he was probably far too hot anyway. She tried to remember afterwards what had been her first picture of him, but had only a blurred vision of a not tall, rather square figure, with blond hair, very straight and fine, and a wide mouth that turned up at the corners (that was, in fact, the first thing she noticed, because Archie had once said that it meant that the person had a sense of humour, but she'd never been able to test the theory because nobody after he'd said it had turned out to have that sort of mouth). His eyes bulged slightly like a friendly frog.

'Do you know anybody here?'

'Only my aunt. I don't suppose I know her. Aunts are sort of landscape, aren't they?' Then he seemed uncomfortable about having talked so much and looked at her with something like panic.

The waiter came by and offered Polly a glass.

'I should have got you one,' he muttered, and she saw him going red again. 'Would you like to sit down?'

'Yes.' She sank gratefully on to the window seat.

It seemed extraordinary to her now, but she remembered that then she had felt distinctly sorry for him. She invited him to sit beside her which he did, at a distance, eyeing the gap between them as though he was measuring it. She elicited some information: he had been in the Army, before that had lived in the country with his family, he had one sister, who was married, and his family had recently sent him to London where he was supposed to read law and eat his dinners and become a barrister. He did not sound enthusiastic about this prospect. He'd got himself a flat – in Pimlico. When she asked him what it was like, he said it was awfully small. He said that as though it was the best thing about it. In between these questions and answers – it was a conversation – he kept looking at her intently, and when he saw that she noticed this, looking away.

Eventually his aunt came back to them and said that they must be going or they would be late for dinner with the Laytons. 'I'm afraid I must tear you away. Have you asked Miss Cazalet to advise you about your flat? He's bought the most awful little flat. I was telling Caspar – I said if you can do anything with that you're a genius.'

'Go and have a look at it, dear,' Caspar had said next day. 'Lady Wilmot is not short of the readies, and he's her only nephew. A touch uncouth, though, wouldn't you say?'

'I don't think so. I think he's just rather shy.' And a bit of a weak character, she thought to herself, but she didn't say anything like that to Caspar. An appointment was made, and a few days later she found herself going down the area steps of a house in Ebury Street.

He opened the door to her; he was wearing the same tweeds, and, she thought, the same shirt. He seemed deeply confused at the sight of her. 'I thought one of them was coming,' he said. 'You know, one of those men who gave the party.' He led the way down an extremely narrow dark passage into a room that was also dark since its one window faced north and was heavily barred and looked on to the black-brick wall and the steps up to the street. Excepting two kitchen chairs and a piece of carpet the colour of mud, the room was empty. Without saying any more he led her back to the passage, at the end of which were a clutch of doors. 'This is the other room,' he said. It was smaller than the first one, but lighter since it faced south with a similar barred window. There was a camp bed along one wall. The other doors introduced a minute kitchen that contained an ancient gas cooker, a stained porcelain sink and a water heater bracketed to the wall. It smelt of gas. The third door was the bathroom: small, stained bath, basin and lavatory with another water heater, placed, she noticed, so that one would hit one's head if one stood up in the bath. It, too, smelt of gas enhanced by damp. Taps dripped and linoleum curled upon the floor. 'That's it,' he said. 'It's amazing what you can get in a tiny space, isn't it? It's what drew me to it.'

It was probably all he could afford, she thought. 'It has possibilities,' she said – one always had to say that. They went back to the first room, and she got out her tape measure and notebook.

'I have to measure first,' she said, 'and see which walls are structural, things like that.'

'It's awfully good of you to go to so much trouble.'

'Not at all. It's my job.'

'I thought you would just advise me about colours of walls and curtains – that sort of thing.'

'Well, we do do that, of course, but I think there are some things that need doing before that here.'

'I'm sure you know best. It's my first place, actually, so I don't really know the form.'

He helped her measure, which made it much quicker, and during it, she found that he had been living in the flat, 'Sleeping here, at any rate,' he said. 'It's a bit difficult to do anything else.'

They had coffee in a place round the corner that she knew. She suggested it. 'I say! Would you really? I was wondering whether you'd mind if I asked you.' As well as coffee, he had a poached egg on toast and baked beans. 'Best thing about the Army was the baked beans,' he said. 'We never had them at home. Not that I've spent very much time there.'

'How do you mean?'

'Well, boarding schools since I was seven and then the war and the Army – you know how it is. And then, after Charles, my older brother, was killed, my mother found it difficult to have me about – she said I reminded her too much of him, you see, which is funny,' he added, as though he had just thought of it, 'because I was never really in the least like him.'

'What was he like?'

'He was terribly brainy as well as being good-looking and awfully good with girls and that sort of thing.'

Then, looking at her and as though he knew what she was about to ask, he said, 'No. As a matter of fact, he rather despised me. I wish,' he added hurriedly, 'that you would tell me a bit about yourself.'

'What would you like to know?'

'Oh, anything! I would like to know anything about you.'

She told him about her family and living at Home Place throughout the war. 'Gosh, that sounds fun!' he said. 'Go on.' She told him about her mother dying of cancer and how unhappy it had made her father, and saw his slightly bulging eyes become moist. 'Oh, Lord,' he said. She told him about Simon, now at Oxford, and Wills just gone to his prep school, and about her sharing a flat with Clary. It was surprising how much she had told him, she thought afterwards, but he was such an attentive listener that it was somehow enjoyable to tell him. Eventually, when it was extremely clear that the waitress thought they should leave or have another meal, and she pointed this out, he said, 'That's all right. I'll simply have another poached egg. Wouldn't you like one by now? I mean, my first was my breakfast; yours could be an early lunch.'

So they both had poached eggs and while the eggs were coming, Polly said they really ought to talk a bit about the flat. 'What made you choose it?'

'It was the first one I saw. It seemed about right – nice and small – so I got it. Do you think it was the wrong choice?'

'I think it needs quite a bit doing to it. How much do you want to spend?'

'Whatever you say.'

'No, I mean seriously.'

'What do you think?'

'Have you got any furniture?'

'Those chairs. And the bed.'

'Well, I think you'll probably need to spend about three to five hundred pounds on building and heating repairs, and dealing with the damp. Did you have a survey?'

He hadn't.

Without thinking, she said teasingly, 'You're not very practical, are you?'

He blushed. 'No. The awful thing is that unpractical people are supposed to be very clever or artistic or something of the sort, and I'm not. There's really nothing to be said for me at all.'

But there was something to be said for him, she

thought, as she caught her bus to go back to the shop. She knew about her capacity for feeling sorry for people, and he seemed, on the face of it, a prime candidate, but it wasn't all, or even the first thing she felt.

She was given the work on his flat, as Caspar and Gervase were much taken up with the decorating of three large hotel suites and a very grand house in the country where the owners wanted to move their kitchens from the cavernous basement to the ground floor. 'You do it, dear girl. It will be very good practice, and with such a little henhouse you can hardly go wrong.'

A week later, when she had done her drawings, assembled an electrician and a plumber, she decided that she must see him again to get his approval, and rang him early one morning. 'Oh, good. When?' On the spur of the moment (she told herself), she asked him to supper in her flat. 'It's most awfully kind of you,' he said. He sounded very pleased.

She bought some smoked haddock and made a kedgeree, one of her best things, the night before, and a fruit salad of grapes and bananas. Clary was away and she had the place to herself as Neville, who had spent a good many weeks there, had now gone back to school. That, too, was a kind of relief as Neville was just as untidy as Clary, but also ate any and all of the food in the house, and had filled up Clary's room with a set of drums, a double bass, his trumpet and a portable piano and held interminable rehearsals with his friends every evening until late into the night, which interfered with any social life she wanted to have. Not that she'd had very much. Christopher had been going to come, but at the last minute he had cried off: Oliver had suddenly become ill, and couldn't be left. 'He's got cancer,' Christopher had said. 'The vet says he may have to be put down if the operation doesn't work.' So she'd offered to go down to him for a weekend, but Christopher had said that he'd be better on his own. She'd been relieved because his loving her made her feel sad and uncomfortable with him, and she was afraid if she was with him he might ask her about her hopeless love and that she might lie about it, because she knew that she would never love Christopher, and if he knew that there was nobody else on the horizon he might have hope.

Gerald arrived exactly when she had asked him, and he brought a very beautiful fern as a present. 'I didn't know what you'd like,' he said, 'but I've never liked cut flowers myself, and there wasn't much choice of things in pots. It's funny,' he went on, as they tramped up the stairs to her room, 'but I kept wanting to bring you a cat as a present. Then I thought you might have one anyway. Have you?'

She said no, but she missed having one. 'I haven't got a garden.'

'Oh, well, then. It's yet another drawback to London: the lack of good gardens for cats.'

'There are quite a lot, but not so many where you've got your flat.'

'Are there? I hardly know London. But you do like cats, don't you? I was right about that?'

She told him about Pompey and how much she'd loved him, and he told her about a cat he'd had when he was seven, which had always slept on his bed and went for rides in his bicycle basket.

'What happened to him?'

'It was a her. She had kittens and then my parents had her put down while I was at school.'

367

'How awful for you!'

'They didn't like cats, you see. I'd hidden her from them but, of course, when I was sent to school, they found out.'

Pretty difficult to hide a cat in a house from your family, she thought, but she didn't say so.

He sat in the Victorian chair in her room looking round him and not saying anything.

'Do you like it?'

'I knew I would. It's – elegant and charming. Suits you.'

He was very appreciative of everything: the dark green dining room, the kedgeree – he had two helpings – and the fruit salad. At one point he said, 'I say! I am having a lovely time!' and the slightly bulging eyes met hers with such a frank and grateful pleasure that she was infected by it.

After supper, she fetched the drawings she had made and laid them out on the table. He was far quicker than most of the clients at understanding them, and when she remarked on this, he said, 'Well, it's a bit like map-reading, isn't it? And I had to get very good at that.'

'The war?'

'Yes.'

'Where were you?'

'Moved about. Got dropped into places. From time to time.'

'You were a paratrooper?'

'That's it.'

She stared at him, trying to imagine having to jump out of an aeroplane into nothing. 'I know I don't look the part,' he said apologetically, 'romantic heroes and all that

368

stuff. I look more like a frog, really, which is not much good unless you are one.'

She opened her mouth to say that he didn't look like a frog, but he leaned over the table and put his hand over her mouth. 'Don't,' he said. 'Everything's been so truthful between us. I don't want a kind lie. Imagine me on a water-lily leaf. Look!' And he suddenly crooked his arms and sat hunched with his eyes stretched wide open. He looked so tremendously like a frog that she couldn't help laughing. 'I'm a wonderful swimmer, too,' he said, 'just haven't got my colour quite right.'

'I've never met a frog before.'

'It's not surprising. There aren't a lot of us about.'

'Do you feel OK about the drawings?'

'I trust you absolutely.'

'I suggest we go ahead with the building part, and then you can see what you want to spend money on. You'll need some more furniture and curtains, and something to put on the floors. But we can do a lot of that fairly cheaply if you want – I mean, paint on the wall instead of wallpaper, and sanding the floor instead of carpet, that kind of thing. And there are places where you can buy second-hand furniture quite cheaply. That's what I did.'

'Did you? Well, you did it awfully well, I must say.'

She made coffee and they took it downstairs to her room. By now she had the delightful sensation of feeling that she had known him all her life, plus the certainty that there was a great deal more to know. They talked and talked: about themselves, the state of the world, about themselves again – how much he didn't want to be a lawyer, and how she felt that her job was really a dead end, about whether anything that they ever did would in

369

the least change the world and its dreary, warlike, power-mongering ways, about whether the arts were a politically civilising influence, about whether people had always been the same and the only changes were technological. It was after midnight when they realised the time.

'Can I see you tomorrow?' he asked as she let him out.

'It is tomorrow.'

'Well, later today, then.'

That was the beginning, ages ago, it now seemed. They did meet that next evening: he took her out to supper, but it wasn't a great success – he seemed quite different, nervous, abstracted and ill at ease. There was one lighter moment when, after a rather unpleasantly bossy waiter had tried to manipulate them into choosing something neither of them wanted to eat and had gone away sulking, he suddenly imitated the waiter – his looming shoulders, his patronising expression and his accent – so accurately that she burst out laughing. He smiled, then, and was momentarily at ease, but it didn't last. He saw her home, but when she asked whether he would like to come in, he said no, he had to go home. Then he said that he had to go down to the country to see his parents and wouldn't be about for a few days. 'Ring me when you get back,' she said. 'Thank you for coming,' he answered. If they were in a play, she thought, it was as though he had heard some dreadful piece of gossip about her that had changed his view of her. Of course it couldn't be that. But in the days that followed, while she went to the shop, cleaned her flat, paid a visit to the Duchy and Aunt Rach, wrote to poor Wills at his school and had her father, who was clearly missing Uncle Rupe and Zoë, to supper, she wondered about him – Gerald, she called him now to herself, although they had not used each other's names at all.

Then, the following week, she got a telephone message from the builders who were doing his flat with some query that she knew she could only sort out on the site. So she went to Ebury Street and found the expected mess of plaster dust, broken brick and floorboards up. They were altering the partition walls to make the kitchen larger and this meant moving the services. She noticed that the camp bed had been moved to the middle of the room, as the electrician had the floor up round the skirting boards. It had newspapers spread all over it, held down by some of the bricks, and the telephone, covered with dust, lay beside it.

'Wouldn't it be easier to dismantle the bed?' she asked. 'It's only a camp bed – it would pack away.'

'Can't do that because the gentleman is sleeping on it,' Mr Doncaster said. 'Really be easier if he'd move out for a week or two, but there it is.'

'He's back, then?'

'Mr Lisle? Only went away for one night. He's back, all right. It means getting the services back on for him – barring the hot water, of course – every night. That takes time, you know.'

'Let's look at the problem, then,' she said. She felt dispirited that he had been back for days and hadn't rung her. She wondered whether he had known that she was coming this morning and had gone out to avoid her. She also wondered fleetingly why she minded.

That evening, when she had had supper and was doing her ironing, she decided that she missed Gerald because she was lonely with Clary being away. When she had finished, she found herself sitting at her small davenport with a piece of paper on which she had so far written:

GERALD

cons:

He does look rather like a frog.

He said he was going away for a 'few days' and he didn't (untruthful).

He wears pretty awful clothes. (Must be dirty too, living in that mess.)

He bites his nails.

He doesn't seem to want to do anything (have a career).

He's very changeable. I thought he really liked me, but he can't or he would have rung up. (He pretended to like me?)

He seems to have a horrible family.

Then she got stuck. So she started the other column.

pros:

I like talking to him.

He makes me laugh.

He has extremely considerate manners.

He hasn't made a pass at me like most people after about two meetings.

He doesn't show off at all. (What about? Well, he might have shown off about parachute jumping – being brave in the war and all that.)

He likes cats – and other animals.

He is very uncomplaining.

I actually like him more than most people.

He has a very nice voice.

Good ears.

Good hands except for the nails (a detail).

She stopped there and reviewed the page. He was uncomplaining about what sounded like a fairly horrible life – being the least favourite child, and being sent away all the time, and them killing his cat, and then having all of the war to fight. But was this because he was a weak character and hadn't stood up to his parents or anyone else, or was he simply stoic about misfortune?

Clary – and Louise, ages ago – had said that she should be careful about being sorry for people; Louise had even said that she would probably marry someone simply because she was sorry for them. This used to be true of her, she thought, but she was experienced now: at least four people had made her feel sorry for them because they said they were so madly in love with her and she didn't love them back. Well, Christopher hadn't behaved like that, and it had made her feel sorrier for him than the others, but she still hadn't felt she ought to agree to love or marry him. So she needn't worry about any of that any more. She'd also been through all the misery of unrequited love with Archie; looking back on that, she could hardly understand it. Archie was, of course, a very nice man, but she was actually relieved that he hadn't been in love with her. That afternoon when he'd come back from France because of Clary, she'd been awfully grateful that he'd come because she'd known that he would know what to do for Clary, but looking at him, she'd seen how old he was – looking older, of course, because of his sleepless night – and that he was not someone she wanted to kiss or spend the night with. She had asked Clary what that part of being in love was actually like; in fact, she'd more or less asked her three times, although she'd only put the question baldly once. 'I'm not quite sure,' Clary had said to the bald question. 'I don't feel I've got the hang of it yet – Noël says it's my bourgeois upbringing – but I will tell you, Poll. I won't be like everyone else in our family about it.' The next time that she asked was more round-about: 'How's it going?'

And Clary had thought for a bit before she said, 'I'm not absolutely sure, but I have a sort of feeling that it's mostly for men – only people don't tell you that.' And the last time, just before she knew – or, rather, before Clary had told her – that she was pregnant, Clary had looked at her with a hunted expression. 'It's simply to do with Nature, and you know what Nature's like . . .' Then she said, 'But it doesn't really matter if you love the other person.' Then she had said, 'Do stop cross-examining me!' and burst into tears. So when Archie had turned up that day, she'd been glad to see him, but she'd known that she didn't love him enough to go through all that.

She read through the piece of paper again. At the bottom of the pros, she wrote, 'I would quite like to see him again.' Then, at the bottom of the cons, she wrote, 'He doesn't seem to bother about me much.'

The next evening she rang him up.

'Who is it?' He sounded extremely wary.

'It's me. Polly.'

'So it is!' He sounded pleased now.

'I wondered if you'd like to come to lunch over the weekend.'

'I've got a car. Couldn't we go somewhere and have a walk somewhere where there's grass and trees and I could take you out to lunch?' He arranged to pick her up at eleven on Saturday morning.

It was easy, she thought. If you wanted to see someone, you simply asked them. Why hadn't he asked her?

He arrived promptly, in a different but equally old tweed suit – this one had leather patches on the elbows and a blue shirt with a rather frayed collar. His car proved to be a battered old Morris Minor. 'Where to?' he said, when he had handed her into her seat.

'I thought we could go to Richmond Park. Or Kew – or Hampstead Heath?'

'You choose,' he said.

'Richmond Park is the most countryish.'

'Do you know the way?'

'I'm afraid not.'

'That's all right. I've got a map.'

When he'd finished with the map, he put it on her lap. 'In case I make a mistake,' he said, 'but I think I can remember it. Awfully glad you rang up.'

'You could have rung me.'

'In a way I could. I wasn't sure . . .' His voice trailed off. Then he said, 'I'm really a sort of job for you, I know that. I didn't want to – overstep the mark.'

'I don't think there is a mark,' she said. She felt entirely light-hearted.

They walked in the park for two hours. It was one of the best autumn days that month: mild, with hazy sun, pale blue sky, the trees still thick with bronzed and livid leaves and distant small herds of deer. During the walk he told her that his father was very ill and that that was why he had been away. 'I thought he might want to see

375

me,' he said, 'but he didn't. So in fact I only stayed one night.'

'Is your mother very upset?'

'Can't tell. She's never very anything. She doesn't talk to me much.'

'He will get better, won't he?'

'No, I don't think so.' He didn't seem to want to talk about it. But much later, when they were having lunch, he said, 'Actually, I'm quite worried about my mother, if my father dies. I'm not sure what she'll do.'

A vision of his mother taking sleeping pills or drowning herself came instantly to Polly's mind. 'You mean, she is – will be – terribly unhappy?'

'Not that. No, she's always hated our house, and she's talked for ages now about going to live on the Riviera somewhere. But I don't think she's got much idea about money, not that I'm all that good at it, but I'm pretty sure there's nothing much left.' Then he said he didn't want to talk about that any more, and that she should tell him more about her family. 'They sound much more fun.' So she did; they were back to the same kind of ease with each other that had obtained when he had come to her house, when they slipped easily from one subject to another as though they had known one another for years but had not met for some time, with the result that a great deal had piled up to talk about.

After lunch he said what would she like to do? What would he like? 'I don't mind as long as we do it together,' and he began to blush. 'But perhaps you've had enough for the day.'

They went to the Tate Gallery. 'I don't know anything about pictures,' he said. 'I don't even know what I like. I bet you do, though.'

'We had a governess who used to take us. She especially loved Turner. I'll show you.' This was a success.

'He really is most awfully good. I mean, I like looking at them.'

They went back to Polly's and she made tea and toast with Marmite on it, and then he went out and bought an evening paper to see if they wanted to go to a film. She felt worried about his spending money on her because she knew he wasn't earning any and it didn't sound as though his family gave him much, if anything. But when she said couldn't they share the cinema, he said, 'It's all right: I've got quite a bit of my gratuity, because my aunt gave me three thousand pounds to buy somewhere to live and do it up. So really I'm temporarily flush.'

They found a cinema showing *I Married a Witch* and then they had supper and then he took her home. Their parting was awkward.

He saw her out of the car and up to her front door.

'Thank you for a lovely day,' she said.

'Oh, no! I should thank you.'

They stood for a moment, looking at each other, and then he said, 'Well! Just see that your key works, and then I must be off.'

So she made her key work and he said, 'Well – good. I'll be off.' And went.

She walked slowly up the stairs wondering how, although they seemed to be very intimate in some ways, they were still utterly impersonal. He'd never once made what people in her childhood described as 'personal remarks'. She remembered how, when reproved for making them herself, she had thought how much more interesting they were than many of the other kind. But Gerald – she had not called him that – had never once said anything to her that could remotely be described as personal. He had not even called her Polly. She felt slightly piqued by this. She had taken her usual trouble about her clothes and appearance generally, and she was used to people saying, 'That blue looks lovely with your hair, or matches your eyes perfectly,' things of that nature, that she had not particularly noticed at the time but noticed now because of their absence. She had quite wanted to hug him when they parted because she felt sad that the day had come to an end; it had even crossed her mind to ask him in, but then she'd felt nervous at the idea. He might have thought that she expected him to stay the night, with all that that might have implied, and with the experience of poor Clary fresh in her mind, she was not going to take any plunge. But I suppose I would have liked to be led to the water, she thought. I wouldn't have minded if he'd wanted to kiss me; in fact, it might have been a good idea to find out what it would be like. But, of course, it's no earthly good if he doesn't want to. And he showed no signs of wanting to. Oh dear, she thought, the people who I wish would just be friends don't want to be that at all, and when I would quite like someone not to be just that, it seems to be all they want to be.

The next morning the telephone rang at nine. It was him, and she felt a rush of pleasure when she heard his voice. 'I hope I'm not ringing you too early.'

'No. I'm just having coffee and toast. What about you?'

She was just about to say why didn't he come over and join her, when he said, 'When I got back last night there was a telegram. My father died yesterday morning.'

'Oh!'

'So I'm afraid I've got to go down there and see to things. The funeral and all that. I think I'll be away about a week. I just wanted to tell you.'

'Yes.'

She started to say she was sorry, but he interrupted. 'It's all right. There's nothing you can say. I just wanted you to know. So you wouldn't think I'd just vanished. Not that it would necessarily matter if I had.'

'It would!'

'Would it?' His voice was suddenly tender. Then he said goodbye in his usual tone.

She did not hear from him for ten days. She spent half of that time not thinking about him – that is to say, if she started to she quickly thought of something else – and the other half trying to get his flat more habitable for his return. The wiring and plumbing were finished, the floors were sanded, and she'd had the bars and the black-brick area wall painted white.

After a week, when Gerald had still not returned, she organised the painter for his flat and told him to do the bedroom first in case the owner came back. Caspar gave her another job – a studio flat overlooking the river where the conversion had already been done and she had simply to design and organise its décor. Ordinarily she would have been excited at the promotion; now she was just grateful to have something to do to take her mind off things. What things? she wondered as she boarded a bus to meet the new client on site. Was she beginning to fall in love with Gerald? If so, why? If she thought about him dispassionately, there really didn't seem to be any good reason for this. He seemed aimless, and he certainly couldn't be described as good-looking; he was kind and she enjoyed being with him but that was probably because she didn't know him well enough to be bored by him. Perhaps she had just reached the age where she wanted to be in love with somebody so whoever came along became the object. This was a depressing thought and, because it depressed her, she thought it was probably true.

Her client turned out to be a young man – he said he worked in the City – who wanted the studio as a *pied à-terre*. 'My wife and children are in the country,' he said, 'but I've found commuting a bore.'

He seemed very young to have a wife and children, although he was beginning to go bald. 'It's on the small side, but I was rather taken with the view, and it's handy for getting to the bank. I want it kept quite simple, but I may want to bring people back to it from time to time, so I'd like it to look good.' The studio was quite large, but the bedroom was small and the kitchenette and bathroom barely adequate.

'The bedroom is rather a problem, isn't it? By the time you've got a bed in it, there's hardly room for cupboards.'

'Oh, I thought I'd use it just as a dressing room and sleep in the studio. I like a really large bed.' As he said this, she caught him eyeing her speculatively.

She had brought samples of paint colours and swatches of curtain material which she laid out on the draining board in the kitchen, but he did not seem very interested. She asked whether he had furniture, or whether he wanted it bought for him. 'Oh, you buy it,' he said. 'Get some modern stuff – we're loaded with antiques in the country. Annabel's mad for them.'

When she was putting away the samples in her case,

he came up behind her and said, 'Has anyone ever told you how surprisingly attractive you are?'

She felt hands on her shoulders, which turned her round to him. 'Quite enough people,' she said.

'I was thinking we might have lunch.'

'No, thank you.'

'Don't get on your high horse. I really do find you extraordinarily fetching.'

'Has anyone ever told you how patronising you are?'

His smile faded. 'There's no need to be unpleasant. I only asked you to lunch.'

'No, you didn't.' She shut her case and walked to the door as deliberately as she could manage, but her knees were shaking.

'You have a high opinion of yourself, haven't you?' He said it with a kind of feeble malice; she felt she'd won.

But when she got back to the shop, she found that he'd telephoned to cancel the job. 'I've told you before, you must not be rude to clients,' Caspar said. 'I don't know what you said to him, but you certainly did upset him. Rolling in money, too. Gervase won't be at all pleased.'

'He made a pass at me,' she said. 'I'm sorry.'

'I dare say he did. You're a big girl now, darling. Be your age.' She didn't get the rise that had been hinted at that morning.

On Friday morning Gerald rang her early before she left for work. 'I do hope you don't mind,' he said, 'but I have a favour to ask you. Are you by any chance free this weekend? . . . Oh, good. Well, would it be possible for you to take a train to Norwich tomorrow morning? I'll meet you. I'm still in the country, you see. I've got a bit of a problem about my parents' house. And you're so good at that sort of thing. I thought you would know what to do.'

She agreed to catch the nine thirty from Liverpool Street.

'It's really wonderful of you to come. Bring warm clothes – it's rather a cold house.'

In the train she wondered about the house and why it was a problem. Perhaps his mother was going to live abroad, and he was being left with having to sell it. She had never been to Norfolk. Perhaps it was a farmhouse with beams everywhere and smoky steaming log fires. She was just being romantic; it could as easily be a modern house – a bungalow, even. Anyway, there was such a housing shortage that, whatever it was, it shouldn't be too difficult to get rid of, if that was what they wanted.

He was standing on the platform; she saw him before he saw her and she felt the same rush of pleasure at the sight of him as she had at the sound of his voice on the telephone. He wore a polo-necked jersey under the tweed jacket with leather elbows. 'There's lunch of a sort at home,' he said, 'if you can hold out till then. It's about twenty miles.'

'I don't mind.'

He had a different – somewhat larger but equally battered – car: 'It was my father's,' he said. 'It's marginally more comfortable.'

'Is your mother . . . ?'

'She left immediately after the funeral. A friend has taken her to France for a holiday. It's quite a relief, really. It means at least I can try to sort things out in peace.'

He sounded as though he had been having a difficult time, she thought. 'Is there a lot to sort out?'

'Well, in one way there is. But every decision seems

to depend upon another one, and it's not easy to know where to start, so I thought I'd start with you.'

'How do you mean?'

'I'll tell you later. I don't want to talk about it now. Tell me about your week.'

So she told him about the studio flat and its owner. She thought she made it sound quite funny, but she saw him scowl and then glare ahead at the road.

'Insufferable lout,' he said, 'but I suppose, looking as you do, you come in for rather a lot of that sort of thing.'

'The thing was, I lost the job, and Caspar and Co. weren't best pleased.'

'What's so depressing about that,' he went on, as though she hadn't said anything, 'is that he can't have known what you're like. But I suppose that sort of person doesn't care.'

A few miles later, he said, 'Do women ever feel like that man? I mean, do they mostly notice what men look like?'

'Not so much, I don't think. I mean, of course they do talk about men being handsome and all that.'

'Do they? I thought they might.'

'Well, they do in books. But I don't know how much you can trust *them*.'

After another silence he said, 'At least my mother turns out to have some money of her own. She's all right – she can easily live in the south of France if she wants to. And she absolutely doesn't want to go on living here.'

'So she'll want to sell the house?'

'The house? Well, actually, my father left it to me. That's rather the point. He hasn't left me any money – there wasn't any to leave.'

He turned off the road into what she thought at first

was a cart-track, but when an avenue of large trees began each side of it she realised that it was some sort of disused drive. Beyond the trees on either side there was parkland, studded with more enormous trees, most of which appeared to be dying or already dead. After about a quarter of a mile the parkland stopped and the avenue became woods that arched over the drive cavernously. Then they emerged from the wood and, turning a sharp corner, she saw across further park an enormous building splayed across the skyline. It was a yellowish colour with three square towers. The avenue had stopped, had been felled, and sawn logs lay on either side. The building was further away than she had thought, since they continued to bump along the drive for some minutes without it seeming appreciably nearer, but gradually, windows winked in the cold sunshine, and she saw that it was built of bricks that looked like clean London stock, with stone facings, and that the towers were pink brick, crenellated with stone battlements. It looked as though it might be a hospital or an Edwardian hotel, and was, she thought, the ugliest large building she had ever seen in her life. He had been completely silent, but now, as they got within a hundred yards of the place, he drew up and stopped the engine. In the silence that followed, she could hear the distant cawing of rooks. 'You can see my mother's point,' he said. 'It's stately without being much of a home.' Then he turned to her. 'It appals you. I was afraid it might. That's why I had to show it to you. Anyway, let's go and have some lunch in it.'

He started the engine and they drove up to the front of the house. The front façade – about the length of a tennis court – was flanked by two wings running at an angle. The forecourt, which must once have been lawn, was a desolate and tangled jungle of thistles, nettles and ragwort. The wings, each ending with its pink-brick tower, had an archway where they joined the main part of the house. He drove through the right-hand one of these, to reveal a further courtyard surrounded by buildings that looked as though they had been stables and garaging. 'We go in here,' he said, and opened a glass-fronted door. 'Perhaps I'd better lead the way.'

She followed him down a wide dark passage, and through a second pair of doors. The chill struck her at once. Here, the passage, which continued, was lighter as there were skylights at regular intervals. Towards the end of it, he turned left through a mahogany door into what seemed like a small hall, since it had other doors, all in one wall. He opened one of these and shouted, 'Nan! We're back,' shut it and went to another one, which revealed a small sitting room, with a gate-legged table set for lunch. A very small coal fire burned in the grate. 'It's marginally warmer in here,' he said. 'There's some sherry, if you'd like it. Come and sit by the fire while I get it.'

While he was out of the room, she examined it. It had a very high ceiling, and the walls had beading on them in panels that were painted green with the beading in a paler shade. The chimneypiece was grey marble and there was one very tall window that looked on to a further courtyard with the third pink-brick tower; this was crowned by a cupola below which was a clock whose hands registered twenty past four. The curtains were an oatmeal linen with a pattern of acanthus leaves sparsely embroidered in green wool, and there was a glass-fronted bookcase crammed with a set of dark blue books all bound in the same manner. A wireless, its front fretted like a setting sun, stood on one of the several small tables that were dotted about, beside the sofa, beside each of the two armchairs, in one of which she sat, and beneath a large glass case of dusty stuffed birds. It was all surprising – and rather exciting – she thought. And if the house was as full of furniture as this room, they could have a very enjoyable time choosing things for his flat.

He came back with the sherry, closely followed by an elderly woman in a flowered overall with a tray. 'Now, then, Mr Gerald, you don't want to go wasting the young lady's time with drink. You know what it's like getting hot food along these passages – your soup's none too warm as it is.' She put the soup on the table and cast a shrewd look at Polly. 'Good morning, Miss.'

'We could put some sherry into the soup,' he said.

'Oh! You do as you please, your lordship! The bird is resting. I'll bring it in ten minutes.'

When she had gone, he poured sherry into glasses and said, 'She's always bossed me about. She means no harm.'

'I thought any minute she'd call you Smarty-boots.'

'I could get her to say that simply by answering her back. Nannies' habits die hard.'

'She was your nannie?'

'She was. She's always been here. She's spent practically her whole life looking after us. That's another thing.'

'What do you mean?'

'I must look after her now.'

The soup was tinned mushroom and they both put their sherry into it.

'After lunch, I thought we'd go over the whole place,' he said. 'There are some rooms that I've practically never been in, and I should think a lot of it's in a pretty awful state.'

'I suppose that might make it difficult to sell.'

'Sell? I can't sell it. It's been left to me through some awful trust that means I can't get rid of it.'

'Oh!' She began to see why he'd seemed so abstracted.

'Perhaps something like the National Trust might help?' She'd heard Caspar talking about them.

'They wouldn't touch it with a barge-pole. It's not only in a frightful state, it's frightful anyway.'

'So what are you going to do?'

'I don't know. It depends on – things. I haven't decided.'

The next course was roast chicken with bread sauce and mashed potatoes and swedes.

'When people talk about white elephants,' he said, 'I think how much nicer it would be to have one of them.'

'Wonderful lunch,' she said to Nan, after a slice of Bakewell tart, and was rewarded by a smile.

'I do like to see a nice clean plate,' she said.

'We're going to look at the house now, Nan.'

'Mind yourselves with the ballroom floor. And don't go trying to open any of the windows. You can call me when you're ready for your tea.'

'Might as well do the ground floor first as we're on it.'

He led the way. Another passage with glass-fronted doors opened on to a vast hall from which rose a double staircase with a stone balustrade, and a pair of glass-fronted doors that led to the main entrance. To the left of these was a drawing room, the walls upholstered in damask silk which had faded badly since there were gaps on the wall where pictures had hung that were almost garish pink by comparison. The furniture was mostly covered with dust-sheets; a dead starling lay on a heap of soot in the fireplace. Two doors, one each side of the fireplace, led to the ballroom, the long wall of which had four large windows that looked on to a conservatory. The roof was largely broken; great splinters of glass lay on the floor, which was paved with tiles. A fat rusty pipe, like a python, ran round the room about a foot from the floor. Earthenware pots and glazed urns were full of dusty soil and dead ferns. In one of these she saw a tiny pencil with a silk tassel, the tassel faded to a dirty white. Windows on the outside wall looked on to the wreck of a formal garden and, beyond it, a low brick and stone balustrade.

'This must have been marvellous!' Polly said, as they walked past an ancient camellia whose topmost branches had literally gone through the glass roof. She caught his eye when she said that, and thereafter was conscious of his casting many anxious, enquiring glances.

The next room was what had been the library. The shelves were still there, and it was about half full of books. One wall was decorated by a rather jazzy black and white fungus and the room had a strong mushroom smell. And so on. Two more sitting rooms, a study with a wallpaper so dark that it was almost black, and a vast partner's desk littered with papers. Unlike most of the rooms they had seen this showed signs of fairly recent occupation: there was a smell of pipe tobacco and the fire was freshly laid. 'My father used to spend a lot of time in here,' he said. 'I think we'd better tackle the next floor. The other rooms here are just gun room, boot room, pantry, telephone room and lavatories – that sort of thing.'

'How many bedrooms are there?' she asked, as they went up the staircase from the main hall.

'I don't know. We could count if you like.'

At the top of the staircase was a very wide passage

that ran in both directions, lit by a regularly placed series of round windows set almost at ceiling level. The ceiling was vaulted in a Gothic manner. The bedroom doors were mahogany with small brass-edged frames pinned at eye-level to the wood. In one of them a card was slotted. 'Lady Pomfret' was written on it in beautiful copperplate. 'For weekend parties,' he said, 'they used to put the visitors' names on the doors so that people knew where they were, and other people knew where they were. Edwardian high jinks,' he said gloomily. 'My mother simply loved talking about that sort of thing. When she married my father it was still going on.'

The bedrooms were all much the same. Many had dressing rooms adjoining that each contained a single bed, a chest of drawers, a wardrobe, a smaller fireplace. Again, dust sheets prevailed; many of the carpets were neatly rolled and tied with tape. There were fifteen bed-rooms on that floor and two bathrooms; the lavatory pans were blue and white porcelain. Two of the bedrooms had basins.

'There's an attic floor as well,' he said, 'but perhaps you've had enough for one day?'

'Oh no! I'd like to see it all.'

So up they went.

'I suppose the things in the house belong to you?' She wondered whether the mother would come and take anything nice.

'Oh, yes. Every single thing.' He sounded so despondent that she nearly laughed.

The attics were clearly where the servants had slept – a good many of them, judging by how many attics there were. But in one of them she made a discovery. They very nearly hadn't gone into it – the light was fading and the rooms were all drearily alike. He suggested going down for tea, but there seemed to be only two doors left unexplored, so she said, 'We might as well finish the job.'

The first was exactly like the others: a small window facing the battlements, thus concealed from public view, and an iron bedstead, the mattress gone, a hard chair, a painted chest of drawers, a single lightbulb hanging from the ceiling, the faded flowered wallpaper, the tiny grate never used . . .

'Last one,' he said, as he opened the door. It was exactly like all the others except for one thing. The walls were four deep in very small watercolours, widely mounted and in identical gilt frames. This was so surprising that she went to examine one. It was a sunset over a stretch of wild seashore, and it was somehow familiar. She looked at others. They were all full of skies and light at different times of the day: of landscapes, seascapes, their weather and their seasons, storms, sunrises, thundery winters, sunlit summers, balmy autumns – all by the same hand. She took one off the wall and carried it to the window. 'J. M. W. Turner' was clearly discernible in the bottom right-hand corner.

'Come and look!'

'It's rather good, isn't it?' he said. 'My mother loathed watercolours unless they were done by her, so I suppose she just bunged all these in a maid's bedroom to be out of the way.'

'Have you noticed the signature?'

He looked, and then looked at her. 'Good Lord! The chap we saw in the Tate! What an extraordinary thing!'

'You've never seen them before?'

'Never. They must have been here for ages. It's a good thing, because if my mother had realised about them she'd have sold them like a shot. She sold all the good pictures – whenever she needed money, in fact.' He watched her put the picture back on the wall, then he said: 'I suppose they're all Turners?'

'You could take one to London to find out. I should think that if one of them is they all will be.'

'How many are there?'

They both counted.

'Forty-eight,' he said.

'Fifty-two. There are four behind the door.'

'He must be awfully valuable,' he said; he seemed rather dazed.

'Yes.'

'So – if I sold them, I'd have some money?'

'Of course you would. Only – won't there be death duties?' She'd heard her father talking about them when the Brig died.

'I don't think there will. When Mr Crowther read me the will, it turned out my father left the house and all its contents first to my brother, and then, when he died, to me. He never told us. And, anyway, it's all tied up in some ghastly trust, so it can't be sold or blown up or anything like that. I suppose, actually, these pictures would be worth thousands of pounds?'

'Thousands.'

'Enough to repair the house, do you think?'

'Honestly, I don't know. I should think so.'

'But probably not enough to do that and live in it,' he said.

As they were leaving the room, he suddenly said, 'Have one!'

'Have what?'

'A picture. Choose one. Well, do it tomorrow, when

you can see them better. Choose the one you like best. You found them, after all.'

'I can't possibly. It's very kind of you,' she added, 'but I don't think you've taken in how – well, how valuable they are. And you need the money.'

'I suppose I do. A bit of me would quite like to sell the Turners, buy Nan a cottage and just lock the doors here and never come back. What do you think of that?' They had reached the main staircase now. He said, 'Would you mind awfully sitting on the stairs while I talk to you about something? If we go down, Nan will interrupt us with rock cakes.'

'All right.'

'First, I really do want you to have a picture. If you won't choose one, I'll have to, and I'll get it wrong.'

Before she could answer, he said, 'Otherwise, what do you think of what I said just now? About leaving the house, and all that?'

'I suppose,' she said slowly – she was trying to imagine being him – 'it depends whether you love it at all. Because if you do, and you abandon it, it might haunt you, rather.'

'If you were left it, what would you do?'

'Oh, I think I'd try to live in it. I'd make bits of it, at least, comfortable, and then I'd see how it went.'

'Would you?'

She remembered then his saying something like that on the telephone to her – and just in the same way. This time she could see him. He was fixed upon her, earnest as well as tender. 'Then I must take the plunge – would you live here with me? Would you marry me and do that? Would you at least consider it?'

'I don't need to consider it,' she said, discovering how little she needed to do that.

'You mean it? You really will actually marry me?'

'I want to marry you.' It seemed to her then that she had always wanted to marry him – had never had a single doubt.

'I've wanted to marry you from the moment I saw you,' he said. 'And then, the more I saw you, the more I wanted to. But I didn't think I had a hope. And then, just when I was beginning to hope that I had a hope all this happened about my father dying and getting saddled with this place and not having any money . . . I thought you ought to see it all . . . and then the Turners . . .'

'I would have married you without a single Turner.'

'Would you?'

When he had kissed her – a sweet and long kiss – and they had drawn a little apart she saw how his radiance transformed him.

'Your eyes are like stars – like those sapphires that have a star in them,' he said, as she put her arms round his neck.

They spent an unknown amount of time on the stairs in a state of joyful ease, not saying very much until the dusk had become dark and they were interrupted by the distant booming of a gong.

'That'll be Nan with our tea.' He took her hand and they crept carefully down the staircase to the door that led on to the passage where he felt for and found a light switch. Weak yellow light illuminated the passage that led back to the room where they had had lunch; the fire had been made up and the table set for tea.

Nan appeared at once as if by magic. 'I took the

liberty of calling you because as we all know drop scones won't wait for anyone,' she said. She had given them one shrewd glance, and then busied herself with a covered dish and a silver teapot on the table.

After one long look at Polly, he said, 'We're going to be married, Nan, and you're the first to know.'

She straightened up from setting the table and wiped her hand on her overall. 'I did wonder,' she said, and shook Polly's hand. 'I hope you'll be very happy,' she said. 'I've known him since before he was born and there's not an ounce of vice in him.'

'You make me sound like a horse!'

'Don't be silly,' she said. 'Your young lady can see you're not a horse.' She turned to Polly. 'You have your nice tea if his lordship will condescend to pour you a cup. You can call me when you're finished.'

'She approves of you, my darling Polly – may I call you Polly, by the way?'

'Unless you want to stick to Miss Cazalet – or,' she found she enjoyed saying this for the first time, 'I suppose, in due course, Mrs Lisle.'

'Well, actually, that's another thing. I'm afraid you won't be Mrs Lisle. You'll be Polly Fakenham. Chronic association with me turns you into a lady.'

'You mean when she said your lordship she meant it?'

'We could be called Lisle if you prefer it. Being a lord usually turns out to be more expensive, and as you know, I've hardly got a bean. All I can offer you is the froglike devotion of a lifetime.'

'No. I think I should enjoy being Lady Fakenham. It sounds like someone in an Oscar Wilde play.'

'It goes with the house,' he said. 'And, after all, when we're quite alone, you can always call me Gerald.'

Hours later she lay in a surprisingly comfortable bed in one of the many spare rooms, clutching a stone hot-water bottle to her and wearing an old white long-sleeved nightdress, procured for her by Nan, and thought about this amazing day during which so much had happened to change her life. She lay in the dark so crammed with memories that were randomly of this day and of days long gone before it – of lying on the grass at Lansdowne Road with Louise telling her she'd marry one of the people who proposed to her out of sheer kindness, and for years afterwards being afraid that that might actually happen . . . and here she was, with Gerald, and kindness didn't come into it. And Dad, at his club when she was having dinner with him saying that one day she would fall in love and get married 'but you have to meet people to find the right one'. And she had gone to that party that she hadn't wanted to go to and met him. Tomorrow she would ring Dad and say that she wanted to bring someone to meet him and he would guess at once why, and then when he met Gerald, of course he'd be fearfully relieved at how wonderful Gerald actually was. Here, the thought intervened that her mother would never know that, and grief, which had seemed deeply buried, sprang freshly from its grave. I've simply got used to missing her, she thought, but I shall always miss her. I'm far luckier than poor Wills, because I have so much more of her to remember. Then she thought about Gerald again to comfort her. She thought how funny he was when he felt at ease. There had been no shortage of personal remarks that evening, either: he had never stopped making them – in fact, he thought she was much more beautiful, interesting and charming than she really was. What would Clary think of it all? She felt she knew now that Clary could not really have been in love with Noël: she had been far too anxious and unhappy throughout the whole affair to have been that, and the end of it had been awful for her. After the abortion, when she had seemed sunk in a kind of stupor, Archie had made her go and live in a cottage he had found for her and write her book. He went down at weekends to cheer her up and urge her on – at least, that was what she supposed, because when she had suggested going down, Clary hadn't seemed to want her to come. They had grown apart, and she was afraid that the contrast now between their lots would make this worse. It won't. It can't. I really love her, she thought. She had told Gerald about Clary this evening – all of it – and he had listened properly and seemed really to mind. Clary would like Gerald and she would come and stay. The house would make her laugh, though: it was so unlike the house that Polly had so often carefully described to her that one day she was going to have, it was almost the opposite; rather a challenge, she thought slowly – she was getting rather drowsy. There were so many rooms, it would probably take her all her life . . . she thought about some of the new things she had learned about Gerald. He could play the piano and he rode very well. These pieces of information had come from Nan, and had been the only two occasions when he had reverted to blushing – something that had otherwise stopped. 'I was so in awe of you,' he had said, 'you seemed such a marvel. You know, like looking closely at a butterfly's wing – every detail is perfect.'

Tomorrow they were going to explore outside. There

was a lake, choked with water-lilies and weed, he said, and a rose garden, but the roses hadn't been pruned for years and it was full of weeds, and there were four glass-houses, falling to bits, and a walled garden for vegetables (this had been when they had discussed the possibility of growing asparagus as a way of making money). There was a bluebell wood, and other woods, but most of the farmland had been sold off. His mother had been a deter-mined seller of anything that would raise money. This had come out when Nan, chatty from her glass of champagne, had arrived with a small brown-paper package that she had dumped before Gerald.

'Twasn't my business,' she said, 'but there's such a thing as right and wrong, and some of us knows it and some don't. When her ladyship sent all the family jewels up to London to some sale, I couldn't stand the idea that this should go. It was your grandmother's and, as you know, I first went into service with her when I was thir-teen. Your grandmother gave it to your father to give to your mother when they were engaged, but it was too small for her ladyship's finger and she never cared for it. It walked – and nothing was said. If you hadn't married, Mr Gerald dear, I'd have given it to your lordship just the same, though the dear knows what you would have done with it.'

Inside the brown paper was a dark blue leather box and inside that, wedged on its dirty white velvet, was a ring – an oval star sapphire surrounded by diamonds. She felt it with her fingers, remembering what he had said about her eyes after he had kissed her, and was beset by a surge of such pure happiness that she thought she loved not only Gerald, but everybody in the world.

THE WIVES

December 1946–May 1947

'How was your Christmas? Really?'

'Oh, darling! I don't know where to begin.'

Jessica had come to tea, which had been taken with Miss Milliment, and therefore Christmas had been discussed with the stock cheerfulness that said nothing about emotional undercurrents. Jessica had described Nora's Christmas tree with a present for every inmate, and how Father Lancing had brought some of his choir to sing carols, and how she, Jessica, had made four dozen mince pies that had been consumed on this single occasion, and how the pipes had frozen just before the holiday began, and burst just in time for Christmas Eve. Villy had told Jessica about cooking her first Christmas dinner (Miss Milliment had said how good it had been), and how the children had played Racing Demon all over the drawing-room floor and Lydia had accused Bernadine of cheating and Teddy had got very angry. 'And I made a Christmas cake that was like a bomb shelter,' she had said.

Now, Miss Milliment had tactfully retired to her room, Lydia and Roland were out having a Christmas treat with Rachel, and she had Jessica to herself. The room was reasonably warm since, although there was practically no coal to be had, Cazalets' sent a lorryload of off-cuts, and the sisters sat each side of the log fire, Jessica lying on the sofa with her elegant shoes off and she, Villy, in the only comfortable armchair.

Seeing Jessica lying there, looking so well groomed in her beige and green tweed suit with a jumper exactly matching the green, their mother's pearls round her neck and her newly set hair, she felt a pang of resentment. How the tables had turned! Now it was she whose hands were rough with kitchen work, who never seemed to have time to get her hair done, whose clothes each day were chosen for their suitability for housework and keeping warm. It was she who had Miss Milliment to look after, had young children unused to London, who had to be fed and entertained and looked after, and worse, she was having to do this all on her own, whereas Jessica, with her neat little Chelsea house, had a daily maid and a husband.

'I don't think I can begin to convey to you how awful it was,' she said, and instantly, as she had known that she would, Jessica started upon a flurry of flimsy silver linings. 'It must be nice to have Teddy home,' she said.

'Of course I'm glad he's back. But I'm worried about him. Edward' (she pronounced his name with a new, bitter clarity) 'doesn't pay him enough. He has the most awful struggle to make ends meet. And Bernadine – I have them to supper once a week – told me that *that* woman has a housekeeper, a daily woman and someone to look after her child! Something of a contrast to here.'

'Well, darling, you did choose this house—'

'When I thought I was going to live in it with my husband!' There was a short silence, and when she had lit a cigarette, she said, 'And he's bought her a new car!'

'He did give you one, didn't he? The Vauxhall?'

'It's hardly the same, is it? I need one. She has

someone to chauffeur her around.' She smiled then, to show that however awful everything was, she could take it.

Wanting to give her something to smile at, Jessica said, 'Judy says Lydia is tremendously popular at school. She said she was wonderful as Feste. Such a pretty voice. How pleased Daddy would have been.'

'Yes, he would, wouldn't he?' For a moment they were amiably united by nostalgic affection. 'But I expect Mummy would have been simply shocked at her playing a member of the opposite sex. Which would knock out Shakespeare completely for any girls' school.'

'Oh, it didn't,' Jessica said. 'They simply cut out the rude bits and most of the men wear sort of robes anyway. I don't think Shakespeare counted when it came to decorum – even with Mummy.'

'How's Judy?'

Jessica sighed. 'Going through a difficult phase. She argues with Raymond, which he doesn't like at all, and she somehow seems too big for the house. She's always knocking things over and shouting when one can hear her perfectly well if she simply speaks. I think sixteen is almost the worst age.'

'And Angela?'

'Good news. She's having a baby.'

'Darling, how nice for you!'

'If only she wasn't thousands of miles away, it would be. I want to go over, of course, when it's born, but Raymond won't let me go by myself, and he hates the idea of the voyage. I must say I sometimes almost envy you being free to make your own decisions.' Looking at her sister's face, she retreated from this notion. 'Of course I know it's awful, darling, I really do. But Raymond doesn't like to let me out of his sight, and honestly I do find it claustrophobic. He doesn't like parties, or concerts, or any fun, really. All he wants to do is sit in that coach house he's converting, grumbling about what Nora has done to his house, and bullying the builders.'

There was a silence during which Villy looked at Jessica and thought how astonishingly insensitive she really was. It was all part of what she now had to endure – passing sympathy of the kind one might proffer to someone who had mislaid something, and then reams of stuff about the petty inconveniences of *her* life.

'How is Louise? Isn't it about time—?'

'She hardly comes near me. I think I told you that she was in cahoots with her father about the whole wretched business behind my back – he talked to her before me – and when I did see her she admitted that she'd met that woman, actually had dinner with them, so it's quite clear to me which side she's on.'

'Have you seen him?'

She sensed sympathy. 'Not since some time before Christmas. He asked me to lunch because he wanted me to divorce him.'

'Are you going to?'

'I don't know. Why should I? I don't want a divorce.'

When Jessica didn't reply, she said, 'You think I should?'

'Well, it does sound as though you're in rather a strong position. I mean, if he wants it and you don't. You might get him to make rather more generous provision for you in return for agreeing.'

'I'm not interested in money!'

'Darling, if you don't mind me saying so, that's because you've always had enough of it. I haven't, as you know, and it's made me realise that being unhappy with not enough money is infinitely worse than being unhappy with more. That's all I meant.'

She was trying to help. She was wrong, of course, but she meant well. 'I'll think about it,' Villy said, to close the subject. 'That's a very pretty suit. Did you get it from Hermione?'

'Yes. She's got some very nice tweeds. And it's bliss not to have to stick any more to the utility thing. I always loathed those frightfully short skirts. You should go and look.'

Villy offered a drink, and Jessica said one would be lovely, and then she must go. For the rest of her visit, they stuck to safe subjects . . . Christopher, who had spent Christmas with Nora to help, seemed to have become rather religious, and Father Lancing, who was very High Church, had taken rather a fancy to him, or he to Father Lancing – at any rate, Christopher was always doing things for the parish, running errands and so forth, 'although I think that was partly to get away from Raymond,' she finished. Roland was having lessons with Miss Milliment, but of course next autumn he would really have to go to school, Villy said, although she was not going to send him away. Miss Milliment, apart from being a little deaf, was much the same, although her sight did seem to be worse. Jessica divulged the fact that Raymond and Richard had got rather drunk together on New Year's Eve and that Nora had been outraged. 'But for once I think Raymond was right, and it was good for poor Richard to have a little fun.' Then she had added that it was rather awful to think that getting drunk with Raymond constituted fun, and they had both laughed.

They had become friends again. She felt quite sorry when Jessica left.

Armed with her own clothes coupons and some that the Duchy had given her at Christmas, she did go and see Hermione. She decided to ring up first to be sure that Hermione would be there. She was, and immediately asked her to lunch. She left lunch for Miss Milliment and the children, and promised to be back in time for tea. Lydia had protested, 'Honestly, Mummy, it's terrifically boring having lunch with nobody of my age,' but she was placated by being allowed to make a cake. 'Only you'll have to use dried eggs.'

It was a raw, cold January day; there had been a heavy frost and the sky was dense with what looked like snow; there was ice on the lake in Regent's Park and the grass was white with rime. People waiting for buses in Baker Street looked pinched with cold; it was even cold in the car, and Villy was glad when she reached the cosy shop in Curzon Street. Hermione, as usual, made her feel both distinguished and welcome. 'How too, too lovely that you were able to come! And it's so lucky because my divine chestnut has gone lame so no hunting this week. Miss MacDonald! Look who's here!' and Miss MacDonald, wearing the jacket that matched her pinstriped flannel skirt, appeared from the depth of the shop, and smiled and said how nice it was to see her.

'I'm sure Miss MacDonald could rustle up a cup of coffee – in fact, we'd both like some, if you'd be an angel.' Miss MacDonald smiled again and disappeared.

'What's happened to your neck?'

'I broke it last week. Rory and I rather misjudged the most enormous hedge that turned out to have a horrid ditch on the other side of it. We both came down, but our respective vets have said the damage is superficial. Rory has to rest and I have to wear this horrid collar. Sit down, darling, and let's consider what you would like to see.'

Villy sat on the fat little sofa, newly upholstered in grey damask, while Hermione lowered herself stiffly on to a chair. 'I don't need party clothes. There aren't any parties these days.' She looked up from getting a cigarette out of her bag and met Hermione's shrewd, cool gaze. 'I'm not being sorry for myself,' she said. 'It's simply a matter of fact.'

'I always think the English concept of best clothes that are hardly ever worn is one of the chief reasons why they look so dowdy. One should wear one's best clothes all the time. I think what you need is a really ravishing tweed suit, and perhaps a cosy woollen dress that will lend itself to some of your beautiful jewellery. But we'll see.' They saw for about two hours, at the end of which she had acquired a suit of charcoal and cream tweed with charcoal velvet trimming, a dress in fine facecloth the colour of blackcurrants with long sleeves and a high neck, and a short coat in black doeskin lined with artificial fur. Of course, she had looked at, and tried on, many other things – including, at Hermione's insistence, a long straight evening skirt of black crêpe with a multi-coloured figured-velvet jacket. 'It is lovely, but I'd never wear it,' she said, and realised that for the past two hours she had not, until now, remembered her altered state.

Hermione took her to the Berkeley, where they had a secluded corner table with the head waiter behaving as though Hermione lunching there had filled his cup. When they had settled for hot consommé and a casserole of grouse, Hermione said, 'Now we're out of Miss Mac-

404

Donald's earshot, I really want to know how you are and what is going on. Are you knee-deep in lawyers?'

'No. Edward's lawyer wrote to me once about money, but that's all. Why?'

'Divorces usually have lawyers attached to them. I imagined you were divorcing him.'

'I don't know. He wants me to.'

'That's not a good reason. I think it should be entirely for your sake.'

'Why?'

'Darling, he has behaved abominably. Unless, of course, he has recognised this and wants to change his mind . . .'

'Oh, no. He's set up with her now. They have a household.' She heard, and disliked, the bitterness in her own voice. 'Oh, Hermione, I find it so hideous! I can't stop thinking about it. To know that he's in London, a few miles away, getting up and making plans with her at breakfast – he must drive almost past the end of my road going back to her in the evenings, and his taking her out, going to his club with her so that all the members can see her – they've even been to dinner with people who used to be our friends – and then going back to their house and their bedroom—' She could not go on; her imagination by no means stopped there, but she was ashamed of the disgusting thoughts that so easily took possession of her, night after night, and so frequently rendered her sleepless until they had run their revolting course. Not here! Not in this restaurant, in broad daylight, with Hermione opposite her. She picked up her glass of water and sipped it while she tried to think of something pretty and harmless. 'It's all been such a shock,' she finished lamely, because she had said this so many times before. 'Daffodils', she thought, that cliché-ridden poem of Wordsworth's that Daddy used to love so much. But it was too late. Looking at Hermione's attentive, carefully expressionless face, she felt exposed.

'It is vile for you . . . I can't help feeling that you need to be entirely shot of him so that you can do something else with your life.'

'But what could I do? I'm years past dancing, even if I'd been doing it all my life. I gave all that up for Edward.'

'You might teach – children, perhaps. More and more little girls seem to want to do ballet.'

'I don't think anyone would have me. I'm fearfully rusty.'

'You don't know that.'

For the rest of lunch it seemed to her that every time she explained – with a practical reason – why she would not be able to do something, Hermione simply presented her with something else, until she felt hedged in by possibilities.

As they got back to the shop to collect her new clothes, she said, 'I suppose one of the reasons why I don't want to divorce Edward is that it would mean I was giving in, just doing what he wants and becoming nobody in the process.'

To which Hermione in her light, rather amused drawl, answered, 'I don't think you would. I'm divorced, after all – have been for ages when it was far less acceptable, and I am not a nobody. Never have been.'

'Oh, darling, I'm sorry! Of course you aren't but I'm not glamorous and entertaining and all the things you are.'

'Oh, my dear! What an abject refugee! And here is Miss MacDonald with your sackcloth and ashes.'

She drove home full of the conversation at lunch. Of course, it had not changed her mind but it had provided food for thought. She felt uncertain, excited and fearful; the future branched out before her with more prongs to it than she had been envisaging. Perhaps she could start a small ballet class? This had nothing to do with a divorce – she could not see why Hermione had connected the two things. Perhaps she would talk to Sid, who taught at a girls' school and might have ideas about how one set about getting teaching work.

But when she got home it was to a strong smell of burning cake – and freezing cold, since Lydia had opened all the windows to get the smoke out, she explained. She found Miss Milliment on her knees before the sitting-room fireplace, trying to clear out the grate – the fire had gone out – in order to re-lay and light it. Oh, Lord! she thought. How could I ever think of doing anything? 'I leave you for a few hours and look what happens!' she scolded. 'All those cake materials wasted, and the kitchen looks as though you've been cooking for about two days, Lydia! And why did you let the fire go out? You were in here, weren't you?' She was helping Miss Milliment to her feet as she spoke.

'I fear it was my fault,' Miss Milliment was saying. 'I fell asleep over the crossword after lunch and did not keep an eye on everybody as I should have.'

'You shouldn't have had to. Lydia is quite old enough to have dealt with things.'

'It was Roland who burnt the cake,' Lydia said. 'He turned the gas up to make it cook quicker. I could have told him how stupid that was.'

'And don't tell tales. Will you never learn not to do that?'

'I think at my age it's too late now for me to learn that kind of thing.'

'It was my fault, Mummy. I'm really sorry. We were playing Racing Demon and we forgot the cake. And I'm afraid I fused the lights upstairs because I was doing my experiment and there was a bang. Sorry, Mum. I'll do the fire for you.' He stumped on to the tiled fireplace and there was a scrunching sound that turned out to be Miss Milliment's spectacles, which had fallen off when she was being hauled to her feet.

'Have you got another pair, Miss Milliment?'

'I believe I still have the ones that I had before I left London. They are in my father's old case, as they were his frames. Somewhere. I cannot quite recollect where.'

Hours later, Villy had mended the fuse, got the fire going, shut the windows – it had begun to snow – set Lydia to clearing up the kitchen and Roland to help her with the washing-up, spent ages searching through Miss Milliment's battered and capacious luggage for the spare spectacles, which proved almost useless when they were found, made tea for everyone with toast and potted meat instead of the cake, cleaned the oven and got more wood from the shed in the garden, sent Roland up to have his bath before supper and had another confrontation with Lydia about the state of her bedroom, which resulted in Lydia bursting into tears and then coming to her and saying that she had rung up Polly, who had invited her to supper and she was jolly well going. As this meant one bus down Abbey Road and Baker Street, she allowed it on the understanding that Lydia came back in a taxi for which she gave her money. Lydia went off, white-faced and sulking, and Villy felt miserable about it. As she had been coming downstairs from Roland she had overheard

Lydia on the telephone saying, '. . . it's horrible here', and the phrase, and her daughter's voice saying it, kept repeating in her head. After all her efforts it was horrible!

Roland said he didn't want any supper, and proved to have a temperature. He couldn't have caught cold already – must have been cooking up some ailment before that. She settled him down with an aspirin and a hot drink, and then began to make supper for herself and Miss Milliment who, it was clear to her, could hardly see at all. 'I'll take you tomorrow morning to the optician,' she said, 'and we'll have two pairs of glasses made.' She made herself an extremely strong gin before dinner. It meant that she was going to run out of it before the grocer would let her have another bottle, but she was so tired and dispirited, she didn't care. She gave Miss Milliment her sherry, but the glass got knocked over before she had had more than one sip of it. 'Oh, my dear Viola, what must you think of me?'

'It's quite all right, but I'm afraid there's only a drop left.'

She went to the kitchen to get it. It would probably take a week for the new glasses to be made and she realised that everything about Miss Milliment's life would be a hazard until they were. I shall be more pinned to the house than usual, she thought, as she put the potatoes on to boil, scorching her finger with the match. 'Oh! Damn!' The sudden pain brought tears to her eyes.

When she had given Miss Milliment what remained of the sherry, she topped up her gin without thinking. 'The other half', Edward had always called the statutory second drink. But no sooner had she settled herself upon the sofa than unmistakably she heard Roland crying. 'I don't think he's very well,' she said, and then, as she was pounding upstairs, realised that Miss Milliment had not heard him and therefore hadn't understood what she had said.

He was sitting up in bed, crying. When he saw her, he cried, 'Oh, Mummy! I want you to be with me!'

She sat on his bed and put her arms round him. He was hot and his hair was damp with sweat. 'Darling! How do you feel?'

'Crumbly.' He thought for a moment. 'I feel like a weak old biscuit. Hot and crumbly.'

'Biscuits aren't hot,' she said, stroking his head. His ears stuck out in spite of Ellen taping them back when he'd been a baby, and with his feverishly bright eyes and the widow's peak of his hair that grew, like hers, just off centre, he looked like a small monkey. 'Would you like a drink?'

'A cold drink. There's toast in my bed scratching me.'

She picked him up and put him in a chair wrapped in an eiderdown with a thermometer in his mouth while she tidied his bed which, apart from undeniable crumbs of something, contained his two bears, a dismantled torch, his favourite tin tip-up lorry and some sticking plaster that had come off his knee. 'You've got so many things in your bed, no wonder it's not comfy. Now. Let's see.' His temperature was a hundred and one, in spite of the aspirin.

He began crying again. 'I don't want you to go!'

'I won't be a minute, my darling. Let's put you back in your nice tidy bed, with Tedward and Grizzly.'

When she came back with the drink, he said, 'Why can't we go back to living with Ellen and Wills and Jules and everyone? Why do we have to live in a house by ourselves?'

She explained – not for the first time – about all the family returning to London because the war was over, and coaxed him to drink a little. He was snuffling now, and she helped him to blow his nose. But when she started to tuck him up, he became frantic again. 'I don't want you to go!'

'How would it be if you slept with me tonight? With Tedward and Grizzly in my bed? I'll get you a night-light, and then when you wake up I'll be with you.' That seemed to go down well. She carried him to her room, went downstairs again and found a night-light, which she put in a saucer. When she got back to him, he was lying quite peacefully in her bed. She kissed him and he received her kiss with a dignified satisfaction. As she was leaving the room, he said, 'Mum! I know why Dad doesn't come here.'

'Oh?'

'The ceilings are too low for his head. It might be better if we got a taller house.'

'I'll think about it. Sleep tight.'

She went to tell Miss Milliment that she was now going to get supper, but in the kitchen discovered that the potatoes had boiled dry, had begun to catch on the bottom of the pan. She tipped them out, and cut the burned pieces off them. There was neither milk nor margarine to mash them. She put them on a tray with the remains of a meat loaf she had made. It would have to do. She was too exhausted to think about any other vegetable. She finished her gin; she wasn't hungry, but luckily Miss Milliment wouldn't see if she hardly ate any supper.

But Miss Milliment seemed to know some things whether she could see or not. After they had discussed Roland – she would ring the doctor in the morning – the current strike of the road hauliers, and the food shortages, the desirability or not of using the Army to distribute food supplies and the imminent shortage of potatoes, she said, 'Viola, my dear, there is something I wanted to discuss with you—' but then the telephone rang.

It was Lydia. Polly had asked her to stay the night, was that OK? She'd be back after breakfast. 'Well, for lunch anyway,' she said.

'You haven't got anything with you,' she heard herself weakly (and pointlessly) saying.

'It's OK. Polly will lend me a nightdress and I took my toothbrush just in case she asked me.'

'All right. Have a good time.'

'I am! It's lovely here.'

And horrible here, she thought, as she went back to the sitting room. 'That was Lydia,' she said, as she sat down at the small gate-legged table. 'She's staying the night with Polly,' and then, without any warning, she burst into tears.

Up until now, she had preserved a tight-lipped silence on the subject of being abandoned: she had had, of course, to tell Miss Milliment that Edward was leaving her and going to live with someone else, but she had done it in such a way as to preclude any discussion – or, indeed, any further mention of it. Miss Milliment had listened, had said quietly how very, very sorry she was and that had been that. But now, it all poured out – she could not stop herself: the need to confide her terrible sense of humiliation and failure, her anger at being lied to and betrayed, her resentment that, having been, as she felt, a good wife for all these years and having therefore, in a sense, earned the peace and security of old age in the married state, she should now be faced with the anxiety

and fear of ending her life alone – not that she felt she
had any life to speak of anyway, but now, she felt, she
was going to have to be grateful and obliged to people for
any stray consideration or kindness, neither of which
could, in any case, even assuage her loneliness because
nobody would ever know or care about how desperately
unhappy she was . . . She had stopped there for a moment,
staring at Miss Milliment with streaming eyes. They could
neither of them see each other, but Miss Milliment groped
with her hand across the table until she found Villy's and
held it. And now, she said, Edward wanted her to divorce
him so that he could marry this woman who had
destroyed her life. And people seemed to think that this
was perfectly reasonable. She should not only lose her
husband, but virtually give him to someone else! Jessica,
her own sister, thought something of the kind. And the
friend she'd had lunch with today had seemed to think
that divorce would stimulate her into starting some sort
of career in ballet again – and teaching – since having
given up her real career entirely for Edward she was, of
course, too old to resume it. Think what Mama would
have said about divorce! She stopped here, feeling that
this was the cue for Miss Milliment's shocked agreement.
But it wasn't. 'I do not feel,' she said, 'that Lady Rydal's
views upon such matters can be of much use to you now,
Viola. A very great deal has changed since her day. Had
changed, in fact, long before her death. Divorce no longer
carries the stigma that once it did. It cannot, since there
are now so many – nearly a hundred thousand in the last
two years, I remember reading in the newspaper. No. I
am concerned for your unhappiness. I am acutely aware
of that. It is what I wanted to talk to you about.'

Lydia saying 'it's horrible here' recurred, and she

said, almost angrily, 'Oh! You mean I've been going about with a long face making everybody feel miserable! Well, I don't see what I can do about that. I can't change what has happened.'

'No, you cannot.'

'So?'

'You have to think about what you can change.'

She was silent. She did not know – did not particularly want to know – what her old governess meant; she was almost back to sulking in the schoolroom, remembering how Miss Milliment used to lead, coax, invite her to arrive at conclusions, as it were by her own volition.

'Responses?' Miss Milliment said, after the pause. 'It is possible to change those, and sometimes this can lead to a better understanding.' She waited a moment. 'I think of you as having so much generosity of spirit. I know of no one who takes the trouble to be so constantly and unobtrusively kind as you, my dear Viola. And I have admired this all the more because, ever since you took me in during the war, I have been conscious that your life has disappointed you or, perhaps I should say, has not presented you with the opportunities to realise to the full your considerable gifts. Is that not right?'

It was. It had always been true, but it was a bit late now to change that. 'I'm nearly fifty!'

'My father did not die until I was fifty-three and it was not until his death that I started to earn my living.'

It was different for her. She had had to – there was no money – but Villy did not like to say this.

'Of course, it was necessary for financial reasons. But there are other kinds of necessity, aren't there?'

'You think I should find some work – get a job?'

'I think you might enjoy having something to do that

interested you beyond the domestic round. It is worth thinking about.'

'But even if I did – find something – what has that to do with divorcing Edward? Do you mean I should shake that dust off my feet and say good riddance?'

'Oh, I don't think you would ever do or say that. It is not in your nature. No, presumably that is what he wants and it would be in keeping with your character if you made that gesture towards him.' She was silent for a moment, and then she said: 'I fear you may think that a monstrous suggestion. But whatever you do now will be difficult. Since Edward has gone, and you could not prevent that, remaining married to him in name will keep you trapped, as much as it will him. You will not be able to rid yourself of the idea – however unlikely – that he will return to you, and I fear you may come to hate him because he does not. It is extraordinarily difficult not to hate someone when one feels powerless with them.' A small smile eddied its way from her mouth down into her chins. 'Goodness! How I used to hate my father some-times! And how miserable and wretched that made me feel! My dear Viola, I am afraid I have fallen into the trap of being wise after my own events, as it were. It was so clear to me afterwards – after he died – that I had never made my own wishes known to him, so how could he know that I had any? I saw myself as the dutiful, un-married daughter, sacrificing my life to his comfort. It came to me afterwards that martyrs are not really good domestic company. Poor Papa! How dull it must have been for him.'

Villy became conscious of her hand being stroked. 'I have great love and admiration for you,' Miss Milliment was saying. 'You were always my favourite pupil in those days. Such a good mind! So quick to apprehend and then apply yourself, as I remember telling your dear father. You were his favourite as well.'

Lying in bed beside Roland, with the night-light burning in case he woke (his fever seemed to have broken – his forehead was damp with sweat), she felt the same kind of feverish relief. For the first time in months she could feel the weight of her own body – a welcome lassitude, a fatigue that was certain to be recompensed by sleep. She turned on her side so that she could face her son: the sight of him made her feel weak with love.

∞ ∞ ∞

'I'm afraid I spilled a teeny drop or two, but I think it only went on to the sheet. Not the blankets.' She smiled reassuringly at her daughter and dabbed her mouth with her napkin still in its napkin ring. She was having break-fast in bed, her pink bed-jacket draped round her shoulders. She could not put it on as she had broken her right arm when she slipped getting off a bus some weeks back; it was still in plaster and she had to wear a sling. This had meant, of course, that she was unable to dress or undress herself, had to be helped in and out of the bath, have her food cut up for her and, worst of all, was unable to knit – a pastime that she had so come to rely upon that Zoë recognised its impossibility as a real hardship.

'I'll go and get a cloth.'

'I think it's too late for that, dear. I did it just after you brought my tray, but I didn't call you as I didn't want to be a trouble.'

This remark or, rather, refrain – since it occurred at least half a dozen times a day – had almost, but not quite, ceased to irritate her. There were variations – a burden, a nuisance were two of the other things her mother said she didn't want to be – but in this respect, her wishes seemed doomed. She had been living with them now for nearly three months, and there was no doubt at all that she was quietly, persistently, sometimes unobtrusively one or all of these things.

'I'll take your tray out now and come back later to help you get up.'

'No hurry, dear. At your convenience.'

While she washed the breakfast things, Zoë thought despairingly of the sort of day she would once have had, before her mother came, and the sort of day she would have now. She had known it would be difficult, but the difficulties had been of a different kind from those she had envisaged. She knew now that her mother had changed a great deal since the days in the Earl's Court flat. Years with Maud in the Isle of Wight had accustomed her to being the centre of unremitting attention. She had been treated as a semi-invalid; Maud had made all the dull or difficult decisions for her and, while allowing her to think that she was sharing the chores, had taken on the bulk of them.

When Zoë had brought her mother back to London in November, she had indeed been pathetic, sad, thin, tired, extremely anxious and also – particularly to Rupert – touchingly grateful for being taken in, as she put it. But as she became used to the situation she had gradually encroached upon Zoë's time. She was always talking about Maud – in relation to herself. 'She was such a one for little *treats*,' she would say. 'She would ask somebody to tea and not tell me till the last moment, or I would guess because I could smell her flapjacks in the oven.' Or:

'She loved surprises. She was always thinking up little ways to cheer me up. Once she drove me all the way to Cowes to have tea in Coffee Ann's. And then we went to such a good shop to spend our sweet ration. In summer, she would sometimes make us lunch in the *garden*! She had a sort of rustic bower and a seat – not very comfortable, I must say, but she had an air cushion, which made all the difference. "If you don't mind the earwigs, Cicely," she would say, "we'll have lunch *al fresco* – if you're game." Of course I always was. She took me to the hairdresser once a week. "We must keep up appearances," she would say, "war or no war."' It had been going to the hairdresser that had resulted in her fall. She had, of course, gone on her own, not wanting to be a burden.

The worst of all this was that Zoë felt her exasperation and, indeed, boredom mounting, and hated herself for it. She would tell Rupert this when they were alone, and his responses had changed from defending her mother – 'She's really rather pathetic' – to a wry acceptance that she was, in fact, a bit of a killjoy. Yesterday – the weekend – they had all been having tea, and Juliet had been explaining how at school they fed the birds, but the bread got all hard and frosty for their poor beaks, and then she had said: 'I've got a very good wonderful kind idea for birds, Mummy. I shall spend the whole of next summer collecting worms and keep them in a box and then in winter I'll give the birds one or two at a time – like rations.'

Mrs Headford had said, 'I don't think that worms are very nice for a little girl.'

'I'm not going to eat them, Gran.'

'I mean to talk about, dear.'

'I think they're very nice. I often talk about them. I talk about anything I think of.' And seeing her grand-mother's head shaking at her with a maddening smile, Jules had added, '*You* needn't talk about them if they frighten you.'

Rupert had caught her eye and winked.

They had tried very hard in the early days. Had taken her to the cinema – Anna Neagle and Michael Wilding. That had been a success: she had remarked that Maud had used to say how like she was to Anna Neagle. But when they had anyone to dinner she managed to infest the evening with gentility, with clichés, with a kind of trivial egocentricity that reduced everyone to dull compli-ance. After a particularly unfortunate evening when they had invited Villy and Hugh and she had held forth on her own (and Maud's) views about divorce and refused to be deflected by any attempts on Rupert's part to change the subject, they decided that dinner parties at home were temporarily out. 'It's not just that she puts her foot in it,' Rupert said gloomily, 'she *keeps* it there.'

'I should have told her more about Villy,' Zoë said. 'I did tell her that Edward had left her, but I didn't say that there was going to be a divorce.'

'Well, I think that if we want to see people in the evening, we'd better take them out.'

'But that's terribly expensive, and anyway, Rupe, it's not fair on you.'

'It's not *your* fault.'

'Hugh seemed in good form, though.'

'Yes, he's very pleased about Poll's engagement. He really likes the chap.'

After Mrs Headford broke her arm things got better

about that, because she announced that if there were guests, she would rather have dinner in bed as she found having her food cut up for her embarrassing.

But then first Juliet and then Ellen were ill: influenza, the doctor said – it was raging; people were suffering from being cold nearly all the time since fuel shortages made it impossible to keep either houses or offices warm and the weather continued to be raw. It was the coldest February since 1881. Mrs Headford had knitted her grand-daughter a thick cardigan for Christmas, but, unfortu-nately, she had chosen a pale pink wool, and Juliet hated pink. She stood miserably in the middle of the room while her grandmother admired her.

'Aren't you going to thank your gran with a kiss?'

She walked over to the armchair, shut her eyes tightly, and gave her a quick peck.

'You look so pretty in pink.'

'I don't want to look pretty, Gran.'

Mrs Headford thought this was a joke. At tea, Juliet reappeared minus the cardigan, wearing her father's tweed cap the wrong way round, and a large charcoal moustache. 'This is how I want to look,' she said. She flatly refused to wear the cardigan at all, although every day, without fail, her grandmother asked why she wasn't wearing it, until, in desperation, Zoë embroidered red poppies all round the cuffs and edge.

But now she could not knit, and the problem was how she should pass her time. Zoë offered books – novels that she thought light enough – but Mrs Headford simply opened and shut them and said she really only liked library books. This mysterious distinction involved regu-lar trips to the library to select books which, in some cases, they already possessed. Rupert bought her a wireless for Christmas, and this certainly helped, although she remarked plaintively of this – as of reading – that one could not do it all the time. What she liked were little chats about her life in the Isle of Wight and little outings – rendered difficult because of the weather, and when influenza struck, impossible through lack of time. It seemed to Zoë that she spent all her time on freezing excursions to buy food, and then long hours preparing it, followed by exhaustive efforts to get the invalids – and her mother – to eat whatever it was. 'I know I'm a rotten cook,' she wailed to Rupert in the evenings, 'but they each don't like different things. Jules hates fish and milk puddings, and Mummy says stews give her indigestion, and Ellen won't eat anything except Bovril made with powdered milk.'

Ellen recovered, and Rupert said that she had confided that she would like to spend a week with her married sister in Bournemouth.

'I didn't know she *had* a married sister!'

'That's where she always goes for her holidays. And she's looking very frail – I think some sea air would do her good.'

'Of course she must go.' But she thought that she would still be doing everything, just when she had hoped that Ellen might take over the cooking again, at least.

Then, in the middle of that week, when Juliet was better but still not back at school and therefore bored and fractious, Hugh suddenly asked them to a party he was giving for Polly and Gerald.

'Of course I can't go,' she said. 'But you must.'

'Darling, of course you can. Juliet will be tucked up in bed, and your mother will be here.'

'She's not very good with Jules.'

'She won't have to be anything with her, if Jules is asleep. Anyway, we can give her Hugh's telephone number.'

So she agreed. She hadn't been to a party for ages, and looked forward to it. 'Don't worry about *me*,' her mother said, 'I can always boil myself an egg.'

'You won't need to, Mummy. I'll leave supper for you in the kitchen and Juliet will be asleep before we go.'

When Rupert came home from work, she was riffling through her wardrobe hopelessly. 'I've nothing to wear!'

'I'll choose for you, then.'

'You've got to wear black tie.'

'I know.' He was going through her dresses. She had far fewer clothes than she used to have. 'You never wear this.' He pulled out a short black silk dress. It was the one she had bought for her first evening with Jack.

'I can't wear a short dress!'

'Well, nobody will have seen you in it because I certainly haven't. And it looks pretty dressy to me. You should wear your hair up with it.'

In the end she did wear it. After all, she thought, either I should have thrown it away or I should wear it. It was simply taking another step away from Jack, and that was what she wanted to do.

They explained to Juliet that they were going to Uncle Hugh's and that Gran would be there. This did not go down very well. 'I really don't want to stay here just with her. I want to come with you and see Wills.'

'Wills is at school. You wouldn't see him. And you haven't got to talk to Gran. You'll be asleep.'

'I won't! She might come into my room. She really *smells* so *awful*, Mummy.'

'Jules, that's nonsense – and rather unkind.'

422

'It's not unkind to say what people *are*. She smells
...' she wrinkled her nose as she thought '... she smells
sort of like Irish stew with violets in it.'

'Don't you dare say that to her. It would hurt her
feelings.'

'I don't want to say anything to her. She's not good
with children, my dear. That's what.'

Rupert laughed when she retailed this exchange, but
it worried Zoë. 'Supposing she has a bad dream, or
something?'

'She won't. She sleeps like a top, and your mother
can always ring us at Hugh's. After all, we're only a few
minutes away.'

Her mother was sitting in her armchair next to the
gas fire. Zoë had undressed her earlier, and she was
wearing her thick quilted dressing gown. 'I can't seem to
get into this book,' she said. 'It's all about a clergyman
with a difficult wife – a depressing story.'

'Well, perhaps you should give it up and listen to
your wireless,' she said, as she put the supper tray on the
card table in front of her mother's chair.

'Oh, no, I don't think I'd better. The batteries have
run right down so that I can hardly hear it.'

'You should have told me.'

'I didn't like to be a trouble.'

'Here's our telephone number at Hugh's in case you
need it. We're just down the road, we can be back in a
minute. Juliet is in bed. We'll wait till she drops off.'

'Don't worry. I'm perfectly capable of looking after
her. Mind you don't catch cold in that dress, Zoë. It looks
very skimpy to me.'

Rupert had said that he would tell Jules a story to
settle her, and Zoë went upstairs to the sitting room to

wait for him. Once, she thought, she would have wanted passionately to go to this party; she would have thought about it for weeks, would probably have made or bought a new dress to wear, and would have been utterly cast down if anything had happened to prevent her going. It seemed to her now to be a very long time since she had felt anything of the sort about anything at all. Ever since that evening before she had gone to the island to fetch her mother, her relationship with Rupert had been in limbo: had altered neither for better nor worse; they were courteous, kind to each other and he had been, she recognised, immensely generous about having her mother, in spite of the many disadvantages this entailed. It cut down the time they could have alone together, but she thought, sadly, that perhaps that was a relief to him as well as to her. Certainly he never protested about it, any more than he teased her as he used to do. They were most at ease with or about Jules, whom he adored; but the rest of the time she sensed – not so much any more that he was withdrawn as that he was resigned. Looking at herself in the mirror over the fireplace, she saw her image – the piled-up dark hair, the thin black shoulder straps emphasising the whiteness of her skin – and remembered looking at herself in Archie's flat, when she had dressed there before she had gone to meet Jack, the stranger she had met on a train that morning. Then, she had worn her pearls twined in her hair as she had no other jewellery with her; now, she wore the paste earrings that Rupert had given her years ago the Christmas before they had gone skiing with Edward and Villy. She was looking at her reflection but she hardly saw it, because it came to her then that the feelings she sensed in Rupert were a reflection of her own for him. She was no longer withdrawn, but a kind of resignation had taken the place of withdrawal. She was becalmed, trapped by responsibility and goodwill – but without anything more heartfelt. The nearest she had come to natural, spontaneous feeling had been that evening before she had gone to her mother, when she had thought that Rupert did know – somehow – about Jack. She remembered her instant terror when she had asked him how did he know, and then the extraordinary tide of hysterical relief when she had realised that he was talking about her mother – he had known nothing about Jack. Now, she recognised that she also had been stabbed by a disappointment: it had been as though she had been dragged to the edge of a cliff and there had been nothing for it but to take the plunge, only to discover that it was not a cliff, merely a dreary slope. If she had been forced to tell him more about something he already knew, it would be over, one way or another – there would have been some movement, some release from careful immobility. But to do it in cold blood. I simply have not got the courage, she thought, and her image looked back at her with contempt.

'She's off. I say, that is a good dress!' He picked up her overcoat and helped her into it.

'Is there really going to be dinner for everyone?'

'A buffet. His secretary has done all the arrangements. She's pretty efficient so I expect it will be all right.'

Hugh's house seemed transformed. The large L-shaped drawing room had a fire burning logs that had a wonderful fragrance, and the room was full of blue and white hyacinths. Hugh stood by the fireplace with Polly. She was wearing a pearl-grey satin damask dress with a tight bodice and a long full skirt below her tiny waist.

'This is Gerald,' she said, after she had kissed them, and a young man with rather bulging eyes blushed.

'I say, Poll! You do elevate prettiness to an operatic level!'

'It's my dress, Uncle Rupe. Dad gave it to me.'

Zoë saw Hugh smiling with pride, and thought how much younger he looked when he smiled. When she said how lovely the room was, he smiled again and said that Mrs Leaf had done it all. 'She's here, as a matter of fact,' he added. 'I couldn't let her arrange everything and then not come to the party.'

Simon, very tall and elegant in his dinner jacket, appeared with a tray of champagne; more people were arriving, and the party began.

Throughout it, the drinks, the greetings, the buffet – everyone went down to the dining room to collect a plate and a glass of wine – she was conscious of, fascinated by Polly and Gerald. Even when she could not see them, the power of their happiness radiated the room: their love, which seemed bewitchingly mutual, engendered love from everyone else. She remembered her first dinner at Chester Terrace, to meet Rupert's parents and brothers. How much she had been in love with Rupert then! And Rupert? *Then* she had been sure that he adored her, but now her sense of what that meant had changed; now she could see that she had been in love with a man far older than herself who had a dead wife and two of her children. She had been clear that he wanted her, and she had equated that with love; her mother had brought her up to believe that appearance won everything that could be desired. When she had married Rupert, she had been in love with his desire for her; now, she was no longer sure what else she had felt. It had taken Philip and his sexual revenge upon her vanity, and then Jack (for a moment, she could not bear to think what Jack had felt about her) to teach her anything about love. Jack . . . *had* he loved her? Not enough to stay with her, at any rate. But perhaps that was not fair; perhaps he had loved her and she had been part of the life that he gave up. I did love him, she thought, for the first time without anguish. I wasn't enough for him, but I loved him. It was some comfort.

In the car going home, Rupert was very quiet. When she asked him what he was thinking, he said, 'I was just hoping that Clary would find someone she could love like that. But I'm afraid she's not like Polly.'

'She will get over it.' She knew that Clary had fallen in love with a married man and that he had called an end to the affair.

'Yes. But getting over something doesn't mean that you're the same person that you were before. Clary loves people very seriously.'

They got home to find that Juliet was up, barefooted in her nightdress. The back door to the kitchen that led on to the garden was open and she was chopping up a loaf of bread. 'I'm feeding the poor birds,' she said; her teeth were chattering. 'I took them out one bowl, but it didn't look enough, so I'm doing some more.'

While Zoë shut the door, boiled a kettle for a hot-water bottle and wrapped her in a blanket, she said that she had woken up because she had dreamed about a horrible seagull who stole all the food 'and bit the other poor birds with his horrible beak, so I had to make some breakfast for them, Mummy'.

'Why didn't you go into Gran's room?'

'I did. She was asleep, all muddled in her chair with the lights on. She doesn't like birds.'

'Let's put her in a hot bath,' Rupert said. 'The fastest way to warm her up. I'll do it, you go and see to your mother.'

She found her mother as Jules had described, but with the added horror that her library book had fallen from her lap and been partially charred by the gas fire.

'Oh dear! I must have dropped off.'

'And you nearly set fire to the house, Mummy – look at your book!'

'Oh dear!'

'And Juliet woke up and you didn't hear her – she came into your room and you were fast asleep, and now she's probably caught her death of cold going into the garden.'

'That's very naughty of her. She shouldn't have done that. I was here all the time. She had only to wake me.'

'Oh, Mummy! You were meant to be looking after her! We go out for one evening and she might have died!'

'Don't shout at me, Zoë, I couldn't help dropping off. How was I to know that she'd wake? You said she never did!'

Before she could stop herself, she completely lost her temper. 'And *you* said you were perfectly capable of looking after her! And apart from possibly being burned to death, she's probably caught pneumonia! After all these months, this is the first time I've ever asked you to do anything for me, and look what happens! Well, I'll never ask you to do anything again, you can be sure of that!'

Her mother's face, her trembling mouth and frightened eyes, stopped her. She was standing, ineffectively tugging at the zip on her dressing gown.

'I'm sorry. I'll do that for you.'

'I think I'd better pay a visit to the bathroom first. You needn't wait for me. I can put myself to bed.'

Zoë picked up the supper tray and took it out to the kitchen. Then she went back to her mother's room, turned out the gas fire, and took the counterpane off the bed. Then she waited; she felt shaky and sour, but she couldn't leave things like this, she wanted to apologise and get the hell out.

Her mother was a long time in the bathroom, and when she returned, Zoë saw that she had been crying.

'I'm sorry, Mummy. I shouldn't have lost my temper like that.'

Her mother let herself be helped into bed without saying anything. 'Shall I take your sling off? You don't need to wear it in bed.'

She unpinned the silk scarf. As her mother lay down, she said, 'I did my best for you. You may not have thought it much, but it was the best I could do. In the circumstances.'

'I know you did. I didn't mean to make you cry.'

'I was missing Maud,' she answered with shaky dignity. 'It's hard losing your only friend when you're my age.'

'I know – I do realise that. We'll talk in the morning.' She kissed the soft pouchy cheek, an empty gesture that would only have been significant if it had been absent. 'Shall I turn off your light?'

'If you wouldn't mind.'

When she and Rupert had settled Juliet, he took her arm on the stairs up to their bedroom.

'Darling! You're shaking! I'm sure she'll be all right.'

'I lost my temper with Mummy. It's my fault – she's

not capable of anything after all these years of being looked after by her friend. Maud did everything for her – encouraged her to think of herself as an invalid. And now that's just what she is.'

'Ellen will be back soon,' he said.

'It will be easier when Mummy's arm is out of plaster,' she said.

'Jules is a tough little egg. And, after all, the back garden is only about the temperature of the bathroom at Home Place. She's used to being cold,' he said, trying to coax a smile out of her and failing.

'Let's get to bed. It's after one, and you're dead beat.'

She thought she wouldn't sleep, but she did – at once – and woke in the morning because Rupert had brought her a cup of tea. It was Saturday so he didn't have to go to work. Jules was fine, he said; he was giving her breakfast. But there was still her mother's tray to do. She drank the tea, put on her dressing gown and went down to the kitchen, where Rupert and Jules were sitting at the table.

'We're having kippers,' Jules said.

'Kippers?' They couldn't be.

'Madam ordered kippers,' Rupert said.

'And this is a hotel splongdeed where you can get everything, Mummy.'

She held out a piece of toast spread with anchovy paste from her plate. Rupert had cut the toast into a fish shape.

'Guests don't usually eat meals with the waiter,' she said.

'I'm the manager,' Rupert answered, 'and this is a very special guest.'

She made her mother's breakfast tray, and with a

rather shaky determination to be bright and kind, went into Mrs Headford's bedroom.

She was up – and partially dressed. That is to say, she was still wearing her bedjacket, but she had managed to get into her roll-on suspender belt and her knickers, and was struggling to fasten her stockings. She had lit her gas fire and drawn the curtains, whose window looked on to the back garden.

'Oh, Mummy! You should have waited for me.'

'You know I don't like to be a burden.' There was resentment in the familiar phrase.

'You're not, honestly. You can't help your arm. Anyway, it will soon be better.' She had put the tray down and knelt to do the suspenders.

'The doctor said next week. So it won't be long.'

'No. That'll be nice, won't it? You'll be able to finish your jumper.'

She hooked her mother into the bust bodice that half-heartedly encased the drooping white breasts, slipped the camisole over her head and eased the Viyella shirt-sleeve on to the plastered arm. While she was buttoning up the front, her mother said: 'I've been thinking, Zoë. I think I'd rather go home – to the cottage – when my arm is out of plaster. I can perfectly well manage for myself and Maud left me the cottage, after all. I don't like to think of it empty.'

'But you know the agent said he could let it for you in the summer, Mummy.'

'I don't like to think of it full of strangers among all Maud's things. And anyway, dear, you have your own life, and you don't really want me in it. You never have.' The faded pale blue eyes met hers with an irrefutable

431

directness. 'I know', she said, 'when I'm not wanted. And there's no need to tell me that I am. I may be useless, but I'm not a fool. As soon as I've got back the use of my right hand, I shall write to Avril Fenwick and she will tell Doris I'm coming back and get the cottage ready for me. I don't want to argue about this. I've thought it all out in the night. Would you pull that curtain further back, dear? It's taking the light.'

Zoë went to the curtain and the window. Outside, snow, like coarse greyish sugar, lay in the little runnels on the blackened grass, and the bread that Jules had scattered sat in frozen lumps. She felt confused – because with the guilt about her failure there was irrepressible relief that her mother might leave (she realised then that the worst part of having her had been the feeling that it was for ever) – to which was added deep shame – that she should have such a feeling, and that she had behaved so badly in the first place as to make her mother consider such a course. 'I'm sorry,' she said at last. 'I don't know what to say.'

'I don't think there is anything to say.'

'I shouldn't have been so cross last night, but I was frightened about Jules, you see.'

Her mother took a sip of tea and then put the cup back in the saucer. 'Do you know, Zoë, ever since you were a little girl, you hardly ever apologised for anything, and when you did, you always made an excuse for what you had done to show that it wasn't your fault.'

All of that day, which seemed interminable, she struggled with this indictment. Was it fair, or true? If it was true, it must be fair. Whatever it was, it rankled bitterly inside her. She could not tell Rupert of her mother's decision because she didn't want to talk about it in front of Jules. She sent them out shopping while she tidied the flat and prepared lunch; she remembered to ask Rupert to get some batteries for her mother's wireless. At least she had remembered that. But when Rupert returned with them and installed them of course it was he whom her mother thanked.

As a treat she had used the week's meat ration for a Sunday joint. She had chosen pork, because Ellen, who was very good at that, had told her how to cook it. With it she had made apple sauce, mashed potatoes and cabbage, which always seemed to turn out rather watery but at that time of year there was not much choice of vegetable.

Rupert carved. 'I say! This is a bit of all right!' he said, in the cheery voice she noticed he seemed always to use when her mother was present.

'No crackling for me,' Mrs Headford said.

'PLEASE DON'T CUT MY MEAT UP!' Jules shouted.

'It's not yours, darling, it's Gran's.'

'Oh. Can I have her crackling?'

'No. You'll have your own crackling.'

'No cabbage! I hate it. I—'

'Cabbage is good for your complexion,' Mrs Headford observed.

'What's that?'

'Your skin,' Rupert said, putting her plate of food in front of her.

'My skin? My *skin*? A funny thing, Mummy. You know how people sweat? When they have little blobs on their forehead when they get hot? Well, why don't blobs of rain go in? Because Ellen says they don't. She said skin's waterproof, but if sweat comes out it can't be, can it?'

'I see what you mean,' Rupert said. 'Perhaps some does go in and you don't notice.'

'I don't think we want to talk about that at lunch-time.'

'*I* do, Gran.' She seized a bit of her crackling in her fingers and bit into it with her sharp white teeth. 'What would you like to talk about?' she asked. 'Oh, I know! Dad says that Polly is getting married. It's in June. Can I be a bridesmaid, Mummy? It *is* my turn. Lydia was last time, and she's *far* too old now. She's marrying a man called Gerald Lord.'

'No, darling, he *is* a lord. He's called Gerald Faken-ham.'

'What's a lord, Dad?'

'It's a title. You know, like Dr Ballater being called doctor.'

'What are lords good at?'

'A good question. Well, the same things as other people, really. Or not, as the case may be.'

'I expect he has a very nice house and grounds,' Mrs Headford said, 'and plenty of money. Very nice for your niece.'

'I don't think he's got any money at all, but Hugh says he's a very good egg and they both seem very happy.'

'A good *egg*, Dad? How can a person possibly be an egg?'

'It's just a phrase. It means a good person.'

'Jules, darling, do eat your lunch.'

'I am, Mummy, bit by bit.' She speared a slice of meat with her fork and bit a piece of it.

'Cut it up first, Jules.'

'It sounds silly, marrying an egg.'

'And don't talk with your mouth full.'

'Mummy, I can't do both the things you say. I can't eat my lunch and *not* talk with my mouth full.'

And so it went on, the atmosphere saved by Juliet's prattle. At least Zoë's mother didn't bring up the subject of her going then.

Afterwards, they took Juliet to Kensington Gardens to see if there was ice on the Round Pond. Zoë had got some stale bread from the baker's without coupons so that Juliet could feed the ducks – one of her favourite occupations. Mrs Headford, invited to come, said that she would have a little rest.

Home before it was dark. It had been freezing in the park, and standing about, while Juliet fed the ducks, she had nearly told Rupert about her mother, but each time she was about to start, Juliet claimed their attention.

'What's up, darling?'

'Nothing.'

'Something's worrying you.'

'I'll tell you later.'

They had tea and toast with Marmite to conceal the taste of the bright yellow margarine. Then they played games with Juliet; Rupert tried very hard to get his mother-in-law to join in, but she said she couldn't play cards with one hand, and when he suggested Pelman Patience, she said she could never remember where any of the cards were. 'Pegotty, then,' Rupert said, and they played that, although Jules said she didn't like it.

Eventually, and by what seemed tediously slow progression, Juliet was bathed and put to bed, supper, mostly left-overs, was laid on the table, eaten and washed up, and then Mrs Headford said that she was tired and would go straight to bed and listen to her wireless. So Zoë helped her mother undress, filled her hot-water bottle, waited while she went to the bathroom, and helped her into bed. During all this, nothing was said about the future, beyond that tomorrow she would have breakfast in bed and wait there until Zoë had returned from taking Juliet to school to give her her bath. Eventually she escaped upstairs to the sitting room, exhausted.

'There's a spot of brandy left. Would you like it with soda or neat?'

'With soda, I think.'

'Coming up.'

'Now, then,' he said, when he handed her her glass. 'What's going on? The atmosphere was pretty sticky at dinner, I thought.'

She told him.

'Perhaps she doesn't really mean it,' he said. 'It might just be because you were cross with her.'

'She does. I mean, I'm sure it is to do with me being cross with her, but she does mean it.'

'Do you think she can manage by herself?'

'Well, she couldn't before.'

'I must say, I can't see her cooking much, or that sort of thing. She didn't do a thing to help you today.'

'She can't with no right arm. But she says, as soon as the plaster is off, she's going to get in touch with Miss Fenwick – the friend who lives nearby – to get the cottage ready.'

'I suppose she couldn't just go back there for the summer when it would be easier for her, no fires, et cetera, and spend the rest of the year with us?'

'Oh, *God* – I don't know. It's just so awful, day after day. I don't know what to *do* with her, and she doesn't get on with Jules – or Ellen, come to that.'

'Poor darling, I do realise how difficult you find it.'

'Well, you do too, really. You're much nicer about it than I am, but meals are awful just with her, and we've tried having people and we know that's out. And it's going to go on for years and years! She's not sixty.'

'It's partly this flat,' he said. 'There's not enough room. If she had her own sitting room it would be easier.'

'I don't think it would. She would be wanting to be with us all the time, so even when she wasn't I'd feel guilty.'

There was a short silence while she watched him take a cigarette out of a bright blue packet and light it. Then she said, 'If I'd been nicer to her when it was easier to be it – I mean, when I only had to see her sometimes – I wouldn't feel so bad about her now. Goodness, that smells far better than your usual cigarettes. Could I have one?'

He offered her the packet and lit one for her. For a moment it reminded her of Jack's cigarettes, but only for a moment: these did not have the slightly burnt-caramel taste of the Lucky Strikes.

'How do you get French cigarettes?'

'A place in Soho. I only smoke them occasionally.' He sounded defensive.

'I don't mind what you smoke, darling.'

'The fact is that you've never got on with her, and of course she must know that. I'm not *blaming* you,' he added hastily. 'I'm just saying that that's what makes it so difficult. Perhaps it would be better if she did go.'

'But, Rupert, that's the problem. I feel I can't let her go and I feel I can't stop her from going.'

They talked in this way for some time. He offered to talk to her mother, but she refused. She was afraid of what her mother might say about her; she was in that state when every suggestion that he made seemed unavailing. Eventually, he gave up and she could sense that he was aggrieved at the lack of a solution.

'I think you just feel everything is insoluble because you're dead beat,' he said. 'Come on. Bed.'

As she followed him into the bedroom, she thought of all the different ways in which, long ago, he had made that suggestion.

A few days later, she took her mother to Dr Ballater to have the plaster taken off her arm. Yes, he said, she could use it normally; the muscle tone would soon return. 'But don't go hopping on and off buses in this weather,' he had added, looking at Zoë as he spoke, as though, she felt, *she* had made her mother go in buses.

Mrs Headford spent the afternoon writing letters – or, rather, although she had described this activity in the plural, one rather long letter, which she asked Zoë to post when she went to fetch Juliet from her dancing class. The subject of her mother leaving was still not mentioned between them.

She took her shopping – to her favourite old-fashioned drapers, Gaylor and Pope, where when you paid the lady at the counter wherever you bought what you wanted, your money and bill were put into a small canister and whizzed away along wire to the cashier, returning with your receipted bill and any change required. Mrs Headford had made a list and they ploughed through it: knickers, warm stockings, bedroom slippers, some petersham ribbon to trim her summer hat, buttons for the cardigan she was now able to finish, bias binding, elastic, some hairnets, a bath-cap, and a bag to keep her knitting in. She was indefatigable, and kept remembering things that she wanted that she had not put on the list.

Zoë had resolved to be infinitely patient about the expedition, and to take her mother out to lunch after the shopping was done.

'Oh, I should like that,' she said, when this was proposed. Marylebone High Street also contained one of those places where chiefly women went, generally for elaborate cake and tea or coffee, but which also served simple, genteel luncheon dishes, such as omelettes or cauliflower cheese, and they went there, and sat at a very small round table so surrounded by carrier bags that the waitress could hardly reach them.

'I seem to have bought the shop up,' her mother said happily.

'Shopping clearly does you good.'

'And things are much better now, aren't they, Zoë, now that you know I'm going.'

'You know I'm worried about that.'

'Yes, dear. But I shall be all right. Doris is very good to me, and she will help me with the cooking, and, as Maud always said, Avril is a brick. And I think I shall get a cat for the company.' Later, she said, 'And of course you must bring Juliet for a visit. As you know, we're not far from the seaside.'

'She's absolutely *determined*,' she told Rupert that night.

'Perhaps you'd better take her down and make a point of seeing this friend of hers and asking her to get in touch with us if she's worried.'

'Oh, God! I suppose I'd better.'

'I'm only pointing out that if you're worried about her this would be something you could do about it.'

439

She sensed that they were nearly quarrelling and that it was because she was so full of conflicting feelings about it. She did not tell him that, in the taxi coming home after the shopping spree, her mother had said, 'You know, Zoë, I don't think you appreciate how lucky you are to have your husband back from the war. You're not faced with being a widow at twenty-four as I was, with a little girl to bring up on my own. He's a very nice man and you should do everything you can to make him happy.'

'I think he *is* happy.'

'Do you, dear? Well, I'm sure you know best.'

Nothing more was said, but again, this parting shot of her mother's unnerved her. Was he happy? He was devoted to Juliet and when he was doing things with her he was the old Rupert she had married – kind and funny, full of small jokes and sweetness of temper. With her he was patient, gentle and, she now felt, somewhat bored; there was nothing light about their relationship – it seemed to be composed of myriad small duties, and whenever these seemed, temporarily, to come to an end, there was a kind of void, a feeling of tension and uncertainty. With Ellen back, there were fewer tasks for Zoë, and consequently more of the tension.

The letter from Avril Fenwick arrived promptly – she must have replied by return of post, Zoë thought, as she took it in on her mother's breakfast tray.

When she went to fetch the tray, she found her mother still in bed, the letter spread before her and her breakfast untouched.

'Oh, Zoë!' she cried. 'Such news! Such a wonderful letter! I've never had such a letter in my life. Poor Avril! She didn't want to tell me because she thought I would be so upset, but when *I* wrote to her she says she saw her way clear at once! And she *was* ninety-six, after all. As Avril says, it was a good age and she had a wonderful life. But it's so *kind* of her! I can't get over it!'

'Mummy, perhaps I'd better read the letter.'

'Do, dear. It's such a wonderful letter, do.'

She did. She had gathered that old Mrs Fenwick had died, and read through the paragraph that enumerated her many – Zoë felt hitherto well-concealed – virtues. Her courage, the way she always spoke her mind, never mind to whom or the circumstances, her zest for life – and here there was a menu of the foods she had most enjoyed – her high standards about other people's behaviour, her wonderful endurance of a difficult marriage, to a man who was always either working or obsessed by his collection of butterflies and whose early death had proved a blessing in disguise – Mother had never really seen the point of men . . . Zoë gave up at this point and went on to the next page. Here, Miss Fenwick suggested at some length that Mrs Headford might like to 'team up' with her, share her cottage and 'stick it out' together. She said how much she would enjoy looking after her, what a lot they had in common, how, if they pooled their resources, they would have more money, and all kinds of little trips might be arranged, and finally what a kindness it would be if Cicely were to accept, since she contemplated living alone, after all these happy years with Mother, with such dread. Finally, she begged Cicely to think it over carefully without hurrying about her decision, and meanwhile she would be delighted to get Cotter's End ready for her return. The letter ended 'with ever so much love, Avril'.

'Isn't it wonderful of her? When she had her own grief to bear, to think of me.' She was trembling with excitement. 'If you don't mind, Zoë, I shall send her a telegram. I should go at once. To think that she's gone through the funeral weeks ago and I never knew! So the sooner I go the better.'

'Would you like to speak to her? You could ring her up.'

'I couldn't, dear. She's not on the telephone. Her mother didn't like the idea. They had one for a bit, but her mother said that Avril talked on it too much.'

The telegram was sent, and in it she arranged to leave in two days' time.

'I'll come with you.'

'Oh, no, dear. Avril will meet me. Either at Ryde, or she will come over on the ferry and meet me at the station in Southampton.'

All day, she talked about Avril and her letter. She had no hesitation about her decision, she said. It was the most wonderful opportunity. And then came out – streamed out – how frightened she had been at the prospect of living alone: the long evenings, the noises at night, the absence of anyone to talk to, the fear that she might not manage if anything went wrong – the gas cylinders, for instance: they were so heavy and could be dangerous, they could leak without you knowing it – and the shopping when she didn't have a car and could not drive and so on. All of it made Zoë feel she had felt so unwelcome in London with them – with *her*.

When Rupert got back from work and was informed, he made Martinis and entered into her mother's spirit of festivity. He listened to an account of the letter, was given it to read and then told its contents all over again; throughout, he was patient and charming to her, while she, Zoë, was virtually silent. When Ellen sent Juliet up to say goodnight, her grandmother said: 'I'm going back home,

Juliet. I'm going back to the island. Will you come and visit me in the summer?'

'Will there be other people on it?'

'Oh, yes, dear. All my friends. It's a big island. You've been there, you remember.'

'I don't because I was a baby.' She shut her eyes tightly to kiss her grandmother and escaped.

'Well!' Rupert said, when Zoë's mother had gone to bed and they were on their own in the drawing room. 'All's well that ends well. Are you taking her down?'

'No. She wired her friend, and she's coming *here* to escort her home. She seems to want to, and that's it.'

'Well, that seems to me a good thing,' he said tiredly. 'Obviously this Avril person is fond of your mother.'

'She said – Mummy, I mean – how nice it would be for us to be on our own again.'

'And will it?'

'I don't know, Rupert. Will it?' She looked at him; there was a moment when they both seemed frozen. It came to her that that was how it had been for a very long time, and also that they could stay like that, or move on to something better or worse.

She said, 'We've never talked about what it was like for either of us all those years that you were away. I want to now. I have to tell you something.'

He had been standing by the fireplace fiddling with the fire. Now he straightened up, looked quickly at her and then sat on the arm of the chair opposite – almost, she thought, as though he was poised for escape.

'You sound very serious, darling,' he said, and she recognised the voice that he used when he thought she was about to make a scene.

'Yes. While you were away, I fell in love with

443

someone. An American officer I met on a train coming back from seeing Mummy on the island. He asked me to have dinner with him – and I did. It was the summer of 1943: I'd heard nothing from you for two years – not since the note that the Frenchman brought. I thought you were dead.' She swallowed; that sounded like an excuse, and she didn't want to make any excuses. 'Anyway, that's not the point – I think I would have fallen in love with him anyway. We had an affair. I used to go to London to be with him, telling all sorts of lies to the family. Only for short times – he was taking war pictures for the American Army, so he was often away. When it got to the Normandy landing, he was away a lot.' She thought for a moment; she was anxious now not to gloss anything over, leave anything out. 'He wanted to marry me. He wanted to meet the family – and particularly Juliet. We had our first – row – well, really the only one we ever had – about that. Because I wouldn't agree—'

'To marry him?'

'No. I wanted to do that. But to tell the family about it when we didn't know whether you would come back or not. And then, the following spring, nearly a year after the invasion and still we heard nothing from you, he had to go to photograph one of the concentration camps, I think it was Belsen. About a week later, he suddenly rang me at Home Place to ask me to go to London that night, and I couldn't because I'd said I'd look after the children while Ellen had a weekend off. By then the war was so nearly over and I was – I was imagining going to America with him. I got back from taking the children for their afternoon walk and there he was, sitting next to the Duchy at tea. The Duchy was wonderful. I think she knew but she never said anything. She told me to take him into

444

the morning room after tea so that we could be on our own. He was different – unreachable, somehow. He said he had to go back to London at once as he was flying the next morning. He was going to another camp. He said,' for the first time she felt her voice trembling, 'he said he was glad he'd seen Juliet. He said he was going to be away for a long time. Then he went.' She stopped. 'I never saw him again.'

'He went back to America without a word?'

'No. He died.' It was a great effort to tell him how Jack had died, but she managed it. 'About six weeks later, you came back. Oh. There was one important thing I've left out. He was Jewish. That's why. Why he killed himself.'

There was a long silence. Then he got up and came over to her, took her hands and kissed them. 'You're still in love with him?'

'No. I don't think I could have told you if I was.' Then she became anxious that some element of truth would elude her. 'I shall always have love for him.'

'I understand that,' he said; she saw tears in his eyes.

'It's a great relief to have told you.'

'I admire you so much for telling me. *Love* and admire you. You have been far braver than I.'

And while she was still trying to understand what he meant, he began to tell her his tale. As he told it, she could not imagine why none of this had occurred to her before. He had been away so long; he had been left by Pipette with this woman who had taken them in, and on whom he had in the immediate future to depend. When, in the telling, he lapsed from Michèle to the diminutive – his pet name for her – she felt a dart of jealousy and was almost glad of it. Then, as he told her about how the

445

woman had gone to so much trouble to get him painting materials, she thought how little she had ever supported him in that, but when he described the visits of Germans to the farm, she realised how potent this isolation plus danger must have been. And then he came to the difficult part. The invasion, and his continued stay at the farm, and the reason for it. For he did not gloss things over, or excuse himself, or pretend that he had not loved her. She had wanted him to stay and see the child, and then she had sent him away. He did not even say that it had been he who had made that decision. 'I am really trying to match your honesty,' he said. 'I can't match you in any-thing else. It was not excusable to you,' he said, 'leaving you all that time without knowing. I owed Miche a great deal, but not, perhaps, that. But that is what I did. Archie said I should tell you,' he said, 'but I couldn't.'

'Archie? You told *him*?'

'Only Archie. I told no one else.'

'Archie knew about Jack. I took Jack to have a drink with him one evening, and it was Archie who Jack wrote to before – he died. He came down to Home Place to tell me.'

'He certainly has been a repository of family secrets.'

'But that's hardly his fault, is it? He's simply the sort of kind, loyal person who gets told things.'

'You're right. Oh, Zoë, how much you have changed!'

'Do you,' she said – she was dreading the possible answer – 'do you keep in touch with her?'

'No. Oh, no. It was agreed that we should part completely. No letters, no visits, nothing at all.'

'You must have found that very hard.'

'It's been hard for both of us.'

'For her? How do you know?'

'For *us*, my darling. Things have been hard for *us*.'

'I suppose we made them worse than they need have been.'

'I don't know. I feel as you do. I couldn't tell you about Miche until it was over for me. Or over enough.' He touched her face, stroked her cheekbone with one finger. 'Oh, the relief! To know you again! And you began it. You were the brave one.' She wanted to catch his gaiety – his relief – but she could not. She was not finished, and now, what was left to tell him seemed the worst of all. She remembered the Duchy saying that one should not burden other people with the responsibility of one's experience – or something of the kind. The whole business of Philip had happened to someone she scarcely recognised as herself. But then she had had the baby that had turned out to be Philip's – and she had put Rupert through all the misery of her pregnancy, labour and subsequent loss, and through all of that he had attended to her, had never once claimed any of the grief or loss for himself. She had to put that right, whatever it cost.

'What is it? What's the matter?'

She felt herself blushing – with shame and fear – but she made herself look at him.

'That first baby,' she began, haltingly, trying to find the right words.

His expression changed, and for a moment it was as though he looked far into her and saw all that was there; then he took her hands again and said in a voice that was both gentle and casual, 'It was rather a changeling, wasn't it? I think we should both let it lie. Will you do that with me?'

Tears rushed to her eyes, and with the first spontaneous gesture since his return, she threw herself into his arms.

∞ ∞ ∞

'You stay put. I'll get Mrs Greenacre to bring you some breakfast.'

'I only want tea. I couldn't face anything solid.'

'Poor darling!' he said heartily. 'Perhaps you'd better give the doctor a ring.' He had bathed and shaved and dressed, and was standing in the middle of the room, poised to go for his breakfast.

'No need – it's just gastric flu. You go down, darling, or you'll be late.'

'Right.'

When he had gone, Diana crept out of bed to go to the lavatory, where she had spent a good deal of the night. He had left the bathroom window open, and the gale had knocked the Bakelite tooth-mugs off the window ledge into the bath. She bent to pick them up and felt a wave of nausea. She shut the window. Grey clouds were scudding across the sky at an unearthly rate, and the garden was full of the tiny petals from the pink may trees. It looked as though it would rain again. She ran a basin of hot water and laved her face. She looked awful. Once, she would never have allowed Edward to see her like this, but now she supposed it was different – or very nearly different. The divorce was in hand, thank God, but she had been warned that it would take months. Villy was divorcing him for adultery; when she had questioned this, he had said that the lawyers had said that it was either that or desertion, which would take a great deal longer.

448

Her face was not even romantically pale; it was more grey with a yellowish tinge, and her hair looked matted and dull. She cleaned her teeth and picked up Edward's comb, but it was thick with his hair oil. She went back to the bedroom to find her own comb; by then she was shivering.

Mrs Greenacre duly arrived with a tray of tea and lit the gas fire. She also shut a window – Edward insisted on sleeping in a draught. Diana asked for her handbag and, when she was alone, found her dry rouge and dabbed a bit on her cheekbones. Edward would be sure to come and say goodbye to her before he left for the office.

'You look better already, darling,' he said, when he did so. 'Better warn you – the government's latest decree is that we can't have any fires from now until September.'

'Oh, Lord! Turn it out, then.'

'Nonsense! You're ill. I'm not having you cold. Get better, sweetie. I'll be back a bit later because I'm going to the doc.'

'Oh, yes.'

He bent to kiss her and she smelt lavender water and hair oil – scents that used to excite her about him. 'Look after yourself.'

'I'm sorry I look so awful.'

'You don't look awful! You look beautiful. I love you – remember? – as always.'

'I love you.'

He was gone. She heard him talking to Mrs Greenacre, and then the front door slam. As she drank some of the tea she reflected how often they said this to one another these days. It was a kind of ritual refrain, not so much a declaration as a staunching process; without it, everything might leak away. This thought frightened her: it seemed extraordinary, almost inconceivable, that

449

something she had wanted for so long was not making her deliriously happy. It was more that *not* having it would be so terrifying that she could not contemplate it. She had thought that her discontent was due to uncertainty: first, that he would not ever leave Villy and live with her and then he had, and then that even if he lived with her, he would never press for a divorce, and then he had. But the feeling of – disappointment persisted, compounded now by the moral obligation to be desperately in love with someone who had done all that for her. And somewhere, buried, because she did not want it to be a certainty, she was afraid that he felt the same – had the same disappointment, felt the same necessity to reiterate his tremendous love for her to justify what he had done. So every day, often several times a day – or, rather, evening – this ritual of love was declared aloud between them, although she derived less and less comfort from it.

It was not even as though they lived a life of sweetness and light, artificial or no. There had been ructions . . . Now, because she was feeling rotten and there was nothing else she had the energy to do, she must lie and contemplate them.

There had been the awful half-term when Ian and Fergus had come to them. They were at the same boarding school, and spent most, if not all, of their holidays with their grandparents in Scotland. The moment they arrived at the house, she had sensed their hostility, not only to Edward but to her. With Ian, the eldest, nearly seventeen, it had taken the form of taciturnity, and the determination not to be impressed by anything. With Fergus, two years younger, it had been rather senseless boasting, accounts of how he had beaten people at games or exams, or simply by some clever remark. When Edward spoke to them, they barely answered. He had been good to them, had taken them all to *Nicholas Nickleby* and out to dinner afterwards. He asked them what else they would like to do, and they had said they would rather go off on their own. Which they did, for nearly the whole of Saturday, and were uncommunicative about where they had been. Jamie, who had got very excited about their visit, was also snubbed.

She had prepared a large room for them on the top floor of the house and when she showed it to them, had said, 'This is to be your room, so you can keep things in it for when you come.'

And Ian had answered, 'There's no need, Mum. We won't be coming. We'd rather be in Scotland.'

When she had taken them to the station in the car with Edward and seen them off, she had cried. He had been very nice to her about that, said that she couldn't help the fact that due to the war and everything of course it had been better for them to be in Scotland. But she'd lost them, and somewhere, because she felt so guilty about it, she had wanted to blame Edward.

Then, and far more recently, they had had an actual *row* about the nights he spent in Southampton. He went once a week, and two weeks ago, had rung to say he would have to spend an extra night there. Instantly, pictures of his wartime deception of Villy occurred to her. He had used to ring *her* up, or tell her he'd rung Villy up, with some story that he said had 'made things perfectly all right'. Perhaps that was what he was doing now, with *her*, she had thought, and once she had thought it, she could not get it out of her mind. She knew, better than most, how susceptible he was; she also knew, better than anyone, that he was not going to bed with her with the

same enthusiasm and frequency. So, surely it was obvious
– or at least very likely – that he was going to bed with
someone else. She tried ringing the hotel where he said he
was staying, and they said he was out. When he came
home she confronted him with this. 'I was in the dining
room!' he exclaimed. 'Silly buggers, why didn't they look
for me there – or page me or something? Why did you
want to get hold of me anyway?' he asked a moment
later.

'I wondered where you were.'

'I told you where I was.'

'Yes, but then I couldn't get hold of you.'

'Not *my* fault,' he said. 'I'll speak to them about that
next week.'

'Where did you *think* I'd be?' he then asked.

'I didn't *know*. Well, of course I thought you'd be at
the hotel, or I wouldn't have rung it.'

'I meant when you didn't get me there.' His eyes had
become quite hard, which she knew they did when he
was beginning to get angry.

'I had no idea, darling. I was worried.' If only, at this
point, she had said something like, 'After all, I am rather
attached to you' or 'I was really worried about your poor
tum' (his indigestion, though intermittent, was sometimes acute), things might have calmed down, but she
didn't. There had been a brief pause while Mrs Greenacre
brought in the cheese and celery and then he had continued to press her: where did she *think* he might be?

'I suppose I thought you might have gone off with
some bright young thing . . .'

He was outraged, not in the least flattered, simply
angry. His anger had all the exaggerated resentment that
she had associated with people accused when they were

innocent of something they habitually did. In the end, she apologised – abjectly, with tears in her eyes – and he forgave her. Afterwards, she reflected wearily, all she had done was put the idea into his head.

There had been brighter moments – or, rather, better times. Easter at Home Place, for instance. The Duchy was spending a few weeks there during the holidays, and she and Edward were invited down for a long weekend.

'Who will be there?' she had asked. She felt both nervous and excited at the prospect.

'Rupe and Zoë, and my sister Rachel and poor old Flo – that's the Duchy's sister – and Archie Lestrange, an old friend of Rupe's, well, of the whole family, really. And Teddy and Bernadine – I don't think she's been before, either, and she'll be far more of a fish out of water than you'll ever be, darling.'

'It's a lot of people to meet at once for the first time.'

'You know Rupe and Zoë.'

'Will Hugh be there?'

His face clouded. 'No. He's taken Wills off on some boating holiday with friends.'

And so, on a Friday evening, they drove down. It poured with rain until the last few miles when the sun came out suddenly, making all the fresh wet greens of trees and fields glisten, and bluebells were like wood-smoke on the ground in the woods. 'It is the most lovely time of year,' she said. She associated the country with being cold and lonely; now she was going with Edward to be received into his family. She had some minutes of pure happiness.

Edward smiled, and laid a hand on her knee. 'This is rather different from those times when I used to drive you down to Isla's cottage,' he said, 'isn't it, sweetie? This

is a bit of all right.' He had stopped at Tonbridge and
spent all their sweet coupons on expensive chocolates,
two boxes. 'Violet and rose creams for the Duchy,' he
said, 'she does love them, and truffles for the rest of us.'

They were driving now down a hill with high banks
each side of the road, and woods on their right. White
gates appeared on the right and they went in.

The house, rambling and rather shabby, was larger
than she had expected. A small man with bandy legs met
them and carried their luggage.

'Evening, Tonbridge. How's Mrs Tonbridge?'

'Keeping very nicely, sir, thank you. Good evening,
madam.'

They followed him through the wicket gate to the
front door.

In the large hall Edward led her straight to the Duchy,
who was arranging daffodils on a long table. She was
greeted kindly; Edward had said that his mother was
nearly eighty, but she did not look it, and her eyes, the
same colour as Edward's, looked straight at and, Diana
felt, through her with a direct simplicity that was unnerv-
ing. 'I think Rachel has put you in Hugh's room,' she said.
She had wondered whether they would be allowed to
share a room, and was relieved as well as surprised.

They met Rachel on the stairs. Like her mother, she
was dressed in blue but she was taller and extremely thin.
Her hair was shingled in a very old-fashioned manner –
nowadays one associated that kind of hair-do with les-
bians, she thought.

'Darling! You've cut your hair off! When did you
do that?'

'Oh, not very long ago. You know you're in Hugh's

room, don't you? We've put Teddy and Bernadine in your old one.'

She had gone faintly pink – the hidden allusion to Villy, Diana supposed.

'I'm so glad you could come,' Rachel was saying; her smile was warm, her gaze like her mother's.

Diana followed Edward along the gallery landing to the end where there were two doors and the passage turned to the left.

'Here we are!' The room looked out on to the front lawn where there was a monkey puzzle tree with daffodils under it. 'The bathroom's along the passage, down two steps and turn left,' Edward said. 'And the lavatory's next door to it.'

She went along the passage to the lavatory. Clouds of steam were creeping out from under the bathroom door and there was a smell of expensive bath essence. As she returned, she heard peals of laughter coming from the room next to theirs. Then the door opened and there was Rupert in white shorts and a shirt. 'Oh, hello, Diana! You didn't by any chance notice whether the bathroom is free, did you? I've just had a rather humiliating game of squash with Teddy, and Zoë says I smell like a very expensive horse.'

'How I imagine an expensive horse would smell,' Zoë said as she appeared behind him.

'Hello.' She smiled at Diana. She was wearing a pale green bath towel like a sarong; her hair hung down her back and she looked extremely beautiful. When she said that someone was having a bath, Rupert said, 'It's Bernadine. She's been in there for hours.'

'I expect Teddy's in there with her.'

'Oh, is he, indeed?' He stalked along the passage and banged on the door. 'Are you in there, Teddy? Well, hurry up. I need a bath.'

'Although I expect the hot water will have run out,' Zoë said. 'I hope you don't want one.'

No, she didn't.

Back in the room, she asked, 'Do we change for dinner?'

'Only a bit, not much. We change more on Saturdays.' He was mixing up some white stuff in a glass of water. 'I thought I'd be on the safe side,' he said. 'I'd rather knock this back and not worry about what I eat.'

The room was quite cold. She unpacked and put on her petrol-blue woollen dress with long sleeves and settled at the dressing table to do her face.

'Darling, I'll leave you. They'll want me to make drinks.'

'Where will you be?'

'The drawing room. Bottom of the stairs and then opposite you on the left. Don't be long.'

While she combed her hair, powdered her face, and added a discreet touch of blue mascara to her eyelashes, she thought how extraordinary, in fact, it was to be there, the place where she had miserably imagined Edward weekend after weekend during the war. When Rupert and Zoë had come to dinner with them she had thought how unlike Edward Rupert had been, and that although Edward had said how pretty Zoë was, she had seemed rather lifeless. This evening, draped in that peppermint towel, she had looked like a film star, effortlessly fresh and glamorous with that wonderful creamy magnolia skin and those clear green eyes. Of course, she was years older than Zoë, and one's hair when it was permed and tinted, never looked quite the same. She tied a mauve chiffon scarf loosely round her neck to conceal it and went down to find Edward.

In the drawing room she found him talking to a very tall dark man, who rose from his chair when she came in.

'Archie, this is Diana,' Edward said. 'I've just made a splendid Martini.'

'How do you do?' He had a limp, she noticed, and a domed forehead from which his dark hair was receding, and very heavy curved eyelids. He looked at her in a manner that was both penetrating and impassive, and she felt wary of him. It was clear, though, that he was much appreciated by the family. The Duchy made him sit next to her at dinner, during which there was a good deal of general conversation. They ate roast lamb, which reminded someone of the frightful floods – 'two *million* sheep were drowned,' Rachel was saying, 'poor dears.'

'I don't suppose it was any worse for them than being killed any other way,' Teddy said. He was sitting next to Bernadine, who wore what could only be described as a cocktail dress, of turquoise crêpe with bands of gold sequins round the sleeves and neck. She kept putting pieces of skin and fat on his plate and he obediently ate them. On her other side was Edward, with whom she was flirting in a worn, girlish manner that made him dull and breezy. They talked – briefly – about the violence and uncertainty in India: Archie said it looked as though we were going to divide and *not* rule for a change, and Edward made his usual remark about what a damn shame it was that we were casting off the Empire as fast as we could. But what could you expect, considering the government we had?

'I love our government,' Rupert said. 'Don't you think

it's fascinating that the moment the war is over, we stop having dramatic chaps like Churchill and Roosevelt, and opt for quiet little men who look like bank clerks – like Truman and Attlee? It makes peace comfortingly middle class. More roast drowned lamb, please.'

The Duchy said, 'Stop teasing your brother, Rupert.'

Bernadine fitted a cigarette into a long holder and lit it. This, Diana saw, did not go down well with anybody, and after a moment Teddy muttered, 'We don't smoke until after the port.'

Bernadine shrugged, gave him an angry look and then smiled and shrugged again as she stubbed it out on her side-plate. 'I shall never get used to your British ways.' So she had to wait, sulking through the rhubarb tart and cheese.

'That was all right, wasn't it, darling? They liked you – that was plain to see,' Edward said when they were going to bed. 'You fit in a jolly sight better than Teddy's wife.'

She opened her mouth to say that she hoped she *did*, but desisted. Instead, she said, 'It must be very difficult for her. I think she was bored, poor thing.'

'Oh, well, I expect she's wonderful in bed,' he answered. 'And you know what it's like when you're young.'

'She's not young! She looks older than Zoë. Is she the kind of girl you'd have gone for when you were Teddy's age?'

'Lord, no! When I was his age I was madly in love with a sweet, innocent girl called Daphne Brook-Jones – we got engaged, in fact, but we didn't dare tell our families.'

'Why not?'

'We knew they wouldn't approve,' he said. She sensed that he didn't want to tell her why.

'We used to go riding in the Row before breakfast,' he said. 'Otherwise we just met at parties.'

'What happened to her?'

'Oh, she married someone else,' he said.

'And you?'

'I met Villy,' he said shortly.

So his marriage had been a kind of rebound, she thought after he had made rather perfunctory love to her and gone to sleep. She had the feeling that there was more to his first love affair (if that was what it had been) than she would ever find out. But the knowledge that his marriage had been a rebound made her feel more sure of herself.

The weekend was pleasant but uneventful. 'It seems so strange to be here without any of the children,' Rachel said at one point.

'Except me,' Teddy said; he was consuming an enormous Sunday breakfast.

'Well, yes, darling, but you are grown up now.'

'So is Louise. So is Simon. So are Polly and Clary.'

'Yes. There are only the babies left.'

'They're not babies, they're what we used to be.'

'Well, I miss the long table in the hall and the nursery meals,' Rachel said. 'Thread this needle for me, would you, Zoë? I need new specs – can't see a thing.'

'Even Lydia thinks she's grown up,' Teddy said. 'Oh, Lord, I nearly forgot Bernie's tray.' She preferred to have breakfast in bed, he had earlier explained, and he put far more than her share of butter on the tray when he took it up. The Duchy, Rachel said, who deeply disapproved of people having any meals in bed unless they were too ill to eat anything, had said that he must be responsible for bringing the tray down to the dining room so that it could be cleared away with the rest of breakfast.

Diana went round the garden with the Duchy, who showed her her gentians. 'They aren't doing as well as I had hoped, but it's lovely to have them. Do you like gardening?'

'I think I should like it, but either I haven't had the garden or when I had a cottage during the war there never seemed to be time.'

'Ah. But you have three children?'

'Four. Three sons and a daughter.'

The Duchy asked their ages, and Diana explained about the older ones being brought up by grandparents. 'I have Jamie, but he's just started prep school. So only Susan is at home.'

'And how old is she?'

'Almost four.'

'And she is Edward's child,' the Duchy said tranquilly. It was hardly a question.

'Yes – yes, she is.'

There was a pause, and then the Duchy said, 'I don't think that Edward's wife knows this, and as there is to be a divorce, there seems to be no need to broadcast the fact. I hope you agree?'

'Yes.'

She did not tell Edward about this exchange.

A great deal of the conversation consisted of family affairs. Polly's wedding, for instance. Everybody seemed pleased about it, and the wedding was to be in July. Diana felt rather out of this, because she thought she was the only person who had not met Polly's fiancé. 'A nice young man,' the Duchy said.

'He's no pin-up,' Bernadine confided to her, 'but she'll have a title, and they say he's got no money, but it sure doesn't sound like it. He has a house as big as a *hotel*, so she can't be short of dough the way Teddy and me are.' (The remark about Polly had come out of a fairly long ingenuous 'chat' that she'd had with Diana about making ends meet and the meanness of Cazalets' in this respect, which she knew she was supposed to hand on to Edward.)

'Hugh is so pleased. He's become a different person since Polly's engagement,' Rachel said. 'He looks ten years younger.'

'Clary will miss her,' Rupert said. 'They've been such friends for so long. When *is* she coming back to London, Archie, do you know? Archie?'

He had been knocking out his pipe against the grate, and seemed not to have heard. 'I think she'll come back when she's finished her book,' he said.

'The best thing is that they're so tremendously in love,' Zoë had exclaimed, and Diana saw Rupert give her a very loving look. They're in love, she thought. They really are. And envy briefly possessed her.

But on Sunday evening, when they were alone, Edward said, 'Don't get too excited about this wedding.'

'I'm not, but why not? It sounds very happy.'

'We shan't be attending it, I'm afraid.'

'Why not? I've met everyone now, and they seem to have accepted me.'

'Because Hugh wants Villy to go. That's why. Villy was awfully good to Sybil when she was dying, and Hugh has never forgotten that.'

'Oh. Does that mean he'll go on refusing to meet me?'

'I don't know. He may do. He's stubborn as hell about

461

some things. And there are other differences between us. It's not just you.'

'I'm glad of that,' she said.

'Are you?' He looked hurt. 'You know there are.'

Of course she did. It was all about capital investment and Southampton and things which, although he had told her about them, had seemed so tortuous, unresolvable and actually rather boring that she kept forgetting how much they preyed upon his mind. 'Darling! I'm sorry! I know it worries you. I only wish there was something I could do to help.'

'Sweetie! You do help. I love you very much, you know.'

'I know. And I love you.'

Then, when they had returned to London, there had been the fearful business about John. The hospital had rung about an hour ago, Mrs Greenacre said, but when she had rung Home Place she had been told they had left. It was about Major Cresswell. He was in the Middlesex Hospital.

'I'll take you,' Edward had said, and they had gone straight away without even ringing the hospital.

'Do you think he's been in a car accident or something?'

'I don't know, darling. He could just have had a particularly bad attack of malaria.'

'They wouldn't have rung us about that, surely?'

'Or a heart attack or something like that. It's no good worrying about what it is, we can't know. Just have to get there as fast as we can.' It was pouring with rain again, but there was not much traffic.

'He took an overdose,' the ward sister told them, 'but fortunately, he was found in time. We've pumped him

462

out, and he's quite comfortable. Your name was in his address book so, naturally, we telephoned your number.'

She was leading the way down a ward. He was in a bed at the very end of it. Edward said he would wait for her outside. There was a chair by the bed and she sat on it. He lay, looking very grey and pinched with his eyes shut, but he opened them when she said his name. 'Johnnie! It's me, Diana.'

He looked dazed. 'Awfully sorry,' he said. 'Couldn't think what to do.' She took his hand. He gazed at her earnestly. 'It's no use,' he said, 'I simply can't – find . . . Haven't even managed that, though, have I? Here I am again.' He tried to smile and a single tear slid slowly out of one eye.

She stroked his hand. 'Darling Johnnie, it's all right. I'm here.'

'There isn't anyone to talk to, you see.' He shut his eyes again, then, with them still shut, he said, 'That was one good thing about the camp. No shortage of that kind of thing.'

'I think you should get some sleep now. I'll come back tomorrow and we'll talk properly.'

'Poor old chap. What an awful thing!'

By dint of much questioning she discovered that no, he wasn't much good at the job he had at Cazalets'; that they'd kind of *made* a job for him, but it wasn't really working out. He kept worrying about how to do it, and asking other people. Hugh had thought he should go, and Edward had persuaded him to let things run for a bit longer.

'Tell you what. Why don't you talk to Rachel about him? She's really good at that kind of thing.'

And she had been. Diana had rung her and she had

come round the same day and they had had a long talk, and Rachel had said she would go and see him. 'He sounds as though he is too lonely, poor fellow,' she had said.

Diana felt grateful and relieved. Then she began to worry about where he should go when he came out of hospital, which, she had gathered from her second visit, was to be as soon as possible. Obviously, she could suggest his coming to her, but her heart sank at the prospect, and although she guessed that Edward would agree to such a scheme, she knew that he wouldn't want it.

But Rachel had fixed everything. 'I hope you don't think I've been too bossy,' she said on the telephone that same evening, 'but Sister Moore said there was really no point in his remaining in hospital so I've arranged for him to go and stay with an old colleague of mine – a retired sister, who takes people in from time to time for light nursing or convalescence. She lives in Ealing, so you could visit him there. But I've told her what's been going on, and she's a very sensible person. I'm sure she will get him over the next stage. And, meanwhile, we can find him something more congenial to do than sit in a cubbyhole at Cazalets' struggling with figures, which he says he's not good at. I think what we should aim at is getting him a job in some community or institution, somewhere where there is built-in company for him. Sister Moore said that he was underweight, and his kidneys are not too good, so he needs a good rest first. I've talked to him a bit about this and told him that I'll go and see him when he's in Ealing.'

When she tried to thank Rachel, she was interrupted: 'Oh, no. It's the kind of thing I enjoy doing. I only hope you don't think I've been too bossy. He's such a sweet fellow and he deserves a better deal. There must be hundreds of people like him, mustn't there? Who've really been wounded in the war, but in ways that don't show so they simply don't get the right attention.' She paused for breath. 'There was one rather sad thing. He gave me his address book because he wanted me to ring his dentist to cancel his appointment. The only addresses and numbers in it were the dentist and you.'

The morning had almost gone. As she got up, with the notion of having a bath, she thought about her visit to Johnnie the previous week. A fortnight with Sister Crouchback had worked wonders. He looked less shrunken and less generally pathetic; there was some colour in his face, and his clothes looked well cared-for – a properly ironed shirt, and his trousers pressed, his sparse hair neatly combed, his shoes polished. 'He's been learning to knit,' Sister Crouchback declared. 'Taken to it like a duck to water. And he's cut my privet for me quite beautifully. I'm beginning to wonder what I'd do without him.' And she saw him turn pink as she ended, 'There's nothing like having a man about the house.'

How lucky I am, she thought, compared to Johnnie! And she lay in the bath, counting up her blessings: a nice large house, not beautiful but convenient, a housekeeper who relieved her of all the shopping and cooking that had dominated her life for so long, four healthy children, and Edward, who had given up his marriage to marry her. What more could she want? But somehow she did not feel up to pursuing this question.

PART FOUR

PART FOUR

LOUISE

Spring 1947

She sat at the built-in dressing table on which was a shallow cardboard box and a large bottle of nail-varnish remover. The box contained five very small turtles whose shells were thickly covered with bright green or bright yellow glossy paint. She had bought them that morning from a man who stood on a street corner of Madison Avenue and 48th Street with a tray of them. They cost five cents each and she was buying them to save their lives, since, covered with the paint, their shells were unable to breathe. She got a wad of cotton wool out of the dressing-table drawer and soaked it in the acetone. It took a long time to clean each turtle: the top layers of paint came off quite easily, but there was always a good deal left in the minute cracks and crevices. The turtle withdrew its head, which was a good thing, she thought, as the fumes of the acetone might also be bad for it. When she had got all the paint off, she took it to the bathroom and washed the shell with warm water and a bit of soap. Then she dried it on her face towel, and finally tipped some almond oil into a face cream lid, dipped her finger in it and gently massaged the oil into the shell. Then the turtle was ready to join the others – already cleaned – who sat in the bath. They had been in the hotel for nearly three weeks and now she had thirty-five of them cleaned.

Michael had been very nice about it. The turtles had

to be moved every day for them to have baths and she used a dress box from one of her numerous shopping expeditions to house them. She fed them on chopped-up greens, which she ordered every day for breakfast: 'A green salad with no dressing.' Her plan was to take them back to England on the boat, and give them to the zoo. Michael had pointed out that the more she bought, the more the street vendors would procure, and although she recognised the logic of this, she simply couldn't bear to pass the trays of the miserable little creatures and do nothing. Anyway, cleaning them passed the time.

They had come to New York for Michael's show at a gallery on East 57th Street. The show had been a success: portrait drawings of well-known people had been bought, and commissions placed for oil portraits. Michael was out all of every day fulfilling some of them (he was going to have to return to do them all). Today, he was painting Mrs Roosevelt on behalf of a charity that she sponsored. In the mornings, Louise stayed in bed until after breakfast, and then got up very slowly. She felt ill most of the time because the food was so rich. Even if she asked for a boiled egg for breakfast, two arrived, and it seemed a fearful waste not to eat them. Then, most evenings, they were invited out – to large dinner parties chiefly full of people at least twenty years older than she, where enormous meals were presented: great steaks dripping over the plate, fish in rich creamy sauces, elaborate and delicious ice creams. All this would be eaten after at least an hour and a half of Martini drinking, and, she had noted with surprise, many of the men would accompany their dinner with huge glasses of creamy milk. Unlimited butter had contributed to her ill health. It seemed so wonderful and extraordinary to have as much as she liked

– and what was called French bread to spread it on. There were amazing salads for one accustomed to a few limp lettuce leaves, a slice of cooked beetroot and half a tomato. These salads had little pieces of fried bread in them, and dressings made of blue cheese or mayonnaise. She ate an avocado pear for the first time in her life, stuffed with prawns and covered with a thick pink sauce. She ate aubergines, which she found delicious and tasting like nothing else. Best of all were the plates of oysters or cherry-stone clams with which many dinners began. For the first two or three days she had eaten everything put in front of her, but after that she was forced to be more prudent. But she still felt sick, and her back ached. Michael had been incredibly generous; he had given her *carte blanche* to go shopping, and she had made a list in England of people's sizes, and was buying everyone presents. Nylon stockings, lovely idler shoes made of kangaroo hide, beautiful underclothes, trousers, innumerable pretty cotton shirts, clothes to last Sebastian at least two years. The stores, as they were called, were intoxicating; not being bounded by clothes coupons made choice far easier, and things seemed incredibly luxurious and cheap. She knew that there were five dollars to the pound, but the money seemed quite unreal – like playing Monopoly, it hardly counted. She bought herself a black velveteen raincoat, and a pale pink oilskin – and one for Polly, trimmed with dark blue corduroy. There were leather belts in every imaginable colour; she had bought them for all the people she could think of. She bought yards of soft thin raw silk for Aunt Zoë and Polly and Clary, and one length for herself. She bought cotton quilted housecoats for the girls and herself. Every morning she staggered back with boxes and bags of these things and entered the appropriate gifts against her list. She bought pyjamas and shirts for Michael. She walked and walked until she was exhausted. People were very nice to her. Her accent seemed to amaze people. 'Can't you speak English?' a bus conductor had said, after trying to understand where she wanted to go, and when she said no, he seemed convulsed and said lady, she sure was something.

She had gone on like this for about ten days, although sometimes somebody she met at the gallery or at dinner took her out sight-seeing: to Radio City, in a ferry to Ellis Island, where the immigrants had once been landed and sorted out, to the Frick Museum, where the pictures were shown so that each one was like a jewel. The bookshops were full of books printed on white paper – as white as the bread. It was spring, the sky was blue and the air was sharp and exhilarating, and when she walked down the narrower streets, the towering buildings made it very cold. Often she stopped at a drug-store for lunch and drank large tumblers of pure orange juice, which seemed to her the height of luxury.

She did not remember about her cousin Angela until two days before they sailed home. She had never been particularly close to Angela but, still, she felt she should see her. She looked her up in the telephone book; there were pages of Blacks, but she found them – 'Earl C. Black' – and the address was Park Avenue, which she had been in New York long enough to know was smart.

Angela answered the telephone and immediately invited her to lunch.

'Today?'

'If you're free.' The flat – she was learning to call it an apartment – was in an imposing building. 'Take the elevator to the eleventh floor,' Angela said, when she had pressed the buzzer marked 'Black'. She was there at the open door. She wore a narrow black skirt and a scarlet smock. 'What a lovely surprise! Yes, it's due in a couple of weeks,' she said, as Louise, embracing her, encountered her stomach.

She led the way into a large, long sitting room, with windows all the way down one side. A pale carpet covered the floor; one wall had an enormous glass-fronted cabinet filled with blue and white porcelain, and at the far end, over the mantelpiece, hung a portrait of Angela, in a man's green shirt, sitting in a chair with her hair down, that was somehow familiar.

'Rupert's picture of me,' Angela said, seeing her look at it. 'He gave it to us for our wedding. I don't care for it much, but Earl's mad about it. So.' She gave a happy shrug, implying that anything went that he was mad about. 'You look lovely, Louise.'

'So do you. I've never seen you look better.' It was true. Her pale skin glowed faintly with health, her hair shone. She wore no make-up excepting a pale pink lip-stick.

'I've never felt better. I feel as big as a house, but it doesn't seem to matter.'

She wanted news of the family, and Louise, in trying to give it, realised how much she had cut herself off from them. 'You know that the Brig died,' she said.

'Oh, yes. Mummy wrote me about that. And Christopher's given up his farm job and gone to live with Nora and Richard. How's your baby? Only I suppose he isn't a baby any more – he must be about three?'

'Yes. He's fine. Walking and talking and all that.'

'Oh, I can't *wait*! I must show you the nursery I've

made. Earl let me do it just as I liked, and I've finished it just on time. We're having a chicken salad for lunch. I hope that's OK. Earl thought I might like to have you to myself,' she explained, as they went to collect the lunch laid out on trays in the kitchen. 'He sent you his love and hopes you're enjoying New York.'

'Is he out of the Army?'

'Oh, yes – ages ago. He's back in practice.'

'Of course – he's a doctor.'

'He's a psychiatrist. He has a small apartment on the ground floor of this block where he works. He has so many patients now that he has to keep referring people. He says we'll be rich enough to buy a cottage out in the country so that the baby will get to have a nice open-air life. I feel so lucky, Louise.'

'I think you were awfully brave to come out here by yourself and get married without your family about.'

'I had a funny trip out, I can tell you. The worst crossing they'd ever had, according to the captain, and everyone threw up practically, except me. I didn't miss a single meal. There were four hundred of us.'

'How do you mean "us"?'

'GI brides. Except, of course, I wasn't one. I was just a fiancée. It was an awful trip. But then Earl met me on the quay and brought me back here, and we got married the following day. It was wonderful. No, I wasn't brave. I knew I wanted to marry Earl. I *knew* I was in love with him.'

Later, when she had shown the nursery – 'I made it blue, because it would be silly in pink if it's a boy' – she said, 'I didn't think I *could* be happier until I got pregnant. Did you feel like that?'

'Not exactly.'

Angela gave her a quick look and fell silent. She had asked about Michael earlier, and Louise had told her about the exhibition being a success. 'Would you like to bring Michael to dinner?' Angela asked – with some diffidence.

'We're leaving in two days, and he's made plans for the last two evenings. I'd much *rather* come to you.'

Then, because she was in a strange country, and because she was leaving so shortly, and perhaps, most of all, because so much of her life seemed unreal, she said: 'I don't feel like you at all. I didn't want my child when I had him. So now I'll never know whether I would ever have wanted him. I don't think I love Michael. I think I may have to leave him.' And then, the enormity of what she had just said was too much for her, and she burst into tears.

Angela moved to her – they were back in the sitting room – took the coffee cup from her shaking hand and put her arms round her, holding her without saying anything until she had stopped crying. 'I'm so *sorry*,' she then said. 'It must be so awful for you – so difficult and awful. I wish I could help.'

'Would you like to talk to Earl?' she said, when Louise had dried her eyes. 'It can be a help to talk to someone who is outside the situation. And he's really kind and good.'

'No. I tried that. You won't tell any of the family, will you? I mean – I haven't made up my mind about what to do. I must do that on my own.'

'Of course I won't. Will you keep in touch, though?'

She said she would.

At the door, when she was leaving, Angela said, 'I meant it about keeping in touch. You could come and stay with us.'

'Thank you. I'll remember.'

Happiness makes people much nicer, she thought as she went down in the lift. I wonder what that makes me?

She decided to walk back to the hotel so that she wouldn't have to talk to a cab driver. Angela's suggestion that she should talk to Earl brought up painful thoughts. Earl was a psychiatrist, like Dr Schmidt had been, and remembering him still made her feel raw. He had seemed such an answer: an old man, with white hair and a moustache and dark brown penetrating eyes with dark marks under them. She had gone to his gloomy ground-floor flat where he practised. It was cold and the daylight that filtered through the dirty net curtains was like fog. But he had seemed so wise, and so kind, and he really listened to her – an experience she felt she had never had before in her life. She sat in a rather hard armchair, and he sat opposite her in its pair, with a small rickety round table between them. Dr Schmidt had come into her life not through Stella, although it had been she who had first suggested such a course, but through Polly and Clary, who had an Austrian friend who knew people like that. So she had asked them to ask 'for a friend of mine', and saw Clary shoot a quick look at her, although nothing had been said. But, quite soon after that, one of them had rung her with Dr Schmidt's telephone number and address. She had told Michael that she was going to see him, and he had seemed quite pleased. 'Good idea,' he had said. 'It might help to sort you out, darling.'

'Supposing he wants to see you?' she said.

'Oh, I don't think he'll want to do that. I should think that very unlikely.'

Anyway, she rang up.

'And how do you hear of me?' she was asked.

She mentioned the Austrian friend.

'Ah, so! A dear friend of mine.' His foreign voice sounded warm. He made an appointment for her at once.

At first she had not known what to say, had sat twisting her fingers in her lap and looking over his shoulder. 'You are nervous,' he remarked. 'It is natural. You do not know me.'

'I don't know where to begin.'

'You may begin anywhere. Tell me how you are feeling with your life.'

And after that, she found it quite easy to think of things to say. To begin with, she was very much afraid that he would think her so worthless and wicked that she would tell him something and then make some remark to pre-empt any adverse judgement. Things like 'So, you see, I didn't even want to have a baby although I knew that Michael might be killed.' And about her affair with Rory: 'So, you see, I was unfaithful to Michael about two years after we were married.' She rushed headlong through her misdemeanours, attacking them not in chronological order but, rather, in order of their gravity. She watched him carefully for any reaction, but his expression of attentive interest did not change. She went twice a week for an hour, and after the first two or three sessions, she began to look forward to the time when he would pronounce upon her life and tell her what to do. But this continued not to happen; he occasionally asked a question, but that was all. This was beginning to irritate her, and when, some six weeks after she had started going to him, he asked – out of the blue; it had no reference to anything she had been saying – how she got on with her father, something snapped in her. 'Why do you simply ask me questions? Why don't you *tell* me what to do? I don't care if you think I've behaved badly because I know that anyway, so why don't you say what you think?'

He looked at her for a long time without speaking. Then he smiled. 'I am not here to judge you,' he said. 'There seem to be enough judges in your life, beginning with yourself. I shall not join them.'

'So what – what do you do?'

'I am here to listen, so that you can unpack your mind and look at what you find there. If I were to say, "That is good, that is bad," you might find it difficult to take everything out. I think you find it already hard.'

'Do I?' She was beginning to feel frightened.

'I think you have not yet told me what has made you most unhappy – what has most disturbed you.'

'No.'

'Breathe,' he said, 'it is good to breathe.'

She let out her breath. 'I haven't told you, I haven't told anyone. One person knows it *happened* but I didn't tell her what it was like because I couldn't bear to. It made me so very unhappy, sad, miserable for a long time and then, at the end of it, it felt as though a bit of me had died, as though I couldn't feel any more about it, or much about anything else.' She felt her throat closing and swallowed. 'It was so awful! So horrible! And I loved him so much!'

'It is natural to love one's father.'

'My father? I'm not talking about my *father*! *No*! I'm talking about someone called Hugo. I told you about

Rory, which didn't really matter, but I didn't tell you about Hugo.'

She told him all of that. Every single thing she could think of; when she got to the last few minutes that she had spent with him, tears began streaming out of her eyes but she continued right through the sojourn in Holyhead, and Michael's destroying Hugo's letter, up to the luncheon party at Hatton, months later, when she had discovered Hugo's death because casual mention was made of it at lunch. Then she broke down utterly – sobbed herself dry. Then he said she must go, but she could sit in the next room for a while to recover herself. 'If you wish.' She went and sat in an even darker room that had a divan in it and a wardrobe with a long mirror set in one of its doors, and an open, empty violin case lying on a table. But after a minute or two she didn't want to stay there, and left. She felt light and parched and silent inside.

The next time she went, he asked her to tell him more about the Hugo affair as he called it. She didn't want to – she felt she'd told him everything – but he said that this time he wanted to know how she felt about it at the different stages. There was an impasse. She sulked and he remained silent until the end of the session. The next time she asked him what more he could possibly want to know about all that, and he said, 'The things I do not know.'

'Or,' he added, when she had not replied, 'things that you have told me that I have not understood.'

So she went through it all again; this time, although she had tearful moments, she did not break down. When she got to the bit about Michael destroying Hugo's only letter to her she did not feel so sad, much more furious with Michael. Afterwards she felt exhilarated and very grateful to Dr Schmidt, who seemed to her then to be the most wonderfully trustworthy, intelligent and wise person she had ever met in her life. It was extraordinary to have someone to whom one could say anything, *knowing* that one could entirely trust them. By now he knew all kinds of things about her that she had never dreamed of imparting to anyone. The fact that going to bed with Michael had never worked, for instance. 'Or with Rory?' he had asked. 'Or with Rory,' she had answered. 'Most people aren't like that, are they? Like me, I mean?'

'When you say "most people", you imply that you should be one of them. Why do you think like that?'

'It would make one fit in more easily, I suppose.'

'Ach, so. But sometimes we are not like most people. What then?'

'*I* don't know. I feel you keep asking me questions when you know the answers to them perfectly well. I can't see the point of it.'

He sat quietly, looking at her. The skin under his black eyes was almost like purple grapeskin, she thought. 'I do know why, of course. You want *me* to know the answers . . .'

One day she went, full of the news that she was going to New York – for some weeks, she thought, she didn't know for how long. He said nothing to this; he seemed abstracted. At the end of the session, he asked her if she would mind changing the time at which she came. Could she come at five o'clock instead of three? It made no difference to her. She had become used to knowing when her session was up, because the doorbell would ring, and he would answer it and put the newcomer into his small back room until she had left. She never met another patient.

But the next time she went, she noticed that he was wearing a different suit and bow tie and that the table, which was usually between them, had been moved and was now covered by a coloured embroidered cloth on which were a plate with two slices of cake and two wine glasses.

'Are you going to have a party?' she asked; she felt glad at these signs of his having some ordinary social life.

He smiled. 'Oh, yes! Perhaps. We shall see.'

His assault, when it came, was utterly without warning of any kind. One minute he was opposite her, head slightly hunched between his shoulders, and the next he was on his knees, surprisingly powerful arms enclosing her, pushing her head – by the back of her neck – towards his face until his mouth met her cheek and moved sideways and downwards until he reached her mouth. The shock was so great that, for what seemed a long time, while these physical manoeuvres took place, she was paralysed, but as he fastened his mouth on hers she began to fight him, pushing weakly with her hands since he had pinioned her upper arms, clenching her teeth against his tongue, and finally dropping her head and butting his face with her forehead. He fell back at this and she freed her arms to push him suddenly and hard so that he fell sideways on to the floor. She got up from the chair to her feet just as he was beginning to sit up.

'Wait,' he said. 'You have not understood. I adore you—'

'I hate *you*!' she tried to say but, like a nightmare, no sound came out.

Without her coat or bag, she ran from his room down the passage to the front door, which she wrested open, down the steps into the street. She ran the whole length of the street and at the corner looked to see if he was following her, but he was not. She turned the corner and continued running, and when she reached the main road by the park, she realised that she had no money to get either the bus or a cab. It was late, and the park would be closing; she leaned against a pillar box trying to get her breath back and then renewed fears that he would pursue her took hold and she hailed the first empty cab that came. Someone would have the money for it at home, was her last coherent thought. When she reached home, she called Nannie, who produced the money for the fare, and, saying that Mummy looked really tired, offered her a nice cup of tea in the nursery. 'Sebastian would love to have tea with his mummy.'

'I'm sorry. I don't feel well. I may have caught something. I just want to go to bed.' Michael was not back from the studio; she threw herself on the bed and lay there while it got dark.

She never saw him again. The next day, her coat and bag were returned to her by some young man of whom she knew nothing, but who announced himself as Hans Schmidt. 'My father asked that I bring you these,' he said. She took them without a word and shut the door on him.

When Michael enquired how she was getting on with Dr Schmidt, she said that she did not like him and had given up going, news that he received with a kind of weary indulgence: she was full of whims – she would never stick to anything.

Since then she had had a series of nightmares about him that always took the same form but with variations, so that there was always a shock attached to each dream. She would be going about her life and he would materialise from nowhere, and he was always coming towards her. Once it was on a moving staircase, when she was on the descending side and she saw him ascending – watching her with his dark, intent eyes. When he reached a level with her he seemed to disappear, but then the man standing on the stair below her would turn round to face her – and it would be him. Another time she was running from him through a series of rooms with doors that led into one another, and when she reached the door that led out of the house, it would open and he would be standing there. The nightmares stopped exactly when she had tried to scream and discovered that she could make no sound. These dreams, although they slowly became less frequent, continued throughout that winter. Looking back on that time, she knew now that it had changed things. She remembered how that winter when she and Michael went to large dinner parties, she would look at the men alternated with women round a dinner table and wonder whether, when they were alone with a woman, they behaved in some way or another like Dr Schmidt. If this was so, she had to find some way of dealing with it. One way would be to look so awful and behave so unpleasantly that no man would want even to talk to her, but there was a serious flaw in this solution. She felt so worthless and guilty – about Sebastian and also about Michael – that the only times when she felt any better were when someone paid her any kind of admiring attention. She knew that people thought her beautiful, and although she did not agree with them (she would not have chosen her appearance which struck her as too bony and otherwise dull), she relied upon even small, casual remarks about it to give her fleeting moments of self-esteem. She had also a reputation for intelligence that privately she knew to be unfounded but, again, it helped that some people thought this and said so. So she could hardly afford to be entirely unapproachable. The situation remained miserably unresolved.

She had been lonely that winter: Stella, having landed a job with a London newspaper, was immediately sent abroad as a foreign correspondent, which meant that she came back to London rarely and only for fleeting visits.

She saw Polly a bit at the flat, but Clary was hardly ever there and when she was had turned into someone it was very difficult to talk to, although Polly was comfortingly the same. Sometimes, after she had spent an evening with her, she felt envious of Polly's life: her own place, a job where she was taken seriously enough to earn money, and her being able to choose exactly how she spent her spare time. All the efforts Louise had made to get employment had come to little or, in most cases, nothing: an amateur reading of a communist verse play in Ealing, a couple of small parts in radio plays, and three auditions for parts in the theatre, none of which she got. There had been no film work and she had stopped trying to get any.

They had spent the first Christmas after the war at Hatton. She had wanted to stay in their own house, but Michael was adamant, and since she knew, although nothing was said, that he was cross with her for stopping seeing Dr Schmidt, she neither dared nor felt up to arguing with him.

After that – which was three weeks of being disapproved of, for smoking, for drinking alcohol, for not being pregnant, and for being a bad mother, all indisputable bull's eyes, she thought miserably – they came back to London, and she resumed her life of trying to think of meals for Mrs Alsop to cook, things to do with Sebastian on Nannie's day out and, occasionally, going off on her own to some of the places she'd been to with Hugo. One day, in Portobello, in the window of the shop where he'd found the Pembroke table, she saw a piece of red and cream striped silk draped across an inlaid table. It was the remains of a curtain, the man in the shop said, a bit frayed at the edges but a nice piece of material. He wanted three pounds for it and she bought it simply because she loved the stripes. The red, which was both soft and bright, was of satin; the cream stripe was watered taffeta. She took it to her dressmaker who said it was just possible to make a dress of it if she had an almost straight skirt and a bodice with ribbon shoulder straps. It was a romantic dress with a faintly Regency air, and the first opportunity to wear it came when Michael arranged a dinner party, which included, among others, his mother and stepfather and a well-known conductor, who was one of Sebastian's godparents. The latter insisted upon Louise taking him to see his godchild. 'He'll be asleep,' she said, as they climbed the stairs to the nursery floor.

He was asleep. Together, they gazed at him in his bed, the only light coming from the open door to the passage. She turned to go and felt his heavy hand on her shoulder trying to ease off her shoulder strap. As she backed away it broke, and she found herself facing him, holding her dress over her breast. He was still groping for her, 'You're such a damned attractive girl,' as she fled down the passage to the day nursery, where she got Nannie to repair the shoulder strap. This incident was useful to her because she found that it did not induce panic; she simply felt angry. All through that evening she found herself looking at parts of him – his oiled black hair which, she realised, was so black it must be dyed, his hideous hands, which would have been suitable for an ogre they were so large and knobbly, his polished hypo-crisy, 'What a little angel I have for a godchild,' and other creepy remarks he made to Zee, and the way that his eyes slid furtively over her without engagement.

Then there had been the party for Angela . . . and thinking of that, she realised how much Angela had changed. Then she had been thin as a stick, pale, with mascara and startlingly red lips, very cool in her responses to the congratulations, hardly smiling or talking. Now she was altogether more solid: rounder, softer, spontaneously warm. Perhaps there is such a thing as a happy marriage, she thought. Of course, there must be – it was she who had made a hash of it.

She was reaching the corner where the man had the tray of turtles. She had promised Michael that she would not buy any more as he said that no more would fit into the dress box in which they were to travel. He had been so nice about the turtles that she felt she ought to stick to his ruling. After all, if she bought, say, three more, there would still be at least a dozen on the tray and more of them tomorrow. So she kept on the wrong side of the street for the turtle man.

Michael was back in their room. 'Where *have* you been?'

'To see Angela – my cousin. I had lunch with her.'

'But it's nearly five o'clock!'

'I walked back. It was quite a long way. Anyway, what does it matter? We're not going out till eight.'

'Well, we are, as a matter of fact. We're having drinks with Maimie and Arthur Kesterman – you know, we met them with the Ameses'.' She didn't know, but there seemed no point in saying so. 'So, darling, you'd better start changing. Oh, damn! Someone's coming to photograph us before the dinner. We'll have to get him here earlier, or to see us at the Kestermans'.'

'Why do they want to photograph us?'

'Ah, well,' he answered. He was tying his black tie. 'It's because we're so awfully famous.'

'*You* are. I'm not.'

'You *are* – because you're my wife.' He caught her eye in the dressing-table mirror. 'At least, I wish you were *more* my wife than you seem prepared to be. Have you made up your mind about that?'

'About what?' she said stupidly.

'About going to bed with me, darling. It's pretty rough, you know, living cheek by jowl, everybody saying how ravishing your wife is when she won't play with you.'

'I suppose it must be . . . I'm sorry.' To have this sort of conversation at the same time as having to take off her clothes made her feel shaky and sullen. 'I think I'll have a bath.'

'You won't have time. We've got to be there in three-quarters of an hour and you know how long it takes to move all those turtles.'

So she didn't. She changed into the dress he chose for her – he was good at picking the right outfit for these occasions, which always seemed to her very much like one another but were, he insisted, full of subtle distinctions.

It was a long evening and she ended it a little drunk. The prolonged drinking before the dinner party and her inability to think of fresh answers to the questions she had been asked for the last three weeks – 'How do you like New York?' 'What is it like to be married to such a famous and charming husband?' 'How many children have you got?' followed by 'I expect you miss him terribly, don't you?' – made her drink too much before dinner, and not want to eat when the food arrived.

Michael drank a good deal as well. They did not get back to the hotel until after one, and while they were undressing, he said, 'Don't bother to put on your night-dress, I'm going to make love to you.'

I don't mind! she thought, when it was over and he had turned away from her to sleep. I didn't even feel anything about not liking it. I simply didn't feel anything at all. This, surely, must be a step in the right direction. Just not to care a damn, one way or the other.

On the boat, going back to England, it happened several more times – with the same result.

At Southampton, Zee met them with Sebastian and Nannie. Zee and her chauffeur drove back to London with Michael, and Louise, Nannie and Sebastian went by train. 'You don't mind, darling, do you?' Michael said. 'Only Mummy hasn't seen me for so long, she wants a little time with me to herself.'

She didn't mind.

She returned to life at Edwardes Square. Stella was still away, Polly was going to be married, Mrs Alsop gave in her notice the morning after her return. 'There are people in this house, madam, who seem to think they should be waited on hand, foot and finger,' and as she had been alone in it with Nannie and Sebastian, her meaning was clear. After Mrs Alsop had left the bedroom – she was in the throes of unpacking – clearly disappointed that her bombshell had not had more impact, Louise spent the rest of the morning allocating the presents she had bought for everyone in New York. When Michael rang at lunchtime to say that he would be out in the evening, she decided to take Polly's and Clary's presents to Blandford Street.

Neville – surprisingly – opened the door to her. He was wearing a pyjama jacket and half of his face was covered with shaving soap. 'Oh, hello, Louise. Polly's on the telephone, as usual, so she asked me to answer the door. I stay here in the holidays,' he continued as they went up the stairs. He towered above her now – must be over six feet – although, with his tufted hair and sticking-out ears, he looked otherwise the same. 'Do talk to me while I finish my shave,' he said, when they reached the open bathroom door. 'You'll have to sit on the stairs if you want to sit. Poll hates being interrupted when she's talking to her lord.'

'Why are you shaving at this time in the evening?'

'I'm off to work in a minute. Anyway, it doesn't matter when I do it. I can see it's going to bore me most frightfully for the rest of my life. I was thinking of growing a beard, but they aren't fancied at Stowe – except for the art master.'

Quite soon he cut himself. 'When I have to do it every day, my face will be like a railway junction,' he complained.

'What's your work?'

'I wash up at the Savoy. It's absolutely tedious, but I get a free meal and paid in cash. I'm saving up to go to Greece and Turkey and a few other places like that.'

'Are you going on your own?' It seemed wonderfully adventurous.

'I'm going with two friends, Quentin and Alex. Quentin's father was in some embassy in Athens so he's got quite good at Greek. We're buying an Oldsmobile from a man in Bletchley. It's quite old, but the man says it's the most remarkable car he has ever had pass through his garage. He only wants ninety-eight pounds for it. Hence the washing-up.' He mopped his face and dried it with a tea-cloth. 'What do you think of Polly marrying a lord?' he said.

'I haven't met him. Do you like him?'

He shrugged. 'He seems all right. Of course, Polly thinks he's super-wonderful. People always think that before they marry people, don't they? They don't seem to notice that secretly they're just like everyone else. I don't think I shall marry. I would, if I were Polly, because I should be interested to go to a coronation. Although I expect she'll be so old by the time there is one she won't enjoy it. But there isn't anyone I could marry that would give me the *entrée*.'

'Why do you want to go to one?'

'Partly the trumpets. They have marvellous trumpets at things like that, I'm told – the man who teaches me the trumpet told me that – and partly all the dressing up, fur, you know, and velvet and wearing a coronet. I suppose I have a thirst for experiences that are out of reach – the ones I *can* have are mostly too tedious for words.'

'Do you know what you want to do?'

'Do? I don't want to do anything. Well, I want to get into university if I can because at least it will put off the ghastly National Service, and by the time I've finished at Cambridge, or wherever I get into, they might have stopped having it. Quentin thinks there's a sporting chance. Simon is loathing it. He's in the RAF and he says the officers *moult* in the bath.'

He took off his pyjama jacket – he had on a shirt underneath.

'She's off the telephone and I'm off to work. You couldn't sock me sixpence for the bus, could you? I haven't got any money.'

'You don't change,' she said, as she gave him the sixpence. 'About money, anyway.'

'No, I don't – haven't found the need. And I've been short of cash all my life.'

'Scrounging again.' Polly had come noiselessly down the stairs and now stooped to give Louise a kiss. 'If he'd had the slightest chance, he would have asked me for the bus fare as well and then he would have bought something to eat.'

'Quite right. I'm well known.' He smiled with sudden, dazzling charm, threw his pyjama jacket carelessly on to the floor of his room and went.

'Come up. Sorry, I was on the telephone.'

She was looking particularly lovely, even in her oldest blue jersey with the elbows darned in a lighter blue and her coppery hair tied back with a crumpled piece of blue velvet ribbon. All the evening, she glowed: she shone as though she was full of sunlight. 'I hadn't the slightest idea that one could feel like this,' she said, 'as though the rest of my life is going to be a magic adventure. I feel so lucky to have met him – I very nearly didn't.'

At one point she asked Polly if she was *sure*, absolutely sure, and she answered serenely, 'Oh, yes. We both are. We both feel the same.'

She showed her clothes. 'And the best thing is – but I haven't got it yet – my New Look suit for going away. Someone in Paris started it. It's the opposite of all the dreary utility clothes. A huge full skirt and tight waist and lovely rounded shoulders. I'm having it in a very fine broadcloth – peacock greeny blue with black braid on the jacket. You should get one made, Louise, it would suit you perfectly.'

Later, she said, 'You know how you feel completely excited and completely at home with someone? That's how I feel about Gerald.' Then she added, almost shyly, 'Is that how you feel? Felt when *you* were engaged?'

'I can't remember. I expect I did. I don't know.'

'Tell me about New York. Was it wonderful?'

She tried to remember what it had been like and failed. 'It – of course, it was all completely different. All clean and gleaming, with masses of food and shops full of everything.' As she spoke she discovered with the beginnings of panic that the whole time there had not really impinged upon her, seemed as dull and unreal as a distant dream where nothing is sharply remembered, events seemed to have no consecutive significance, and people were simply faceless crowds with the same voice. It had been nearly four weeks of her life, and not very long ago, and nothing of it remained with her.

'I brought you some things,' she said, or thought she said, as the terrifying idea that perhaps, sometimes, she simply did not exist occurred to her. Then she remembered the turtles, grotesque in their dreadful green and yellow paint, how their tiny antique heads set with a pair of eyes like minute black beads retracted with fear when picked up, but would slowly emerge if she scratched the undershell gently, while the front rounded flippers and smaller back legs would make little scooping underwater movements, and how beautiful their shells were when the paint was removed, and she was able to tell Polly about them. 'They only cost five cents,' she said, 'two for a dime, so I bought a lot of them.'

'What have you done with them?'

'I took them to the London Zoo, except for four that I've kept for Sebastian. But he doesn't seem to care for them much.'

Polly said that Gerald had a lake; it was very weedy and generally in a mess, but if the turtles came from North America they would probably be all right in a Norfolk lake. So if Louise got tired of them, at any time, she would look after them.

Polly had been pleased with her presents. They had talked a bit about Clary, who, Polly said, was living like a hermit in a cottage that Archie had found for her. 'She doesn't like being here any more,' Polly said. 'It reminds her of all the wrong things.'

'Is she still very unhappy about the man she was working for?'

'I don't know. But you know how whole-hearted Clary is. When she loves someone, she really *loves* them.'

Unlike me, Louise thought.

Just before she left, she said, 'Do you have to pay all the rent while Clary isn't here?'

'No. Uncle Rupe kindly said he'd pay Clary's share because Neville comes here quite a lot.'

'So what do *you* have to pay?'

'Half. Seventy-five pounds a year. It's quite cheap, really, because of all the poultering that goes on in the basement. It smells, rather, sometimes.'

Going home in a cab she realised that she had not the slightest idea whether seventy-five pounds (a hundred and fifty, if you counted the whole flat) was cheap or not. I would have to earn money, in any case, she thought, regularly, not just the odd broadcast, because that wouldn't even pay any rent – let alone all the other things! That night, she tried to make a list of what the other things might be. Gas, electricity, a telephone (although she supposed that she could do without one), bus fares, having sheets and things washed by a laundry. She had enough clothes to last for ages, but there were still things like having shoes mended (she was rather proud of thinking of that), and then there were things like electric lightbulbs, lavatory paper, Lux to wash her clothes, and toothpaste and Tampax and make-up . . . She began to wish she had asked Polly what she earned; then she remembered that Uncle Hugh gave her an allowance, anyway, of a hundred a year, so whatever Polly earned *she*'d need to earn a hundred more . . .

She couldn't go home because she no longer had one. She knew that even if her mother stopped being so angry with her for knowing about her father leaving, she would not be able to bear living in that dark, unhappy little house. But now that her father was settled with Diana, who had seemed disposed to be friendly, she might go and see them and find out what they thought she could do. He might pay for me to do a typing course, she thought. If I did that, I would be able to get some sort of work.

She rang her father at home and got Diana. 'I'm afraid you can't,' she said. 'He's gone to bed early. He hasn't been very well.'

'What's the matter with him?'

'He had a rather bad appendix operation. He only got back from the nursing home yesterday.'

'Poor Dad! Could I come and see him?'

'I should leave it for a bit. He's feeling pretty awful, and I'm not letting him have visitors.'

She said she would ring the next day, which she did. Diana still put her off. After two more days of this, she rang her uncle Rupert at the office.

'He's been awfully ill – he damn nearly died. A burst appendix – horrible thing – poor old boy. It happened while you were away or I suppose Diana would have told you.'

'She doesn't seem to want me to go to see him.'

'Well, I suppose she's been very worried about his getting too tired.' Then he said, 'I should just go, if I were you. The nurse told me he'd been asking for you. Kept saying, "Is my daughter in the house?" and the nurse didn't even know that he had a daughter till the house-keeper told him. So perhaps you should just go.'

She went in the afternoon, late enough for him to have had a rest, and took him a bunch of white lilac and yellow irises. She felt, when she was getting it, that it might well be the last bunch of flowers that she would buy for a very long time so it might as well be an expensive one.

The housekeeper said that Mr Cazalet was resting and Madam was out.

'I've come to see my father.'

'Oh! That will be nice for him!'

He was lying in a large bed propped up by pillows and awake. A book lay open on the bed, but he was not reading it. He seemed very pleased to see her.

The housekeeper suggested bringing some tea.

'Why not!' he said. 'You'd like some, wouldn't you, darling? Oh, it is good to see you!'

She sat in a chair by the bed. He had lost a lot of weight so that his eyes looked much larger in his face, which seemed otherwise to have shrunk.

'I knew you were going to America,' he said, 'because you rang, Diana said, but I didn't know when you'd be back.'

She knew that she'd told Diana it would be for four weeks, but she didn't say this.

'Anyway, you're back,' he said, 'that's the great thing.'

He put out his hand and she took it. 'I didn't know you were ill or I would have come the moment I got back.'

He squeezed her hand faintly; he seemed very weak. 'You would, I know you would.'

There was a pause, then he said, 'I nearly copped it. To tell you the truth, I thought I'd got cancer so I put off going to the doctor, although I felt bloody awful. My fault really.'

'Poor Dad.'

'And you know,' he shifted himself up a bit in the bed, which clearly hurt him, 'after the op when they were giving me some pretty fierce painkillers the night nurse – she was a real brick – said that I went on and on about having my medals cleaned because the King was coming to have tea with me! She said she had to say that she'd taken them away for a thorough cleaning because, of course, they weren't in the hospital at all, they were here, at home. Funny what one thinks at times like that, isn't it?' He had a pathetic, boyish expression that she'd never seen before.

'Yes. I suppose, somewhere inside you, you *wanted* him to have tea with you.'

'To thank me,' he said. 'All those awful things that happened – all for King and country, you know. There hasn't really been a way of making up for it.'

496

'The war?'

'Tell you something, I had to *shoot* people. Not the enemy – our own blokes. I had to go out at night and put a bullet into them. Put them out of their misery. Never talked about that to anyone – not even Hugh.' He looked at her earnestly. 'Perhaps I shouldn't have mentioned that. Don't want to upset you. That's the last thing I want in the world.'

'It doesn't upset me,' she said. 'I'm glad you told me. Shall I get your medals? Would you like to see them?'

'They're in that drawer.' He indicated it.

There were three boxes: two fat square ones and a long thin one.

'Those are just for pinning on to evening dress,' he said, discarding the long box. 'These are the real ones.'

He clicked open one box and there, on the grubby, bruised blue velvet, lay the white enamel and gold Military Cross.

'That's the bar,' he said. 'I got it twice, you see.'

'And you were recommended for a Victoria Cross, weren't you?'

'I got the bar instead.'

They were interrupted by the sound of voices, Diana's and the housekeeper's, on the stairs.

'Have them,' he said. 'I'd really like you to have them. I won't be able to leave you anything. Put them in your bag. Quick!'

She did as he asked. His wanting to be surreptitious about it shocked her.

The door burst open and Diana came in with a tray.

There followed an uneasy tea. During it Louise came to realise that Diana actually disliked her – was jealous? Disapproved? She didn't know. But, worse, she also sensed her father's nervousness, his desire to please or, at least, to placate Diana. He constantly said how wonderful Diana was and had been to him; the story of his illness and going in an ambulance was told by both of them, the postponement of a summer holiday in France – much lamented by her father, on the grounds that Diana needed a well-deserved rest, and made light of by Diana, in a way that reminded her curiously of her own mother.

This did not last long: as soon as tea had been drunk, Diana said that the invalid must be given respite. 'You have a little rest and read your book, darling, and I'll see Louise out.'

He had looked at the book lying face downwards on the bed. *The Judge's Story* by Charles Morgan.

'I'm afraid it's too highbrow for me,' he said. 'I can't seem to get into it. I think I'll just have forty winks.'

'Come again, won't you?' he said as, watched by Diana, she bent to kiss his face. As she straightened up she met his beseeching eyes: he looked exhausted. 'My two favourite women,' he said, in a voice uneasily meant for both of them. She felt a lump in her throat. When she looked back at him from the door, he caught her eye, put his fingers to his lips and attempted to blow her a kiss.

'Of course I'll come,' she said.

In the hall, Diana said, 'He gets tired very quickly. That's why I don't feel that he's quite up to visitors yet.'

'He is all right, though, isn't he? I mean – he is going to get well?'

'Of course he is. It will just take time, that's all.' She smiled in a conclusive way. 'How was America?' she asked, with massive incuriosity. Before she could reply, a door burst open and a small girl said, 'Mummy, are you going to read to me or *aren't* you going to read to me? I've been waiting and waiting and waiting.'

'This is Susan. Say hello to Louise.'

'Hello to Louise. *Now*, Mummy.'

'Yes, I will. Just saying goodbye to Louise.' She brushed the air an inch from Louise's face. 'I'll let you know when he's up to another visit.'

No, you won't, she thought, as she walked down the street. She felt bewildered by Diana's animosity, and uneasy about her father. Apart from looking far iller than she had expected, he did not seem happy. Instances of the difference between his behaviour when he had been alone with her and when he was not came back to her with uncomfortable clarity; he seemed vulnerable – something she had never thought of him being – and also somehow trapped. What right had Diana to decide whether she should see him or not? She remembered Diana's friendly behaviour to her on the only other occasion when they had met – at her father's club – and began to dislike her more. The way he had talked about his war, almost like a confession, had made him seem as young and vulnerable, she realised, as once he must have been. Whatever he had done, whatever had happened to him, whatever wrong moves or choices he had made, she discovered then that she still had affection for him – still loved him. It was an extraordinary relief.

But it was useless to suppose that he was, or Diana would allow him to be, in any position to help her now. She would have to fend for herself. This felt uncomfortable, but right. On the long journey home, which involved two buses and a wait for the second one, things began to take shape.

499

She was going. If she left Michael she would have to leave Sebastian and Nannie. She could not possibly cope with looking after them as she would have no money to start with, no job and nowhere to live. If she tried to think about all of this, she felt sick. It would be best to think about one thing at a time. The place to live seemed a good start. If she could raise the rent money for it, perhaps she could take over Clary's half of the flat in Blandford Street. But, then, Polly would also be leaving it when she married and she couldn't possibly afford the whole thing. Perhaps Stella would return and she would need somewhere? She might, but it couldn't be counted on. Then she remembered that once, in a restaurant in the winter, a card had been sent over to her and Michael's table. It had said: 'Would you be interested in modelling for *Vogue*?' She had lost the card, but she could ring them up and see if they would employ her. Or I could do what Neville was doing, she thought. Anyone can wash up. And I did learn a bit about cooking once. Perhaps I can be a cook.

She decided to write to Stella and tell her.

It seemed very odd to be going back to Edwardes Square – to Nannie and the end of Mrs Alsop – and a dinner party in Markham Square that night with Michael. I can go on seeing Sebastian every week on Nannie's day out, she thought, as long as I get a job that gives me that time off. This did not seem any more difficult than getting a job. She began to have wild ideas. She might write a play; she had always meant to do that. Or she might try far harder to get work in the theatre. She was nearly home before she wondered what Michael would say or do when she told him. Whatever it was, she knew, somehow, that he would not really mind, might even be relieved, particularly as she was the one who was doing it – leaving him so that he would seem the good person. I've let him down so much, she thought, that really leaving him will be stopping doing it. He can divorce me and marry Rowena. She had discovered that he was seeing her just before they had gone to America and that, too, had been a relief. It made her feel less guilty about him, at least. There seemed to be nothing she could do to feel better about Sebastian – nothing. Somehow, she could not bear to think about him. She seemed to have let him down from the start – by the mere process of having him at all. She had a feeling that she was going to pay for that all of her life.

But going, otherwise, seemed to her a new air – freedom – as though she was taking the paint off her own back and starting to be what she was meant to be in the first place. An impoverished divorced woman of twenty-four (well, she would be even older before she was actually divorced), with no skills, no qualifications; it all sounded pretty frightening, but it was a challenge and she had to risk meeting it.

CLARY

1946–47

'It might interest you to know what Rupert said.'

She had been so angry, she had just looked at him.

'He said, there was no point in your turning me into your father when you had a perfectly good one already.'

That had been the beginning of the worst row she had ever had with anyone in her life.

She said she had never heard anything so stupid.

'Well, as it seems to you equally preposterous that I might have been treating you as an adult—'

'You mean, having an affair with me—'

'*Yes*, that might have come into it. Of course it didn't – but I think it was reasonable that Rupert should think so.'

'Do you? Well, it simply seems disgusting and idiotic to me.'

'I see. So that leaves me as merely a kind of mother's help. Sorry, Clary, I didn't mean that.'

'You did. You're trying to be as nasty as you possibly can. I thought you were my *friend*! There's no need to treat me like a child!'

'Oh, yes, there *is*.' She remembered how grim he had sounded when he said that. She had hunched up over her jig-saw again (which she had done the moment her father had left the room, with Archie seeing him out), but now he walked over to the table and swept most of the puzzle on to the floor.

'I treat you like a child because you go on behaving like one. If you want me to treat you like a friend, you'll have to bloody well listen to me. You were pretty unpleasant to your father, but I expect you're so wrapped up in yourself you didn't notice.'

'You weren't particularly nice to him either. In fact, I think you're a fine one to talk.'

'Yes, I am. And I'm going to. You've got to stop, Clary.'

'Stop what?'

'Stop being so sorry for yourself, making everyone else pay for your mistakes, expecting everyone to make allowances for you without even doing them the honour of telling them why. You've got to stop *wallowing*. I know you've had a hard time—'

'Oh, thanks very much for that. You call falling in love with someone who turns out not to love you or want your child and having an abortion "a hard time"! You can't have the faintest idea what any of that feels like!' She was crying by now, but it was mostly from outrage.

'There you go again! Now, you listen to me – as your *friend*, since that is what you say you want. You fell for someone who was already married, which might have been some kind of warning, but who also turned out to be a selfish bastard. You decided not to have the baby and so you had to go through all that. You knew, really, that he never had any intention of leaving his wife for you, but you wanted to think that he might. You *have* had a hard time. But you've had it now, and it's time you moved on. You've got to start making yourself eat, stop these crying jags, start fending for yourself.'

'Oh! If you're sick of me, why don't you jolly well say so instead of beating about the bush like a craven brute?'

This made him laugh, which she hadn't meant at all.

'I'll go,' she said. 'I'll go and pack now and you'll never see me again.'

He seized her hands and stopped her getting to her feet. 'There you go again! Trying to make someone else responsible for your behaviour. Sit still. I haven't finished with you.'

She blinked the tears from her eyes so that she could see his face, which did not look as grim as he sounded.

'Sweetheart, I am your friend. I know everything seems completely bleak for you, but it won't go on being like that. And it will get better just as soon as you start wanting it to.' He put out his hand and smoothed some hair from her forehead. 'People do fall in love with the wrong person and suffer for it. It happens. And you're rather a headlong sort of person, so it's hit you very hard.'

'When I love people, they die, or they go to France, or they simply turn out not to love me.'

'*Clary! Who* has died?'

'My mother. Of course I think I've got over that. It doesn't really count any more.'

'Everything counts, love. But nothing is everything.'

She thought about that then, and often afterwards.

'What do you think I ought to do?'

'Well, you could go back to the cottage – on your own for the weekdays, and I'll come down at weekends. You could start writing your book. You could make the cottage more comfortable, and you might tidy up the garden. If you do some physical work, you'll get nice and tired, and then you'll go to sleep. And writers need food. You'll write awful weedy stuff if you go on trying to subsist on

504

lettuce and black coffee. I shall come down on Friday evenings and expect an enormous hot dinner.'

So she said she would do that. And next morning, he saw her off at Paddington. He gave her money for a cab to the cottage and three more pounds for food. 'I'll be down in two days,' he said, 'and we'll stock up with everything for the next week.' He was standing on the platform and she'd pushed down the window. 'Headlong people usually have a lot of courage,' he said.

When the train began to move, she waved quickly and he turned at once and started walking back down the platform. She was in an empty compartment so she could have had a good cry, but she decided not to. She sat with her notebook on her lap making lists of things to do so that she wouldn't mind being alone too much.

It had been very hard at the beginning. When the cab deposited her at the end of the lane that led to the cottage and she'd paid him and he'd backed out and gone, she stood for a moment where he had left her at the small gate that opened on to the mossy little path that led to the kitchen door. It was very cold: there had been a heavy frost. An October sun, belyingly flushed for it seemed to give no heat, was poised in the sky beyond the beech trees and willows, and the only sound she could hear was the curious metallic chinking of coots on the canal. Inside, the cottage seemed colder, and the silence was complete. She dumped her cases and set about lighting the fire in the sitting room, filling the log basket with armfuls of logs from the lean-to shed outside. Two days ago she had been here by herself when Archie had left on Monday morning. She had stuck it out until tea-time and then suddenly decided that she could not, would not stay there alone. The cottage had no telephone, so she had simply turned up at his flat. He had been cooking, but everything had come to a halt. She had burst into tears and said that she couldn't bear it, she couldn't cope with being alone. She didn't want anything to eat so it didn't matter about supper – she would have a bath and go to bed; he needn't worry about her. And then, the next evening, Dad had turned up – out of the blue.

And now, here she was, back, and she had to stick it out this time or Archie would despise her. She lit the fire, and then went up to the bedroom and made her bed which she had left in a mess. There were two bedrooms, one large and one smaller, and Archie, who had found and rented the cottage, made her have the large one, which she had liked because it had two ace-of-clubs windows in it.

She made a sandwich with a hard-boiled egg and tomato for lunch, and while she ate it, she looked at her list.

Make a bonfire of all the garden stuff Archie cut
   down.
Look in Mrs Beeton for a stew to make for Friday
   evening.
Housework all the cottage [two bedrooms, the sitting
   room and the kitchen]. Clean bath, clean windows
   [they had got very smoky].
Make a shopping list.
Start novel.

There it was. At the bottom of the list – a bland little note. It sounded no harder than cleaning the bath. But the moment she stopped doing physical things, like collecting wood or dusting, and sat down at the small table with a kitchen chair and the blank paper in front of her, thoughts and feelings that had nothing whatever to do with what she planned to write overwhelmed her: the last time she had seen Noël; his voice, which she now recognised had been as full of self-pity as the hostility that had struck her at the time.

'You know enough about my own childhood to know perfectly well that I am not cut out for parenthood, never have been, never will be.' The dinner with Archie after he had come back from France when she had said that she should not have the baby. The ensuing night when she had wept about the awfulness of not having the baby, had tried to take in the fact that Noël was not only out of love with her now but could never have been much in love in the first place. Then Archie taking her for the operation. Just walking through the streets with him, being taken away and leaving him in the waiting room, and lying on the hard high table while a small, obscenely merry little man assaulted her deftly in his rubber gloves. And then – blood and tears at the end of it. Going back to Blandford Street and not being able to bear being there. Not really wanting to be anywhere, she had told Archie, who had said that if it didn't matter to her, he would make the choice. He had taken her to the Scilly Isles, and made her go for walks with him, had taught her six-pack bezique; had made them take turns reading aloud from *Mansfield Park*, had pretended not to notice when she picked at her food, when she suddenly wanted to cry, when she withdrew or snapped at him. He made her talk about Noël – and Fenella. Quite soon he called Noël 'Number One' and she found herself following suit. It distanced him, but this seemed to increase her senses of humiliation and failure. She moped, and he let her. He had, indeed, been her friend, she thought now, as she looked at the bland white page on which anything might be written. She had even told Archie what she did want to write. 'It is sort of Miss Milliment's childhood and youth,' she explained. 'I mean, what it must have been like to be plain and have nobody who actually cared about you. She had a brother who everybody thought was marvellous. And even *he* was awful to her about her appearance.'

'What about her mother?' Archie had asked.

'Oh – she died. She had an aunt who brought them up, but then she died too.'

'Oh.' She noticed Archie looking at her intently, and said, 'Of course, poor Miss Milliment isn't really like me. I had Dad and he did love me.'

'I should think he's still at it.'

She agreed that he did, of course, in a way, but privately she thought that what with Zoë and Jules, he could hardly have much time for someone like herself. She had changed the subject back to Miss Milliment and her Victorian youth. It was not that she planned to write about what happened to Miss Milliment, which would have been extremely difficult since she knew only the bare outline of her life, it was more that she needed to know about the mid to late nineteenth century during which she had grown up. Practical things, like the times of meals and what was eaten, and clothes and what houses looked like and what people did in their spare time. Archie had suggested that she go and talk to Miss Milliment about that sort of thing, but she felt this was out of the question. She was not *really* writing about Miss Milliment but she was afraid that Miss Milliment might think she was. In fact, she said, she had the idea of writing about Miss Milliment's time and her own, with, roughly speaking, the same character living in both of them. 'I don't worry about making the main person,' she had said. 'I know how to do that.' But for days, weeks even, that was about all she did know. The bones of the story jangled about in her mind without seeming to knit themselves together.

Today she decided to stick to getting the cottage straight, washing her other jersey and cleaning the sitting room, which got very dusty with wood ash.

Cleaning was made more arduous by lack of utensils. The carpet-sweeper hardly worked until she found that the small wheels each side of the brushes were tightly encased in long red hairs that had to be unwound one by one. The duster was itself so dirty that it seemed to transfer a different kind of dirt to whatever she used it on. In the end she used the only tea-cloth. The place had been more or less furnished when Archie found it, but that really meant that you could sleep in a bed, fry an egg on the old electric stove and sit at a rickety table to eat it. There was a battered old sofa and armchair in the sitting room, one standard lamp, a threadbare carpet and a small shelf of books that kept falling sideways as there was nothing to prop them up. It was when she was dusting these that she made the discovery. A dark red book, larger than the others and therefore the one to put at the end of the row, she thought. It was called *A Book With Seven Seals*, the author anonymous. She opened it, and was lost. It was the account of a mid-Victorian clergyman's family in Chelsea and she became so absorbed in it that she read till it was dusk and she discovered that she was cold because the fire had gone out.

Mindful of her promise to Archie, she opened a tin of

baked beans and ate them cold from the tin with a teaspoon, while she read in her overcoat – she couldn't be bothered to relight the fire. Eventually, she made herself a hot-water bottle and took it, with the book, to bed. She fell asleep before she finished the book and slept all night without a dream.

The next day she began to write.

When Archie arrived on Friday, she had cleaned the cottage and made an Irish stew. 'And you've even washed your hair!' he exclaimed, after she had hugged him. 'Am I glad to see you!' he said. 'Looking almost human. Well done.'

He had brought a load of things in the car: more blankets, bath towels, his gramophone and a box of records and another box containing books, 'I got you some Victorian novels. Thought they might be a help,' as well as two bottles of wine, his painting equipment and his bezique packs. The stew was the best bit of cooking she'd ever done. They both had two helpings, drank a bottle of wine and played two records – 'We take turns to choose and then there can be no ugly scenes,' he had said. She told him about the book and he asked her about her own work and she felt suddenly, nervously, shy, and said she might have made a start but it was probably no good.

On Saturday they went shopping, for food and things for the cottage, and paint because he said he thought the walls of the sitting room should be yellow. They had lunch in a pub and after they'd got back and unpacked the car, he made her go for a walk along the towpath the other side of the canal. 'We'll do five bridges and then we'll turn round,' he said. It was a mild, grey afternoon and the towpath was thick with livid leaves that had fallen from the trees growing on the steep banks. The grey, still water was speckled with them. A pair of coots that lived on the water just outside the cottage swam ahead of them towards the first hump-backed bridge. The stone coping that edged the towpath was broken in places, leaving muddy inlets with rushes. Every now and then they heard the explosive, raucous sound of a pheasant.

They walked for a while in comfortable silence, and then he said, 'I've decided to give up my dreary old job.'

'And go back to painting?'

'I'm not sure. Probably. If I can make a living at it.'

'You were before the war, weren't you? Of course, you were in France then. I suppose that's different.'

'I still have to eat food and live somewhere. I've still got my place there.'

'Are you going back there to live?'

'Don't know. Haven't decided anything.'

The faint stirrings of alarm in her subsided. 'I should think you'd be jolly lonely if you went back there now,' she said, and felt him glance at her before he answered.

'Perhaps I would.'

Later, when they were toasting crumpets, she asked him when he would be leaving his job.

'Christmas,' he said. 'I've got to stick it out until then.'

Christmas seemed a long way off. She was content to leave it at that.

It was hard when he left very early on Monday morning. He brought her a cup of tea in bed at half past six, kissed her forehead and said he was off.

'Work hard, eat a lot and get the lawn mowed,' he said. 'I'll be back on Friday. I shall *notice* all those things.'

She listened to his car start and then to the engine noise becoming fainter until she couldn't hear it. It would be five days and four nights entirely alone. She got up and looked out of the little window. There was a white mist rising from the canal and a lumpy thrush was hauling a worm out of the grass with short, irritable tugs. She decided then that the best way of not thinking about him driving back to London was to get her work and read over what she had written before the weekend. This became a routine. She would get up, make a mug of tea and go back to bed with it and her novel, which she read aloud to herself because she found that this was a good way of hearing uneasy passages, repetitive words or sounds, or simply finding out what she had left out. Miss Milliment – she decided to call her Marianne rather than Eleanor – was now seven, rather fat with skimpy pigtails. Then she thought that perhaps girls in those days didn't have pigtails but flowing hair streaming down their backs, and poor Marianne's hair was not the kind that flowed – any more than her own had been.

After her breakfast – porridge and more tea – she got a mirror and had a long, careful look at her face. Her forehead was broad but rather low, with a widow's peak off centre. 'Low forehead, greasy hair growing to a point,' she wrote. Eyebrows. Hers were quite thick and Polly had made her pull bits out towards the middle so that there was more of a gap between them. 'Sparse eyebrows growing too close together,' she wrote. Eyes. Her own eyes, large, grey and calculating, she critically surveyed them, were really just ordinary eyes. 'Small, grey, rather beady eyes,' she wrote. Nose. Pudgy. 'Pudgy.' Noses were very boring to describe. Shape of face. She seemed to have wide cheekbones above a round face and a firm-looking chin. 'Pudgy face with chin and sub-chin,' she wrote. When she had finished she read the notes again.

The funny thing was that they didn't really give a picture of a face – they stayed stubbornly being bits of a face. She shut her eyes and started remembering Miss Milliment's *now* – in her extreme old age. (It was very difficult not to call her Miss Milliment; she decided to change Marianne to Mary Anne – much better for a plain child.)

Remembering her old was much better: her vast face, the colour of grey custard, her surprisingly soft skin, her eyes like tiny pebbles behind the small thick water of her glasses, her descending arrangement of chins, her strained-back, oyster-shell-coloured hair, the intricate network of wrinkles like crazed china all over her face, her expression of gentle anxiety born of a lifetime of not being absolutely sure at first what she was seeing, punctuated by a glance minutely penetrating and kind that somehow made one forget any or all of her separately unattractive features. I think my eyes are my best feature, she thought, but I suppose most people's are. She could not remember looking either penetrating or kind, but there it was. One knew less about oneself than other people realised, although one couldn't consider other people in a novel without considering oneself. This seemed to be because one could never be *quite* sure about getting other people's feelings right unless somehow one *became* them. And this in turn meant that one was pulling things out of oneself; it was a maze and she felt lost in it, but extremely interested.

So, that first week passed surprisingly quickly and then there was Archie again and the weekends were lovely. He always brought some kind of treat: chocolate biscuits, a poster of Madame Bonnard in her bath (the cottage had no pictures), a new record, the desk that Polly had given her years ago that he had collected from

Blandford Street. 'She'd love to see you,' he said. 'I thought you might come up with me one Monday and spend a night or two with her?' She might.

Just before Christmas, she did. They went on Sunday evening, so that Polly would be there when she arrived: she couldn't face going there alone. Polly, looking wonderful, received her with open arms. 'Oh, it's so lovely to see you,' she kept saying. She was wearing a scarlet corduroy skirt and a raspberry-pink shirt, and a very flashy ring of smoky blue with what looked like diamonds round it.

'They are,' she said. 'Gerald gave it to me. That's what I've been dying to tell you. I'm in love with him and we're going to be married.'

It was a shock.

'Are you sure, Poll? Really *sure*?'

'People keep saying that. Of course I am. I don't think it's something one is unsure about. Either you are or you aren't.'

'Are what?'

'In love.'

She was silent. She knew then that it was the kind of untruth that everyone had to discover for themselves. But perhaps Polly would never have to do that. She was the kind of person who got things right, she thought, seeing Polly's shining eyes and air of joy.

'I've asked him to come after supper to meet you,' she was now saying. 'He knows you're my best friend as well as my cousin.'

All through supper Polly told her about him. About his enormously ugly house, and how she'd nearly not met him, and how they were to be married in July and he was going to take her to Paris for her honeymoon, and how good he was at imitating people, and how he wasn't conventionally good-looking (that probably means ugly, she thought; people's appearance and the consequences of it were her profession these days), and the more Polly talked about him, the more she thought about Noël and the worse she felt.

Goodness, she thought, love can make people rather boring.

'I'd rather not,' she said, when Polly said she wanted her to be a bridesmaid.

When Polly began asking her about herself, she could find little or nothing to say. 'Yes, it's a good place to work,' she said of the cottage.

The book was getting on. (What could one say about a less than half-written book? She didn't want to say anything about it at all.) Talking to Archie about it was different.

Yes, she said in answer to the most serious question. Yes, she was over Noël. 'But that's what I mean,' she added, suddenly finding something to say. 'I am over him – more or less – and once I thought I never would be. I thought I was completely in love. Don't you see?'

'See what?'

'That it isn't as simple as you think. You are in love with Gerald now, but how do you know you'll go on feeling like that?'

'I see what you mean. But I *do* know, Clary. I really do. It is awfully difficult to explain—'

'What about Archie? You *thought* you were in love with him, didn't you? It went on for ages.'

'That was different.'

'You didn't think so at the time.'

'I see what you mean,' Polly said again. 'I suppose

everyone has to go through falling in love with the wrong person, but that doesn't mean that they can't find the right one. If they didn't nobody would be married.'

'That might be a very good thing.'

'Don't be silly! Of course it wouldn't be.'

'Well, I'm not going to marry anyone.'

'I think you're just saying that because you've had such a rotten time. I do admit it was far luckier to fall in love with Archie than with Noël.'

At this point the doorbell rang and Polly rushed down to let Gerald in.

Clary had felt divided about whether she wanted to like him or not. Of course, in a way she did, but there was a stubborn, contrary part of her that resented having to fall in with Polly's complacency and happiness. 'I know you'll like him,' she had said, more than once. How could she know that? Why should she, Clary, like people just because Polly thought she would? But she had to admit to herself that he did seem all right; moony about Polly, of course, but very nice to her as well. When Polly told him that she didn't want to be bridesmaid, he looked quite disappointed, and then he said, 'I can't blame you. I should hate to be one myself.' And he asked her about her cottage much more than Polly had, so that Polly said, 'Why don't we come and see you there? One weekend?' and she heard herself saying – quite rudely, 'Oh, no! I can't have people there. It's far too primitive, especially for you, Poll. She's always wanting to do things to houses, decorate them and all that.'

And he had said, 'I know. Well, she's taken on either a life's work or her Waterloo with mine.' He had looked at Polly, and they had both smiled. They were continually meeting each other's eyes and smiling. Once he picked up

Polly's hand and kissed it, and Polly sat looking at that hand with a look of contented bliss that went straight – and painfully – to her heart. Noël had never, at any point, treated her like that.

The atmosphere was so full of this sort of thing, evoking all kinds of painful contrast, that in the end she couldn't deal with it. She said she was tired and would go to bed.

'I've made up your bed,' Polly said, after she had insisted upon taking her downstairs. 'I'm afraid Neville has made rather a mess of your room, but at least the sheets are clean.'

And then the inevitable question.

'You *do* like him?'

'Oh, yes, of course I do. I think he's – jolly nice,' she finished.

'Oh, good! I thought you would. Sleep well. See you in the morning.'

But she couldn't sleep. To be back in this room, where she had occasionally spent nights with Noël – where, in fact, their last meeting had taken place – brought back a weight of misery and anguish that she thought had gone. That she had cared so much for him, that he had never, in fact, loved her, that she had not recognised this until it was too late, engulfed her more painfully than ever before. This was because she now knew all three of these factors, whereas before they had occurred one after the other. Again and again she heard Noël's cold and irritable response to her saying she was pregnant; again and again, she played her memory record of Fenella's voice on the telephone with its precise blend of indifference and hostility that had so confounded her – they were not, had never been, her amazing, dear, close friends. She supposed

517

dimly that she had been used, although she did not understand why, but in any case she had been stupid enough to be a willing, an enthusiastic victim. All the events connected with her pregnancy came back, and remembering how she had bled and wept after the abortion, she wept again as pride leaked out of her until she was nothing but her humiliation. The whole night her losses ganged up on her. Her mother who had left her for ever by dying – left her with a single postcard and memories that were not to be talked about because of upsetting her father. And then Dad – going off and leaving her for *years*. He would never know what his absence had cost her. And then, when he did come back, of course he had a new, far more beautiful daughter to look after, and she, now ostensibly grown up, was meant to look after herself. And now Polly was going off to be married which really meant that she wouldn't want the same kind of friendship any more that they had had all these years. She had reached the stage of misery where she searched for yet more reasons to justify it. And I just don't look like Polly, so nothing like that would ever happen to me anyway, she thought, as she put on the light to search in her chest of drawers for a handkerchief. But her chest of drawers turned out to be full of Neville's things – dirty shirts, sheet music, half-eaten packets of biscuits, broken pencils, rolls of film . . . Her chest of drawers! Full of the wretched Neville's things! And he had not even asked her if he could use her room! She found one of his handkerchiefs – a Cash's nametape with N. Cazalet sewn on it. I'll use it and I'll keep it, she thought. Then she saw that she was behaving like a cross little girl of ten and not at all like a grown-up with tragic events behind her.

At this moment, she heard the front door slam downstairs. So Gerald did not spend the night with Polly. She turned off her light again; she did not want Polly coming in to talk to her.

She must have slept a bit, because when she came to it was beginning to be light. She got up, packed the rucksack she had brought and wrote a note to Polly. 'Am going back to the cottage to work. Sorry, but I don't want to be in this place at the moment. Nothing to do with you – it's other things. Love, Clary.'

She took the note upstairs and put it outside Polly's room. It was half past six. She let herself out of the house and walked to Baker Street station to catch a train for Paddington and her journey back to the cottage.

It was raining heavily and she was soaked on the walk to Baker Street; she had just enough money to buy the two train tickets, but not enough for a taxi at the other end. This would mean a three-mile walk unless she got a lift. The train was unheated, and she sat in a compartment to herself, wishing that she had a hot drink to warm her up and hoping that the rain would have stopped by the time she reached Pewsey.

It hadn't, of course. It seemed set for the day, if not for ever. Only one other person got off the train at Pewsey, and was met by an old man in tweeds with a pipe; he carried her off in an old Morris Minor before Clary had a chance to ask them which way they were going. She would have to walk it. Up to now, the journey had felt like an escape; even shivering and damp in the train she had felt that everything would be different and better when she got off it. But now as she tramped wearily towards the cottage, its emptiness and silence began to weigh upon her. She would be alone for at least four days, and Archie, who had expected to drive her down the following Friday, had not left the usual five pounds for housekeeping. She would not have money to buy food and there was very little in the way of stores. She realised then that for weeks Archie had been providing for her, since she'd had no money of her own once her job had stopped. She simply had not thought about this before, but now it frightened her. She was completely dependent upon Archie turning up when he said he would, and supposing he was cross with her for running away from London (and without telling him – she could have rung him up, she now thought), he just might not come on Friday.

She had reached the wooded part of the road and, although this meant some protection from the rain, great flurries of larger drops fell from the branches, making straight for the back of her neck until she felt sodden – wet to the skin. The only traffic she encountered was a farm tractor coming the other way, whose driver asked whether it was wet enough for her.

The key to the cottage was under a stone near the back door. She felt light-headed with exhaustion, but she was back.

She made a pot of tea. She knew that the next thing was to light the fire, but she felt too tired to do it. She took the tea upstairs and got out of her wet clothes. It seemed easiest to get into her pyjamas and then to bed, but once there, she could not get warm. Her feet were icy and her teeth actually chattering – like people in books, she thought. So she got up again, made a hot-water bottle, dried her hair a bit on her bath towel and found some woollen socks. Back in bed she gradually began to thaw, until she was warm enough to fall asleep.

She woke when it was already dark, very thirsty and, she thought, hungry. But when she sat up, her head ached so violently that she couldn't face going downstairs. She drank what remained of the cold tea with two aspirin she got from the bathroom and went back to bed. The hot-water bottle was cold, so she got up again and refilled it from the hot tap in the bathroom. These two trips had made her cold again, and it took ages to get warm.

She spent a night full of feverish thoughts and dreams. It was hard to tell which was which – what she was thinking and what she was dreaming. There was Archie saying she'd let him down and he was going to France that day, and there was Noël saying she'd let him down and he didn't want to see her any more, and Polly saying she was so happy she didn't need her friends, and somebody whose face was turned away and whose voice she did not recognise who kept saying she didn't belong anywhere. And then she was running along a street towards a crowd of people but when she reached them the ones nearest threw up their arms in horror as though to ward her off and all the others melted away and there was the empty street again, only it had turned into a lane and at the end of it she thought she saw the cottage but when she got nearer there was just a black place and she fell into it and as she fell it got hotter and hotter until she was burning and there was a drumming, beating sound coming from her head and someone was telling her to open her eyes, but she was afraid that if she did that, it would be just the same – no dream, no difference.

'. . . it's all right, darling, wake up. I'm here with you.'

It was Dad. He was sitting on the side of the bed, and

he was stroking her forehead with his long thin fingers. She looked at him with terror that it might not really be him, and then with fear that he might be angry at her being in the cottage away from home although she couldn't remember where that was . . . 'Oh, Dad!' she said. 'Oh, Dad! I'm so glad you've come!' But then as she looked into his face, that had been smiling, she thought, and saw his serious eyes, it wasn't Dad at all – it was Archie.

'It's Archie,' he said.

'I know. I can see you now. I was having a dream, I think. Such an awful dream.'

He put his arms round her as she began to cry, and held her with small rocking movements as she tried to tell him – but the whole thing went into jagged pieces and made no sense.

'It doesn't matter,' he kept saying, as she repeated hopelessly that there wasn't anybody – anybody at all – she couldn't find a single one. 'I saw some people, but they melted.'

'I'm not surprised,' he said. 'You're burning hot. Now, lean forward and I'll make your pillows comfortable.'

'Is it Friday?'

'Tuesday, as a matter of fact.'

'Nowhere near Friday.'

'Not really, no.'

'Why are you here, then?'

He straightened up from collecting her tea-tray off the floor and looked at her for a moment – considering, she thought.

'I came to see you.'

'Oh. To see me.' She felt a different kind of warmth.

'Especially to see you,' he said, and went with the tray.

She leaned back on the pillows: relief, contentment, pleasure filled her and she hardly felt ill.

He stayed all that week. The first two days she was in bed because she had a fever. He made her pots of tea and brought her a bottle of Robinson's lemon barley water and a large jug of water to mix it with. He made a fire in her room, and in the mornings, after a bath, she lay in bed reading a book called *Animal Farm* that he had brought her, while he sat and drew her. 'Got to get my hand in,' he said, 'and there you are. You might as well be useful.'

After lunch, he tucked her up and went out to shop and do other chores while she slept. She slept deeply and without dreams each afternoon, and would wake when it was dusk and the firelight was coming into its own.

Then he would bring their supper up on trays, and afterwards they would play bezique: they had kept the score for months and he said she owed him two hundred and fifty-three pounds.

When she was better, their ordinary life resumed, and when he left for London the following Monday, she went back to her book.

He asked her why she had left Blandford Street, and she told him about Polly and Gerald – a bit, though not much, about hating her room because of Noël.

'Did you know about Poll and Gerald?' she had asked him.

'I did, actually. But Polly wanted to tell you herself.'

'Do you think it's a good thing?'

'I think it's a very good thing. He's a very nice chap and she'll make a splendid countess.'

'*What?*'

'Didn't she tell you? He's a lord. So, of course, she will be a lady.'

'Lady what?'

'Fakenham. Didn't she tell you about his house? It's enormous and in an awful state – just the thing for Poll.'

'Yes, it would be. I can see the house part of it. I was just worrying – I mean, supposing she married him and it all goes wrong? They stop loving each other, or even *one* of them stops . . .'

'Well, then it would all be sad and an awful mess, wouldn't it? It's a risk, of course, but people have to take them, and in their case I think it's a pretty small one. But it's their business, Clary. You can't tell anyone who to love or not love.'

'No.'

'Would you have taken the slightest notice if I had advised you *not* to take up with Number One Noël?'

'I wouldn't. I see. OK, you win.'

They spent Christmas at the cottage. He asked her if she wanted to go to Home Place or be in London for it, and she said no, she wanted to stay where she was. The book had reached the stage where things were working in it that she had not envisaged when she began, but she had started to worry about the end, and didn't want a holiday away from it. But she also – although she did not tell Archie – felt superstitious about leaving the cottage where she felt safe and cut off from her old life. She wanted simply to write, to make the garden and to have Archie every weekend. He taught her to make a proper vegetable soup, and interesting salads with things like potato and egg and anchovy in them. She began to grow things from seed and she planted bulbs to come out at Christmas.

She did one day talk to him about the fact that she had no money and that he was having to pay for everything. To begin with, he said that she could pay him back when her book got published, but, having worked in a literary agency, she knew that writers did not get paid much for their first book – or indeed, sometimes for many books after that. When she pointed this out, he said he thought that her father would probably give her a small allowance if she asked for it. So she suggested asking him down to the cottage, but Archie did not seem to want this, and said no, she should go to London to talk to him.

After Christmas, Archie had stopped his job, and although he had not given up his flat in London, he began to spend more time at the cottage, and was out painting whenever the weather was fine enough. 'I could go up for the day,' she said.

'No, for a night,' Archie said. 'Unless you go at a weekend, otherwise he'll be working. Go on,' he said, 'don't be feeble.'

'Why don't you want him here?'

'He might get the wrong idea.'

'Oh, that! I could tell him.'

'What would you tell him?'

'I'd tell him – I'd tell him that we're *friends*! Well, we are, aren't we?'

'I think you could say that.'

'You don't sound very pleased about it.'

'What am I supposed to be? Hopping up and down with excitement? Like you?'

'I'm not hopping,' she said. He was making her feel

525

grudging and sulky, which she hated. They had parted company for the afternoon. He went off to paint by the canal, and she collected branches that had fallen from the trees on to the piece of woodland garden where all the snowdrops had been and primroses were to come. All the time she was doing this she felt worse and worse about him. She thought of how kind he had been, how he had looked after her, how he had found this cottage and supported her living in it, encouraged her to write her book – really done every single thing for her for months and months. She thought of how good he had been with Neville when their father was still away; how tactful he had been with Polly when she was in love with him. He was the kindest and best person she had ever met. And there she was, making difficulties about doing one thing the way he wanted her to.

When she went back into the cottage, he was standing at the kitchen sink washing his brushes.

'I want to apologise,' she said. 'I was foul to you. Of course I won't tell Dad about our life. If he asks me I shall simply say that you have been terrifically kind – like a sort of second father to me.'

There was a silence. He did not turn round, but eventually she heard his croaky laughter, so she felt things were all right.

She went to London for the night, which she spent with Dad and Zoë in their rather grand new flat that looked on to Ladbroke Square. They both seemed very pleased to see her, and Juliet rushed in from playing in the square to give her a hug.

'You've grown your hair long!' she cried. 'You're grown up. Why aren't you wearing lipstick? Mummy, a boy called Hastings is coming to stay because he's running away.'

'Why is he running away?'

'His parents are very cruel to him. He stood on a wall 'cos he wanted to jump off it and they didn't want him to so when he jumped, they spoiled it and *caught* him! I'm going to be a bridesmaid at Polly's wedding! If you come to it you'll see me in a long dress, and probably – ' her voice dropped and slowed dramatically ' – I almost surely . . . perhaps . . . may be . . . wearing lipstick. A bit.'

Zoë bore Jules off and Dad took Clary upstairs to the drawing room for a drink.

'Let's have a good look at you,' he said. 'You look quite different since I last saw you – although, heaven knows, that's far too long ago. You've got very thin.'

'Have I? I didn't notice.'

'It suits you. What have you been doing? Archie told me that you were writing.'

She told him about the book. Well, not *about* it, but about doing it. Then – he brought it up – he asked her how she was managing about money, and she told him that she hadn't got any. 'I haven't even paid Polly for the rent for the flat,' she said (a thought that had only recently occurred to her).

'Don't worry about that,' he said. 'I'm paying it for Neville. He seems to like staying there – doesn't want to be here, and it seemed sensible.'

'Oh.' How could she ask him for more money after that?

'But that's another matter. You must be needing some for yourself, though. I suppose Archie has been subsidising you. We can't let him go on doing that. He's probably saved a bit from his job, but he told me that he was thinking of giving that up, then he'll be off to France and he'll need what he's saved to get started again. It's the devil going back to something like painting when you haven't been doing it for years.'

'Did he tell you he was going to France?'

'He said he was thinking about it.'

'When?'

'Oh, darling, I don't know when! Sometime in the autumn, I think, after he'd found that cottage for you. I seem to remember that he said the cottage was dirt cheap – twenty-five pounds a year. Are you going to stay in it after you've finished your book?'

'I don't know.' She was suddenly feeling so frightened that she couldn't concentrate on what Dad was saying. If Archie was going, why hadn't he told her? All he had said, months ago, was that he hadn't decided. So had he changed his mind?

'It was just before Christmas, I remember now.'

'What was?'

'When Archie talked about France. Clary! Do listen to me! What I propose is . . .'

The rest of the evening, although she tried to conceal it, she felt completely desperate. Zoë arrived to say that Juliet wanted her to say goodnight, and she went downstairs to Juliet's bedroom. It's probably a mistake, she thought, as she went, a misunderstanding. He wouldn't lie to me.

'Mummy said you live in a cottage? Do you like it?'

'Yes.'

'I wouldn't. I shall live in a boat. Or an aeroplane. Yes, an aeroplane because I don't want to have a garden and weeding to do. You're my sister, aren't you? Sort of?'

'Yes, I am. We have the same dad.'

'Where's your mother?'

'She died.' She found that she could say that as though she was talking about somebody else.

Juliet flung her arms round her and she was tightly squeezed. 'I'm very, very, *very* sorry for you.'

'It's all right, Jules. It was a long time ago.'

'Oh. I suppose it's gone into history. We do history at my school and people die all the time. They keep doing it, and then we have to learn about a new person.'

She went back on the train next morning. She should have felt relieved. Dad was giving her an allowance of a hundred and twenty pounds a year, and he produced two hundred at once to pay Archie back. 'You'll probably have to get some sort of job, you know,' he said. 'It's not easy to live on writing books to begin with. Come back soon. Don't disappear again.'

Archie met her at the station. He bent to kiss her, but she turned her face so that he only got her ear.

'What's up?'

'Nothing's up. Dad is giving me an allowance. And he sent you this cheque to pay you back for all the money you've spent on me.'

'I've hardly spent any money on you.'

She didn't want to have it out with him while they were in the car, so she didn't reply.

'I'll tell you what we'll do,' he said, as he dumped the shopping he had done on the kitchen table, 'we'll buy you some new clothes. You badly need some. I'm getting rather sick of those two torn old jerseys and those baggy corduroys.'

'Well, when you go to France, you won't have to see them any more, will you?'

'Oh! That's what it is! Clary! You are one for making mountains out of molehills.'

'I'm not! It isn't you *going* that I mind particularly, it's you not *telling* me. Telling other people, and not me.'

'I didn't. I haven't.'

'Dad said you did, so don't try to get out of it.'

'He asked me if I was going back – no, he said, "I suppose you'll be going back," and I said that I hadn't decided, but I might.'

'To live there?'

'Well, yes. If I go back I'll expect to do a spot of living.'

'Don't be facetious! You see, you are serious about it. And I notice,' she added, and could not stop her voice from trembling, 'that you don't ask me.'

'Whether I may go? No, I don't.'

'No! Whether I would like to go with you.'

There was a dead silence. He was leaning against the sink, his back to the light. She could not see his face. She was sitting on the kitchen table fiddling with a paperback from the shopping basket.

'I couldn't stay in this cottage alone,' she said. 'I couldn't be here all by myself for months and months. I'd go mad with – with nobody to talk to! Surely you can see that!'

He walked over to the table suddenly, put his hands on her shoulders, and then, surprisingly, folded his arms.

'You could go back to London,' he said. 'You'll need to get some other work to support you while you write. For a bit, anyway.'

'I know about that,' she said. She felt her eyes filling with tears. 'I know I've got to find a job, and I will. It's just – I don't think I can do anything if you simply aren't there. You tell me what to do, you see. And then I can do it.'

'You've got accustomed to having two fathers.'

'I suppose I have.'

'Well,' he said briskly, 'you've got to grow up. You've got to stand on your own feet. One father is quite enough for most people.'

'Why did you look after me if that's what you think?'

'Because you were in a bad way. But you're not now, you're over that and ready for the next thing.'

'What next thing?'

'Oh! You'll find a nicer man than that ghastly Number One, and fall in love like a normal grown-up girl. Now stop snivelling and help me get lunch.'

'I don't want any lunch,' she said, and could hear herself sounding like a sulking child, and felt angrier and more despairing than ever.

'Well, I do.'

So she peeled potatoes and washed lettuce, and nobody said anything. When she had put the potatoes on to boil, she went upstairs to change out of her London clothes – her only skirt and a flannel shirt that had belonged to Archie. Then she put on her cotton trousers and one of Dad's old shirts and didn't comb her hair. Trying to tell her not to be dependent and then saying, 'We'll buy some new clothes!' Trying to have it both ways. If he thought she would muck about with her appearance just to please him, he could think again. She could perfectly well get a job, not live here or at Blandford Street; she could start all over again. However awful life was it kept on going on. It was not a comforting thought. She took off the shirt and put on her holiest jersey. There is never really another person, she thought, only yourself.

When she went down again (which she found quite difficult – her dignity felt dangerously precarious, but she was bloody well not going to break down and 'snivel', as he called it), he looked up from mashing the potatoes and said quietly, 'Clary. I would never do something like make plans to go away behind your back. If you thought that, then I apologise.' And he looked at her and seemed quite friendly again.

For weeks after that she worked and worked – or rather re-worked. She had become a perfectionist: nothing she wrote seemed quite right or good enough, and she became obsessed with getting at least the first chapter right.

And then, in April, he announced that he was going to Home Place for the weekend. He had come back from one of his visits to London, which he made most weeks, and he told her during supper.

'Why?'

'Because the Duchy asked me. Edward and his new lady are being invited together for the first time, and she asked me to be there.'

'Oh.'

'You could invite Poll for the weekend. I'm sure she'd like to come.'

'I could if I wanted to, of course.' She thought about it: having anyone, any outsider, would mean that she couldn't work.

'It would do you good to have a couple of days off,' he said, as though he knew what she was thinking.

'It wouldn't. I'll ask her when I've finished the book.'

So he had gone, and it felt very strange. She spent one morning reading all that she had written, and then decided to copy out the first chapter on the second-hand typewriter that he had given her for Christmas. If it was typed, she felt, she might be able to see it better. But when she had done that, it still didn't seem right. She felt despair, and on Sunday evening she decided that she would show it to Archie – get him to read it and see how it struck him. If he says it's absolutely no good, I'll have to stop, she thought. But at least I'll know.

He came back in good spirits. Yes, he had had a very nice time. Her father had been there, and Teddy with his incredible wife. She asked about Uncle Edward's new lady, and he said that she seemed anxious to please, and he supposed she was all right as far as she went. 'Which wouldn't be far enough for me,' he had added.

After supper she gave him the typed chapter. 'I really want to know what you honestly think,' she said. 'Because if you don't think it's any good, I'd rather know and I'll stop.'

He had looked up suddenly from the papers she had put into his hand and said, 'Of course I will be honest with you, Clary, but *you* must remember that it will only be my opinion – not some cosmic edict. You mustn't take *too* much notice.'

She could not bear to be in the room with him while he was reading it, so she went and washed her hair. When she came back to dry it in front of the fire, he had finished.

'Well?'

'Well, there's some very good writing in it. Some of it almost felt *too* good.'

'How do you mean?'

'As though you are more concerned with how you are doing something than what it is you are doing. I like

533

the simpler bits best. Tell me what you wanted to have in this bit. I mean, what you wanted me – the reader – to end up knowing.'

She told him. It didn't take long, seemed quite small and clear.

'Yes, well, that all seems quite right. But sometimes you have obscured that by getting too elaborate about it. Take the bit where Mary Anne realises that her father isn't interested in her. That's a shock. I don't think she would think about what the room looked like and her earliest memories of everything else just then. I think she would be too upset by what her father had said. But, that's only a minor criticism. It reads as though you have had a number of second thoughts and so the feeling has got a bit lost. I think.'

'In the first draft I just said: "So she was not loved." That was it.'

'You see? That's far better. The feeling is there. Goodness, I'm no literary critic. Could I see your first draft?'

'You won't be able to read my writing.'

'I think I can just about manage it.'

But she said she would type it out for him.

When he had read it and said he thought it was better, and why, she felt enormous relief.

'Oh, Archie! That does cheer me! I was afraid you were just going to say it was bad in a different way.'

'And what would you have done then?'

'Don't know. Given up, I expect.'

'Don't let me ever hear you say that. If you're going to make writing your life, you've got to start depending on your own judgement. You may take notice of other

534

people, but ultimately, it's what you think is right that's right.'

'You often ask me what I think of your painting.'

'Yes, but I'd still go on doing it whatever you said.'

She thought of all the times when he had shown her paintings and drawings accompanied by his own disparaging remarks about them, about the innumerable, often absurd, alternative careers that he then devised for himself when he said that he would throw in the sponge.

'What are you smiling at?'

'Nothing. I think in some ways we're rather the same.'

Archie was painting a lot now. He took some pictures to London to show to galleries and came back rather gloomy. Only one had been at all interested, he said; it was the one where he had had a show before the war, and they wouldn't give him one although they said they would take a couple of landscapes to put in a mixed show.

'Well, that's a start,' she said.

'I can hardly live on it, though, can I?'

'We *are* living,' she pointed out.

'Just. But, of course, I'm expecting you to be a combination of Agatha Christie and Jane Austen and make thousands, while I shall simply be frightfully good – like van Gogh – and hardly make a penny.'

'Funny. I was planning for you to be Mabel Lucie Attwell or Burne-Jones while I was Virginia Woolf.'

This became a game she enjoyed where insults – elaborate and oblique – could be exchanged.

Then, at the beginning of June, everything went wrong. Afterwards, when she tried to think what had started it, she could only come up with rather petty things, like it being a heat wave and Archie saying he hadn't been sleeping well. What happened was that she'd put the kettle on for breakfast before having a bath and then she'd forgotten about it. Archie was out painting a picture he worked at before breakfast on fine days, so he didn't smell the burning. Anyway, she finally smelt it, and tying her bath towel round her, ran down to the kitchen to find black smoke. She turned off the stove, and then, without thinking, she tried to pick up the kettle and, of course, burned herself. She cried out with the pain and went to the kitchen sink to put her hand under water and in doing this, her bath towel slipped and fell on the ground. So when Archie, who had heard her cry of pain, came into the kitchen, she was naked. He found the tube of tannic acid and made her pat her hand dry while he tucked the bath towel round her and then dressed her hand. It was quite a bad burn: the skin was going to come off. In spite of this, he seemed almost cross with her, saying she was bloody careless and – not quite saying it – implying that it served her right. He put on a saucepan for boiling water – the kettle was ruined – and said for goodness' sake go up and put some clothes on. Not at all the way that *she* would have behaved if he had burned himself getting their breakfast. But when she pointed this out to him, he snapped at her again, saying that they didn't feel the same about a lot of things, although he absolutely refused to say what.

That evening he announced that he was going to go away for a bit. 'I want to sort things out,' he said, 'and I think you should too.'

And while she was wondering what he meant, he said, 'Well, we can't go on like this for ever.'

'Why can't we?'

'Clary, for God's sake, grow up! I've got to make a decision about my flat in London – and France. I can't possibly afford both, which is more or less what I'm doing now. And you've got to learn to cope with your own life and not depend on another person for everything.'

'I *can* cope.'

'Good. Well, you won't have any trouble while I'm away, then.'

'Are you going to stay in France?'

'I might. Haven't decided. But part of the deal is that I don't have to tell you where I am. Nor you me.'

'I don't mind telling you. In the least.'

'I know that.'

'How long is this going on for?'

'I'll be back for Polly's wedding.'

'That's not until half-way through July. That's six weeks!'

'Just about.'

'I can't see the point of it at all.' Then she said, 'You said you'd help me to choose the clothes to wear for the wedding!'

'Supposing the cottage catches fire? Or I get awfully ill?' were some of the other things she said at intervals. But he only looked at her, shrugged, smiled, and said, 'Well, if the worst comes to the worst, you've always got your dad in London. I agree that you're no good at clothes, but Zoë will help you and she's much better at that sort of thing than I am. And forgetting about kettles is the sort of thing that people of seventy-two do rather than twenty-two. You must take any advantage that can be found in being so pathetically *young*.'

He was so calm and maddening and unsympathetic that she felt more angry with him than sad, and when he left the following morning, she kissed him quite coldly on the cheek.

THE OUTSIDERS

Summer 1947

She felt quite fagged and no wonder. She had been up half the night as, apart from little journeys to the bathroom, she had had to repack her cases. She had started packing the moment Kitty said they were to go, but by the time she had taken everything off the mantelpiece and out of her two top drawers, the case was full. 'But how do I know what I shall need?' she had exclaimed, as she watched hopelessly while Rachel unpacked the case and started again.

'You're only going for a fortnight or possibly three weeks, darling, you won't need *all* the photographs, and I think the china dogs might get broken so we'd better leave them. Shall we just put in the nice one of Flo?'

She had nodded. Flo had gone, she knew that now – and all she had was this picture taken of her in the summer frock that she, Dolly, had never really liked, with her amber beads that, she remembered having pointed out at the time, were really better as *winter* jewellery.

She had had to let Rachel pack things – and even she had recognised the need for more than one case – but after she had had her supper and they had said goodnight to her, she had got out of bed and started to deal with everything. She was *not* going for a mere fortnight, she was going for much longer – longer, it seemed, than they knew. So she had to take everything she possibly could.

It was very late by the time she had repacked the cases and she was quite unable to shut them. The servants would have to do it, although they hardly ever came near her nowadays, she had noticed. When she finally got back to bed, her hot-water bottle was cold and she had to dispense with it. She had once tried refilling it from the bathroom tap, but there had been something wrong with the stopper because it had leaked very badly in the night.

Rachel had said that sometimes one did not remember things when one got older, and the remark had both incensed her and hurt her feelings. It simply wasn't true. She might not always remember every single little thing, but what she did remember was always sharp and in great detail. Tonight, she was too fagged to think about anything, and for a long time she seemed too tired even to go to sleep, although in the end she must have dropped off because there was Rachel with her breakfast tray saying what a beautiful day it was.

When she came back to her room after washing, her cases were shut, so that was all right. She felt nervous because she was not absolutely sure whether they were going to Stanmore or to Home Place – or, possibly, to somewhere else. This became so worrying that she had to find out.

'I suppose the garden at Stanmore has suffered from our absence?' she said to Kitty, as they sat in the drawing room downstairs while the chauffeur put the luggage in the motor.

'Oh, darling, I don't know. I expect the new people will have looked after it. I don't think we'd want to go back there to see, do you?'

'Oh, no. Of course we wouldn't. It wouldn't be at all like Home Place. The garden, I mean.'

'Oh, I'm really looking forward to my roses there. They will be out, or better still, just starting. Won't that be nice?'

So it was Home Place. She had been to visit there, with Flo, and they had shared a room and Flo had had the bed by the window because she was such a demon about fresh air.

When they got into the car, she discovered that Rachel was not coming with them. 'She is going to have a holiday with Sid,' Kitty said, when they were both safely ensconced in the back. It seemed odd of Rachel to want to have a holiday at all. *She* had never had a holiday in her life – unless one counted the seaside visit to Rottingdean after she and Flo had had the measles. 'It was really a convalescence,' she said aloud, and Kitty answered, 'Well, poor Sid *has* been very ill.'

She didn't reply to this. It was not her fault if Kitty muddled things up, although she ought not to – she was a good two years younger than herself.

But she enjoyed the drive. Tonbridge did not drive too fast, and once they were out in the country there were meadows with buttercups and Queen Anne's lace and country-cottage gardens full of flowers. Kitty looked out of her window and kept pointing things out to her but, of course, she could not see them because by then they had passed – they were on to something else. But she *pretended* to see them, as she did not want to spoil Kitty's happiness. Her husband had died, some time ago, but it did not seem to have upset her unduly; another reason, she felt, for being thankful that she had adhered to the single state. It was odd, she thought, how much she had to pretend these days: to hear what people said, to understand (sometimes) what on earth they were talking about, to feel a great deal more well than she did a great deal of the time, that she hardly needed her spectacles (she could never find them and got quite sick of asking people where they were), that she had slept quite beautifully when this was hardly ever the case, to know who a large quantity of people who came to see Kitty, or stayed with her, were.

Of course, she knew that they were part of the enormous family that Kitty had married into, but that did not help about their precise relationship. And most of all, and this was nearly all the time, to pretend not to be tired. This was a fib if ever there was one: she felt tired nearly all the time; she often woke up tired. Oh, yes, and to being able to digest anything. When she was young, Flo had always said she had the digestion of a horse. This had not been very kindly meant at the time, but it was infinitely better than not having a digestion at all, which she felt had become the case. But, 'Away with care,' she said aloud, and Kitty looked at her and said, 'Yes, away with it. We shall both feel the better for a little country air.'

She was glad when they arrived, and they had tea on the lawn, although it seemed a bit chilly to her, but Kitty got Eileen to fetch her thicker cardigan, on which she unfortunately dropped some strawberry jam but she knew she had another cardigan in one of the cases.

After tea, she insisted on doing her own unpacking, although Eileen offered to help her. It tired her but she felt that she would learn where things were. There were no other people there, excepting the servants, of course, and so she insisted upon dining with Kitty who would otherwise have been alone. But soon after it she said she thought she would go up to her room to settle in. Kitty accompanied her, which meant that she had to take the stairs faster than she would have wished, and when she had been kissed she subsided on her bed, quite breathless. She had made a very good meal: Mrs Cripps had produced a roast chicken – which had always been a treat when she was a girl – and new potatoes and spinach from the garden. This had been followed by a rhubarb tart, and she had always been partial to rhubarb and forgot that it did not any longer seem to agree with her. She had a touch of indigestion. She sat on her bed for a few moments' rest. The window was open, and the sky was the lovely soothing colour of lavender; it was still quite light. She was really quite fagged, as dear Papa used to say, but a trip to the bathroom was essential and she got up to make it. When she had been unpacking, she had thought there was something missing about her room, although she could not think what it might be, but when she returned from the lavatory she knew at once. Flo's bed was gone. It had been by the window, and now there was simply a space where it had been. This distressed her: it was as though whoever had moved the bed was denying Flo's existence. Not her existence now: she knew that Flo had gone – to her Maker, to Papa and Mama and their dear brother killed in the war – but her existence at *all*. She had always shared this room with Flo, and her bed being gone made her feel much more alone. Then she had a very good idea. She would move *her* bed to the window and sleep where Flo had slept. It would not matter if there was a gap where her bed had been because, after all, she knew *she* existed. She looked at the bed and wondered whether she would have the strength. 'Nothing ventured nothing won,' she said aloud, and set about it. The bed was on casters, so sometimes it moved quite easily although sometimes it got stuck by a ruck in the carpet, but she persisted, moving it a bit one end at a time until with one last heave, it was exactly where Flo's bed had been.

She sat suddenly on it. She had a frightful twinge of indigestion high up in her chest and shut her eyes tightly to endure it. When she opened them, the room seemed to be full of tiny flies – coming in, no doubt, from the open window. She turned her head to look. The light, which had become a greyer, darker lavender, seemed without flies, but her chest still hurt, and she turned to prop up her pillows so that she could sit upright, but when she leaned back against them, it was as though someone was pushing her chest, a painful shove with a heavy weight that was going to crush her if she didn't look out . . . She heard a distant, rather gasping voice telling her to keep calm (could it be Flo?) and turned again to the window, but the dusky lavender had become quite dark – no colour at all – and was then succeeded by a light so white and blinding that with a cry – of fear and recognition – she fell towards it . . .

∞ ∞ ∞

'Are you awake?'

There was no answer from below. No wonder – it had been a momentous day for her as well as for Rachel. But it had been Rachel who had borne the brunt of the most tiring part of it. When she had seen the Duchy and Dolly off to Home Place that morning, she had had her own packing to do. She had had to shut up the flat, and then she had come round to Abbey Road to help *her* do the same things. She still had to rest in the afternoons and she had begged Rachel to do the same but, of course, she hadn't – had spent that time tidying everything up, throwing away food that would go bad in their absence, washing out the tea-cloths, going to the local newsagent's and paying the bill for papers. She brought tea at five just when she awoke from a long, refreshing sleep. That was when she had told her about the Duchy's possible future plans. To begin with, she had thought that this would mean that Rachel would be incarcerated at Home Place, and had waited, with a sinking heart, to be told what little snatches of privacy would be afforded. But Rachel had said that the Duchy was perfectly happy to be in Sussex on her own, with the family coming at weekends, and that Rachel could either keep the Carlton Hill flat if she liked, or sell it and buy somewhere else. She still felt so weak that any strong feeling made her want to weep, and Rachel had most tenderly forestalled this by sitting on the bed and putting her arms round her. 'We've got lots of time to talk about it,' she had said. 'Now let's concentrate on catching our train.' They were going to Scotland, by night sleeper, putting the car on the train to Inverness, and once there – they had made no plans – were simply going to explore and stay where they pleased for two whole weeks. Rachel had taken them out to dinner in a very charming restaurant in Charlotte Street that she said Rupert had recommended, and they had sat at a table with a little red-shaded lamp and had a most delicious French meal. She still had to be very careful to eat things with as little fat as possible and she was not allowed to drink, but she did not care in the least. She felt intoxicated with the senses of adventure and freedom, and her darling looking as happy as she. 'My friend has been ill,' Rachel had said to the waiter, 'so we want a very *simple* meal.' And he had understood and helped them choose:

consommé julienne, grilled sole and raspberries. Then they had driven to King's Cross, seen the car on to the train and repaired to their sleeper. There had been just time to prepare for bed before the train started.

And now she lay in the dark, listening to the regular rhythmic rocking, thinking how extraordinary life was.

Just over a year ago, soon after Rachel had come to London with her parents and the Brig had died, she had thought that there was no future of any kind in their relationship. Rachel seemed to avoid her, to be almost frightened of her, and at the same time had seemed so desperately unhappy. She had suffered tortures watching this and being unable to do anything about it but make it worse. She had finally written to Rachel saying that she thought perhaps that they should not meet at all for a while. It had cost her much to do this, and it had been a last resort, but Rachel's ravaged face, and her frequent oblique allusions to her own worthlessness, which she, Sid, seemed unable to alleviate, so distressed her that she felt it was all she could offer. It was accepted in a short, but still incoherent letter. Rachel said that she agreed it might be better 'for a while'; she hoped that with time she might be able to 'deal with things'; she doubted whether she had ever been worth a moment of Sid's time, and she was deeply sorry for the distress she could now see she must have caused her – 'I am simply not worth it!' she had exclaimed at the end. 'I am not. I am so *ashamed* of myself.'

So then, all through that spring and summer, she had seen nothing of Rachel – excepting for one glimpse of her in the street. She worked, she taught, she eventually found an oldish woman to come and clean the house, which had become very shabby without the ministrations of Thelma from whom she mercifully heard nothing. Then, in the autumn, her sister Evie had suddenly descended upon her. Her latest relationship had crumbled and she was at her exasperating and exacting worst. Sid had to help her to find a job. For a short time she worked at HMV, selling records in Oxford Street, but she never ceased to reproach Sid for making her do such a menial job, and soon took refuge in various ailments that precluded her going to work, which, of course, in the end resulted in her being sacked. Then she got indisputably ill, with jaundice, and Sid had to nurse her through it. Then just as Sid was despairing of ever getting rid of her (she owned half of the little house in Abbey Road and there was no way that Sid could buy her out), she got left a small sum by the conductor who had briefly engaged her affections at the beginning of the war. She was transformed. Five thousand pounds! She would go to America where there were so many more orchestras and musicians she might work for. She bought herself a new wardrobe – using all Sid's clothes coupons as well as her own – and went. The relief!

That first evening, when she had the house to herself, when there was only the faint though pungent aroma of Evening in Paris to remind her of her sister's existence, she had had three enormous gins and indulged in an orgy of Brahms on the gramophone. Before going to bed – without supper, she couldn't face doing anything about that – she opened the windows on the first floor to disperse that scent that made her feel positively queasy. It was February, and freezing. She had to get up in the night to close the windows.

She had got so tired, working and coping with the house and dealing with Evie, that she decided to have a late morning and lay in bed listening to the news. Evie had insisted on having the wireless in her bedroom when she was ill, and Sid had moved it into her own room when Evie got better. The main news was the announcement that Britain would quit India by June 1948. There had been stormy scenes in the House of Commons due to Attlee's decision to remove Lord Wavell and appoint Lord Louis Mountbatten in his place to oversee the transfer of the Indian dominion to self rule. Mr Churchill, as leader of the opposition, had been furious, but he failed to get any change out of Mr Attlee. She wondered if the latter knew what he was doing. In spite of the coal mines being nationalised, there was an acute shortage of coal; food rations had effectively been cut again – unless you counted being allowed twopence more corned beef per week. It had been a winter of strikes and power cuts and altogether a good deal of hardship for a victorious nation.

All that day, when she braved the awful weather to do the shopping, stuffed yet more newspaper into the cracks of the old window frames to keep out the worst of the draughts, made a succession of hot drinks to warm herself up, she wondered why she wasn't feeling brighter with Evie gone at last. She should be rejoicing, but in fact she felt more and more depressed, and also unable to eat. At least, she kept thinking she was hungry, but when she actually tried to eat anything, she couldn't manage it. She felt sick, and by the evening had a raging headache and a temperature. She retired to bed and the next day felt very much worse. In fact, so ill that she could not face going down to the kitchen in the basement, and spent the day on glasses of water from her tooth glass in the bathroom.

Later – she was not sure how much later, but something like two or three days – she heard the doorbell ringing more than once. The mad thought that it might be Rachel got her out of bed and she lurched down to open the front door, to find the Duchy wrapped up to her chin and carrying a bunch of snowdrops.

'I was passing this morning,' she said, 'and I saw the milk bottles outside your door and thought perhaps you might not be well, as you hadn't fetched them in. My dear Sid!'

For the sight of a familiar face, and the kind, calm voice that became full of concern, was too much for her. She collapsed on the hall chair. She managed to say that she was not very well, and then she must have passed out, for the next thing she knew was that her head was between her knees and she could hear the Duchy telephoning.

'I've rung the doctor,' she said. 'Do you think if I helped you, we could get you back into bed? My dear, you should have rung us, we are so near and we could have been round in a trice.' Even then, she noticed that the Duchy did not use Rachel's name.

She stayed until the doctor came, who said that Sid had jaundice. The Duchy went down to the kitchen and made a pot of very weak tea. 'No milk, I'm afraid,' she said, 'but a hot drink would do you good.'

She had left, saying that she would be back tomorrow. 'Only give me a key,' she said, 'then I won't have to get you out of bed.'

But it was Rachel who arrived, and not the following day but later that evening. She came with a tin of soup and some fruit, and there was no dramatic reunion. Sid felt too ill to express either surprise or delight, and she – Rachel – seemed intent upon looking after her exactly as though they had been meeting every few days for the last months. She got clean sheets and made her bed; she brought her a basin of hot water to wash; she gently combed her hair. She heated the soup and encouraged her to drink it. 'Don't try to talk, darling,' she said. 'I know how weak you must feel. One of the nurses at the Babies' Hotel had jaundice and she felt terrible. I have made you some barley water: the doctor says it's good for you to drink as much as possible.'

The next morning when Sid woke up she was there, and it transpired that Rachel had stayed the night in Evie's room.

'You shouldn't be left alone,' she said.

Rachel nursed her for weeks. She, Sid, had turned the unbecoming yellow that accompanies the disease, and she felt so weak that she would lie for hours wondering whether she had the strength to push her hair from her forehead. Rachel had been a wonderful nurse. Nothing was said about their recent separation, only one day when she had tried to say how grateful she was, she saw Rachel begin her painful blush as she answered, 'You don't know how much pleasure it gives me to be able to do anything for you.'

She accepted, she basked in the affection and care. When she was better, Rachel would go back to her home in the afternoons. Then, eventually, Sid was up and about and able to sit in the garden on fine days and the Duchy sent bunches of tulips and bottled fruit she had brought back from Home Place. Then she actually went there for a blissful week in April with the Duchy and Rachel. They went by train and Tonbridge fetched them from the station. The Duchy gardened all day, and sometimes in the evenings Sid would play the familiar sonatas with her while Rachel lay on the sofa, smoking and listening to them. They slept in separate rooms, and when they had retired for the night, she would sit by her window with the scent of wallflowers rising up from the beds on the front lawn and feel the stirrings of her old longing for Rachel's arms, for her kisses, for her endless presence, and wish that her lover were a Juliet, for if she were . . . 'the more I give to thee, the more I have for both are infinite' was a line that recurred during those solitary spring nights. And then the Duchy had suddenly to go back to London three-quarters of the way through their week. The person hired to look after old Aunt Dolly could not stay the course: she had some family trouble and rang in distress to explain this. And she had thought that that would be the end of it. Rachel would have to go back with her mother. But the Duchy would not hear of it.

'You are to stay and finish your week,' she had said to Sid. 'It is doing you so much good. It is doing you both good,' she had added, still looking at Sid with that frank, direct gaze that seemed to see so much.

That night Rachel came to her room, sat on her bed, trembling. 'I want to spend the night with you,' she said. 'I always have, but I've been selfish about it.'

'My darling, you are the least selfish person I've ever met in my life—' she began to say, but Rachel had put her hand over her mouth and said, 'I mean, if one loves somebody – there are things . . .' Her shaky small voice had tailed away. Then she took a breath and said, 'I think you ought to show me, because I don't know. I honestly and truly never knew – but whatever I thought about it is probably wrong, you see.' And she could see what it cost Rachel to look straight at her, as she said, attempting a casual little laugh: 'Of course, I shall probably turn out to be absolutely no good at it . . .'

It was then that she had realised the meanness of not accepting this offer – this most loving gift. If she stood upon her pride – she did not want to be presented with any sort of sacrifice however lovingly offered – nothing would change. Rachel had had the courage to risk, and so must she. As she pulled back the bedclothes and Rachel was beside her, Sid put her arms round her shaking shoulders, and said, 'I love you, and if nothing comes of this I shall continue to love you till I die. We are both afraid, but we need not be afraid of that.'

Afterwards she thought of the Ice Maiden, the Sleeping Beauty – the single kiss was not enough, but they had made a beginning.

∞ ∞ ∞

'You said you had something important to tell me.'

She told him.

'But – where will you go?'

She told him.

'But what will you do? How will you earn your living? I mean, you won't be able to afford to pay Nannie.'

'I thought it would be best if I left Sebastian and Nannie with you. I could look after him on Nannie's days out.'

He thought for a moment. 'It's all rather a *shock*, darling,' he said, 'but I suppose you've thought about it all. The implications. Couldn't you live with one of your parents for a bit? Think it all over?'

'No. My stepmother or whatever she is wouldn't want me, and I certainly don't want to live with Mummy.'

'I see. I can't afford two establishments, you know.'

'I know. I'm not asking you to keep me.'

He looked at her. It was a hot grey day, and she wore a sleeveless coffee-coloured linen dress and white sandals and her long silky hair was held back by a brown velvet snood. She was twenty-four, they had been married for five years, and her appearance still gave him pleasure, but almost everything else about her was unsatisfactory.

'I'm sorry you don't love me,' he said, and she answered politely, 'So am I.'

'I suppose it was the war – we should have waited until it stopped. Or don't you think that that would have made any difference?'

'I don't think so.' She was lighting yet another cigarette. She smoked too much, he thought.

'What are you going to do?' he asked. 'Try to get back to the theatre?'

'I don't think so. I don't think I'm good enough. I'll get some sort of job. I suppose we'd better have a divorce.'

'You have no reason for divorcing me. I didn't ask you to go.'

'I know. I thought you'd prefer to divorce me. I don't mind. There are two things . . .'

'Yes?'

'I wondered if it would be possible to have a little money, a small allowance for when I am looking after Sebastian. For bus fares and taking him to the zoo – things like that. Because, at any rate to begin with, I shan't have much money.'

'What's the other thing?'

'Well,' he saw she was beginning to blush, 'I thought that as I haven't really got any qualifications for a job, perhaps you would consider letting me buy a typewriter and I could buy one of those books and teach myself to touch-type. I don't know what they cost, but perhaps I could get a second-hand one.'

'Anything else?'

'No.'

'I can see that you won't miss me,' he said with some bitterness, 'but what about Sebastian? It is surely very odd of you to abandon him like this?'

'I expect it is. But I couldn't possibly keep him in the way he is being kept now. I could never afford Nannie, and how would I earn the money to keep him if I had him with me all the time? Anyway, I'm not much of a mother. I never have been, you know that.'

He thought of all the things his mother had said about Louise's lack of maternal feeling and was silent. This was one of the most unsatisfactory – and unnatural – aspects of her.

'I'll get my secretary to find out about a typewriter for you,' he said. 'And of course I'll give you a small allowance for Sebastian.'

'Thank you, Michael. I really am grateful. And I'm sorry I've been such a failure as a wife. I'm sorry,' she repeated, less steadily.

'When do you plan to leave?'

'I thought some time this week. Tomorrow, probably. Polly is going to her father's at the weekend until her wedding, and she will show me how everything works before she leaves.'

'And you will be alone there?' It occurred to him that that must be a daunting thought to her.

'To begin with anyway. But Stella might be getting sent back to London, and if she is she will share the flat with me, and if she doesn't, I'll have to find someone else. Because of the rent. It does seem better, if I'm going, to get on with it.'

'Yes. I think it would be.'

That was that.

∞ ∞ ∞

'My poor darling! What a thing for you!'

'Well, Mummy, I think it is really for the best. We weren't having much of a life together – haven't for ages.'

'What about Sebastian?'

'She's leaving him with me.'

'She is the most extraordinary girl! He could come down with Nannie to Hatton for the summer. Wouldn't that be a good plan? And you, of course, darling, whenever you feel like it.' She dipped a strawberry into some sugar and then some cream and held it out to him. They were having tea in the small, sunny back garden.

'Of course *you* will have to divorce *her*.'

'Yes. She has agreed to that.'

'And she will go back to her mother?'

'No. She's going to live in the flat that belonged to her cousin – the one who's getting married next week.'

'To poor Lettie Fakenham's son? The plain one?'

'That's it.'

'I haven't heard of her since I wrote when her elder boy was killed. Poor lady, she was absolutely devastated. To be marooned in that monstrous house with the plain son and that husband who was a *howling* bore, and she was really rather glamorous – when she was young, at any rate. But, Mikey darling, back to you. What are you going to do about money? Is she being very greedy? She was very haughty and extravagant when you were in New York.'

'I know she was. But an awful lot of that was presents for everyone, and she'd never had a chance to buy clothes – I think all shops and no coupons went to her head. Anyway,' he added, 'I told her she could.'

'But what happens now?'

'She doesn't expect me to keep her. She asked for very little, really.'

'I suppose she has some new lover.'

'No, I don't think so. She says not and I believe her. You mustn't be too hard on her, Mummy. For Sebastian's sake, if for nothing else.'

'You're quite right. I mustn't be. You're a much nicer character than I am. I have something of the tigress in me.'

This made her laugh. 'Well, my darling,' she said, when he was leaving, 'we must look on the bright side. You have the most adorable son, my grandson. I think the most difficult thing I have ever had to face was the possibility that you might not. I am a happy woman. And grandmother.'

∞ ∞ ∞

'What sort of news?'

'Like most news, I suppose, it depends upon how you look at it.'

'How do you feel?' she asked, after he had told her.

'I don't know. In some ways a kind of relief. Of course, a feeling of being a failure as well.'

They had dined in Rowena's house, and were still in

the dining room. The windows were open, but there was not a breath of moving air; the flames of the candles on the table were motionless and upright. Between them lay a bowl of cream and the palest pink roses voluptuously near their end. The maid had brought the coffee tray and been dismissed for the night. She leaned towards him and he saw her breasts move charmingly in the low-cut dress.

'I'm so sorry, darling Mikey. It must have been an awful time for you. For her as well.'

'Yes. I suppose it must.' He had not really thought about how Louise felt about it: she was doing the leaving, so he hadn't felt the need to consider what had brought her to it.

'What about the child?'

'She's leaving him with me. My mother is going to have him down at Hatton for the summer.'

'Oh.'

'I'm glad I've told you.'

'Tell me as much as you want to.'

So he did. He told her how Louise had sprung it on him that morning, how he had gone to his studio but found himself unable to work, how he had called in on his mother and how good she had been about it, and how glad he had been to find, when he telephoned Rowena, that she was free that evening.

'It must have been a shock. I mean, even if one is half expecting something it's a shock when it happens,' she said.

She had got up from the table once while he had been telling her, but only to get the brandy which she poured for them.

'When is she going?'

'Tomorrow,' he said. 'I was wondering . . . I mean,

the thought of going back there for a ghastly last night, I don't feel I can face it.'

Her face lit up. 'Darling Mikey! You don't have to beat about the bush. You would be very, very welcome.'

∞ ∞ ∞

If anyone had told him two years ago that he'd find work the easiest part of his life and almost everything else about it the most difficult, he wouldn't have believed them.

He was on his laborious journey back to Tufnell Park from the wharf, which was near Tower Bridge, at the end of an arduous week. The weather had been alternately stifling and stormy and whatever he wore at work got soaked with sweat. Bernie had said she was sick of washing his shirts and he'd taken to doing them himself. The trouble was, he thought, that whenever he gave way to her about something, she thought of something else. He had the uncomfortable feeling that she was losing respect for him, although she still liked him in bed. That had become, or perhaps it always had been, their best time: when she was demanding without being rancorous – she was even affectionate. But he was beginning to find, or to notice, that the nights were taking a toll. She wanted so much of it, and his saying that he was tired only provoked her into arousing him yet again. She was too jolly good at that. But often now he woke tired, and unless he nipped out of bed pretty fast she would be awake wanting him to do it to her one more time. This had sometimes made him late for work, and more often meant that he left without any breakfast. He had to admit that she was definitely not domesticated. She kept the bathroom clean, though cluttered with make-up, but the rest of the flat was a mess. She loathed cooking, although in Arizona she had boasted of all kinds of American dishes that she could make. Here, her excuse was that she couldn't get any of the ingredients. She was such a rotten housekeeper that he had taken to doing the shopping on Saturday mornings.

And she was absolutely hopeless about money. Dad had bailed him out once to pay the main bills, and Mum had also come up with the odd fiver, but he felt wretched about asking them. He *had* put the rent and a small amount in a separate account which meant, of course, that he had less to give Bernie. She couldn't understand it. 'You told me your parents were rich,' she said. 'You went on and on about having two houses, and servants, and that means rich-rich, and I come over and you land me in a dump like this!' He didn't think he'd gone on about these things. It was only when she questioned him – cross-examined was more like it – about his family and home that he'd told her anything. He was sick of apologising for the flat, for the lack of money to go dancing or to nightclubs – in taxis, for God's sake, since she was always wearing shoes in which she said she couldn't walk a step although she could *dance* for *hours* in them. She expected to go to the hairdresser every week, in the West End where, of course, they were more expensive, and she was always buying make-up, and complaining about not being able to buy clothes. 'You've got tons of clothes!' he had exclaimed.

'I've worn all of them. In America, we don't *keep* clothes, like a lot of old antiques, we throw them out and get new ones.' She went to the cinema a lot on her own because she said she was bored with nothing to do all day. This cost money as well. He'd been reduced to pawning – well, selling really, because he was never able to redeem them – his gold cuff-links that Dad had given him when he was joining up, and a set of fish knives that the Duchy had given him for his wedding present, and several other portable things like that. He had begun to dread getting back to the flat to find her sulking, sometimes not even dressed, with nothing to eat for dinner and having to have an argument about not going out to a restaurant and then having to go out and buy fish and chips.

Tonight was a Friday and a hot, uninviting weekend lay ahead. The flat was awful in hot weather: it faced south and some of the windows didn't even open. He'd try to persuade her to go to Hampstead Heath with him, and they could take a picnic. She liked lying in the sun and he would be able to go to sleep because she couldn't expect to be made love to with all the people about.

He got off his last bus in Holloway Road and tramped up Tufnell Park Road to the street off it where they lived on the top floor of a tall, narrow house. He let himself in at the front door – there was always a smell of cat on the stairs and sometimes of cooking: there were four flats in the building – and climbed to the top and his own front door. How exciting that had been at first! Being married, having a home of his own . . .

The flat was quiet. Usually she had the radio on.

'Bernie! I'm back!'

There was no answer. She was not in the sitting room, which opened on to the kitchenette, which meant that she must be in either the bedroom or the tiny bathroom. But she wasn't in either of them. It was unlike her to be out,

560

unless she'd gone to a later show at the cinema than usual.

Then he noticed that the bedroom wardrobe – with its doors open – was empty of her clothes. The bed was unmade, but on the pillow, pinned with a safety pin, was a piece of paper. He pulled it from the pin and read it.

I'm off. I can't stand it any longer. I didn't want to tell you this morning so as not to hurt your feelings. I called Ma weeks ago to send me some money to go home. It came yesterday. I'm sure this is best for both of us. Hope you will understand and no hard feelings. Bernie.

He read it twice trying to take it in. She'd gone? She'd *gone*. Just like that! She must have known she was going ever since she'd called her mother, whom she always claimed to have disliked, but she hadn't said a word to him. He had the curious sensation of a surge of emotions without having the least idea what they were. She'd gone, without the slightest warning. Which meant in a way that she had lied to him, because only last night they had discussed what she would wear to his cousin Polly's wedding (she liked him to take an interest in her clothes), but all the time she must have known that she would not be going to it. They were *married*, and she'd left him with just a *note*! Bloody awful cheek! He knew what he was feeling now. He was angry – at being made such a fool of, at her caring so little for him that she hadn't been prepared to do *anything* to make the marriage work. She *was* a liar. She'd lied to him about her age – when they'd left America he saw her passport and she was more than ten years older than she'd said she was. He'd forgiven her for that because she'd been so pathetic about it.

He was wandering about the flat now, with the piece of paper screwed up in his hand. The kitchen sink was full of dirty cups and the remains of their supper from the night before. Her cup had a big lipstick mark on it. He picked it up and hurled it across the room where it hit the top of the gas stove and shattered. She'd never cared for him – he saw it now. Except for sex, she'd had no use for him. Obviously she'd thought she was on to a good thing in marrying him: she'd thought she'd have a big house and servants and any amount of money. Nothing he'd said to her about that had sunk in. She'd been all lovey-dovey with him, saying she'd go to the ends of the *earth* for him – and she hadn't even *tried* to survive Tufnell Park. Then he had to sit down on the chair that had no springs because he found he was crying.

The rest of the evening was awful. He longed for someone to talk to – but the telephone had been cut off because he couldn't pay the bill. He was hungry and tired and thirsty and there was nothing (of course!) in the flat to eat. He went wearily out to a pub and had a pint of bitter, but he couldn't bear the other people talking and drinking and smoking and laughing as though nothing whatever had happened. He went to the fish-and-chip shop and got himself some food to take back to the flat. But the fish, deeply encased in greasy batter, nauseated him. He ate some of the chips, and then he went and lay on top of the unmade bed. It smelled of *them*, and this made him miserable. He got up and cleaned up the kitchen and some of the sitting room until he was so tired that he didn't even care what the bed was like, fell upon it still clothed and passed out.

He woke up very late and remembered that he was alone. He had some faint stirrings of relief, but he banished them. He was an abandoned husband – relief was not in order. He got up and had a bath and a shave, which made him feel much better. Then, just as he realised that he'd have to go out before breakfast because there wasn't any and even the remains of the milk was off, the doorbell rang. They must have rung the wrong bell, he thought. Nobody had ever come to visit them. He went down to answer it.

He opened the door and there was Simon.

'I got your address from Dad,' he said. 'I tried to ring you last night, but your phone doesn't seem to be working.'

It was wonderful to see him, and the unexpectedness of it made it even better. He took him up to the flat and, without any preamble at all, told him what had happened.

Simon was extremely sympathetic. 'Cor!' he kept saying. 'Poor old you. Bit mean of her to spring it on you like that. It sounds as though you may be better off without her. From what I gather from my friends, women tend to be unreliable – on one day and off the next, if you know what I mean.'

He was beautifully dressed in an old tweed suit with a spotted bow tie and sky-blue socks. Teddy felt rather shabby in contrast.

'I've come to London for Poll's wedding, and there's such a fuss going on about it at home that I wanted to get the hell out, and I hadn't seen you for ages . . .'

'I'm really glad to see *you*.'

When Simon discovered that he hadn't had breakfast he suggested that they go out at once and have an early lunch. 'I've borrowed Dad's car,' he said. 'Where shall we go?'

They had lunch in a pub near Hampstead Heath and went out for a walk afterwards, and discussed their futures – which both felt were rather excitingly precarious. Simon had finished at Oxford – 'Of course I don't know how I've *done* yet' – and was faced with impending National Service, which he spoke of with contemptuous boredom, but which, Teddy could detect, he was secretly dreading. He speculated more about Bernadine's departure and supposed he would have to divorce her. 'That's the usual thing, I think,' he said, in as worldly a manner as he could manage, but *he* felt both depressed and alarmed at the prospect. To begin with, he hadn't a ghost of an idea how one set about it. It involved lawyers, he knew, and this was probably expensive, as almost everything nice or nasty seemed to be.

'The thing is,' Simon said – they were lying on a bank in front of a wood – 'that you'd better be pretty careful not to get caught up with another woman too soon. Or at least don't *marry* them if you do.'

'You usually have to marry them in the end,' he said. 'Girls are keen on that sort of thing, I've found.' He did not see the need to tell Simon that Bernie had so far been his only experience of girls – not counting the odd kiss after RAF dances. He was two years older, and tradition had it that therefore he knew more.

'Is it actually *worth* it?' Simon asked later, as they tramped back to the car.

'What?'

'Sex – with someone else. I nearly tried it once,' he added carelessly, 'but when it came to the point, it all

564

seemed a bit – you know – complicated. I was afraid she might get the wrong idea about me.'

Somehow Teddy knew that this had not been the case, but he was fond of Simon, and he also knew, again from the RAF, that people told more lies about their conquests than anything else.

'It can be marvellous,' he said. 'But, of course, you have to find the right person.'

'Yes. And that could take ages,' Simon agreed.

Then they gossiped about the family.

'Polly's tremendously happy. Only she's suddenly got nervous about the actual wedding. You're an usher like me, aren't you?'

'Yep.'

'We could go to Moss Bros together to get our morning coats. Neville was going to be one as well, but he kept calling her Lady Fake and she's had a row with him.'

They were both feeling hungry again so they found a tea shop and had a fairly substantial tea, because the waitress kept offering them extra scones and cakes.

'I expect she's sex-starved,' Simon said. 'We're the only men in the place.'

Then they went back to Teddy's flat.

He asked Simon to come with him. He was beginning to dread returning there alone.

'Course I will. Are you worried she might have changed her mind and come back?'

He hadn't thought of that. But he realised then that he very much hoped she hadn't.

And when he found that she hadn't, that the flat was just as he had left it, he felt tremendous relief. Simon had stood them the lunch and the tea, so he said he would get fish and chips for supper, and Simon bought the beer.

'Do you remember the camp that you and Christopher made without me, just before the war?'

'And you had a fight with him? I do.'

'I didn't really want to fight him. I just hated the way he'd left me out.'

'I didn't really want to run away and live in the camp. It was just that he was so keen.'

'What's happened to him?'

'Dad said he was living with his sister – you know, the one who married that poor bloke.'

'It doesn't sound like much of a life.'

'I nearly forgot! There's a bottle of whisky in the car. I brought it as a present for you. I'll nip down and get it.'

They had had two large drinks each and everything felt very cosy.

'What's it like, working in the firm?' Simon asked casually.

'I think it's *going* to be all right. When I stop being quite so *menial*. Why? Are you thinking of going in for it?'

Simon shook his head. 'God, no! I don't want to be a businessman.'

'What do you want to do?' he asked. He felt faintly nettled at Simon's dismissal of *his* job.

'Don't know. Well, I do, in a way. I'd like to go into politics. I'd like to be a Member of Parliament. You know, change things.'

'Get this government out? That kind of thing?'

'Oh, no. I *approve* of this government. I'd be a Labour man.'

'You mean, you're in favour of all this nationalising of everything?'

'I am. But it's not just that. I'm dead against the Tories. Do you know that the BMA have set up a fund to help doctors who don't want to co-operate with the National Health Service? They say they want to modify proposals in the Bill, but really they don't want the Bill at all. They're Tory to a man.'

'BMA?' he repeated. 'Oh – British Medical something or other.'

'Association. Tories just seem to me against any kind of progress. They don't care about the workers at all.'

'But, surely, *some* Tories are workers. Look at me.'

'Yes, but you know you'll end up in an office bossing the real workers about. There are thousands of people who will work all their lives without a chance of that.'

'You have to have workers as well as bosses. They couldn't all be bosses, whatever you did.'

'No, but you could give them a better deal. A share of the profits. That's the point of nationalisation. Everybody *owns* the railways. Everybody *owns* the coal mines.'

He went on in this vein for some time, and Teddy began by listening and then he didn't listen, and occupied himself getting a jug of water from the kitchen tap to add to their whisky. He began to wish that he had been to a university. There wasn't anything he could talk about for such a long time with such an air of authority as Simon had. Well, he knew quite a bit about Hurricane fighters, but that wasn't turning out to be much use in a peacetime world. And one day he would know a lot about timber – be like Dad.

When Simon had stopped talking about politics and accused him, but in a rather bleary way, of not being interested, they both had one more drink and got back to

– he thought – the far more interesting subject of their own lives.

It started with talking about their fathers. He told Simon how ill his father had been, and he added that it seemed that Hugh and Dad were not getting on and said that he thought it was a bit unfair on *his* dad on top of his operation and all that.

'I didn't know. Of course I haven't been around much, but Dad seems much happier to me. I think he's finally got over Mum. Or perhaps he's just so pleased about Poll.'

'Whatever it is, if you got the chance, you might just mention to him that my dad would like to see him – I mean, not in the office, but on their own somewhere.'

'Right. You'd think they'd be old enough to sort things out for themselves, though, wouldn't you?'

'Perhaps you just get too old to be able to.'

'That would be like life. You spend all your youth being made to do horrible things, and then I suppose you get a few years when you can *choose* what you do before you get too old and weak to enjoy anything.'

'And when you *can* choose, you choose wrong,' he said. He was beginning to feel awful about Bernie again, and wondering where she was, and whether he ought to try and find out and go after her. He said some of this to Simon, who advised against doing anything.

'She's the one who's gone,' he said. 'She's not likely to change *her* mind. And you don't even know if you want her to. Of course, I may be wrong,' he added, but in tones that sounded as though he thought it unlikely, 'but *I* think you'd be better off without her. Would you like me to stay the night here? I don't think I could drive home anyway – I'm too tight.'

He said he would. He staggered to his feet and found some clean sheets, and Simon offered to make the bed with him but they simply couldn't do it. The sheets went all over the place with each one pulling in the wrong direction, and they collapsed laughing.

'Do you remember when we had that ghastly drink in the wood? And we drank to Strangways Major?'

'And Bobby Riggs? I do. And we smoked a bit of one of the Brig's cigars.'

'*You* did. I was sick. And you said it was the fish we'd had for supper.'

'I knew it wasn't really,' he said, 'but you looked so awfully rotten, I wanted to cheer you up.'

'And *I* want to cheer you up,' Simon said, so affectionately that Teddy felt tears coming to his eyes.

'You've been wizard,' he said, 'absolutely *wizard*. I think men are much easier to get on with than women,' he said, when they had settled, head to tail, on the bed.

'Oh, they are, old boy. Absolutely. They don't fuss about the wrong things.'

'What sort of things?'

'Oh, you know, weddings. And spiders. And what they look like all the time . . . How many women have you found who you could talk about nationalisation to? Because, speaking for myself, I haven't found one. Not – a single one. I say, this bed's very *rocky*, isn't it?'

'Bernie wasn't interested in fighter planes. I tried to interest her but she never was. What's wrong with the bed?'

'It seems to be waving about rather.'

'It's not me. You're drunk – that's what it is. I am, too,' he added.

'We're both drunk. We drank the whole bottle, you

know. Not counting the beer we drank while we were getting the beer for supper. We'd better get some sleep.'

'It seems worse if I close my eyes.'

But Simon fell asleep very soon after that, because he didn't notice the next thing that he, Teddy, said to him, and after thinking that perhaps he was going to lie there all night worrying about Bernie, his marriage being over and being on his own again, he didn't remember any more either.

∞ ∞ ∞

Jemima knew that it was because she felt – apart from very much else – a little bit *tired*, but somehow, for the last week or so, her life had seemed to be composed of stopping things, finishing them, casting them off, closing things down, shutting things up, in fact, making all the preparations for something completely different that had not yet begun. Yesterday she had cleared up the office. It was the kind of odd, old-fashioned room that did not respond to being cleared up. It simply looked emptier but resolutely the same, with its dark, panelled walls that were hung with dozens of faded photographs in narrow black frames, its vast mahogany partner's desk, its long black chesterfield that was prickly with errant horsehair, and the enormous dining-room chairs (with arms – she supposed they were carvers), and its window that never seemed to be clear of London grime with a dark green blind that was always sticking half-way, and its once brilliant but now worn Turkish rug on the polished floor – it all seemed designed for a gloomy giant. She felt tiny in it – well, she was small, but she felt ridiculous. And even the things on the desk were dwarfed: the blotter, the silver-framed calendar that she had just set to Friday, 18 July, and his family photographs. There was one of each of his children when quite young: Simon, in shorts with a toy yacht on his knees, and Polly, who had got married last week, as a serious little girl in a sleeveless summer frock, and William, a toddler in a white linen hat, held by his mother on a lawn. She was wearing a rather shapeless flowered summer dress, and there must have been a breeze, because tendrils of hair were escaping from the bun at the back of her neck. William looked as though he was trying to get away, and she was gazing at him with a kind of resigned affection. The larger one of her by herself was no longer there, she noticed.

There were also inkstands, wood samples, and trays for papers in various stages of completion. She had put all of these things straight, even symmetrically upon the desk, had answered the morning post when she could, clipped the letters for him to see and placed them in the middle of the blotter. She had felt strange doing these things because it was for the last time, and because nobody else in the office knew that this was so.

Then she had covered her typewriter in the small black office that was behind this room, collected her hat and her bag and slipped out. 'Going early, are you?' the office boy had said.

'Yes. Mr Hugh's not in today,' she had replied. But why had she even bothered to say that? It wasn't Alfie's business.

She went home to pack up for the boys. Home was – had been for nearly seven years now – the bottom half of a house in Blomfield Road by the Regent's Canal. She had chosen it because the rent was cheap, and because there was a large back garden for the boys. It had two bedrooms and a sitting room on the ground floor, and a dining room and a tiny kitchenette in the basement. It was damp, and difficult to keep warm, and some very strange people lived in the flat above, of whom she was slightly afraid, but it had been their home since soon after Ken had been killed.

She got home well before the boys were back from school, which was good because she could get their packing done far more peacefully without them. They were excited at the prospect of going away to camp for two weeks; the only thing that was worrying them was whether there would be an adequate supply of poplar leaves for their elephant hawk-moth caterpillars. She got out the battered old leather case that had belonged to Ken. It no longer shut properly and had to have a leather strap round it. She'd done all their washing last weekend, so it was simply a matter of counting out enough of everything. Two vests each, two pairs of shorts, four shirts each and a pullover. They could travel in their sand shoes and just take sandals. Perhaps one pair of socks each? But she knew they wouldn't wear them. They could travel in their macs – only they wouldn't wear *them* either, and she'd have to beg them not to leave them behind in the train. Ration books would be required, and into them she pinned an address and telephone number in case she was needed. She finished the packing with their hats, bathing suits and a towel each. They could have the little case for their books, pen-knives, and any other clobber. Tom had a magnifying glass, with which he was mad keen to start a fire, and Henry would want to take his Box Brownie camera. Then, of course, they would take Hoighty the grey monkey (Tom's) and Sparker (Henry's teddy). How the caterpillars were to travel, she didn't know. What seemed so odd, she thought, was that they were not just going away from here for two weeks; they weren't coming back here. They knew this and seemed simply excited by the prospect, but looking round their overfilled, untidy room that was so crowded by their possessions and interests, she felt a pang. It was the end of an era.

They were back. The boys' room looked on to the street, and she saw Elspeth, the girl she paid to take and fetch them to and from school, at the garden gate. She opened it and they surged through like a high tide. Elspeth waved and turned to walk back to the main road. A good thing she'd paid her and explained that she'd get in touch in the autumn, she thought, as she sped down to let them in.

'We've got to pack!' they shouted. 'We've got to collect everything to pack!'

'Not everything. Just enough for your fortnight in camp. You won't need everything for that.'

They looked at each other. 'Yes, we will.'

'We will because we don't know what we *will* want.'

'You've got one small case. You can fill that, and that will be it. I've packed your clothes.'

'We'll hardly need any. Mr Partington says there's a huge lake and we shall go on it most of the time.'

'And in it,' Henry added.

'You go up and wash for tea.'

'What's for tea?'

'Baked beans on toast.'

'Oh, *Mum*! *Again?!*'

'You love baked beans.'

'We *like* them,' Tom conceded. 'But we have them so often we've stopped loving them.'

'I can't help that. That's all there is. I'm saving the eggs for your breakfast.'

'Tell you what,' Henry said, following her to the kitchen. 'We could have the eggs now, and the baked beans for breakfast. It would be just the same.'

The whole evening was like that. Sometimes she stood firm and sometimes she gave in; they accepted defeat with good humour and success with whoops of joy. They were so excited that she sent them out into the garden after their tea to work off steam. By the time she'd got them in to do their packing, run them a bath and got them into it, the negotiations had quite worn her out. There was a very early start tomorrow – she had to get them to Paddington by eight o'clock – and she still had her own packing to do. She left them in the bath while she cleared up their tea, and when she came back they had got into their pyjamas and were sitting side by side in Tom's bed, picking a torch to pieces and trying to make it work. Their sandy hair was damp, and they did not seem to have dried themselves much, but they had that look of rosy polished virtue that seemed only to occur just after a bath.

'Henry pretended to be blind,' Tom said. 'He could do up his pyjama buttons by feel, but he kept bumping into things. It must take a long time to be blind.'

'A long time to do things,' Henry agreed. 'But if people practised every day, then when they were blind it wouldn't matter.'

'But think of all the other things you'd have to practise,' she said. 'Having one leg, like Long John Silver, for instance.'

'Don't mention him at night, Mum. You know I don't like it.'

'But it would be fun to pretend having one leg,' Henry said. 'Could you swim with one leg, Mum?'

'You could if I held you up,' Tom said.

They were so alike, she thought, but the moment either of them spoke she knew which one it was. A lot of the time she knew anyway, but nobody else did. Tom had always protected Henry and Henry always listened to Tom.

When she had read them another chapter of *Bevis*, a book they never tired of, and kissed them goodnight, it was well after eight.

For once she would have liked a drink, she thought, as she went to find something to eat for herself, but she had never been able to afford drink. With her pension, and the salary, she had just about got by, but it had always been a struggle. It was worse with twins, because they always needed new clothes at the same time. She had made her own clothes, and taken the boys home to her parents for holidays. Her mother knitted them all jerseys and her father had paid for her to take a secretarial course after Ken was killed when she was pregnant and it had seemed as good a way as any other of getting from one bleak day to the next. They had had barely a year together, far less if one simply counted his leaves, which was really all the time that they had had. The rest of it had been anxious waiting – except that she was a WRAF and therefore working in the ops room on one of the east coast stations for bombers. They'd had a heavenly ten days after they were married, but that was the longest time they had ever spent together. Afterwards, it was usually forty-eight hours and, once, a week because he had flu.

So, of course, he never saw the boys, who were born

five months after his death. He had *known* about them (but not known that it was *them*); the news that she was to have twins was broken to her about a week before their appearance). By then, of course, she was out of the WRAF, and in a panic about how she was going to be able to manage everything. She had thought that she would get a job as soon as they were weaned, but when it came to the point, she could not get any job that paid enough to pay someone else to look after the babies. Her mother offered to have them, but she could not bear them being so far away, and she felt that going back to live at home was admitting defeat. So she got a few bits of copy-typing that she could do in the evenings at home until the boys were old enough to be going to school, and then she had applied for the job at Cazalets' – and got it.

She didn't feel hungry, so she made a pot of tea and took it up to her bedroom to drink while she packed. This would not take long: she did not have many clothes and most of them were pretty worn out. Her parents had given her the money to buy her outfit for tomorrow and she had chosen a linen mixture in a blue the colour of cornflowers for a very simple suit with a short jacket and longish skirt. She had decided against a hat, and now worried that she should have got one. Too late now. Her friend Charlie was lending her best handbag – a navy blue affair in the most beautiful soft leather that her husband had brought back from Rome. Their husbands had been in the same squadron, but George had survived and become a wing commander – she thought, then, that if Ken had survived he, too, would have reached that rank. His photograph, in a leather frame, stood on the mantelpiece. It had been taken when they were engaged and he was twenty-two, the same age as herself. He was in uniform with his cap slightly askew, nearly smiling but with that look of restless energy, of wanting to get on with whatever might happen next, that she remembered so well. How many times had she looked at this picture and prayed that his death had been too quick for agony? And how many times had she wept because she knew too much to believe that? He was a navigator in a Wellington. They'd gone on a day raid and his plane had been met by fighters well before they reached their target. They'd lost one engine, had had to jettison their bomb load over the North Sea as they limped home on the remaining engine; their rear gunner had been hit, and Ken had gone aft to minister to him. They had reached their home base, had made a clumsy landing. Two of the crew got out in time, before the plane, still laden with fuel, blew up, but Ken had not been one of them. The flight lieutenant who'd served with him had come to tell her about Ken. She remembered she had said, 'He would have died at once?' and John had answered, 'He wouldn't have known a thing.' But she always remembered how he did not look at her when he said that. The last, perhaps the very last, tears came to her eyes. It was time to stop them, to cast off this old grief – it was done and nothing could alter it. She picked up the picture, gave him a kiss, and put it in the case that she would not be taking with her tomorrow. She would keep the picture for the boys.

∞ ∞ ∞

'Are you excited? You must be,' Charlie answered herself. She had come to help her dress. She had got the boys off: breakfast, a taxi called from the rank – they *loved* going in a taxi, which happened very rarely. They journeyed to Paddington with the elephant hawk-moth caterpillars in a shoe box – its lid spattered with holes – resting on both their knees. A paper bag with spare leaves picked from the back garden that morning was in one twin's sponge bag. 'They eat an awful lot, you know, before they pupate,' Tom had said. They had seemed unconcerned at parting with her, but they had each other, and she was glad they were so simply happy.

'Have a lovely holiday,' she had said, as she hugged them both.

'We will,' Henry had replied.

'You, too, Mum,' Tom had added, and Henry had nodded.

'If we actually found a rabbit that was tame, could we bring it back?'

'If it really wants to come,' she said. Then the man who was taking them said they must all get on to the train, so she left.

Back home, she had a bath, and washed her hair, and then Charlie arrived looking very smart, and bringing a small bunch of yellow and white roses. 'I've made you an egg sandwich,' she said. 'I bet you didn't have breakfast.'

She thought she would not be able to eat it, but found she could. 'You are a good friend.'

'I'm just so happy for you. You deserve a really good time for a change. Let me just trim your fringe – it is a tiny bit long.' She tied a bath towel round Jemima's neck and snipped across her forehead. 'That's better. What about your make-up?'

'I haven't got anything much. Some lipstick.'

'You need a spot of rouge too. You're very pale, darling.'

So Charlie applied the make-up. 'Nothing will stop you looking about fourteen,' she said.

She was dressed, and it was time to go, and Charlie drove her to Kensington.

'He's twenty-one years older than me,' she said, as they drove over Campden Hill.

'That doesn't worry you, does it? Not if you love him.'

'I do love him,' she said and, as she said it, was flooded with love for him: for his sweetness, his whole-hearted kindness to the boys, the way in which his gentle, haunted expression dissolved to tenderness and fun when he looked at her, his startling sincerity ('I want always to know what you feel,' he had said. 'Even if it turns out that we don't agree, or feel the same about any particular thing, I always want to know it'), his surprising capacity for both love and affection, the sense that his loyalty was boundless, and then the discovery, made once – a few weeks ago – that he was for her the perfect lover, patient, sensitive, delightful and full of ardour. He had asked her whether she wanted to go to bed with him before marrying, had said that it should be her choice. '*I* am quite sure,' he said, 'but I would like you to feel the same.' And so, because she had had lingering fears – she had been celibate since Ken died, had had neither time nor opportunity to be in love, and was afraid that she would disappoint either herself or him – she had agreed. Charlie had had the boys for a night, and he had taken her to an hotel on the river on a hot June evening, and when they were in their room he had said, 'Let's go to bed now, and then we'll have dinner.' And he had been right about that, because she had felt very strung up. Afterwards, full of a happiness extraordinary to her, she had said how glad she was that he had proposed it that way round. 'Ah! I didn't want you to have the chance to feel *dogged* about it,' he had said, opening a bottle of champagne – she was amazed at what he could do in that way – and when he handed her a glass he said, 'Darling Jemima, *will* you marry me?' And she had said that, in view of what had happened, she had no alternative, and he had said that he had hoped she would say that. They had drunk the champagne and gone down to dinner, which had been full of joyful plans about this life they were to embark upon.

And now she was about to embark upon it.

'Oh, yes, I really love him.'

And Charlie answered, 'Then there is nothing to worry about. You've always been a worrier. Now you'll have to learn to stop.'

He was waiting for her at the register office, with his younger brother and his wife who, with Charlie, were to be witnesses. They stood in the small office-like room, and then she laid her hand upon his black silk stump where his hand had been and they walked up to the registrar, who at once began the ceremony. It was over in minutes; he bent to kiss her, and then the others kissed her as well. Their names were signed, she signed her new name for the first time.

'It was over so quickly,' she said, as she walked with Hugh to his car.

'But the really good, long part has just begun,' he answered. He stopped in the street. 'You're not worrying about the leaflets, are you? We can send them postcards tonight.'

'I'm not worrying about anything at all,' she said. 'Nothing in the world.'

It was true.

∞ ∞ ∞

'Are you *sure* you don't want us to go with you to the station?'

'Absolutely sure.'

They were all three standing outside the restaurant where his parents had taken him for a farewell lunch. It had not been an easy occasion, but he had realised that it had been far more difficult for them than it was for him, and he had tried his best to keep things on an even keel. He had been calm about his father's hostile ruminations about his future, and reassuring about his mother's – he thought – irrelevant and frivolous anxieties on the same subject. He had deflected them by asking them about themselves, a worn trick that none the less worked with most people (another thing he had learned from Father Lancing). Also, talking about Polly's wedding had been a distraction: his mother had enjoyed the whole thing enormously, and his father had been impressed that Gerald had a title. It was odd: his father, who had once been such a terrifying and dominant force in his life, was now of no real account; that he was also a snob struck him as just one more pathetic aspect. But at least he, Christopher, could not be bullied any more. There had been small incidents at the lunch. His father had offered him a drink, and when he had refused, had pressed him, had tried to *make* him have one whether he liked it or not. It was when his mother had intervened – 'Oh, Raymond, can't you see he really doesn't want one?' – that he was taken

581

back to those innumerable times in his childhood when she had tried to protect him and had often made things far worse. He had looked at her then with a sudden affection: money, and disappointment with her husband (painfully apparent) had aged her; she had the look of haggard brightness that he could now associate with inner discontent. He felt sorry for her as well.

'You'll keep in touch, won't you, darling?' she was now saying again – she had said it several times during lunch.

'I expect he'll be back with us before you know where you are,' his father said then. 'Do you want a taxi?'

'No, thanks. I'll get a bus.'

'What station are you going to? Because if it's Victoria, we could give you a lift.'

'It's Marylebone, Mummy. I'm fine, really. Thank you very much for the splendid lunch. It was splendid,' he repeated. He shook hands with his father, and put his arms around his mother's bony shoulders. 'Of course I'll write to you. I'm not going to the ends of the earth, you know.' He smiled and then kissed her as he saw her eyes fill with tears.

'Darling! I do hope you will be happy. All right, at least?'

'I shall.'

'Come on, now,' his father said. He put his arm round her protectively. 'I'm going to take you to a nice film to take your mind off it.'

Everybody said goodbye again, and he turned and walked away down the street to the nearest bus stop. It was done.

On the bus that eventually went down Baker Street, he could not help thinking of Polly whom he had loved so much. After that weekend in the caravan, he had suffered *for* her as much as about her: she, too, was enduring the pain of unrequited love. When Oliver fell ill and, in the end, in spite of all the vet could do and his nursing, had had to be put down, he had returned from the vet with the body which he had buried in the wood behind the caravan. It felt as though he had lost his only friend. He had held Oliver in his arms for the last moments of his life, feeling his poor body, his ribs like a toast-rack, his fur dull and staring, and then Oliver had looked up at him, his brandy-snap eyes still glowing with entire trust and devotion as the vet put the needle in. Seconds later he felt the body go slack. He had managed not to cry until he had got Oliver in the back of the car.

The caravan seemed awful without Oliver. He mourned and withdrew from the Hursts who kept inviting him for meals.

Then one day, Mrs Hurst – Marge – asked him whether he would take an old infirm neighbour to church in the car. 'Tom takes him usually, but he's got a terrible cold. I don't want him going out.'

So he did. He was a widower, a very old man with arthritis. All his movements were full of pain and he used crutches.

'It's good of you,' he said. 'I don't like to miss my Sunday prayers.'

As he was in the church, he thought he might as well try to pray. He prayed for Oliver, and afterwards he felt calmer and much better about him.

That evening, he decided that he would take the plunge and ask Nora if he could be of any use in her establishment. Might as well try to be some use somewhere, had been what he had thought.

Yes, she would be delighted if he would come. There was plenty to do. 'I'm run off my feet,' she had written. 'You could be a great help.'

It had not been at all what he had expected. He did not have to nurse people, Nora said, when she fetched him from the station, except for lifting them sometimes – her back had got quite bad doing it. 'And there's the garden,' she added. 'It would be wonderful if you could grow the vegetables. And you could talk to Richard sometimes. He gets rather bored because I'm so busy.'

It was Richard who shocked him. Outwardly, he looked much as he had at the wedding – a bit puffier in the face and his hair was thinner – but it was the rest of him, his frightful unhappiness, which it took time to perceive. To begin with, he thought that Richard was rather spoiled and peevish; he also seemed to take an almost infantile delight in irritating Nora. His main objects in life were to get cigarettes and smoke them when she was absent and to drink anything he could lay his hands on. He recruited Christopher to help him in both these ploys. 'You don't have to tell *her*. I only want a bit of fun, which, God knows, is in short supply in this place.' When Nora discovered that he had been enlisted, she gave him a tremendous talking-to. 'It's bad for Richard,' she said. 'People who can hardly move have trouble enough with their lungs anyway – and smoking would be the last straw.' And 'We simply cannot afford drink here. And it would really be most unfair if Richard had some and the others didn't. I do want to be fair.'

So the next time that Richard asked him to buy cigarettes, he said he thought he should not, and explained why. He was naïve enough to think that that would be that, but, of course, it wasn't.

It was winter, and he spent a good part of the day sawing wood into logs for the communal day-room fire. One late afternoon, he went into the small sitting room that Nora kept for her and Richard's use, with a basket of logs, and found him slumped sideways in his chair. It was in its usual position in a corner of the room so that he could look out of the window, which Nora said that he liked to do. When he went to help him upright, Richard said, 'Been trying . . . no bloody good . . . not a thing I can do.'

Tears of frustration were rolling down his face, and mucus from his nose. Christopher got a paper handkerchief to mop him up.

'Blow my nose,' he said as, at the same time, they both heard Nora coming.

'Goodness, it's cold in here!' she exclaimed. 'Christopher, you might have kept the fire up. We don't want poor Richard getting pneumonia.' (He had just sneezed.)

'I've only just got in,' he said, as he knelt to make up the fire.

'Soon it will be tea-time,' Nora was saying. 'Mrs Brown has made some lovely scones and there's that rhubarb jam you like so much.' Richard sneezed again. 'Oh, darling! Are you getting one of your colds?'

'Oh, I think I'm *aiming* at pneumonia,' he answered, in the special tone, both childish and sardonic, that he used so often with her, and to which, Christopher had noticed, she seemed impervious.

'Well,' she said comfortably, 'we'll do everything we can to prevent that, but if you should get a touch, even of bronchitis, the doctor says there is a brilliant new drug that kills the bug off. So, there's no need to worry. I'll go and get the tea.'

When she had gone, Richard, without any expression, said, 'I don't *want* the bug killed off. I want to die. It's about the only thing I do want.' He had met Christopher's eye at the end of saying this. There was no doubt that he meant exactly what he said, and Christopher was appalled.

He went and sat by him. 'Isn't there *anything* I can do?'

'Well, you could help me to drink myself to death, which would be marginally more pleasant than pneumonia. I don't think that Dr Gorley has a new drug to cure one of that. And I think there's a fag left behind the books up there. You could light that for me. There's just time before the Angel of Life returns with the exhilarating scones.'

He fetched the cigarette. It was the last in the small packet. He lit it for Richard and put it between his lips. He inhaled deeply and nodded for Christopher to remove it. Then he smiled. 'You're a good sort of chap, I know you are. One of the worst things about being me is other people knowing all the time what's best for me. They don't. I'll be the judge of that. Another drag, please.

'I begin to see what polar bears must feel like in a zoo,' he said, after the second inhalation. 'Trapped. Unable to do any of the things that normal polar bears would do if they weren't kept prisoner. Of course, I'm supposed to have resources unavailable to bears so far as we know. Intellectual, spiritual resources – or so Father Lancing would say. But unfortunately,' he smiled again and, for a second, Christopher saw how charming he must once have been, 'they seem to have passed me by. I can't even *read*. I'd be better off if I was a *dog*.'

At once he thought of Oliver's death, of holding him while the fatal injection was delivered.

'I think I see what you mean,' he said, as he administered the cigarette for the third time. 'She does *mean* well,' he added: he felt sorry for Nora too.

'Oh, yes. I don't think,' he said wearily, 'that I ever forget *that*. One more drag. She'll be back in a minute. And then put it in your mouth if you wouldn't mind. She always smells the smoke, and she'll think it's you. Do you believe in God?' he asked, after his last drag.

'I'm – wondering about that.'

'You're an honest sort of chap, aren't you?'

'Do you?'

'I do my damnedest not to. If he exists, and therefore is responsible for my condition, the implications are too bloody terrifying—'

'Here we are!' Nora barged open the door with the tray. 'Oh, Christopher! It's not very kind of you to smoke in front of Richard.'

'Sorry.' He threw the butt into the fire and caught Richard's eye; he had been watching Christopher, and winked.

The next time Christopher saw Father Lancing – he had taken to visiting him after supper sometimes – he told him about this occasion. 'He is so desperately unhappy. When he told me he wanted to die, I could quite see why.'

'Yes.'

'And while I can see that Nora is wonderfully selfless, I do sometimes feel that she is wrong.'

'Not incompatible.' Father Lancing was packing his small black pipe.

'And I can see why he doesn't want to believe in God.'

'So can I.'

'Nora does. She once told me that her greatest comfort was being able to talk to God.'

There was a short silence. 'You know, talk's a fine thing but, when it comes to God, listening is probably more important.' He was lighting his pipe. 'That is partly what prayer is for. To indicate that you want to listen.' Then he added ruminatively, 'People are often dubbed selfless when they do things that we wouldn't want to do. To be selfless is a high state. Most of us only manage it for a few minutes at a time.'

'What can I do for them?'

'Do you love them?'

He thought. 'No, I don't think I do. I just feel awfully *sorry* for them.'

'Try to love them. Then you will have a far clearer idea of what to do.'

By the time this conversation took place, he knew Father Lancing quite well. Father Lancing brought communion to some of the inmates of the house, and there were one or two people who were able to be taken to church – Christopher was assigned this task by Nora soon after his arrival. He had been confirmed at school, but he had not gone to church – except for that one time in Sussex – since the end of his education. After a few weeks, Father Lancing suddenly asked him to tea, and he went. The priest lived in a large, dank house with a small, silent housekeeper, who was like a wispy little ghost, he thought, since when she spoke, which was seldom, it was in a tiny high-pitched whisper. Father Lancing worked extremely hard. Christopher did not at first recognise that the invitation was squeezed between parish duties, and it did not occur to him to wonder why he had been asked;

he innocently thought that his host must be lonely, living alone as he did, but he slowly became aware that this was not so: when he was not conducting services, he was visiting, going to meetings; he loved children and music and much of his energy was spent upon promoting his choir and helping the local elementary school with their outings and festivities. He was High Anglican and some people in the village did not like this, and journeyed to another church on Sundays, but his church was comfortably full and he heard confessions there twice a week. The first time that Christopher went to see him, Father Lancing asked what had brought him to Frensham, and he had explained about feeling useless after Oliver's death, and wanting to be of some use to somebody. During those sessions, he was always encouraged to talk about himself, and quite soon he felt that Father Lancing knew more about him than anyone else and, soon after that, than *he* knew about himself.

Their conversations always graduated to philosophy – or, rather, Christian philosophy. For instance, after Christopher had told him about Polly and the blow of discovering that, after her unhappy love affair, she had found someone else who was not him and she was to be married – 'So she would never have loved me' – Father Lancing had said, 'But you loved her, and that was a gift.'

'A *gift*?'

'Surely. Love is a great gift.'

'Like faith, you mean?'

'Well, you could say that faith was another kind of love, couldn't you? How does that strike you?'

And so on.

After the conversation about Richard and Nora, he went back to the house full of determination to love them.

CASTING OFF

It was easier to love Richard, he discovered, than his sister. He tried talking to her about Richard, saying that it might be good for him to be allowed some pleasures even if they were not particularly good for him, but she had talked him down at once. 'I know you mean well, Christopher,' she had finished, 'but, unfortunately, meaning well isn't the whole story. I've worked with these people for years now, and I really do know best what is good for them.'

'You *mean* well, then,' he had not been able to resist saying and she had answered blithely: 'Of *course* I do! How could you think anything else?'

By now, he was going to church because he wanted to. He also suggested to Father Lancing that he go to confession, and the priest said that it was on Tuesdays and Fridays, and gave him a book. 'That will give you some idea of the form,' he said.

He went. He had thought to begin with that he had not a great deal to confess but, when it came to the point, there seemed to be a surprising amount. He was also surprised that Father Lancing did not make any moral comment, but confined himself to asking quite practical questions like 'How many times?' After it, when he had been given his absolution and penance, he went into the church and prayed, incandescent with good intentions.

He quickly found that they did not last or, rather, that in the wear and tear of daily life, he forgot them. He seemed to be surrounded by sad and unhappy people, and when he found how hard it was to make anything better for them, he resented their unhappiness.

Then one day, when he was in the woodshed, sawing away at a particularly intractable piece of elm, it came to him that he wanted a quite different kind of life, and something that Father Lancing had said that a monk had told him came back. 'You can put yourself in the centre of the universe, or you can put God. You cannot put another person there.' At the time, though he had listened politely, he had not thought he agreed, but now, suddenly, it was clear to him. He most certainly did *not* want to be the centre of his universe – and that left God.

He rushed to Father Lancing with this news. It was received calmly; he was almost piqued by how calm the priest was about it.

'But what do you want to do about that?' he asked.

'I thought I should go into some community. I thought I should become a monk.'

'Did you, now?'

'Yes. I don't seem to be much good in the world. I think I'd be better out of it.'

Father Lancing did not reply at once. He was engaged upon knocking out his evil-smelling pipe. Then he said, 'Well. I don't think anyone will want to receive you if you're running away from the world. It's more a question of running towards something than running away.'

'Towards God? Yes – that's what I mean!'

Father Lancing put his hands on Christopher's shoulders.

'I could send you to someone who would talk to you,' he said. 'It might clarify things for you and it will do no harm.'

So he had gone to Nashtun Abbey. He spent two days there, and had several long sessions about his possible vocation. The place both enchanted and charged him. There he discovered, as well as much else, that if he was accepted, he would spend two to three years as a postulant and eventually become a novice during which he would be free to leave at any time.

He returned to Frensham in an exalted state of mind; he had no doubts, no fears, he *knew*. It only remained for him to be accepted.

Weeks passed, and he heard nothing. He went to Father Lancing.

'Father Gregory has written to me about you,' he said. 'He feels that you need time and instruction to understand more about what you want to do – to know whether you have a vocation. I see your face fall. Do you think you know everything? Well, people do think that. Spiritual fantasy is much like any other kind. Repetition and you always come out on top. Is that it?'

It was a bull's eye. He felt himself going red.

'If you want further instruction, I have been asked to give it to you, so don't despair, St Christopher.' But he smiled so sweetly when he said this that Christopher was able to laugh with him.

'You and Father Lancing. What are you up to?' Nora asked, when Christopher asked for time to go and see him.

'He's teaching me things.'

'Oh, good. He's a wonderful man, I think. And it makes me very happy that you've started going to church.'

Richard was not so happy. 'I can see you're getting sucked in. You'll soon have first-class reasons for denying yourself – and me, come to that.'

'No, I won't.' He'd decided to collude about the cigarettes and he bought half a bottle of whisky every month which he pretended to share with Richard – actually, he cunningly drank cold tea.

He told Father Lancing that he did not want to tell anyone yet of his intention. By now he was having arguments with him, and once, when he had an appointment to see him and he was not there, he felt furiously angry – which, when they next met, Father Lancing knew at once.

'You're angry with me because I had to do something else. Why? Are you more important than the next person?'

'I thought you could have let me know.'

'Perhaps I could have done that. I was at the hospital, and I didn't want to leave the person I was with. That's about the colour of it.'

'I see.'

'No, you don't see, but you will.'

There was the turning to Polly's street. He looked down it as the bus passed, but he was not sure if he could see her house.

He had not wanted to go to the wedding, and when Father Lancing asked him why not, he said because he was afraid of how it might make him feel.

'If that is the reason, you'd certainly better go. Anyway, what about your cousin? Didn't you say she was very fond of you and won't that mean that she would want you to be there?'

'Well, yes, but I didn't think that was the most important thing.'

'The most important thing is you, is it? Your spiritual state?'

He looked at his friend dumbly, trapped, because he *did* think so and realised that Father Lancing didn't.

'I'm trying to give things *up*,' he said at last.

'Ah, that's it. The problem with that is that it's when your spiritual pride gets a real look in – has a field day, you might say. God can do without you congratulating yourself for loving Him.' But he said it with such kindness that Christopher found he could bear it.

'I do see,' he said. 'I'll go.'

It had been a very strange occasion for him. He had knelt in the church, praying that she would be happy – had chosen the right person. It seemed odd that she would have children whom he would never see, that he would know nothing of her from this day on. She had arrived, and was being led up the aisle by her father, followed, he could see, by Lydia and, he thought, Uncle Rupert's youngest daughter. Her face, covered by a veil, was not visible. But her voice, as she made her vows, was absolutely clear. After they had been into the vestry and she was walking back down the aisle with her husband, her veil was thrown from her face and he saw her and how happy she was.

When, at the reception, he eventually reached the end of the line waiting to congratulate her, her face lit up, and she stepped forward to kiss him, saying, 'Gerald, this is Christopher – my most dear cousin.'

Whether it was the glistening white satin, the veil, the pearls round her throat, her radiant dark blue eyes or all of these things, he did not know, but light seemed to stream from her – he felt struck, and speechless from it, and for a second he was afraid that he still loved her. And then he was simply glad that he loved her and this was accompanied by a feeling of living peace.

'. . . and you must come and stay,' she was saying.

And her husband was smiling and saying of course he must.

He wanted to tell her then, but it was neither the time nor the place. For the rest of the party, during the speeches, the toasts, the general rejoicing, he tried to see as many of the family as possible – say his silent farewells. Clary, thin and with long hair and wearing a green dress, was the only one who regarded him steadily (he had never noticed before how lovely her eyes were), was the only one who noticed that he had changed. 'I don't know exactly *how*, but you have. You look as though you've found something good,' she said.

'I have.'

Then she had grinned at him and looked more like the girl he remembered – whose face was smudged and whose clothes seemed always to be torn or spattered with fruit juice. The Duchy, who seemed a little smaller but otherwise just the same. And Uncle Hugh, who looked so different he seemed almost jolly – 'The last wedding we met at you were wearing my trousers, do you remember?' he said – and more cousins. Simon and Teddy, resplendent in morning dress, pleased to see him, and both mentioned that camp in the wood. He'd been trying to get away from things then – he'd always been trying to get away because he had not found what to go *towards* . . .

The bus conductor shouted up the stairs that this was the stop for Marylebone station, and he got off. My last bus, he thought, not caring, just noting the fact.

'It does seem to me a way of not facing up to things,' had been one of his father's sallies at lunch.

As he walked to the station he thought that, curiously,

it had been harder to leave Richard than anyone else. He had told Nora that he was going to a retreat, but she knew too much about these things, and after she had asked for how long, and he had answered he didn't know, but months anyway, her eyes had widened, and she'd said, 'Oh, Christopher! I understand now. Oh, I do hope you have a vocation!' Then she said – almost shyly, 'One thing. Would you mind *not* telling Richard that you are going for good? He has got rather attached to you, and it would make him so sad. It will be easier for him to know when he has got used to doing without you.'

She did love him – in her way. So he'd agreed to that. He didn't feel good about it, would rather have been honest, but Richard's distress about his going at all was so evident that he recognised that perhaps, for once, Nora had been right.

'I can't say it won't be the same without you, because it *will* – it will all be exactly the same. Bloody awful.'

Nora had left them alone together on his last evening – a piece of tact, of which, Christopher recognised with shame, he had not thought her capable – and they'd had a last drink together and Richard had smoked three cigarettes.

'It's not just the booze and the fags,' he said. 'I like *talking* to you. Still, if you're coming back, I've got something to look forward to, which I suppose is the next best thing to having it in the first place.'

On impulse, he'd bent down and kissed Richard on leaving, and Richard had started – almost as though he'd *hurt* him. 'Get on with it, then,' he'd said.

Perhaps he could write to Richard. But, then, Nora would have to read the letter to him and that, he knew, would change the sort of letter it could be. If I'm allowed to write letters at all, he thought, and was possessed with a nervous dread of what might lie ahead.

But once in the train, with his small suitcase on the rack, he returned to the sense of adventure and challenge that this journey to the interior – the centre of his universe – exacted, and he thought then that the things he had to give up were not either things or even people who had been in his life, but mysterious, as yet not known things, that lay inside himself, for only that could make room for a new inhabitant.

ARCHIE

1946–47

Until now, he had always thought that if one could not make up one's mind about what to do, it was because one was not sure what one wanted. How untrue that is, he thought, as he drove down the familiar lane, away from the cottage, through the wooded bit and then past the drive leading up to the station. Three miles away . . . He could still turn back, but he knew that he would not. He would continue the boring, well-known, dull road all the way to the suburbs of London and thence to his empty ill-kempt flat. Six weeks was not so very long, he said, as though to someone else. It seemed interminable. But this morning had been the last straw. Seeing her naked in the kitchen with her burned hand – the imagination of a body in no way impaired the impact of a first sight of the real thing – had brought home to him as nothing else had seemed to do that he could not continue this life with her which had become so beset by dishonesty.

If he tried to think about it, he could not pin down the moment when he had begun to love her. Certainly, when he had come back from France and found her so wrecked and desperate, he had dropped everything to care for her, had managed to put aside or at least conceal his fury and loathing for the wretched man who had caused her such anguish. Was this love? Or was it simply that he *knew* her – her intense, whole-hearted capacity for love, and the deprivation she had already endured? He could think of no one less equipped to withstand total rejection and pregnancy. The first thing that he had known about her, before he had even seen her, was that she had lost her mother. He remembered how, on one of those long walks in France with Rupert, shattered by Isobel's death, there had come a moment when he had been able to suggest to him that the daughter, the little girl, Clarissa, wasn't it?, must also be very bereft and needing his love. And Rupert had said: 'There's the boy as well, two of them.' And he had said, 'The boy is a baby. The girl is old enough to grieve. You must go back and see to her.'

Which Rupert had done, clearly to much effect, because when Archie did actually meet her, she was sixteen and suffering very much from the loss of him, whom everyone, including Archie himself, thought probably dead. Not she. Her faithful love had touched him then, had transcended her childish, unkempt appearance. She had always been careless of that, had no vanity. He remembered his first sight of her, tidied up for dinner his first evening at Home Place, in a shirt with odd buttons sewn on it, and her hands, bitten nails and ink stains almost, but not quite, obliterating their shapeliness, and the ill-cut fringe just above those amazingly expressive eyes. He had observed these things with no more than a professional eye and friendly interest. This was his best friend Rupert's daughter. And as he became embraced by the whole family – he had the Duchy to thank for that – and he had had time to know all of those children, as he thought of them, she seemed always to be the odd one out. She had none of the Cazalet good looks – the blue direct gaze, the fair to fairish hair, the clear complexion, the height, the long arms and legs; she was small and sturdy, round-faced, with her mother's eyes and heavy brows and fine dark hair, which was always untidy and needing a wash. He had not loved her then. But when that little Frenchman had arrived with his tale and the message for her and he had seen its effect – her eyes like stars, her utter joy that had been dashed (momentarily) by Pipette saying that the message was eight months old, how after a moment she had looked up at him and said that it was 'just a question of time – waiting till he comes back'. He had been touched by her, because by then he knew something of the intensity of her love and longing. After he had broken his leg, she would come to his room, because, he thought, he was the only person who let her talk about her father and he had been amazed – and sometimes amused – by her detailed imagination of his exploits. And then there had been the diary she wrote for Rupert. One day, she had showed him a few pages and he learned much more of her. She had a graceful mind, even though she was clumsy in everyday life – knocked things over, tore her clothes; she was passionate about quite small things. The night after Pipette had come, he had found that he actually respected her, recognised her knowledge of what it was to love, and he thought now, but could not remember, that it had been then that he had felt anxiety that it might get wrongly bestowed.

After that, he supposed wryly, he had tried to be a father of sorts to her. Little did he know how that would rebound. When the girls had come to London, he had taken them out, sometimes together, but later separately . . . Why? At the time he had told himself that it was hard on her always being with the beautiful, immaculate, charming Polly. He remembered that pathetic time when Polly had had a perm, and so she thought she should too, and how deeply unbecoming her frizzy hair had been – like the make-up that she attempted, when in no time her eyes would get ringed like a panda with mascara that always ran because she either cried or rubbed her eyes, or laughed too much, and her lipstick would be eaten off in a trice. She would still spill food on her clothes; she had still been, at seventeen, unconscious of her appearance. But this was *not* true. He remembered one evening when he had taken her to Lyons' Corner House and she had asked him if beauty mattered – by now she had cut off the awful perm and her hair was short and straight again, and whatever it was that he had said had upset her and he had made it worse by saying that he liked her as she was, and she had tried to be rude to him which she always did when she was afraid of crying, and then she had told him that Rupert had once said that she was beautiful and how it had made her seem less ordinary. She would have to fall back on character, she had said. And she had told a story about herself and Neville and the discovery that she just wanted to be pretty. And he had then – suddenly – because she seemed so vulnerable, been overwhelmed with affection for her, trapped by what she thought of as her unpleasing appearance, and also by her unerring honesty. He had wanted to take her in his arms and comfort her with any old nonsense that had enough truth in it to conceal the lies, and she had mercifully prevented this by saying he looked soppy. Did he love her then?

He remembered, and she must have been nearly nineteen by then, how Lydia saying she'd like to go to France with him had given him the idea that perhaps he might take Clary there – to get over Rupert's death, if need be. At more or less the same time, it had been he who told her not to give up hope about her father. It had been a very hot night in May, and she had arrived in a linen tunic, terribly hot, but even so, when he had said how pleased he was to see her, he noticed that she blushed with pleasure. And it had been then that she had seemed to see him as somebody in his own right. 'I feel amazed at how little I know you,' she had said. It had felt almost like a compliment.

They had talked about her having stopped writing and he had been hard on her about it. She'd gone off – to cry, he guessed – to the lavatory. When she came back, he'd tried to cheer her up about Rupert, and at once she'd thought he believed as she did, a trap he might have seen, but he had lumbered out of it somehow.

And then VE night. She'd arrived at the restaurant looking unexpectedly *soignée*: she was growing up, her hair was better cut, the black skirt and a man's shirt suited her, and her hair was wet, so at least she had washed it. They'd had a good and extraordinary evening, had stayed with the crowds outside the Palace longer than he'd intended because she was enjoying it so much, and he knew his leg was going to give him gyp on the long walk home. They'd stopped and sat on a bench in Hyde Park, and it was then that he'd realised how old he must seem to her. She told him that she knew about Polly falling in love with him, and said how ridiculous it was that she should be in love with somebody of his age. When he had said he must seem incredibly ancient to her, she had given herself away by saying, not *incredibly* – he didn't seem to have aged since she met him. Then she understood that she had upset him, and said she was sorry. She hadn't meant that he was *old*, she'd meant he was too old for *Polly*. (Polly and she, he reflected, were the same age.)

She'd stayed the night with him because she could never have got home, and sat up in bed wearing his pyjama jacket and he had brought her cocoa. And she'd told a story about her father eating the skin off her cocoa, which showed, she said, that he loved her, and immediately, not to be outdone, he'd done the same thing. If Rupert was dead, she would need his love.

And then, without warning, she had touched him to the core. It began about Zoë trying to give her Rupert's shirts, and how she'd only taken the worn ones, because to take the others would have been like giving in. But she thought she should make a pact with him that if Rupert didn't return a year from now she would have to accept that he never would. And then she told him how her love had changed about her father: from missing him so much, to wanting him to be alive for his own sake. He found it very difficult to say anything back to that. But he managed, and by the time he came to say goodnight, she had become almost a child again, turning her face up to him to be kissed. 'After all, darling Archie, I've always got you,' she had said. And lying in bed that night, it occurred to him that what she had said about her father had moved him so much because a part of him wished she would say it of him. Love of a kind began, he thought now, that night. He had made a pact with himself then that if Rupert was dead, he would do everything possible to take his place. The possibility of his return, however, might mean that things could be very different. Yes, that had been the beginning or, at least, the moment when he had acknowledged that he did not want to be her father.

Rupert had returned, and he had thought then that this would radically alter his relationship with her. It did not, and he blamed Rupert for it: he was so absorbed by his own problems, which were, he thought crossly, entirely of Rupert's own making. But then, of course, people's problems *were* usually homemade, he had thought wryly, so why not his own?

He had gone to France, and been dissatisfied; he had not clearly known what he was missing, except that the prospect of living alone there did not seem desirable. It was when Polly sent the telegram, and he tried to speak to her, and she said that Clary was in trouble, that he realised thoroughly that he loved her.

Seeing her, when she let him in at Blandford Street, had been a fearful shock. She looked dreadful, as though she had been dealt a mortal blow. But, then, she had looked pretty ropy for months now – she had, as might have been expected, taken to being in love with exhausting intensity, and his instinctive dislike of the man she had chosen, the whole dreary squalid set-up, had filled him with ill temper. But now, something had gone wrong. For a minute he thought that it had simply come to an end, that she would need comfort and support through the stock sad time that people endure in those circumstances. He had not thought of her being pregnant – still less that the couple would unite in abandoning her. When he had discovered that Number One did not want to have anything to do with her he felt rage as well as relief, but that left the question of her pregnancy, he felt, to him. He would not, did not, influence her. He calmed her down, and made her have a rest. She had been being so sick that she needed an evening meal, and he felt that it would be good to do something with her. Of course he didn't want her to have this ghastly man's child, and he soon discovered that Polly felt the same. But they agreed that she must not be influenced, must choose herself.

She had chosen to have an abortion, and he had taken her, waited, and collected her. After it, she seemed to fall into a different despair. He had taken her away to the Scilly Isles, to a small beautiful island, and made her walk a lot, made her learn to play complicated card games, and take turns reading a novel – and, most of all, talk about Number One and his wife. But although all these things seemed in some ways to help, in others they made her feel worse. He quickly found that ridiculing Noël, although it made her less in love with him, made her feel more deeply humiliated. He dropped that, and tried to get her interested in her writing – which Number One had also virtually destroyed. She snapped at him, refused to eat properly, and often withdrew into intractable silence for hours, but eventually one day, when he snapped back, she had said: 'What shall I do? I don't *want* to be like this, but what shall I *do*?'

So, when they returned, he got the cottage, rented via an acquaintance who was glad to have it inhabited – 'Hardly any mod cons and it gets fearfully damp in winter.' The rent had been twenty-five pounds a year. He'd settled her into it and gone back to his dreary job from which he had already taken too much leave. He would spend weekends with her, he had said, but she'd confounded him by turning up on the Monday evening following the first weekend after barely a day without him. And then, the next evening, to top it all, Rupert had turned up, and there had been that awful scene when Rupert had thought him responsible for the pregnancy. What had struck him – and by God, it *had* struck him – was the way in which she seemed to think it so *absurd* that Rupert should think such a thing. And then he, Rupert, had twisted the knife when he'd said on leaving that there was no point in her turning him into a father when she had a perfectly good one already! He'd wanted to yell then that he damn well didn't *want* to be her father, but caution had prevailed. And I am nothing, he thought bitterly, if not cautious.

It was that evening that his battle for her independence had really begun. They had had a row, and he'd said that he treated her like a child because she behaved like one. He'd told her to stop being sorry for herself and much more. The trouble was that when he was managing to do that quite sternly, she would say or do something that turned his heart over, and he would have to keep a tight hold on himself to hang on to being sensible and firm. Because that worked. He sent her back to the cottage on her own, and when he went down the following Friday, she'd cooked a proper meal and he sensed was full of her new book, although she didn't want to tell him about it.

He told Rupert what he had done about her, and Rupe, who was having mother-in-law trouble, said, 'Thanks awfully, old boy. Let me know if there's anything I can do.'

All that autumn he went every weekend. He remembered now – it seemed such a long time ago – how agonised he'd been about sending her back to the cottage that first time. He'd very nearly driven down to see if she was all right, but that would obviate the point of everything. She *had* to learn to fend for herself.

Getting her to go and see Polly in London had not been a success. When he discovered the following morning that she was not at Blandford Street – or, at least, was not answering the telephone – he'd rung Poll at work in a panic. When Polly had told him she'd gone back to the cottage he'd been relieved, at first, but then he had started to worry about her, and in the end, he'd got up at six and driven down to find her in a fever. He'd woken her from a nightmare and he'd been on the point of taking her in his arms and telling her he loved her but at first she'd thought he was her father, and that had stopped him cold.

She was in no state for that: she was sick, and frightened, and when he took her in his arms it was for her to cry and tell him the jumbled fragments of the bad dream. He'd stayed and nursed her and told his office a string of lies. By now, he'd given his notice, and was working it out, and he really didn't care a damn.

She was beginning to grow up. She had come to and realised that she had no money, and although part of him enjoyed being responsible for her in that way at least, he recognised that it was a step for her in the right direction. If she needed money now while she was writing the book, it was her father she should ask. So he sent her off, and she came back with two hundred pounds, in a temper about something. It turned out to be about the possibility of his going back to France. He had told her he was giving up his job, and he had mentioned France then, but now she thought he'd arranged to go without telling her.

To begin with he had thought, Here we go again. She's still expecting me to be there to support her.

The trouble was that, although he hadn't decided, he had to keep France as an option; he had to have some sort of long shot – or maybe not long at all, some necessary resort – if things went wrong. Which they showed every sign of doing. She'd called him her second father just before she'd gone to see her real one. But it was clear that the idea of his going away filled her with fear – something like panic. When she said that she couldn't stay in the cottage alone without him, he very nearly blew it, was touching her before he pulled himself together. He'd been brisk and tough with her, even telling her she'd fall in love with a nice man like a normal grown-up person. She sulked then, which he could deal with more easily than her fear.

But during that afternoon he'd thought it was wrong for her to feel he would make major plans behind her back – and apologised.

He'd reached his flat by now, got out his case and went in. The place seemed infinitely dreary. What was she doing now, he wondered. It was a good thing he hadn't even tried to get a telephone installed, because he knew that the temptation to ring her would have been too much for him.

Anyway, talk of people standing on their own feet, what about him? He had to decide what to do, how to earn a living beyond his small inheritance and what he had saved and any pictures he might sell. Rupert knew a good deal about how to survive and try to paint, he thought. He would start there.

His relationship with Rupert had undergone a considerable change. This had been largely because he had taken the plunge with him when they'd been at the weekend at Home Place designed to welcome Diana into the family. 'I should be so grateful if you would be there,' the Duchy had said. 'You know us all so well, and you are such a *diplomat*.' So he had gone, and then there had been a chance of going for a walk alone with Rupe, as Zoë had a headache and the others didn't want to come.

'Not that I'm a marvellous walker,' he had said, 'but I really wanted to talk to you on our own about something.'

'Fine.'

'Actually,' he said, minutes later, 'I think I'd find it easier if we were sitting down.'

So they sat on the old tree that the children had always played on in the copse behind the house.

'You look worried about something. What's happened? You know that you can trust me.'

'What do you think?'

Rupert had looked at him, and then he smiled slightly, and said, 'I think you've fallen in love with somebody and you're not sure if it's a good thing. I bet it is, though.'

'I wouldn't be too sure of that.'

'I'm right, then?'

'Yes. I have. It's Clary,' he said quickly. 'Hang on a minute. I haven't said a word to her. She has no idea.'

'*Clary!* Good God! You don't mean that!'

'Of course I mean it. I'd be bloody daft to say that to you if I didn't.'

There was a silence. Then Rupert, clearly trying to tread carefully, said, 'Don't you think you're a bit old for her?'

'I knew you'd say that. Zoë is a good deal younger than you, though, isn't she?'

'Twelve years. But you're – you're the best part of twenty years older than she is. That's different, surely?'

'It's certainly different, but I don't think it's necessarily worse.'

There was another silence. Then Rupert said, 'How long has this been going on?'

'Nothing's *been* going on. How long have I been in love with her? God knows. Since she was about eighteen, I should think – only I didn't realise it.'

'And how does she feel about you?'

'That's the trouble. I sort of stood in for you all that time you were away, and she still thinks of me like that.' He looked at him – he could feel his eyes pricking. 'One doesn't choose exactly about this sort of thing,' he said. 'You know that. It – strikes you.'

'Yes. Archie, I don't know what to say. It must be awful for you. All this time – after Rachel, and all that – to have it happen again—'

'Look. Nothing's happened.' He added wearily, 'I don't think she has the faintest idea.'

'Well – wouldn't it – I mean, well, I suppose it might be better for you if you *did* talk to her. Then at least you'd know.'

'I can't – now. I just know it's not the right time. And anyway, I don't think I can face it. If I talk to her and it's absolutely no good, it'll be the end of everything for me with her – I know that, and I can't face it.'

'Why are you telling me?'

'I suppose I sort of hope that at least you would not feel bad about it. My intentions, I mean. Entirely honourable.' He had tried to smile – and broken down. Until that point, he hadn't known what a strain the whole thing had been for so long and how isolated he'd felt trying to deal with it. He tried to tell Rupert this, and he'd been really good about it. He'd sat by him and let him say all these things – and more – without interruption or argument. 'The stakes seem so high,' he had said. 'I really do love her – everything about her – but she's got to grow up, be in charge of her life and make a choice, you see, which isn't based on being dependent on me and all that.'

At the end of it Rupe had said, 'You've made me see

610

that you do love her. That's what matters. We're the same age. I think if I were in your position, I'd feel the same.'

He could have kissed him; they did embrace. Rupe swore he would not tell anyone. 'Even Zoë?' Not even Zoë, he had said . . .

He would ring Rupe now and see if they could meet *à deux*.

He did this, but Rupert was not able to help much about what he could do about painting and earning some money. 'I always found it was one or the other,' he said, 'and with a family, I thought I'd better opt for the other. You could see if there's any supply teaching at any of the art schools, I suppose.'

'That's a good idea.'

He had explained how he was leaving Clary on her own for six weeks – on purpose – and that they would not meet until Polly's wedding. 'Then, I expect, I'll have to risk it, but I'll wait and see.'

And Rupe, who he knew found it difficult to make up his mind about anything, said he could see it was a good thing to give her time on her own and to wait. By now Rupe – possibly because he thought the situation was hopeless – seemed to be fairly on his side.

He'd gone back to the cottage after that weekend at Home Place somewhat lightened by having told Rupert and not been lectured or rejected – not, he knew, that that would have changed things about how he felt about her, but it was good that Rupert knew.

And there she was, really into her book, and wanting him to read some of it. Of course he had – and been surprisingly disappointed with the first chapter: it had not seemed like her at all, was more self-conscious and convoluted than he'd expected. But then she'd said how many times she had written it, and he'd seen her first attempts and that was her, and clear and simple – and gifted. How marvellous it was to be able to say sincerely that he thought it was good. But again (even in this context!) he had had to warn her not to take too much notice of what he – or anyone else – said about her work.

It was soon after that he'd taken some of his own work to London in the hope of interesting a gallery. No dice. Or, rather, two miserable little dice. His old gallery said they would take a couple of landscapes for a mixed show.

He got through the first week without her by various abortive attempts to find work – teaching, no good; a few more galleries, no good. One of the bad things about his flat was that he could not paint in it. The weekend was awful. He missed her, he worried about her, he wanted to be at the cottage. He was lonely and he didn't want to see anyone. He went to *Annie Get Your Gun!* by himself and kept wondering what she would think of it; he went to the pubs where, when he talked to people, he seemed always to get into some futile argument about whether the government was dealing with the severe dollar shortage – rumours were that rations were to be cut yet again, they were putting a tax of ten pounds a year on cars, and who was behind the letter bombs that the Foreign Secretary and his opposite number had received? 'It's the Reds or the Jews,' one morose and slightly drunken man had kept on repeating, until he knew that he'd have to hit him or leave. And then there was India. People in pubs seemed to consider that the whole idea of India becoming independent was (a) a crime and (b) didn't matter a tinker's cuss because they were only bloody foreigners anyway.

He stopped going to pubs on his own. He read, and ate out, and went to bed tired from walking – why did his leg seem worse in London? And on Sunday evening, he thought, it might not only be six weeks of this, it might be for ever. In bed he thought, Here I go, keeping on about *her* being independent of *me*, when perhaps it ought to be the other way round.

So, when Rupert rang him on Monday to say that old Aunt Dolly had died and would he feel like going down to Sussex and giving the Duchy some support, he said of course he would.

But he had been right to go away from her, he thought the next morning, as he drove down to Home Place. He could not go on being avuncular, or give the impression of calm disinterest when he felt none of these things. That moment in the kitchen recurred – again and again. It had been when her beauty, her shock from the burn and her utter unawareness of him had hit him so hard that he simply couldn't take any more. If he stayed, he'd blurt everything out, and his chance of *that* being a success would, he felt, be nil. He *had* to go.

It was soothing to be in the old house. The Duchy was really pleased to see him. 'I think she died quite suddenly,' she said, 'a heart attack, or a stroke, but I don't think she had any pain.'

'But you will miss her,' he suggested.

'Well, you know, I don't think I shall, really. She had become so dependent. It is difficult to maintain a connection with somebody when that is the chief ingredient, don't you think?'

'Very difficult.'

When those of the family who had come down for the funeral had gone their various ways, and he was preparing to do the same, the Duchy had said, 'Rupert told me that you had given up your job, and were going back to painting. Where are you going to do that?'

He said he wasn't sure. He couldn't paint in London, he added.

'You're returning to France? You have a house there, I think you said?'

'A sort of house. The top two floors over a café. I don't know. I thought I'd stay here until after Polly's wedding anyway.'

There was a pause. The Duchy was scraping a very small amount of butter on her toast. 'If you would like to spend that time here and paint, we can make you a room for it, and I should very much enjoy your company in the evenings.'

So he did. He made one journey to London to collect his painting gear and went back. All the weekdays there was just the two of them; the Duchy gardened and he painted outside when the weather permitted; there were frequent thunderstorms, but after them the peculiar beauty of country deluged from violent rain, reviving, glistening in the returning sunlight. There was heavy dew in the mornings, as though the lawns were inlaid with tiny diamonds that dissolved to show daisies opening flat and unwinking in the sun. In the evening, if there had been enough heat, a pearly mist shrouded the ground. All day it seemed to him that everything he saw was changing, on the move. He took to working on two or three pictures at once, for different times of the day and the changing weather. For the first time in his work he became sharply aware of what he was not seeing. It reminded him of the countless times he had tried to draw her without once achieving anything that satisfied him. It was something, he now thought, to do with the first look at anything that had to embrace the whole view and not simply record part of it. He said something of this – about landscape – in response to the Duchy's enquiry about how he was getting on, and found her unexpectedly understanding of his dilemma.

'It is something to do with trusting that first sight, isn't it?' she had said. 'One gets embroiled in a part of what one has seen and then forgets the rest.'

He was so surprised that he could not help saying, 'How do you know that? You used to paint?'

'Oh – everyone painted a little when I was a girl. It was very much the done thing. But I wanted to do it more seriously. I wished to go to an art school, but my mother wouldn't hear of it. And after I was married it was somehow easier for me to play the piano, you see. It was regarded as a more useful accomplishment.'

She played in the evenings, and he drew her, and then, one day when it rained a great deal, asked her if he might paint her while she was practising. So the drugget that protected the drawing-room carpet from sun was brought, and he put his easel on it.

But what she had said about the first sight remained with him, and one day he drew Clary from memory – quite quickly. The next day when the Duchy brought him his jug of flowers – she felt all rooms in use should have flowers – she saw the drawing (he'd used charcoal on a darkish paper) and said, 'Clary! That is Clary to the life! When did you do that?'

'Not long ago,' he had answered, as casually as he was able.

No more was said. But a few days later, when they were having tea, she said, 'You seem to be profiting from

615

this rest, although I know you are working. I feel that you were much in need of respite of some kind. Is that right?'

'I think so.'

'My dear, I don't wish to probe, but for so many years it seems to me that this family has leaned on you – for love and support of many kinds. I should be sad if when you needed those things you did not get them from one of us.'

'Why do you say that?'

'Oh. I feel that you are not very happy, and I cannot help wondering whether you need to be.'

After a pause, during which he wondered wildly whether to confide in her, she said, 'You have been so good – to Rupert and his family particularly, to him and to Zoë, to Neville about his school and to Clary. I shall never forget any of that.'

So he told her – some of it. That he was in love with a girl so young that he did not know how to approach her. He was very careful to keep her anonymous – was very general, and lame.

She put down her teacup and regarded him thoughtfully.

'I was far too young when I married,' she said. 'I knew nothing. I suppose you could have described me as an overgrown child. And William seemed incredibly old to me then. He was only seven years older than I, but it seemed like a generation.' A faint smile, and she added, 'It has done me no harm. I grew up in due course. I have even achieved old age.' She was still looking at him with that disarming frankness; then her eyes gleamed in a way that reminded him of Neville, although he had never before perceived a likeness between them, as she said:

616

'You don't value yourself enough. In my day you would have been described as a *great* catch.'

That night he went to sleep feeling better than he had for weeks.

∞ ∞ ∞

He was nearly late for the church, and by the time he got there it seemed almost full. He looked to see whether she was sitting with Rupert and Zoë, but she wasn't.

'There's a bit of pew next to Neville,' Teddy said: he was being an usher. When he had found it and Neville had greeted him – 'We wouldn't *have* weddings if girls were allowed to dress up in ordinary life' – he saw her sitting with Louise and a thin dark girl diagonally across the church from him.

'We're this side because Lord Fake hasn't got so many friends as Poll,' Neville said, lowering his voice because the organist had begun the entrance of the bride – not Wagner, thank goodness, he thought. Then everybody stood up and he could not see her at all.

Afterwards, as she walked down the aisle Polly saw him, and he got a quick little smile and he thought that anyone who was clearly as happy as that would look dazzling.

'Do let's get out,' Neville was saying. 'You never know how much food there's going to be at parties these days.'

He waited, outside the church while the photographs were being taken, for her to emerge.

'Have you got your car?' Neville was asking.

'Yes.'

'I'll come with you, then.'

'Well, you'll have to wait, I might want to give other people a lift.'

She came out with Louise and the other girl. She was wearing a green dress with a rounded neck and tight sleeves to her elbows, the slightly full skirt falling well below her knees, and what looked like brand new, pretty but rather painful shoes. The outfit was spoiled by a ridiculous hat – a small boater with green ribbon in a streamer at the back. There was nothing wrong with the hat, it was just that hats did not suit her. She seemed to know this, because as soon as she got outside she pulled it off, looked round and deposited it on the spike of a railing. He saw Louise laugh and pick it off. Then they all seemed to see him at once. He knew from the Duchy that Louise had left her husband. 'I fear she may be embarking upon a desert,' the Duchy had said, 'and, as we know, they are full of wild tribesmen.'

So he greeted Louise first, who introduced the thin girl as Stella Rose. 'We're going to share Polly's old flat together,' she said. All the while, Clary stood a little behind the other two, and when he caught her eye, he sensed that she had been looking at him.

'Hello,' he said, nerving himself to go and give her a noncommittal kiss. 'You're looking pretty splendid, I must say.'

'Zoë chose it for me. But she made me wear the hat.' She had gone faintly pink, and now he was near her, she didn't look at him. Pride, he thought – she's not going to admit that she's missed me.

'I missed you,' she said in an offhand voice. 'But I must say, it has been very good for work. You know – no distractions like cooking and all that.'

618

'Oh, come on!' Neville was saying. 'Honestly, we really ought to get there.'

He took all four of them squashed in his car. Neville sat in front, because Louise said if he sat with them he would spoil their clothes.

There will be plenty of time, he thought, as he drove to Claridge's Hotel, for us to talk after the reception. And he began to imagine driving down to the cottage with her that evening. So he made no particular effort to talk to her while they were at the reception, and neither did she.

After he had been received and met Gerald for the first time, he concentrated upon doing the rounds, or covering the ground or whatever they called it.

Miss Milliment was arrayed in a jersey suit the colour of blackberry fool, which did not look its best backed by the salmon pink damask of the large chair she had been parked upon. 'What a happy day!' she said, when he greeted her. 'It's Archie, isn't it? My eyes are not quite what they were.' And later, 'Oh, Archie, I fear a little piece of bridge roll, or possibly just the filling of it has escaped my clutches and may perhaps be visible to you down the side of the chair? Thank you so much. I was pretty sure I was right.'

Lydia – in a bridesmaid's dress – and Villy.

'Mummy, if it's at all possible I want never to see Judy again in my life. Hello, Archie! Do you like my dress? I was just telling Mummy about my ghastliest cousin. She's furious because she's not a bridesmaid and if you ask me she's most unlikely ever to be a bride because I can't think of anyone stupid enough to marry her.'

'That will do,' Villy was saying. 'Go and hand some things round to people.'

'How are you, dear Villy?'

'Better, I think. Busy, anyway. Zoë and I are trying to start a small dancing school, as we both have different skills in that field. I'm not sure of it, but it will be very good for Zoë to have something constructive to do.'

Rachel and Sid.

'The Duchy simply loved having you to herself,' Rachel said. 'We suggested going down, didn't we, Sid, but she wouldn't hear of it.'

'No, she wanted you to herself. But we're taking her down this evening and staying the weekend to soften the blow of your departure.'

'Sid is teaching me to drive,' Rachel said, 'and I'm afraid it has emerged that I don't know my right from my left.'

'She's pretty shaky,' Sid said fondly, 'and has about as much sense of direction as a gadfly.'

'Oh, darling! I think that's a little unkind!'

But nothing between them was unkind, he thought.

Zoë, looking exquisite in a very pale pink suit with a nipped-in waist and long skirt and a broad pink straw hat that lit her complexion to yet another delicious pink. 'Archie!' She kissed him. 'Isn't it a lovely party!'

'I hear you and Villy are starting a dancing school.'

'A small one. I don't know if it will work, but the idea of it has cheered Villy, which is the main thing.'

'Archie, let me introduce you to Jemima Leaf.' It was Hugh with a very small, neat blonde lady.

When he asked was she a friend of the bride-groom, 'She's a friend of mine,' Hugh said, before she could reply. He said it, he thought, as though it was extraordinary to have one. Hugh got called away and he stayed talking to her. She had two children, she said, and she was working for Cazalets' – for Hugh, in fact. He wondered afterwards about that. But eventually Polly went away to change, and fewer people remained to say what good speeches they had been and how well everything had gone. He had been seeing her out of the corner of his eye for some time: she had been talking to Christopher, wasn't it, the cousin who'd had the breakdown and who owned a devoted dog? He went over.

'It's Christopher, isn't it? It's so long since I've seen you.'

'It's very long since anybody's seen him,' Clary said.

'How's your dog?' he asked, after a pause when neither of them said anything and he began to wonder whether he had interrupted something.

'He died.'

'Oh, I'm sorry.'

But with a smile of singular sweetness, Christopher answered, 'He had a very good life and I'm sure he's all right now.'

'Christopher believes in a dog heaven,' Clary said, 'but I don't think they would enjoy it much without their people.'

'Perhaps one day I'll have to join him, then. I must go,' Christopher said a moment later, 'got a train to catch.'

'Well,' he said, when they were alone. 'Shall we have some supper before we drive down?'

'We must see Poll off first,' she said quickly, and began to go to the door of the large room. 'We have to go outside,' she called. He followed her.

But when all that was over, when the small crowd of them were left waving and then turning to one another, she said, 'Could we talk in the car?'

'Why not?'

621

He put her in the front seat and went round and got in beside her.

'The thing is', she said, still not looking at him, 'that I have very, very nearly finished my book and I think I'd better be on my own until I have. If you don't mind?'

He was taken aback. 'You haven't stopped working because I've been around before. Why now?'

'Oh, well . . . The end is quite difficult, and I think I would be better off really concentrating on it. It'll only be about two weeks.'

'All right. If that's how you want it.'

'It is. If that's all right.'

'Don't keep saying if that's all right if you know you're going to do it anyway.'

'All right. I won't. What I would like,' she went on, 'would be if you could get me a taxi and I'll be off. I wouldn't have come at all, only I knew Poll would mind.'

'I'll drive you.'

'I can easily get a cab.'

'I dare say, but here I am. I'll drive you.'

The drive was curiously uncomfortable. At one point he said, 'What's up?'

'Nothing's up. I just want to get back to my work.'

'Everything all right at the cottage?'

'Everything's the same, if that's what you mean.'

He was almost glad when they got to Paddington. She slipped out of the car, waved to him, said, 'Thanks for the lift,' and had turned to go when he called, 'Clary! How will I know when you've finished?'

'I'll send you a postcard to the flat,' she said, and was gone without a backward glance.

So, during that fortnight, he thought almost bitterly, that if he'd wanted her to be independent, he'd certainly got his wish. She hadn't even seemed especially pleased to see him. She'd always gone for extremes, he thought at intervals: she was an extreme person – nothing happened by halves. Anyway, if he faced up to it, he had to recognise that he would not be proposing to a sick or frightened little girl: she'd acquired poise in the last six weeks and a passion for her work which, though admirable, was slightly daunting.

He thought everything about her during that time. He thought about her passionate nature, her determination, the way her hair sprang off centre from the widow's peak, her endless curiosity that could apply itself to anything and hung on until she got some satisfaction, the glimpse he had had of her small, round, perfectly white breasts, her marvellous eyes, which when he looked into them were such a mirror to her self – only there had been no chance of that at the wedding, so really he did not know what she was feeling. It was as though he'd lost a part of her. The trust? Was that what had gone with her dependence? Or had she changed in some other mysterious way? It even crossed his mind, during those days, that she had fallen in love. God forbid, and who with, after all? They knew nobody down there; there could have been a walker – people did walk along the towpath at weekends – but if she'd been working so hard, she would not have had time to meet anyone. Anyway, she would have told him. She did not tell lies, had never withheld anything that mattered to her from him. It was madness even to think of such a thing.

By the time he got her postcard – a full fourteen days later on a Friday morning, the very day, as his morning paper informed him, that 'The Sun sets on the British Raj' – he felt that perhaps he was a little mad.

623

Deliberately, for reasons not clear to himself, he did not arrive at the cottage until mid-afternoon. It was another hot, sunny day, and when he got out of the car, it was wonderful to smell the warm clean air – a hint of caramel from drying hay, and the peppery sweet smell of the phlox she had planted beside the mossy path to the kitchen door. He called her, once, but there was no answer. He unpacked the car – the food he had bought that morning and his painting gear – and carried it in several trips into the kitchen; the door was unlocked, so she must be somewhere.

The door to the sitting room that led on to the garden was also open, and he could see her now, lying on the lawn with one of the old sofa pillows under her head. When he got near he saw that she was asleep, but nearer, some sound he must have made wakened her, as she sat up with a start. She was wearing her old black cotton skirt and a sleeveless white camisole thing that he'd never seen before.

'Here I am at last,' he said, and got down on the grass to give her a greeting kiss. He did not get the customary hug in return, and felt vaguely alarmed.

'Aren't you pleased to see me?'

'I am – in a way.'

'I'm glad your book's done.'

'Yes. So am I. In a way.'

'How not?'

'Well, it's a kind of farewell to the people in it. Saying goodbye to them. I'd got used to them. And I hate saying goodbye to people anyway.' Her hands were locked round her knees, and he began to feel the tension.

'There will be other people,' he said.

'That is what I knew you would say,' she said.

'Well, I have something to say to you that you won't know—' he began. He did not feel that the moment was right, but something drove him to say it.

But before he could get any further, she said, 'There is something I have to say to you.'

He waited, but she was silent, and in the silence he began to feel his heart thudding.

'I was going to ask you if you'd like a holiday in France,' he said desperately – a cowardly half-measure, but he was frightened now.

'No,' she said. 'I couldn't, I'm afraid.'

She must have fallen in love, he thought as he scanned her hands (clean), nails (unbitten), hair (shining with care). God! She had all the appearance – glowing, charming – of a girl who has just found the right man . . .

'Clary, you must tell me – however difficult, you've bloody well got to tell me—'

'ALL RIGHT!' she cried, so loudly that he could see it even shocked her. She had been staring at the ground; now she looked up and straight at him.

'You remember what happened with Polly – ages ago?'

He didn't know what she meant.

He saw her swallow and she began to be very pale.

'I can't go to France with you, and I can't go on living like we have. It's something I found out when you went away. I had no idea of it before, but now I know.'

'Darling, do try to tell me what the hell you are talking about.'

'If you laugh at me, I shall really want to kill you,' she said, in much more the old Clary way. 'I found out that I feel like Polly used to – about you. To begin with I didn't believe myself, because I so much wanted it not to be true. But it is. It truthfully entirely is.' She sniffed and one very large tear shot out of an eye. 'I couldn't manage weekends with you being a sort of uncle or schoolmaster or whatever. It's—' Her eyes were full of tears now. 'It's really most unfortunate. For me, anyway. When I saw you at the wedding I sort of got an electric shock. You see?'

For a second he thought he was going to laugh – with an hysterical relief. Instead, he took her hands in his and when he could manage to speak said, 'What an extraordinary coincidence. Because that is exactly what I was going to say to you.'

He thought that would be the end of it, that they would fall into each other's arms at last; he hadn't reckoned with her disbelief, her uncertainty that anyone would love her, her suspicion that he was merely trying to be kind, 'buttering me up', as she put it. He got up and pulled her to her feet.

'I love you so much,' he said, 'and I've loved you for so long.'

Kissing her made him feel faint – light-headed; it was she who said, 'Wouldn't we be better lying down?'

They walked slowly, stumbling a little because they had to look at each other, and stopping at the foot of the stairs, because they were too narrow. He took her hand to lead her, then kissed her again. 'Do you remember the evening that Pipette brought that message from your father? And you said "the second piece of love sent"?'

She nodded and he could see her eyes, clear now of distrust.

'This is the third,' he said, 'the third piece of love.'

'But as you are here,' she said, 'it will be given, not sent.'

The Cazalet Series of Novels

Elegantly constructed and told with exceptional grace,
The Light Years is a modern classic of twentieth-century
English life and is the first novel in Elizabeth Jane
Howard's extraordinary, bestselling family saga
The Cazalet Chronicles.

Every summer, the Cazalet brothers – Hugh, Edward and
Rupert – return to the family home in the heart of the
Sussex countryside with their wives and children. There,
they are joined by their parents and unmarried sister
Rachel to enjoy two blissful months of picnics, games and
excursions to the coast.

But despite the idyllic setting, nothing can be done to
soothe the siblings' heartache: Hugh is haunted by the
ravages of the Great War, Edward is torn between his wife
and his latest infidelity, and Rupert is in turmoil over his
inability to please his demanding wife. Meanwhile, Rachel
risks losing her only chance at happiness because of her
unflinching loyalty to the family.

'Charming, poignant and quite irresistible . . .
to be cherished and shared' *The Times*

The Cazalet Series of Novels

Beautifully and poignantly told, *Marking Time* is the second novel in Elizabeth Jane Howard's bestselling Cazalet Chronicles.

Home Place, Sussex, 1939. As the shadows of the Second World War roll in, banishing the sunlit days of childish games and trips to the coast, a new generation of Cazalets take up the family's story.

Louise, who dreams of becoming a great actress, finds herself facing the harsh reality that her parents have their own lives with secrets, passions and yearnings. Clary, an aspiring writer, learns that her beloved father is now missing somewhere on the shores of France. And sensitive, imaginative Polly feels stuck – stuck without a vocation, stuck without information about her mother's illness, stuck without anything except her nightmares about the war.

'The Cazalets have earned an honoured place among the great saga families . . . rendered thrillingly three-dimensional by a master craftsman' *Sunday Telegraph*

The Cazalet Series of Novels

The Cazalet Chronicles continues with *Confusion*, the third instalment, set in the height of the Second World War, in which chaos has become a way of life for the Cazalet family.

It's 1942 and the dark days of war seem never-ending. Scattered across the still-peaceful Sussex countryside and air-raid-threatened London, the divided Cazalets begin to find the battle for survival echoing the confusion in their own lives.

Headstrong, independent Louise surprises the whole family when she abandons her dreams of being an actress and instead makes a society marriage. Polly and Clary, now in their late teens, finally fulfil their ambition of living together in London. But the reality of the city is not quite what they imagined, and Polly is struggling to come to terms with the death of her mother and manage her grieving father. Clary, meanwhile, is painfully aware that what she lacks in beauty she makes up for in intelligence, and is the only member of the family who believes that her father might not be dead.

'She is one of those novelists who shows, through her work, what the novel is for . . . She helps us to do the necessary thing – open our eyes and our hearts' Hilary Mantel

The Cazalet Series of Novels

The Second World War has finally ended and so begins a
new era of freedom and opportunity for the Cazalet family.
Elizabeth Jane Howard's magnificent Cazalet Chronicles
continues with *Casting Off*, the fourth novel in the saga.

The Cazalet cousins are now in their twenties, trying to
piece together their lives in the aftermath of the war.
Louise is faced with her father's new mistress and her
mother's grief at his betrayal, while suffering in a loveless
marriage of her own. Clary is struggling to understand
why her beloved father chose to stay in France long after it
was safe to return to Britain, and both she and Polly are
madly in love with much older men.

Polly, Clary and Louise must face the truth about the adult
world, while their fathers – Rupert, Hugh and Edward –
must make choices that will decide their own, and the
family's, future.

'She is the most amazing storyteller because she makes
you care' Elizabeth Day

The Cazalet Series of Novels

All Change is the fifth and final volume in Elizabeth Jane Howard's bestselling The Cazalet Chronicles, where the old world begins to fade from view and a new dawn emerges.

It is the 1950s and as the Duchy, the Cazalets' beloved matriarch, dies, she takes with her the last remnants of a disappearing world – houses with servants, class and tradition – in which the Cazalets have thrived.

Louise, now divorced, becomes entangled in a painful affair, while Polly and Clary must balance marriage and motherhood with their own ideas and ambitions. Hugh and Edward, now in their sixties, are feeling ill-equipped for this modern world, while Villy, long abandoned by her husband, must at last learn to live independently. But it is Rachel, who has always lived for others, who will face her greatest challenges yet.

As the Cazalets descend on Home Place for Christmas, only one thing is certain: nothing will ever be the same again.

'A family saga of the best kind . . . A must' *Tatler*